THE LAST

After centuries of pain, t...
tence, he'd found the onl...
from his stupor and retur... ...measurable
strength fueled every movement, and he was no longer
the shade of the vampire he'd once been. The world melted
away until there was only her. He'd found the one thing
he needed to survive in this gods-forsaken world. He took
off after her, his speed surprising even to him. It would be
nothing to catch her, and once he did, he would never let
her go. Her blood was the very essence of life, calling to
him in a way that no other had in four centuries of existence. Stranger or not, she belonged to him now, and he
would not rest until he tasted her again.

THE LAST TRUE VAMPIRE

KATE BAXTER

St. Martin's Paperbacks

This is a work of fiction. All of the characters, organizations, and events portrayed in this novel are either products of the author's imagination or are used fictitiously.

THE LAST TRUE VAMPIRE

Copyright © 2015 by Kate Baxter.
Excerpt from *The Warrior Vampire* copyright © 2015 by Kate Baxter.

For information address St. Martin's Press, 175 Fifth Avenue, New York, NY 10010.

ISBN: 978-1-250-05376-3

Printed in the United States of America

St. Martin's Paperbacks edition / June 2015

St. Martin's Paperbacks are published by St. Martin's Press, 175 Fifth Avenue, New York, NY 10010.

10 9 8 7 6 5 4 3 2

For Nancy. My very first reader
and the ultimate vampire fan.

ACKNOWLEDGMENTS

Thanks to my family for putting up with a 24/7 work-aholic. To Windy Aphayrath, Chelsea Mueller, and Meredith Moore, thanks for your support and feedback, and to Sarah Bromley, thanks for helping me out when I'd hit a world-building wall. To Kristen Painter and Kristen Callihan, your sound advice kept me from freaking out. And mad love for the Writer Chicks who I wouldn't be sane without!

A huge thank-you goes out to my Agent of Awesomeness, Natanya Wheeler, and everyone at NYLA; also to my editor, Monique Patterson, whose mad skills have made me a better writer. Thanks to Alexandra Sehulster for fielding my millions of e-mails and to the amazing cover artists, copy editors, production staff, and everyone at St. Martin's Press. You guys rock!

I take full responsibility for any and all mistakes. I live in a dream world most of the time; it's a wonder I pay enough attention to wear matching socks!

CHAPTER
1

The vampire knew of no one on the face of the earth that he despised as fervently as the Sortiari. Mikhail wondered if his torture somehow assuaged their guilt as the self-proclaimed influencers of Fate? Perhaps it justified the murders they'd tasked their lapdogs to commit? Because as far as Mikhail was concerned, the only thing the slayer had accomplished was to further enrage an already-rabid beast. Careful in his technique, the false priest took great care as he made a show of purifying Mikhail's flesh. A torch burned bright in the dark dungeon, the fire casting inhuman shadows as though revealing the slayer's true face. He touched the flame to Mikhail's skin again and again as he absolved the vampire of sin in preparation for the killing blow.

Mikhail's fangs punched down from his gums and a feral growl erupted in his chest. Pain fueled his rage and gave him strength as he fought to free himself from the bonds that restrained him. The silver chains were woven, it was said, with strands of hair from an archangel's head. Those lies might have worked on the simple folk who lived in the villages, but Mikhail knew that the Sortiari were nothing more than butchers hiding behind the cloister of the Holy See and the church's myths. The slayer wore an elaborate gold crucifix around his neck, which complemented his black and red robes, giving him the appearance of a man of God. But this creature was no priest and neither were the Sortiari holy. No, the members of this secret society were nothing more than zealots with the resources they required to further their cause thanks to the wealth of the church.

Weakened from a fortnight of torture and starved of blood, Mikhail swayed on his feet, the silver chains the only things holding him upright. Once a proud warrior, he'd been reduced to a bloodied mass of flesh and raw nerves. How he wanted to sink his fangs into his enemy's throat and rejoice in the warmth of the slayer's blood as it flowed over his tongue. He ached for vengeance, for the opportunity to deliver justice to the bastards who'd all but annihilated an entire race. Mikhail thrashed against his bonds, strained at the heavy length of silver that weighed him down and stole his strength. Endless black swallowed the whites of the slayer's eyes until no color remained and he laughed. A sound that grated in Mikhail's ears like the scratch of metal on metal.

The slayer paused in his ministrations, a silver dagger dripping with Mikhail's own blood clenched tight in his fist. "By the will of Fate, we have rid the world of your kind." The words were spoken as nothing more than a whisper, yet they resonated with the force of an angry shout. "The Sortiari have killed your females, ripped the wombs from their wretched bodies, and burned the abominations growing inside of them in sacred flames. Your warriors are gone, torn limb from limb, their black hearts speared, and the pieces buried in consecrated ground."

His breath hot and reeking of rancid flesh, the slayer

spoke close to Mikhail's face. A monster stood in this cold, dank dungeon, but it wasn't the vampire. As the creature in the guise of a human sliced the blade across Mikhail's torso, cutting away great sheets of his flesh, he saw a glimpse of the beast that simmered beneath the slayer's skin. Berserker. He could almost laugh at the folly of the church for allying themselves with the Sortiari. Employing the very creatures they sought to vanquish. As pain clouded his mind and stole any sense of reason, Mikhail refused to cry out. He would not show weakness.

"I killed your sire with my own hands, you soulless wretch," the slayer said with pride. "Your whore as well. And as the last of your kind, you are nothing more than the heir to death. The entirety of your race will end with you." He dropped the dagger somewhere at his side and from his robes produced a long wooden spike, tipped with silver. "The future waits to do the Sortiari's bidding. We are Fate." Holding it in both fists, the slayer held the weapon high above his head, raised to the sky as though in prayer. "May God have mercy on your evil soul," he snarled as he drove the spike into the vampire's chest.

Michael Aristov came awake with the setting sun, clutching at his chest. His fingers found the familiar star-shaped scar, burned there by the wooden spike infused with Sortiari magic. Another inch to the left and he would have joined the entirety of his race in whatever afterlife awaited the immortal. Would there be a day of his existence that he didn't relive that wretched night of torture in his dreams? He collapsed back on his pillow as he attempted to rub the ghost of pain from his sternum. Tonight wasn't the first night he'd wished the assassin had been better at the job. Death would have been a welcome respite from the pain of isolation and the promise of an eternity of soulless existence.

He swung his legs over the edge of the king-size bed and let his head hang between his shoulders. How many nights had it been since he'd fed? Twenty? Thirty? Too damned many at any rate. His body ached with hunger, his throat raw and his gut pulsing with a hollow yet acidic burn that damn near brought him to his knees. With effort, Michael reached for his cell on the bedside table. He scrolled through his contacts and hit "send."

"What's on tap for tonight?" a man answered on the other end.

"I'm going out. Bring the car." Michael's own voice was gravel spinning in a cement mixer, and speaking did little to soothe the fire in his throat.

"Ten minutes?"

Michael's head spun. His thoughts clouded. If he didn't feed soon, instinct would overtake him and he'd be unable to control his compulsion to feed. "Make it five."

"Five minutes, then" came the reply before the call disconnected.

Arms braced at his sides, Michael pushed himself off the bed. He wobbled on his feet for a moment, lightheaded. The collective hunger of an entire race exhausted his strength and he wondered, if he allowed them all to perish, would he too finally see his end? The slayers hadn't managed to do the deed four centuries ago; surely he was doomed to the torture of this empty existence for all eternity.

A few stumbling steps took Michael to a control panel on the wall. He pushed a button and the blackout blinds retracted from the floor-to-ceiling windows, revealing the gray twilight that draped the sky as though with the haze of a mourning cloak. Michael gazed out at the gardens beyond his window, and the tension constricting his muscles eased by slow degrees. He didn't miss the sun.

The sun was hot, and bright, and punishing. He had no desire to feel the warmth of it on his skin or see the ocean in the daytime, bright and blue in its reflection, like the vampires did in the movies. Michael didn't secretly yearn for a time when he would meet the accursed yellow orb in a glorious display of morning light. The thing he feared—truly resented—was that he had to shut himself up in a tomb to block out those deadly rays. Even in his spacious house, miles from the congestion of the city, he felt suffocated once the blinds went down. And he had that Sortiari bastard to thank for that.

True to his word, Alex pulled up to the front door just a few minutes later. The human was worth every cent of his considerable paycheck: prompt, discreet, and efficient. He never asked questions and he did whatever was required of him. And in a city where gossip paid very, *very* well, he was a valuable commodity indeed.

"Where to?" Alex asked as he opened the door of the sleek black town car.

A nice open field in Siberia might be nice. "Take me into the city. Club district."

Alex inclined his head. "Anywhere in particular?"

Michael should have found a dhampir to supply a willing vein—that blood would surely sustain him longer—but he didn't have the patience or energy to deal with his own kin. Keeping company with dhampirs would dredge up too many painful memories for him to stomach. "Wherever's hot right now. I don't care about the specifics."

"Can do." Alex closed the door and took the driver's seat. "You do realize things won't heat up at the clubs for a few hours yet. Tongues will wag whether you're fashionably late or way too early."

True, but at this point it hardly mattered. "Like you said, they'll talk either way. Let's just get this over with."

"You're the boss," Alex replied as he put the car into gear and began the long trek down Mulholland toward the city.

Michael leaned his head back on the rest as he relaxed against the supple leather interior and closed his eyes. His control was slipping as the thirst mounted, his sanity on the precipice of collapse. The memories of the Ancient Ones assaulted his mind, remnants of lives extinguished by Sortiari slayers. Once he fed he'd be strong enough to keep the memories at bay, but right now his mind roared with myriad voices, thoughts, and events of lives in a time long since passed.

"Not much farther," Alex remarked from the front of the car. "Just hang on."

Awareness spiked for the briefest moment and a desperate snarl tore from Michael's throat. The scent of the driver's blood invaded his nostrils, tempting him beyond reason. His fangs slid down from his gums and it took every ounce of willpower in his control to keep from attacking the man speeding through the city in an effort to see him properly fed. Michael pierced his tongue with one sharp tip. It had been so long since he'd last fed, he didn't even have a drop of blood in his own body left to spare. His heart was silent in his rib cage, his lungs still. Chest unmoving with breath. He had nothing with which to keep the frenzy in check.

Michael Aristov was the last of the Ancient Ones, untethered and soulless, the lone remaining carrier of the collective memory, and the sole guardian of an orphaned race.

And if he didn't feed soon, he would be the death of them all.

Claire Thompson spread the wad of bills out on the table, smoothing the crumpled edges, and put them in order, largest to smallest. She promised herself this would be her last hustle, just this once until she picked up more hours at the diner. Without the three hundred dollars she'd won off those guys at the pool tables, she wouldn't have been able to make her rent. And there was no way in hell she was living out of her car again.

Truth be told, there was nothing like easy money. The hours at the diner were hard. Her feet ached every day, she was always tired, and half of her customers were filthy letches or undertipping assholes. She was good at hustling and it took a hell of lot less effort than balancing five plates of eggs and hash browns in one hand while trying not to spill the pot of coffee in her other. But she'd made a vow to herself that she was going to walk the straight and narrow from here on out. Well, from tomorrow on out. Tonight was about making her rent and getting the cash she needed for at least a week's worth of groceries. Los Angeles was a jungle. Survival of the fittest, kill or be killed, all of that law of the wild crap counted here, and she wasn't about to be culled from the herd because she couldn't take care of herself.

Claire stared across the street, observing the circus that had begun to set up camp at Diablo, the newest hotspot nightclub. The neon sign glowed bloodred in the encroaching darkness and the lineup of party girls waiting to go inside were a spectacle in and of themselves. What in god's name would possess a woman to leave her house dressed like a sexy stuffed animal? Tall furry boots, shorter-than-short micromini skirts, and bikini tops weren't enough for these hard-core partiers' outfits. Nope. They topped it all off with pointy-eared furry hats and little fluffy tails that stuck out from the backs of their too-short skirts.

Gag.

However . . . with the drum and bass EDM party scene

came a set of recreational drugs that would make a lot of them easy prey for a skilled pickpocket like Claire. And this wasn't the usual down-and-out crowd you came across in the Valley. The clientele who frequented Diablo tonight consisted of overprivileged, spoiled-rotten daddy's girls and unambitious trust fund boys. None of them would miss a diamond tennis bracelet or gold watch. They probably had drawers full of them at home. A single score would set her up for a couple of months. It was an opportunity she couldn't pass up. Besides, after tonight she was going straight.

She looked down at her worn skinny jeans, simple black tee, and cheap Payless heels. Not exactly the type of grade-A hottie who made it past the velvet rope, especially when she was contending with a horde of plushies, all sucking on pacifiers—probably laced with Molly—in a way that would tempt Freud from the grave. *Ew.*

There were other ways to get into a nightclub, though. She didn't need to look like a teddy-bear hooker to get past the gatekeepers. That's what back doors were for. Claire stuffed all but a hundred bucks of her cash into her pocket and headed out of the pool hall and across the street. She passed up the line of clubbers at the front entrance and strolled to the back of the building as though she belonged there. That was the trick to sneaking around: Never look like you're sneaking. A twentysomething guy in a red T-shirt with *Diablo* scrawled across the front in black script was standing outside the rear exit smoking a cigarette. He eyed Claire with suspicion, taking her in from head to toe. She smiled as though she'd known the guy for years, and tucked the two fifties against her right palm. Indecision gave her pause, and her step faltered as she headed up to the door. If she didn't score inside, she'd be out a hundred bucks and she'd have to go out tomorrow night to make up

the extra cash. Which would totally shoot to shit her vow
to make tonight her last night.

"Hey," she said to the guy at the door. "Sup?"

"The line to get in is around the corner," he replied on
an exhalation of smoke.

Claire kept the friendly smile plastered on her face no
matter how badly the smell made her stomach lurch. Scent
and memory were closely tied, unfortunately, and Claire
had a lot of shitty memories to dredge up. "Oh, I know,"
she said, and stretched out her right hand. "I just wanted to
introduce myself. I'm Janae." Rule of the hustle number
one: *Never* give your real name.

"Paul," the guy said, reaching out to shake her hand.

She slipped the bills against his hand and, though his
eyes showed a hint of acknowledgment, he didn't give any
other sign that she'd placed the bills into his palm. Apparently this wasn't Paul's first rodeo. He tucked his hand in
his pocket without so much as a glance at the money. Like
he knew that she'd tipped him well. Then again, Claire had
always had this strange trustworthy quality about her. It
was like she could project an aura of honesty and people
just bought it. It's what made her so good at the con. And
likewise, she always knew when someone was lying. Like
a tingle that spread through her body. Intuition like that
was a godsend when you grew up on the streets.

Paul toed the back door, easing it open to allow just
enough room for Claire to pass through. He didn't budge
from his spot, just took another drag and expelled the
smoke. "See ya around, Janae."

"You're one of the good ones, Paul," she said as she
slipped through the door.

He responded with an amused snort.

Once through the stockroom and in the club proper,
Claire was reminded of why she didn't hang out at places

like this. It always surprised her how high-class debauchery was so much more accepted. This place had the same sex, drugs, and dirty dealings on display as you'd find in a dive bar in the Valley. But in the morning everyone who'd been here would skip along their merry way like nothing had happened, as though money absolved them of all sin, whereas the stigma of bad behavior followed the less fortunate wherever they went. The wealth and privilege here was a painful reminder that these people were the *haves* while she was a *have-not*. She mused, as she took in her surroundings, that by midnight the accumulated net worth of the club patrons could probably pay off the national debt.

Acting as though she belonged in this crowd was tough when she felt so out of place. Her shoes were the most expensive part of her sad wardrobe. She'd saved up tips for two weeks to afford the thirty-dollar black heels, and to tell the truth, they pinched her feet so badly she was considering going barefoot. Dirty floors be damned.

From the corner of her eye she caught sight of a group of girls taking selfies with their top-of-the-line smartphones. Claire couldn't even afford a cheap prepaid burner phone. If she had to make a call, she used the phone at the diner. Besides, it's not like she had anyone in her life who might be interested in talking to her. For several minutes she stood there, staring as the trio made the standard pouty duck-lip faces, then switched to screwed-up gazes with their tongues lolling out of their mouths like deranged poodles. Which, considering the fact they were all wearing fuzzy hats and tails, wasn't too far off.

"Can I buy you a drink?"

Claire turned to the guy who'd sidled up beside her. Rule number two of the hustle: Free is always better. Especially at a high-end club like this, because a glass of white wine probably ran about twenty-five bucks. "Sure.

Thanks," she said, flashing a winsome smile. "I'll take a bourbon and Coke."

As he led the way to the bar, Claire sized up her first potential mark of the night. He wasn't bad looking, a typical Cali guy: blond, blue-eyed, and built. From the looks of his True Religion jeans and Ed Hardy tee, he was comfortable, though not too well off. His watch was okay, Fossil, but not worth more than a couple hundred bucks, which equated to a thirty-dollar pawn. He tucked his cell in his back pocket, looked like an early-generation iPhone, and a little banged up at that. Nope, this guy wasn't what she was after. She hadn't risked a hundred bucks of rent money for chump change. Claire was hunting bigger game tonight.

She accepted the proffered drink and pretended to sip. Rule of the hustle number three: A sloppy drunk makes for a sloppy con. Keeping her wits about her while still looking like she was having a good time was essential. Once you got someone to let down their inhibitions, they made a much easier target.

"What's your name?" Cali Boy shouted over the heart-stopping bass of the electronic dance music. The twenty-foot display screen behind the DJ booth flashed: *BassNectar.* Dude was certainly living up to his moniker.

"Suzette!" she shouted back. "Thanks again for the drink!"

"No problem." He gave her a smile and leaned in. "I'm Steve. So . . . what brings you out tonight?"

"Just livin' the dream, Steve." While he yammered on about whatever it was he did for a living—something in sports management—Claire scanned the crowd for her mark. The dance floor undulated with a mass of bodies, arms raised high, glow sticks clenched in their fists, and heads thrown back, grinding their asses against anything within touching distance like cats in heat. Strobe lights

flashed with each thump of bass and lasers shot out from
the DJ booth, projecting neon pink and yellow shapes on
the walls and ceilings. Through the mass of bodies and
constant movement Claire narrowed her focus. In addition
to her built-in lie detector, she possessed an uncanny
concentration that she could narrow down to almost a
pinpoint. Each distraction melted away until it felt like
everything moved in slow motion, giving her the time she
needed to make her assessment. Like the eyes of a hawk
searching for a mouse in tall grass, her gaze roamed the
crowd until she zeroed in on a man headed to the back of
the club where the VIP tables were.

Bingo.

Dressed in sleek black slacks and a dress shirt that
probably cost more than a couple of months of Claire's
rent. Swaying on his feet as though he could barely keep
himself upright, he looked as out of place with the nouveau-
raver crowd as she did. He stood about a foot taller than
the tallest guys there and made Steve's sculpted body look
puny in comparison. He wasn't there for the music. He
was at Diablo because this was an "it" place and he was an
"it" guy. She'd have to get a little closer to properly assess
him, but that wouldn't be a problem. If her initial impression was correct, whatever she managed to lift from this
guy would feed her for a few months. Hell, maybe she'd
spring for the name-brand mayo this time.

"So, do you maybe wanna get out of here and grab a bite
to eat?" Steve looked at her expectantly, setting his own
drink on the bar as though positive he was about to score.

"Sorry, but no. Thanks again for the drink, Stevie!"
Claire shouted over the music as she headed toward the
VIP room.

"It's Steve!" he called after her.

She lifted her hand in acknowledgment but didn't turn
around. It was time to hunt.

CHAPTER
2

Murmured voices followed Michael through the club, so much louder than the music or the roar of the crowd. He pushed the myriad sounds to the back of his mind, refusing to let the assault of sensory overload further disable him. Eyes tracked him, flashing silver in the darkness, keen and curious. He kept his distance from most dhampirs, and in turn they regarded him with the wariness of a pack in the presence of their alpha. Their draw on his meager energy stores caused his step to falter as he pushed through the crowds to the VIP lounge. His self-inflicted starvation punished them all. In his untethered state, he couldn't be bothered to care.

Michael was an Ancient One. The last of the true vampires. Dhampirs were a product of birth. The only way for a dhampir to become a vampire was to drain the body of blood and replenish it by taking the vein of a vampire. Due to the fact that he was untethered—his soul lost to oblivion until he found his mate—Michael didn't have the strength to turn any of them. Perhaps he wasn't the only one condemned to a state of inertia.

Every vampire had been descended from a single creature. Like a grove of aspen trees were interconnected, the blood that created them tied them to one another. And there was just enough of that ancient blood flowing through every dhampir's veins to connect them all to Michael. Fate could indeed be a cruel master at times.

In the two and a half centuries since the vampires had been all but exterminated, class divisions separated the dhampir covens, pitting them against one another. Some wanted Michael gone from the face of the earth while others waited eagerly for him to step up and fully claim his role as their leader. They craved the gift he could give them, the bite that would transform them from beings that lived between the human and vampire realms into the creatures they were meant to be.

Without being tethered, he was helpless to do anything for them.

Michael's own raging thirst was paltry in comparison to that of the collective mass of dhampirs in the vicinity. Many of them were in the club now, watching, waiting to share in his strength. They saw a savior, while Michael saw himself as nothing more than a soulless creature destined to fall through time in a state of perpetual emptiness. Perhaps that was why he'd persisted in this state of near starvation for the past century. To punish himself for his inability to save his brethren now as well as when the Sortiari had begun their quest to exterminate the vampires centuries ago.

"Hi. Alex sent me. Mind if I join you?"

He looked up to find a woman gazing down at him and once again Michael was reminded why he paid Alex such a hefty salary. He opened his palm in greeting. "Please. Sit."

She smiled seductively and her too-white, veneered teeth were the perfect horrid complement to her collagen-injected lips and unnaturally large breasts. Why would any woman want to defile the soft curves she came by naturally by replacing them with something unyielding and artificial? No matter. He didn't want to fuck the human after all, just feed from her. And whereas her appearance did little for his lust, the scent of her blood set his throat ablaze.

Bide your time. If he didn't get a grip, he'd tear into the woman's throat. "Can I buy you a drink?" It was the least he could do. After all, she was about to supply him with one. "Champagne?" Wasn't that what humans wanted in these ridiculously overpriced clubs? He motioned to one of the waitresses who serviced the VIP room, appropriately outfitted with devil horns and a long red tail that seemed to grow from the back of her short black skirt. Michael reached into his pocket and produced a matte black credit card from his wallet and handed it to the waitress. "Bring us a bottle of Clos d'Ambonnay."

The waitress smiled appreciatively and spun on a heel, no doubt anxious for the tip that would accompany a thirty-five-hundred-dollar bottle of champagne.

"Oh. My. Gawd!" the woman beside him squealed. She stuck out her hand, wrist bent as though he should kiss it. "I've always wanted to try that! I'm Jasmine, by the way."

He looked down at her hand but didn't move to take it. *Charming.* Michael's patience was wearing thin, as was his control. With each second that passed, his thirst mounted. It didn't help that the human was now stuck to him like a strip of duct tape, rubbing her ridiculous fake breasts against his arm in a way that he assumed was supposed to be arousing. She'd been chattering on for at least twenty minutes, about what Michael had no idea. *How the fuck long did it take to retrieve a bottle of champagne anyway?*

She ran a palm up the inside of his thigh but stopped short of his cock when the waitress showed up with the champagne. *Finally. Thank the gods.* He signed the receipt, adding on a hefty tip for their server before he poured two glasses of the pale bubbling drink. His companion's eyes rolled back into her head as she drank, a low moan that was more reminiscent of a wail issuing from her throat.

Humans like her were a prime example of how easy it could be to hunt in the city. It was also a sore reminder that he had no excuse—other than sadistic self-torture—for starving himself. As Jasmine drank and giggled and drank some more, the scent of her blood pushed Michael's need past reason. Around him he sensed the anticipation of the dhampirs, and he almost reconsidered piercing the woman's throat just to punish them for violating his privacy. For the briefest moment he welcomed the pain of madness and starvation. His instinct to feed was far stronger than his will to die, however. Michael nuzzled the woman's throat and brushed his lips against her jugular, causing the dual set of fangs to throb in his gums.

"Oh yeah, baby," the woman moaned as she tilted her head to expose her throat. "Put your mouth on me."

Gladly. Michael sealed his lips over her throat, sucking gently to coax the vein closer to the surface. Her skin tasted of cheap perfume and she reeked of acrid, chemical-laced smoke. At the moment his fangs punctured her flesh, she melted into his embrace, her high, mewling moan inaudible to anyone but him over the pounding bass of the DJ's music. Her head lolled back on her shoulder and Michael gripped the back of her head to support her. Blood, warm and tinged with something foreign—a narcotic of some kind—passed over his tongue. Human drugs had no effect on him. Michael's eyes drifted shut as he joined his prey in the bliss of feeding.

With each swallow he was infused with strength; her scent, her taste, the feel of her in his embrace, enhanced as his senses sharpened. His heart began to beat once again, his metabolism awakening as living blood coursed in his veins. The air around him became charged with a static tension, like the approach of a violent storm, and he felt the utter relief of the dhampirs who shared in what he'd taken from this woman.

With a sudden, shattering impact a scent the likes of which had no equal invaded Michael's senses and he pulled so violently from the human's throat that he nearly tore her flesh. His brain roared with an instinct too strong to resist, but if he didn't close the punctures in the woman's neck she'd bleed out in a matter of seconds. She slumped against his body and Michael quickly scored his tongue, lapping at her throat and healing the bite. He laid her down in the booth without another thought to her welfare as he was inexplicably drawn to the scent of blood that called to him in a way that he'd never felt before in all of his centuries upon the earth.

Want. Need. Hunger. Desire. *Lust.*

Raw, untamed emotion exploded inside of him, something so deep and primal that he was helpless to fight it. The empty void that had opened up inside of him upon his turning filled to bursting and Michael rubbed at his chest as though the change were a physical thing. His mind raced as he tried to make sense of what he felt, the sensation so foreign and shocking. It had been so long since he'd last fed, perhaps his dormant body simply wasn't used to being rejuvenated. Or maybe it was the sheer fierceness of the anticipation of the dhampirs that sent him into a frenzy. His muscles bunched and flexed with every step, as though they'd gone decades without use. The soulless void evaporated, and in the center of his being something secured itself to him as though with a length of unbreakable chain. The past two hundred years of solitude melted away in this moment, his quest for the exotic scent that drove him past reason, and for the first time since the slayer had entombed him all of those years ago Michael experienced the vitality of the warrior he once was. The powerful vampire. The hunter in search of prey.

But beyond that, he felt *alive*. Truly alive, as he had been before he'd been made into a vampire. Before he'd made the decision to trade his soul for an existence as one of the untethered. If he didn't find the source of that delicious scent, the sweet blood that entranced him like a siren's song, he'd go mad.

Through the hordes of humans he swathed a path with one long arm, brushing them aside as though they were nothing more than blades of grass and his arm a broadsword. The dhampirs watched with curious yet fearful expressions, their irises reflecting silver in the low light, giving him a wide berth as they bowed their heads, afraid to meet his feral gaze. He had finally come alive this night, and though his heart beat anew, it wasn't the whore's blood that had brought him from his soulless stupor. No, as Michael's eyes lit on a female not twenty feet away he knew without a doubt that it was her blood that called to him and her scent that had awakened him.

This female had tethered his soul and returned it to him.

As though she sensed him, too, her eyes met his. She looked nothing like the overdone, overused, and utterly underwhelming human females who seemed to frequent these sorts of clubs. Rather, she stood out among them. A breath of fresh air in a stale environment.

Her lips curled into a flirtatious smile. A sly, seductive expression that caused his cock to grow hard and the blood coursing through his veins to warm. She turned from him, winding a path through the VIP lounge toward the less populated area at the back of the club. Didn't she realize that running only made him want to give chase? Or was that what she wanted, to be captured in a shadowy corner where no one would hear her moans of pleasure as he took her vein?

Michael's step faltered. Of course, she couldn't possibly know what he wanted from her, how her scent drove him to the frenzy that made his earlier thirst a mere annoyance in comparison. If she thought to find an exit in this part of the club she was about to be disappointed. In a matter of moments she'd be trapped, and a thrill of excitement coursed through Michael's veins at the prospect.

Claire found herself facing a black wall with *Diablo* painted in giant red script above her. She put her back to it, palms bracing her as though she'd made a fatal error. *Oops!* she had nowhere left to go. Rule of the hustle number four: Let the mark think he's running the show.

He was high as a freaking kite; of that she was positive. Too bad, too. He was much too hot to waste his looks—and probably his wealth—on the life of a burnout. Claire took a moment to observe him as he stalked toward her. Any woman would be tempted to fall to her knees and thank the lord for his creation when she got a look at the one-two punch this guy was bringing. Tall and sculpted without looking like one of those muscle-beach meatheads. She was willing to bet he pretended to be some sort of fitness junkie when he wasn't high. She saw it sometimes in addicts. They looked fit and portrayed a healthy lifestyle to cover up for their illegal extracurricular activities. He probably worked in the film industry. Not on-screen talent, but she figured he was a lawyer or producer. Maybe a moneyman. Or, more likely, private security. An aura of importance surrounded him as if he knew he was the shit and everyone else should, too.

Full, dark hair brushed his brow in a casual style that was meant to look like he'd hopped out of bed and into his clothes. A straight nose, sharp cheekbones, and the most amazing dimple in his chin only lent to his aura of strength. And his eyes . . . holy shit, were they beautiful. A bright turquoise blue that reminded her of a picture she'd seen of the waters off the coast of Cozumel. She felt an instant connection with him. Something deep and obsessive that stole her breath. She'd never felt such an intense spark of interest before. Shame, too, since she was about to rob the poor sucker blind.

Good looks or not, she wasn't here to flirt. Besides, she didn't waste her time on addicts and users. He was mere feet from her now, each step he took a predatory swagger that sent a thrill through her body. Claire's breath returned, quickening in her chest as she sized him up: much bigger up close. For a moment she had the feeling that she might be in way over her head with this one, but then her gaze landed on the gorgeous Patek watch on his left wrist. With the right fence that watch could cover six months or more's worth of rent. Not to mention cupboards full of groceries. She'd hit pay dirt with this guy. *Ka-ching!*

Claire fixed a flirtatious smile on her face, which, considering the guy was a superhottie, wasn't too tough. He closed the remaining feet between them in a couple of long strides and braced himself against the wall with one strong arm, leaning down as he buried his face in her hair. Was he *smelling* her? Okay, that was sort of weird.

"What are you?"

His voice was a low, hungry rumble in her ear that caused chills to break out over her flesh. Dude was trippin' balls, no doubt about it, but oh man, he could use that voice on her any time he wanted. "What do you want me to be?" The suggestive banter was meant to invite physical contact. He was so out of his mind, it wouldn't be tough to lift his wallet or that amazing watch once the heavy petting began. Claire's gaze landed on his full lips and she almost sighed. If she had to, she could sacrifice a kiss or two, *if* it meant ensuring his distraction.

"Don't play with me. I'm not in the mood for games. You're not simply a human female."

Simply a human? She'd underestimated just how far gone this guy was. "Now, why would I play games with you?" She looked up to meet his gaze. Those turquoise eyes—the dark pupils blown—burned with something she couldn't identify, the intensity of his expression bordering on pain. She reached up and threaded her fingers through the silky soft strands of his hair. Claire almost felt bad for the guy. He was so out of it, he was practically begging to be ripped off. "If you're not interested, I'm pretty sure there's someone waiting for you back at your table."

A thought occurred that he might be a pimp for top-of-the-line call girls. The woman slumped over in his booth sure looked like one. And how awesome was he for just leaving her passed out and alone like that? *Creep.* He was drop-dead gorgeous, but that was the thing about sin: It was always seductive.

"What's your name?" Good lord. Wasn't anyone interested in an anonymous hookup? She was running out of creative responses.

"Amy," she answered. "Yours?"

"Michael."

"No, it isn't." The words left Claire's mouth before she could stop them from escaping. She didn't usually call people out on their bullshit, just used it as leverage. But it seemed she couldn't help but point out his lie.

He canted his head to the side and pinned her with a stare that was much too lucid for his drugged-out state. Something silvery glinted in the depths of his dark pupils and Claire gave herself a mental shake. Maybe she was getting a contact high? "Why would you say that?"

Yeah, Claire, why would you? She was supposed to be inviting his trust, encouraging him to lower his guard, not put him on high alert. *Eye on the prize. Get your hands on that watch and get the hell out of here.*

Rule of the hustle number five: Never break character. She was in a club, surrounded by drugs and alcohol. It would throw up all sorts of red flags if she was the only woman in the place who wasn't at least rocking a buzz. She couldn't turn off the hookup vibe she'd been sending his way just because her internal lie detector was flashing. Besides, who was she to judge?

"You just don't look like a Michael to me, that's all." Claire wrapped her fingers around his large forearm, braced against the wall beside her. Holy shit, the guy must have been chiseled from marble. She caressed a path to his wrist and brought his hand down so it rested on her hip. At this angle, she should be able to flip the clasp on the watch. Once it was good and loose, he wouldn't even notice when it slipped off his wrist.

His nostrils flared when their bodies connected, and he stepped in closer, so close that Claire had to crane her neck up to look into his face. A shiver raced across her flesh. Was it the rush of the con or the thrill of that large palm cupping her hip, his fingers squeezing her as though barely restrained? "Your scent is maddening." His voice was a ragged, desperate growl in her ear. "And I want nothing more than to taste you."

Okay, she'd heard weirder. But the way he spoke—his voice slightly accented in a way that made it hard to pinpoint a region—coupled with the formality of his words piqued Claire's curiosity. Who in the hell was this guy, anyway? And just what would *tasting her* entail? As she contemplated the possibilities, she couldn't deny that the prospect of having his lush mouth anywhere on her body made Claire's brain go a little fuzzy. Rule number six of the hustle: Never lose control.

Keeping her wits about her was a must right now and she couldn't let his sexy voice or *GQ* good looks distract her. The whole point of this game was to keep him so occupied that he wouldn't notice that she'd lifted his watch. Her goal had been to get him all hot and bothered and then move in for the kill. Dude was already pretty worked up. So it was time to get on with the show.

"I have to admit, I've been watching you all night." Claire made sure to keep her voice nice and breathy. "Imagining what it might be like to kiss you." She licked her lips as she stared up into those endless blue eyes and let out a sigh that ended on a moan. His brow creased at the sound, and he rolled his hips into her. *Holy shit. Is that a redwood in your pocket or are you just happy to see me?* Her lips parted on a silent *oh*. Okay, she'd definitely gotten a contact high from someone smoking weed nearby. Because she had to be hallucinating her mark's good looks and raw sensuality.

Michael shifted, cupping her ass with his free hand. Claire couldn't help the gasp that escaped her lips as he hoisted her up as though she weighed nothing and braced her back against the wall. She really had no choice but to wrap her legs around his waist, and when her core brushed up against the erection straining against the fly of his high-priced designer slacks every nerve in her body ignited with awareness. His gaze burned with desire and a lucidity that frightened her. Maybe he wasn't as high as she'd given him credit for.

So much for being the hunter. Claire had a feeling that she'd just become his prey.

CHAPTER
3

Not human. How could she be? The thought resounded over and again in Michael's mind as he fought to maintain an ounce of self-control. A vampire had never been tethered by a human as far as he knew. It simply wasn't possible. And yet his soul burned bright at his center, filling the endless void. He wanted to strip her naked and lay her out on the floor. Run his nose over every inch of her exposed flesh and hold her scent in his lungs before he fucked her. A scrap of memory buffeted his subconscious, not his memory, though it belonged to him just the same. It spurred an instinct that he couldn't fight: an urge to take this female, sink his fangs into her throat, drink of her, claim her body, and make her his forever. To *turn* her.

Impossible.

And yet he was frozen in place, unable to tear himself away from her. In fact, merely using her and walking away seemed too great a feat. And why would he? Their souls were tethered. It could all be a lie, though. Perhaps the instinct he thought he felt was merely an echo of memory brought on by his recent feeding. It would pass, as would the madness he felt for this *human*. He was kidding himself if he believed she was anything but mundane. Once he took her vein, the spell would be broken.

He lifted her in his arms and pinned her against the wall. She wrapped her long legs around his waist and he rolled into her hips, his cock so hard it ached. His bite would give her pleasure, but perhaps she would want more? He'd like nothing more than to fuck her while he drank from her, and he doubted anyone would notice if he yanked her jeans down around her thighs and took her right here against the wall.

It had been so long since he'd felt the tight warmth of a female's soft flesh.

Her lips parted as though in a silent moan, and Michael's stomach clenched with lust. Her eyes were wide, limpid pools of amber and her warm golden hair cascaded over her shoulders in straight, silky sheets. Her skin was delicate porcelain, so refreshing in this city of fake, painted-on tans. He let go of her hip and traced his thumb over a jagged scar on her left temple, just above her brow, and a predatory growl rumbled in his chest. He'd kill whoever deigned to harm her.

She reached up and caught his hand in hers, bringing it to her lips. When the heat of her mouth made contact with his skin, the low rumble intensified, and she smiled.

"I've never made a man purr before," she said in a voice as smooth and rich as fresh cream. "I kind of like it."

How could a human hear anything over the sound of the music and roar of the crowd? Then again, did he really care? She laid his palm flat against her ribs and guided him down her torso and back to her waist. A slow, secretive smile crept onto her lips as she pulled his hand away from her body, but only for a moment as she slipped it beneath the hem of her shirt. The skin-on-skin contact spurred him past reason and he pressed his body against hers as he seized her mouth in a desperate kiss.

She threaded her fingers through his hair, fisting the locks as she held him tightly to her. Her tongue thrust into his mouth, and if the scent of her could snap his restraint, the sweetness of her lips was enough to send him to the brink of insanity. As though she was as starved for him as he was for her, she slanted her mouth across his, her kisses bordering on violent, as if a lifetime had separated them and she was punishing him for withholding himself from her for so long. In his fervor, one fang nicked her bottom lip and the taste of her blood on his tongue sent him toppling over the ledge of his meager control.

Ah, gods! He pulled away from her mouth with a lustful snarl, grinding his cock against her sex as he buried his face against her throat. She arched into him, a low moan issuing from her lips as he latched on to her vein and sank his fangs into her flesh.

"Michael!"

She cried out as he pierced her skin, clinging desperately to him as she held his head to her throat. But that was not the name he wanted on her lips, not the Americanized version of his name he'd adopted, but his true name, the name the slayer had stolen the night the bastard tried to put his existence to an end once and for all. Her blood flowed warm and thick into his mouth and Michael held her fast as he took her vein. She was unlike anything he'd ever tasted: sweet and intoxicating. As the frenzy swept him up, Michael shoved his free hand between them, tearing at the button on her jeans and forcing the metal zipper down until he had no choice but to rip the heavy denim to get to what he wanted.

His only thought was of taking her.

A long-forgotten sense of elation swelled in Michael's

chest, his heart thundering for the first time in months. He forced the distraction to the back of his mind. Aware of the eager attention of the dhampirs, they drew on the burst of unparalleled strength this woman had given him. Hell, every last person in the crowded club could have stopped what they were doing to watch him and he wouldn't have given a fuck-all about it. He cared only for this moment, the human in his arms, and the blood that was like an elixir of life to him.

She whimpered in his embrace and he plunged his hand past the elastic waistband of her underwear. As his fingers found her slick center, she bucked against him, nearly breaking the seal of his mouth on her throat. Gods, but she was ready for him. Her heat enveloped him, her sex nearly dripping and swollen with want. As he drew on her vein, he slid his fingers through her swollen flesh and against the tight knot of nerves at her core. Her hips rolled in time with each pull of his mouth and her legs tightened around his waist. She pushed herself from the wall and her breath was hot in his ear as she moaned, "Don't stop until I come."

She'll come for me now with my mouth at her vein? His balls grew tight at those desperately whispered words, so close to begging that it tempted him to stop, if only to hear her beg again. The tension in her arms slackened and her head lolled back against the wall. Panic chased the high of feeding and by sheer force of will he disengaged from her throat. Her lids were heavy with passion and her eyes glazed over as though she'd lost focus. Michael cradled her head in his palm as he pierced his own tongue on one fang and laved at the punctures until they closed.

He'd taken too much from her. The slow thrum of her heart echoed in his ears, thready and weak compared to how it had rushed over his tongue while he drank from her. Michael froze with fear. Caught up in his lust for blood and her body, he'd forgotten himself. And now this beautiful woman would pay the price for his carelessness.

"Please, don't stop."

She gripped his hand with both of hers and urged him to resume where he had let off. The lazy rhythm of her heart increased in speed, no longer weak but rivaling the heavy bass that reverberated throughout the club. How? He'd drained her almost to the point of death, yet somehow she endured.

"Michael, touch me."

He slid one finger and then another inside of her, all the while working the swollen bundle of nerves with the pad of his thumb. She shuddered against him, gripping his shoulders in her hands until her nails bit into his skin through his shirt. He seized her mouth in a hungry kiss as his own lusts mounted to the point that he wasn't sure how much longer he could withhold himself from her. Hips thrusting in time with his fingers, he could only imagine how tight and warm she'd be when he buried his cock inside of her. She sobbed her pleasure as he stroked her, and her sex constricted, squeezing tight around his fingers. Her body went rigid and she cried out, her core pulsing around him as she went limp in his arms. A rich, sweet scent bloomed around them, permeating his senses and awakening an instinct that Michael had never experienced before. Again, he was assaulted by the others' memories, visions of a bond that he couldn't explain nor had ever known. And still, he recognized it in an instant; as inexplicable as it may have seemed, he was tethered. His soul had found its twin and this human belonged to him.

Her breath heaved in her chest as he planted featherlight kisses to her brow, cheeks, and lips. She uncoiled her legs from around him, sliding to the floor, and he pulled her against his chest, his fist wound in the golden length of her hair.

"We're not done here," he growled against her ear.
"You've had your pleasure; now give me mine." She had to
know that she was his now. How could she think of leaving him? She pulled away and he locked his hand around
her upper arm. "Did you not beg for me to touch you? To
taste you? Your cries of pleasure were not false. Don't
withhold yourself from me, Amy."

Her expression darkened as a shadow passed over her
bright amber eyes. The briefest flicker of fear crossed her
face and it sliced through him with the fiery pain of a silver blade. "Let me go," she whispered.

She pulled free of his grasp and ducked under his arm
before he could take hold of her again. Through the crowd
she ran, weaving and ducking this way and that until he
lost sight of her. But Michael didn't need eyes to know the
direction in which she'd fled. They were connected by an
inexorable bond that she couldn't escape.

After centuries of pain, the unending torture of his existence, he'd found the only creature who could wake him
from his stupor and return his soul to him. Immeasurable
strength fueled every movement, and he was no longer the
shade of the vampire he'd once been. The world melted
away until there was only her. He'd found the one thing he
needed to survive in this gods-forsaken world. He took off
after her, his speed surprising even to him. It would be
nothing to catch her, and once he did, he would never let her
go. Her blood was the very essence of life, calling to him
in a way that no other had in four centuries of existence.
Stranger or not, she belonged to him now, and he would not
rest until he tasted her again.

Hands reached out, voices calling out to him, rejoicing.
He dodged, unwilling to let the eager dhampirs deter him
from what he wanted. If they kept him from the female,
he'd rip them apart with his bare hands.

"I swear, Mikhail, if you take another step, I'll stake you myself."

A familiar voice caused Michael to halt and he cursed under his breath. The only dhampir who could stop him in his tracks just so happened to be in this club. Coincidence? Not a chance.

"Ronan." Michael turned, his teeth clenched to keep him from snapping his jaws around the other male's throat, and faced the fair-haired dhampir. "Your timing is—"

"Perfect?" Ronan ventured with a cocky grin.

"Unfortunate." Bodies pressed in as every dhampir in the club converged on him. *Very* unfortunate.

Claire burst through the doors of the club gasping for breath. She could feel him close behind, pursuing her like a beast on the hunt. She gripped the Patek tight in her fist as she kicked off the too-tight stilettos and raced down the sidewalk, ducking into the nearest alley. Thoughts of tetanus, or worse, threatened to send her back for her shoes, but she pushed the fear of cutting her feet and contracting something nasty to the back of her mind. She had to get the hell out of there. *Now.* Before he caught up to her. The last and most important rule of the hustle: Get while the gettin's good.

Truth be told, it wasn't the fear of being caught that had Claire's heart thundering and her breath racing. She'd never let things get so out of hand with a mark before. Especially one as shady as Michael. There was more to him than met the eye and she should have been wary, but instead, she threw herself at him like some kind of sex-starved coed looking for a Saturday-night hookup. Classy.

Despite the prize she tucked into her pocket for safekeeping, she didn't feel any sense of accomplishment. Instead, shame flushed her cheeks at the memory of his kisses, the sting of his teeth at her throat, and the soft touch of his skilled fingers as he drove her crazy with want. She ran out on him not because she had the watch and wanted to make a speedy getaway but rather because she was afraid that she'd shuck her pants right there in the middle of the club and let him do wicked things to her whether they had an audience or not. The truth hit her like a base-ball bat to the forehead as she dashed across Sunset toward Clark and another back alley.

No man had ever given her an orgasm like that, and she and Michael had barely revved their engines. She could only imagine what he could have accomplished given a little privacy and an hour or three of her time. And what the hell kind of magic had he worked on her throat, any-way? Waves of desire pulsed low in her stomach at the rec-ollection. The not-so-gentle bite followed up with a deep suction that sent a shock of searing heat through her blood-stream. She'd been on the edge of orgasm just from that contact. Her body literally *ached* for him by the time he finally went to work on her zipper.

Claire reached down to the front of her jeans and felt the rip he'd made below the seam. Talk about anxious to get into a girl's pants. He'd torn the heavy denim as if it were tissue paper. He had to have superstrength to accomplish the feat. Then again, she'd seen people do some pretty in-human shit while they were high.

Using side streets, she backtracked until she was a few blocks down from Diablo and on Sunset once again. Con-fident she'd managed to shake her pursuer, Claire slowed her pace, giving her tired, pavement-scraped feet a rest until she could hail a cab. "Four Twenty South Westlake," she said to the driver.

"That's out of my way." The cabbie sounded more than a little put out.

No way was Claire going to hop two or three cabs with

bare feet to get home. "I'll make it worth your while. Promise."

He grumbled under his breath but put the car in gear and pulled out into traffic. Money. The timeless motivator. Claire let her head fall back against the seat and her eyes drifted shut. A silver and turquoise blue stare haunted her thoughts, and his voice raw with emotion when he said, "We're not done here. You've had your pleasure; now give me mine."

That sort of entitled male bullshit was usually the thing that made Claire run in the opposite direction. Right after she drove her knee into the guy's nuts. But the way Michael said it . . . the words were more of a plea than an angry demand. She'd stolen the guy's watch and left him with a serious case of blue balls. Was she the world's biggest asshole or what?

Claire spent the entire thirty-minute cab ride replaying the night's events in her mind. There was something about Michael—other than the fact that he'd lied about his name—that spoke to a hidden part of her. As though she'd known him for a lifetime. Or, rather, was meant to know him for a lifetime.

Wow. Way to rock the hopeless romantic vibe. What a loser. Life wasn't all rose petals and rainbows. Claire had firsthand proof of that. And besides, the guy had been high on something and that violated Claire's number one most important dating rule: No drugs. Ever.

The cab pulled up to her building and she dug the wad of bills from her pocket. "That'll be seventy bucks," the cabbie said with a sneer.

Seventy dollars? What a crock. She knew for a fact that he shouldn't have charged her more than forty-five. But the jerk had turned off the meter when they pulled out onto Sunset so she couldn't call him on his miscalculation. She'd been more than willing to give the guy a generous tip—more than the seventy he asked for—for going out of his way to take her home. But instead of trusting her to do as she promised, he'd chosen to rip her off. Typical L.A. bullshit.

"Here." She gave him two twenties and a ten and opened the door.

"What the hell?" he barked. "I thought you said you'd make it worth my while."

"You made it more than worth it," she said as she climbed out of the car. "It's not my fault you calculated your own tip."

She closed the door on the string of profanity he was throwing her way. What a jerk. Without a look back, she took off at a slow jog toward her building. The place was only a notch above condemned and it still cost her nine hundred dollars a month in rent. If she could manage to pick up a double shift or two at the diner, she'd be elevated to "just scraping by" status. And it was a total downer to admit that she aspired to that lowly fiscal existence. Scraping by was still way better than anything she'd had so far in her twenty-four years of life.

Once inside the building, Claire made her way up the stairs to the second story. She paused at unit 216 and pulled the rest of the money and the watch from her pocket. Midnight. Probably too late to knock.

"Hi, Claire!" a soft ten-year-old voice said as the door opened. "I thought I heard someone out in the hall."

Claire gave her young neighbor an apologetic smile. Ever since they day they'd moved in, something about the girl had tickled her instincts. Like an itch that she couldn't quite reach. Maybe it was simply the kinship of their similar childhoods. Either way, it had instantly endeared her to Claire. "Hi, Vanessa. I didn't wake you, did I?"

"No," she said. "Mom's having a bad night, so I was up making her some soup."

Bad night. Right. Vanessa's mom, Carlene, was addicted to oxy and paid about as much attention to Vanessa as she did to their scrawny, malnourished cat. Carlene had sold her daughter's bike last month to fund her fix and Claire was pretty sure that Vanessa didn't have anything but ramen noodles in the house. Why was it so hard for some people to love and take care of their kids? "I wanted to drop off a little something for you." Claire motioned for Vanessa to come out into the hall, extended her hand, and put a wad of bills in the girl's palm. "Go out tomorrow and buy some food. And get a new outfit for school and some notebooks and pencils, okay? Tina will help you if go down to the thrift store at the end of the block. You don't want to start a new year without at least one pretty new dress."

"I know Tina. I play with her new puppy sometimes. But . . . I can't take this," Vanessa said, her eyes wide. "Mom would—"

"Your mom doesn't need to know," Claire interrupted. If Carlene found out about the money she'd spend it on pills before you could say "back to school sale." "Think of it as an early birthday present."

Vanessa's mouth puckered. "My birthday isn't until February."

"An early Christmas present, then. Take the money and hide it somewhere, okay? Don't tell anyone else about it. Just go out tomorrow and buy some stuff."

"Okay," Vanessa said reluctantly.

"Promise me."

Vanessa gave her a sheepish smile. "I promise."

"All right. Now get to bed. It's way past your bedtime." Claire gave Vanessa a peck on the cheek and sent her back inside.

A hundred bucks wasn't enough to buy Vanessa much, but it was a start and maybe if Claire picked up that second shift she could do a little more. God knew the kid needed every bit of help she could get. She turned Michael's watch in her hand and examined the intricate detail of the gears visible through the crystal face. It had to be worth fifty grand, and if she was lucky she could fence it for five or six thousand.

Claire continued down the hall and stuck a key into the lock of unit 219. Being a witness to Vanessa's childhood was too much like reliving her own. Maybe if she'd lived close to a concerned neighbor who slipped her a twenty now and then she wouldn't have resorted to hustling for cash. And maybe, just maybe, if her mom had been marginally more responsible and behaved like an actual parent who, you know, passed a few values on to her kid Claire wouldn't have given herself over to her passions and let a stranger do the things Michael had done to her tonight.

Although, as she turned on the light in her beat-up kitchen and rifled through the thirty-year-old fridge for the leftovers she'd brought home from her shift last night, she was struck with the thought that even if she'd grown up to be an honest, forthright girl with plenty of cash in her pocket she still would have given herself to Michael tonight.

Who in the hell was this man who made her feel things she didn't know she could feel? And how could she find him again?

CHAPTER
4

"If you're looking for a distraction, Ronan, go find one in the city. Otherwise, quit staring at me. You're making me feel like a damned bug under a microscope."

Ronan had been with Michael from the beginning. The beginning of his solitary existence, anyway. He had been starved, weak, his body emaciated after a century trapped underground, and without Ronan's help in escaping Kiev under the nose of the Sortiari Michael wouldn't be standing here now. Of course, also thanks to Ronan, he wouldn't have lost the female tonight. Fate certainly had a way of balancing the scales.

Michael paced the confines of his living room. Sunrise was still a couple of hours off, but already the walls felt as though they were closing in around him. It didn't help that Ronan's gaze followed Michael back and forth, back and forth, like a child watching a caged tiger in a zoo.

"I can't help it," Ronan replied. He crossed to the bar at the far end of the room and poured himself a finger of scotch. "I mean, have you looked at yourself, Mikhail? You're . . ."

"Agitated." Michael massaged his naked left wrist, just now noticing that he no longer wore the Patek. On top of losing the female, he'd lost a sixty-five-thousand-dollar watch. *Lovely.*

"I was going to say 'a walking miracle.' How did this happen? And where the hell is the female who donated her vein, because I want to shake her hand. Maybe even kiss her. Didn't I tell you that feeding from humans wasn't doing you a damned bit of good? A little dhampir blood was all you needed."

Michael shot Ronan a glare as a predatory growl gathered in his chest.

"Someone's wound a little tightly tonight," Ronan remarked before he tossed back the drink. He poured another and crossed the room to resume his vigil in one of the brown leather wing chairs. "I already apologized for stopping you. What more do you want?"

The moment Ronan had accosted Michael, the dhampirs in the club had converged on him in an anxious crowd. All of them eager for more of the strength he'd bestowed on them. Like drought-stricken land after a hard rain they'd nourished themselves on the sudden burst of power, and both a searing guilt and sorrow tore through him for keeping them all in a state of near starvation for so long. Tender emotions had no impact on the untethered. And until his soul had been returned to him tonight he'd not been bothered by such crippling emotions. He felt it all now, though. Every painful one. Under their assault, the dhampirs had brought Michael to his knees, and the massive draw of energy from his stores made it nearly impossible for him to stand on his own two feet. If not for Ronan, Michael would still be there, beneath the press of eager bodies. It was the only reason he hadn't beaten the male bloody for waylaying him.

"You can hardly blame me for my enthusiasm. Or my

curiosity. I feel fucking fantastic. And if I feel this good, then you must be positively—"

"Enraged beyond belief."

"Stop doing that," Ronan complained, this time sipping from the highball glass. "You feel alive. Invigorated. Like you could conquer the world and defeat your enemies with a single blow. I *know* how you feel, Mikhail," he said, low. "And it is *not* enraged."

Ronan was an eager fool.

Michael continued to pace, his frustration mounting with each carefully placed step. Already the distance between him and the human was too great to track her, and with the rising sun he risked the chance that the distance would grow greater still. Ronan's elation would be short-lived once he discovered the female—and the source of Michael's resurging power—had disappeared into the night thanks to his untimely interruption.

A tethering with a human was unheard of. Would Ronan even believe it if he told him? Michael wasn't sure he believed it himself. "Gone," he said, interrupting his own train of thought this time. "The female is gone."

Ronan gave an unconcerned shrug. "How hard can a dhampir female be to track once you've shared blood? Besides, maybe you spooked her with your"—Ronan waved his hand up and down—"dark prince vibe. Once she calms down, she'll come sprinting back to you."

Insufferable. Ronan rambled on, about what Michael had no idea. He pinched the bridge of his nose, eyes squeezed shut. Had Amy been a dhampir, she might have recognized the tethering for what it was and stayed by his side. It was Michael who let her run. Let her slip through his fingers. His own confusion and shock had gotten the better of him. He'd let Ronan distract him. Let the dhampirs overtake him. And it was a choice that soured his stomach with regret.

The memory of her, soft in his arms, full lips parted as sweet gasps of pleasure brushed his face, assaulted his mind and Michael's eyes flew open only to find Ronan staring once again. He quirked a brow, his single set of short fangs protruding from a cocky smile. "You've been resurrected, my friend."

Understatement of the millennium. Michael didn't know how much of tonight's events he should divulge to Ronan. It wouldn't be fair to give the male—any of them, really—false hope. Especially if there was no chance of the race's grand return like Ronan imagined. Even now Michael couldn't make sense of what had happened. The human whore had given him sustenance, encouraged his heart to beat as fresh blood did every time he fed. But the other woman—Amy—she had performed the true miracle. Her mere presence had returned his soul to him and just a taste of her blood had awakened his power. He craved her more with each passing moment. How could his soul possibly be tethered to a human's?

"Seriously, what's got you so riled?" Ronan let out an overdramatic sigh and pondered the amber liquid as he swirled the crystal tumbler in his grasp. He took another sip and pinned Michael with a stern look. "You act as though you've been handed your death sentence."

Like a sword thrust to his friend's chest, Michael's words were sharp as he cut deep. "The female was *human*. Not dhampir. I am not resurrected. I am lost. *We* are lost." *She is lost.*

"Not dhampir?" Ronan repeated the words as though they were incomprehensible. "That's impossible. I felt your power. Feel it still. A human's blood could have never—"

"And yet, she did." Michael didn't understand why or how, but it had happened nonetheless.

"Okay," Ronan said cautiously. "So she's human. It's weird, but whatever." Beneath his overpriced designer clothes was a strong male, a male worthy of Michael's bite. But no dhampir had been turned in over two centuries, and without the continued strength the female's blood had given him Michael could never risk Ronan's life by trying to turn him. He would remain a dhampir, never knowing his true birthright. "She could be a mermaid for all I care. She's changed you. All of us. That's all that matters."

"You think so?" Michael asked. A dhampir would have been easy to track thanks to the blood bond that linked them all, but once the human female put enough distance between her and Michael tracking became problematic. "And how do you suggest I go about finding this . . . mermaid?" She might as well have been a fucking unicorn. The possibility of being tethered by a human was as much the stuff of mythology.

"You can't sense her," Ronan said as the realization struck. He sat for a quiet moment and Michael could almost hear the gears cranking in the other male's head. "But you can still feel her."

Of course he could. Their souls were bound to each other. His body ached for her, his balls tight with unspent seed. *You've had your pleasure; now give me mine.* She'd run from him, all but terrified when he spoke her name. Why? "Yes. But I cannot pinpoint her location." Which was at the same time curious and maddening.

"Did she drink from your vein?"

Michael cut him a look.

"What? Some humans are into it. They think it's kinky."

"Had she taken from my vein, I could have found her no matter the distance." And while the thought of her drinking from him sent a lick of heat up his spine, wishing it had happened wouldn't do a damned thing to help him find her.

"It doesn't matter if she didn't ingest your blood, though. Right? You have hers and that's enough to establish a link. It might be weak, but it's there. We'll simply find her."

Michael gave a derisive snort. "It's easy for you to sport such a cavalier attitude, Ronan. It's not your mate that's missing." Michael stopped midstride as the words he spoke registered.

Ronan leaned forward in his chair, rapt. *"Mate?"*

"No." Michael resumed his pacing. "I misspoke."

"The fuck you did," Ronan said. The dhampir rose from his chair with a wide grin. "What happened between you and the female? And don't even think about lying to me, Mikhail, because I know you did not simply take her vein."

Didn't he, though? Even now her scent clung to his fingertips, but the contact was innocent compared to what Michael had wanted to do to her. "I took her vein." There were things that even Ronan did not need to know. "And nothing else."

"You're *tethered*." Realization accented Ronan's words as he studied Michael with wide eyes. "The human returned your soul to you. Holy fucking shit, Mikhail! I knew you were different, but . . . Jesus. This is a game changer. When word gets around—"

Michael bared his fangs, Ronan's words sparking a protective instinct that spurred him just shy of an act of violence. "You will speak of this to *no one*. Do you understand me, Ronan?" No one could know about his mate. Not yet. Not until he could make sense of what had happened and how. Not until she was by his side where he could protect her from those who would use her. Exploit her. *Gods. My mate?* Again the thought struck him. *Impossible.*

"Take it easy, Mikhail." Ronan raised his hands as though in surrender and crossed to the bar to refresh his drink and pour a second glass. He offered the heavy crystal glass of sixty-year-old Macallan and Michael took it gladly, enjoying the smooth burn and warm glow in his gut that he could only enjoy thanks to the fresh blood that had awakened his body. "I meant no offense. I'm simply saying that we should find her as soon as possible."

"I'm well aware of what has to be done." He bit off the sentence before he was tempted to remind Ronan yet again just who had kept him from the female tonight. "Our enemies wait in the shadows for just this sort of event. The awakening of our kind will only spur them to action. If they learn of the female . . ."

Then nothing would stop them from seeking her out as well. The Sortiari would surely kill her.

His *mate*.

A feral snarl built in Michael's chest. He rubbed at his sternum, feeling the raised flesh of his scar through the shirt.

"They think you dead," Ronan replied. "In fact, I've seen no evidence that the Sortiari even exist anymore."

"They are as real as you are, my friend," Michael assured him. "They're everywhere and see everything. The Sortiari will learn of my tethering. And they will come for her if only to weaken me first. I will find her," he said through a haze of barely restrained rage. "And I will *annihilate* anyone who dares to stand in my way."

Ronan smiled and raised his glass in a toast. "Welcome back to the land of the living."

Michael downed the rest of his drink in a single swallow. "Indeed."

You've had your pleasure; now give me mine.

She was back there, in the club, held tight in Michael's embrace. But in her dream Claire didn't pull away. Didn't run. Instead, she gave herself over to him, desperate for another kiss and the light sting of his bite at her throat.

She writhed in ecstasy, her mounting passion igniting every nerve ending in her body with a delicious heat.

Michael yanked her pants down around her ankles and Claire kicked them off, desperate to be unfettered. The club full of partiers surged with the heavy bass of the music, undulating and moving as a single body. Claire paid them no mind as Michael lifted her effortlessly, positioning her back against the cool wall.

"Submit to me. You are *mine*."

"Yes." The word rang true, resonating deep within her soul. She was his and he was hers. Claire knew it as well as she knew herself. "I'm yours," she said, her voice little more than a whisper.

He entered her at the exact moment he sank his teeth into the flesh at her throat. Claire cried out, a ragged, desperate sound that tore through her. She broke apart. Shattered. A million particles of matter that separated and re-formed, changing her. Pleasure screamed through her, the orgasm so intense she didn't think she'd survive it. Heat radiated from her throat where Michael suckled at her flesh as though the very act was all that could sustain him. He thrust in time with each deep pull, increasing Claire's pleasure. One large hand reached up to cup her breast through the fabric of her T-shirt and she arched into his touch, letting out a low whimper when he brushed his thumb over the sensitive peak of one pearled nipple.

"Oh, god," she gasped. "Don't stop. Don't stop, Michael."

He thrust deeper, impaling her on his hard length. A low growl rumbled in his chest, a wild, animalistic sound that shivered over Claire's heated skin. The sound of her pulse rushing in her ears quieted, though another wave of pleasure crested over her, stealing her breath. She tilted her head to the side, if only to give Michael unhindered access to her throat, which he continued to bite, to suck, each pull of his mouth sending Claire further over the edge until she couldn't form a coherent thought. She never, *ever* wanted this moment to end—

His name burst from her lips, but not the one he'd given her. "Mikhail!" This was his true name, and finally, in some unspoken way, he'd given it to her. As though she was worthy of knowing it. Of speaking it. He pulled away from her throat with a triumphant roar, crimson drops of her blood coloring his lips and dripping from the dual points of two sets of fangs.

Wait. Fangs?

Panic surged within her, banishing the pleasure Claire felt like the wind against blustery clouds. His eyes flashed silver, a predator's eyes glinting in the darkness, and with the same animal ferocity he buried his face against her throat once more, the sharp bite of his fangs piercing her skin. He attacked her without mercy, drawing with ravenous sucks, and Claire's arms became weak at her sides, numb. Her legs fell from his waist, though he continued to pound into her, each deep thrust laying claim. Her head lolled on her shoulders and Claire's thoughts began to cloud as her breathing grew shallow. The slow thrum of her pulse slowed even more. One beat . . . Two. *Thump . . . thump* . . . Until it stilled in her chest completely and darkness swallowed her.

Claire came awake with a gasp, her heart hammering against her rib cage in a violent staccato. She clutched at her throat, her fingertips searching for puncture wounds at the same time that her body was coming down from the high of orgasm. Her sex pulsed, clenching around nothing as though it missed his absence even as her fear and panic sent her blood racing through her veins. Despite the fear, the utter lucidity of her dream, Claire wanted him more than she'd ever wanted anything in her entire life.

Holy shit. She'd had some weird dreams, but this one took the cake. The entire dream was so visceral, every moment ingrained in her memory. It had felt so real. Her body ached as though she'd just spent the last hour having the best rough sex of her life. God, how he'd pounded into her— Claire's breath caught as a rush of wetness slicked her thighs. And though she'd been terrified by the sight of him, fangs protruding, her blood staining his wicked mouth, she'd only wanted more. Wanted the sting of his bite at her throat, yearned for one more deep pull that seemed to fire all of her nerves, thrumming low in her core.

Was she sick, or what?

No one grew wet with desire at such a twisted thought. But Claire was wound tight with the need for release, despite the fact that she'd come again and again in her dream. She was insatiable, it seemed. But apparently only when it came to mysterious strangers who fondled her in public places.

Mikhail.

The name rang with truth. But how could she possibly know that? Claire rolled over and checked the time on her alarm clock: just past seven in the morning. She'd slept less than six hours, but it felt like days spent in another world. A world she was desperate to return to.

How could she feel so connected to someone she didn't even know?

With a couple of bicycle kicks she disengaged the sheet and comforter from her body. Beneath her worn secondhand Nine Inch Nails concert tee, her skin was clammy and slick with sweat. Jesus, she was burning up. She brought her hand up to massage her aching brow and the heavy Patek watch slid down her arm to almost her elbow. A very large wrist had sported this hardware at one time, and it only made Claire remember how big and imposing the rest of his body was as well.

She needed to unload it. In fact, she'd met with her fence twice since the night she'd stolen it, more than ready to collect her cash. But at the last minute she'd changed her mind, unwilling to part with the only thing she had of him. It was certifiably crazy. Especially when she needed the cash. And yet here she was, sleeping with the damned thing. *Sick*.

The cool morning air kissed her skin, helping Claire to come more fully awake. She'd been far too tempted to stay in bed lately, yearning to return to a dream that she had no right to lay claim to. What happened at Diablo three nights ago proved that Claire had lost her edge. That it was time to pack up the con game once and for all. Too bad she was still short on cash. If she wasn't going to fence the damned watch, she was going to have to go out. Tonight. Her rent was already five days past due, and if she didn't pay her landlord by tomorrow she was as good as evicted. One more hustle, she promised herself. After tonight she was calling it quits. Finito. Donezo. No more.

"Claire? Are you home?" Vanessa's tiny voice came on the heels of a knock at Claire's door.

"Hang on, sweetie. Just give me a second!"

Claire rolled out of bed and threw on a pair of sweats as she padded for the door. Today was the first day of school and no doubt Carlene was too hungover or already too high to help her daughter get ready. Crap. Had Vanessa even eaten breakfast? Claire didn't have much, but maybe she could whip the kid up some scrambled eggs and toast.

"Hey, kiddo," Claire greeted as she opened the door. Vanessa was beaming, her long blond hair pulled up in a haphazard ponytail with a bit of pink ribbon. She was wearing a ruffled pink skirt and a matching blouse, white with pink polka dots. Claire's heart constricted in her chest. There was so much pride in Vanessa's young face. And still she was much too young to shoulder so much responsibility.

"Check you out!" Claire stepped back to let Vanessa inside and smoothed a hand over the frilly fabric of her skirt.

"Do you like it? I went down to Tina's store like you said. Did you know she's got designer clothes and stuff? I got this outfit and three others. Plus a backpack!" Vanessa turned to show off the pastel pink bag that hung from her shoulders.

Claire smiled. It wasn't hard to tell what Vanessa's favorite color was. "Awesome," she replied. "You look so pretty. All of the kids are going to love your outfit." Claire had not-so-fond memories of her own first days of school, wearing ratty, dirty clothes and being made fun of by girls whose parents cared enough to buy them new pretty outfits. Or, you know, wash a load of laundry once in a while. "Hey, why don't you turn around and let me fix your ponytail?" Vanessa whirled around and Claire untied the ribbon and removed the elastic band, smoothing out the ridges and bumps as she combed through her hair with her fingers and gathered it back up. "Did you get some supplies? You're going to need pencils and notebooks and stuff, too."

"Yep," Vanessa said with a smile. She pulled a folded-up piece of paper from her skirt pocket and waved it in the air. "I got everything on the school supply list."

"I'm glad," Claire said with affection. She wound the elastic back over the ponytail and retied the ribbon. There were days that she considered suggesting that Vanessa move in with her. But she knew that without going through the proper channels that wouldn't be a good idea. Nothing like effectively kidnapping someone's kid to complicate your life. "Have you eaten anything yet today? I can make you some eggs and toast before you catch the bus."

"I'm okay," Vanessa said. "I had some money left over, so I bought a box of granola bars and some fruit cups. We get to eat snacks before lunch, so I'm saving them to eat at school."

Claire's stomach knotted up so tight she thought she might just throw up. Despite her shitty life, Vanessa was so positive, so oblivious to her circumstances. Either that or she was simply a good pretender. Something Claire knew far too much about.

"Well, I guess I better go to the bus stop. I don't want to miss it. I just wanted to show you my outfit."

Vanessa headed for the door and Claire followed. "Have a great first day," she said as she opened the door. "I want to hear all about it, okay?"

"Okay," Vanessa replied. "Bye, Claire!"

"See you, kiddo."

Angry tears stung at Claire's eyes as she closed the door. On the flip side of wanting to adopt Vanessa, there were days that she wished she lived as far away from Vanessa as humanly possible. The residual hurt Claire felt was just too damned much and it dredged up memories that she had spent years trying to bury.

It broke Claire's heart to think that something as simple as a few secondhand clothes and a cheap backpack had given Vanessa so much joy. That she'd been proud of the way she looked and excited that she had a measly granola bar and some overprocessed fruit to eat for a snack. Claire looked down at the Patek dangling from her wrist. She could buy Vanessa *new* clothes, get her some decent, healthy snacks, if she'd just fence the damned thing. But even considering the possibility of parting with it opened up a cavern in her chest.

You're not her mother, Claire.

True, but shouldn't someone have been?

Claire's mood soured as she got ready for her shift. No doubt she'd be a ray of sunshine today. She hoped no one would give her too much crap. And though her bitterness wouldn't do anything for her ability to provide decent customer service, it would do wonders for her tonight. She might not be ready to part with the watch, but some poor chump in the city was going to give her a helping hand. Whether he wanted to or not.

After a quick shower and an English muffin, she headed out the door. She stopped at unit 216, glaring at the door as though her focus might cause the wood to burst into flames. Claire brought her fist up to the door, ready to pound out her frustration on the planks. A string of angry insults sat at the tip of her tongue. A tirade that she'd been waiting to unleash on Carlene for months. Claire's fist shook with barely restrained rage and a lump the size of a goose egg lodged itself in her throat.

What good would it do to give Carlene a piece of her mind? Would it change her behavior? Drive some sense into her? Would it snap her out of her addiction and transform her into a responsible parent?

Claire knew the answer. The only thing she'd accomplish by tearing into Carlene would be to hurt Vanessa. And that's not what she wanted.

She took a steadying breath and headed down the hallway. Holding on to the anger of her past wasn't doing her any good now. It had taken a lot of effort to move past that and she couldn't let herself fall into old habits. Send positive energy out into the universe and the universe will inevitably send good things your way. She just had to remind herself of that.

Okay, universe. You can start sending those good things any time now.

She was more than ready for a good thing or two in her life.

CHAPTER
5

"Order up."

Claire headed for the window to retrieve the two plates of burgers and fries and flashed Lance, the diner's owner and sole cook, a smile. "Can I get a side salad when you get a second? Apparently, 'It's a salad kind of day.' "

Lance chuckled at Claire's mocking tone. "I'll get right on that."

Waitressing was sort of like hustling in a lot of ways. It was all about managing people. Telling them what they wanted to hear, giving them her undivided attention, making them feel important and in charge. And steering them toward what she wanted from them. In this case, a good tip. Since Claire made all of about two dollars an hour from Lance, the rest of her weekly earnings were determined by tips. So it was vital to her well-being that she convinced every one of her customers to throw down their hard-earned dollars for her.

"Here are your burgers"—she set the plates down in front of the two men at table three—"and I'll be right back with some ketchup and mustard. Can I get you guys anything else?"

She turned her attention to the shier-looking guy and winked. His cheeks flushed and he gave her a wide grin. "I think we're good. Thanks."

"Well, you guys be sure to holler if you need anything, okay?" Let the mark think he's running the show.

"We will. Thanks."

"I've got your salad!" Lance called from the kitchen.

As Claire crossed the diner and headed for the service window, the bell above the entrance chimed. She shot a quick look over to see a man walk in wearing black slacks and a black shirt with a thin white tab collar around the throat. Though she'd never been a particularly religious person, something about the priest's demeanor rubbed her the wrong way. Maybe it was his jet-black hair and equally dark eyes. Coupled with the black of his clerical outfit, his appearance was overall more sinister and less the calm, comforting vibe you'd get from a member of the clergy.

"Hi!" Claire greeted him with a bright smile as she rounded the counter. "Go ahead and have a seat anywhere. I'll be with you in a minute."

The sensation of tiny insects traveling the highway of her spine set Claire's internal warning sensors off. She watched from the corner of her eye as the priest took a seat on one of the high stools at the counter and rested his hands in front of him, his fingers woven together as though in prayer.

"You okay, Claire?" Lance craned his neck through the service window and took quick stock of the dining area. "You look a little rattled."

She gave a nervous laugh and slid the plate of salad off the sheet-metal serving area. "Yeah, I'm okay. Just a little chilled."

"You better not get sick," he chided in a playful tone. "I can't afford to not have you around."

"Don't worry, Lance. You're not getting rid of me anytime soon."

Claire kept her eyes focused on the salad, but she felt the priest's eyes following her. She set the plate down at table five. "Can I get you anything else?"

The woman looked up from her iPad. "No thanks."

"All right, then, enjoy. And let me know if you need anything."

For a moment, her steps faltered with indecision. Her stomach curled up into a ball as she approached the counter, grabbing a menu from a rack near the cash register. She plastered the widest, fakest smile she could muster on her face and slid the menu in front of the priest. "We serve breakfast all day, so feel free to order anything from the menu. Just give me a holler when you're ready."

"I'll do that. Thank you."

His lips spread into a seductive smile that made Claire's skin crawl. *Eww.* If she'd thought the priest was strange before, he'd just cranked his creepy factor up to a ten. He exuded a strange calm and a laser focus that unsettled her, and it took a hell of a lot to throw Claire off her game. No way in *hell* was this guy a real priest. He was working an angle. It took a con to know a con and this guy was on the take.

She just needed to figure out what his angle was.

Her feeling of unease intensified with each passing moment. Claire busied herself by wiping down tables and refilling salt and sugar shakers, but even that wasn't enough to distract her. As far as she could tell, the priest hadn't looked at the menu once. Rather, he seemed more interested in studying her, those dark, emotionless eyes tracking her every movement like those of a predator waiting to pounce.

Hustlers were superprotective of their territories. Like bears in the woods, they didn't play well with others and often patrolled their individual turfs, making sure to keep any squatters from moving in on their hunting grounds. Claire had known it was a mistake to hit that pool hall. Maybe the priest was here to deliver a message. Something along the lines of, *Stay off my street or I'll bust you in the face*.

Not good.

And like animals, a good hustler could smell fear. She'd always had a good bead on people, and the priest was as cool and composed as they came. Which meant Claire needed to pull her shit together. She couldn't show any sign of weakness. If she was lucky, she'd get off with a warning. Worst-case scenario, he'd try to rough her up to drive his point home. It wouldn't be the first time she'd been on the receiving end of a little physical persuasion, but Claire was going to do everything in her power to avoid it tonight.

"Are you ready to order?" She clutched her pencil so tight that she thought it might snap in her grip.

He gave her a wan smile and said, "I'll just have coffee. Black."

Of course. As black as his soul, no doubt. "Sure." Claire infused her tone with cheeriness as she grabbed a cup. "Decaf or high-octane?"

"Whatever you prefer." That same unnerving smile.

She grabbed a pot from the warmer and poured him a cup. She slid it over to him, but he made no move to take it, simply continued to watch her. "Sugar is right over there," Claire said. "Let me know if you need anything else."

Good lord. The *Mona Lisa* had nothing on this guy's smile.

Claire suppressed a shiver as she made the rounds, checking on her other tables. She wished they were busier tonight. If anything, her brain needed the distraction. Salad Lady paid her check and left a fifty-cent tip—not stellar— while the burger guys were still working on their fries. That left Claire nothing to do but spend a little quality time with the priest. *Awesome.*

"How're you doing over here?" she asked with a cheerfulness she didn't feel. "Can I get you a slice of pie? We've got a great Dutch apple today."

"No thank you. The coffee is fine."

His voice was smooth and slick, as though coating her senses with oil. His words weighed her down—or was that just exhaustion rearing its ugly head? Either way, it caused Claire's stomach to curl into an anxious knot.

"Tell me, do you live around here? I know most of my parishioners, but I have to confess, I don't think I've ever seen you at mass."

Right. Like he was even remotely concerned about never having seen her at church. "No, I live across town," Claire replied, the lie slipping with ease from her lips. "And I'm not Catholic."

"A shame. And yet you commute all the way here for work?" The priest quirked a dark brow.

"Gotta take the jobs when and where they're available." Claire made a show of focusing on busywork, filling ketchup bottles and whatnot. Anything to give him the impression that she wasn't paying him much attention. "And bus fare is cheap."

"An honest job for an honest life," the priest remarked. "Tell me, Claire, do you live an honest life?"

She was wearing a name tag, but still the priest's use of her name sent a zing of adrenaline through Claire's bloodstream. The intimate murmur, the way he enunciated each letter, was like an unwelcome caress. Her pulse picked up as a riot of butterflies took flight in her stomach. There was something seriously off about this guy.

"I'm sorry, but the sort of life I live is none of your business." Even if he was a priest, he had no right to ask her a question like that. Nosy much?

"But I'm afraid it *is* my business, Claire."

His eyes met hers and for the first time Claire realized that his irises were so dark, she couldn't even discern a pupil in their nearly black depths. Her intuition spiked. *Dangerous! Get away. Get away, now!*

"Who are you?" Claire asked, her body flushing with heat. She found it difficult to draw a deep breath and her lungs ached.

"I'm just doing God's work." He pushed a five-dollar bill across the counter and slid from the stool. Without another word he turned away and strode out of the diner.

The bell above the glass door chimed in protest with the priest's passing and Claire released a shuddering breath as she slumped against the counter. She leaned over his cup, noting that he hadn't taken a single sip. The five remained on the counter, untouched. Claire didn't want it. Didn't want anything to do with him.

"What was that all about?" Lance asked from the kitchen.

"Maybe he just really loves being a priest?" Claire suggested with a nervous laugh. "We get some interesting people in here, Lance."

"You said it. Let's just hope he doesn't come in again."

Somehow, Claire doubted tonight would be her last encounter with the priest.

"Three nights," Michael growled. His agitation grew by the hour, his inability to find her a burr that had worked its way under his skin. "*Nothing.*"

"L.A. is a big city, Mikhail." Always the voice of reason, Ronan's optimism wasn't so easily squashed. "If you'd let me call in additional help, our chances of finding her would be that much better."

"No." Michael couldn't afford for anyone else to know about her yet. He trusted Ronan with his life, and yet he was one person too many. Michael had nothing of her but a first name—Amy—and her blood in his veins. That alone should have been enough to find her. But since she was human, tracking her wasn't as easy as he'd hoped.

"You're the boss," Ronan said with a sigh. "But we are merely two bodies, Mikhail. There is only so much ground we can cover in one night."

True. They'd been operating on the assumption that Amy lived somewhere near the nightclub. But after the first night Michael couldn't find even a trace of her scent. He didn't feel her presence at all. Which meant she didn't live anywhere near the club district, and that left a vast city for him and Ronan to search. They might as well be looking for a single snowflake amidst a blizzard.

Michael estimated that if she was within a twenty-mile radius he'd be able to sense her. The metropolitan area alone boasted almost five thousand square miles. At this rate, her blood would cycle through his system before he could find her. *Gods damn it.* Would he have to suffer feeling the presence of her soul but never see her again? "We've wasted precious time." On that Michael could agree. "We'll start in the Valley and work our way back."

Ronan settled back into his chair and regarded the liquid swirling in his glass. "It's as good a place as any to resume the search." He cast a sidelong glance at Michael and cleared his throat nervously. "I think that you should feed." A low growl rumbled in Michael's chest and Ronan held a hand up as though to calm him. "Your strength is flagging, Mikhail. I do not suggest this lightly."

"I will not feed again until I find her." Stubborn? Perhaps. But he'd made a decision from that first taste. He'd never feed from another. If he starved himself, so be it.

"What of me, then? What of the others? Do we not deserve to be nourished?"

Dhampirs needed blood much less frequently than vampires. Four times a year. Dhampirs' hearts beat every day, not only when they drank. Their bodies functioned, metabolized food. The drinking of blood wasn't a necessity. Especially when they could draw on Michael's own stores of power for nourishment. "Have a cheeseburger."

"You're a cranky bastard. You know that?"

Michael cocked a brow. "Am I?"

"Yes. You are. And you know what I mean, Mikhail, so don't think you can offer me up a Big Mac and assume that I'll be satisfied."

The onslaught of emotions Michael had experienced over the course of the past few days had begun to take its toll. He hadn't meant to be so callous. Neither Ronan nor any of the dhampirs deserved his disdain. But nothing short of finding his mate would smooth Michael's sharp edge. "Tell me in truth, Ronan. Are you concerned that I find the female for my own well-being or for yours? I know what you expect of me should we find her."

Ronan's face screwed up into a grimace. "That hurts me, Mikhail. After all we've been through?"

Ronan's words tempered Michael's ire. He fixed Ronan with a solemn expression. "Is it not what you desire?"

Ronan let out a heavy sigh. "Of course it is. I've only asked you for this favor for decades. And now that you have the means to give it to me, why shouldn't I want it?"

Why indeed? It was Ronan's birthright, after all. He had a warrior's heart and strength. Surely he would endure the transition with little difficulty. Michael knew from experience what it was, to feel so unfinished. Incomplete. And only one creature on the face of the earth could give him the gift that would turn him into what he was born to be.

A vampire.

It was a gift of strength that only the worthy received. The transition—even for a dhampir—was brutal. Violent. And the sacrifice—that of one's own soul—wasn't something to be considered lightly. Knowing that it could be decades, millennia, before he found the female who would tether him didn't seem to matter to Ronan. Neither did the fact that none of the dhampirs Michael had attempted to turn over the past century had survived the process. But things were different now. If Michael could find his mate and sustain his strength, he was certain Ronan would survive. He was too damned stubborn to die. If anything, he would survive the change just to prove a point. Michael appreciated the male's tenacity. He was more than worthy.

"If we find her," Michael said, "I will turn you. I give you my word."

"*When*," Ronan stressed. "When we find her."

In addition to having tenacity, Ronan was an optimistic fool. "*When* we find her. I swear."

"Well then. Let's get our asses in gear."

Ronan deserved to be turned. So many dhampirs did. And Michael made a silent vow that he wouldn't rest until he found the female. And resurrected the vampire race.

CHAPTER
6

Claire's shift had been brutal. A steady stream of customers all day, which was great for the diner but not so great for her. She'd almost reconsidered going out, but the looming threat of eviction sent her out in search of easy money. Good lord, she was tired. Her final—for real this time—night of hustling had proved to be fruitful, though she'd violated one of her own rules by hitting a place she'd already been to.

She'd made enough to cover rent and then some in just two games. *Grocery store, here I come!*

Claire walked out of the pool hall and stared across the street at Diablo's bloodred sign. It was slow for a Monday night, the horde of weekend partiers absent from the sidewalk outside. As though her feet moved on her own, they took Claire across the street. She was *not* going in. A couple brushed past her on their way to the entrance, and she took a step to the side, craning her neck to get a glimpse inside the club before the doors closed. Just because he'd been there once didn't mean he'd be there again. Which was why she wasn't going inside.

"The cover's twenty bucks tonight."

Not exactly sure how she'd gotten from the sidewalk to the entrance, Claire looked up at the guy holding open the door. If she wasn't going in, why was she handing him a twenty? He grabbed her hand and stamped her wrist, leaving behind a red pitchfork that stood out against her pale skin.

Okay, so she was going in. But just for a second.

The place was considerably less hectic than it had been three nights ago. The clientele a little less highbrow. Claire ordered a five-dollar Coke—*what a rip-off*—so she wouldn't look like a complete freak and also to give her hands something to do so she wouldn't fidget. Because right now she was as jumpy as a grasshopper in a field of tall grass. What would she do if she saw him? Just march right up and say, "Hey, remember me? Probably not, because you were absolutely loaded, but I just wanted to let you know that you gave me the best orgasm of my life. Oh, and I'm pretty sure I'm obsessed with you. And also, I stole your watch."

Claire, you are one classy lady.

It didn't take long to determine that the mysterious Michael wasn't there tonight. Claire fought against the disappointment that settled in her stomach like a stack of too-heavy pancakes from the diner. It had been stupid of her to make an almost-twenty-mile trek across the city tonight. Sure, she'd told herself that the pickings had been easy at the pool hall and that's why she'd come back for round two. But that wasn't why she'd spent forty dollars in cab fare to come down here. She came hoping to find *him*.

It was as unsettling as it was pathetic.

Claire sidled up to the bar, determined to finish every last drop of her five-dollar soda before she left. It wouldn't be too hard, considering the glass barely held a few swallows. Especially with all of the ice the bartender had loaded into the glass. Claire snorted. Bars were a total con. These guys ripped people off nightly and it was all totally legit. Talk about a sweet deal . . .

"Can I get you anything else?"

Claire looked down into her almost empty glass and said to the bartender, "Nah, I'm good. But—" *Don't do it, Claire. Don't be that girl.* "I was wondering, do you remember a guy who was in here a few nights back? Really tall, muscular. Designer clothes. Sort of stood out from the ravers. He was sitting in the VIP section?" Too late. She'd officially crossed over into crazy stalker territory.

"Sorry," the bartender responded. "There are too many bodies coming in and out of here on event nights. You got a name?"

Yeah, but not his real one. "Michael?" she asked more than said.

"That's it?" The bartender laughed. "No last name?"

"No."

So not only did Claire feel like a desperate stalker; she also was pretty sure that now the bartender shared that opinion. He gave her a rueful smile and shook his head. "I wish I could help you out."

"No worries," Claire said with a nervous laugh. She wasn't usually the type to get embarrassed, but this was a new low, even for her. "Have a good one."

"You too," the bartender said with a nod of his head.

God, Claire, you are such a loser.

She left Diablo, only marginally mortified. She was supposed to be the stone-cold hustler. The woman who refused to let her emotions rule her. She'd never once chased after a guy or even worried about her love life. Having food to eat and money to pay for electricity had always been her priorities. There'd never been a man worth her time before— *Before what, Claire? Before him?*

Pathetic.

She hailed a cab and told the driver to drop her off at the bus stop at Sunset and Miller. No way was she going through the bullshit of haggling with a cabbie ready to take her for a fifty-dollar bill. She'd already wasted forty dollars to get to the club district and another twenty-five bucks on a miserable fifteen minutes inside of Diablo. The cab fare just to get her to the bus stop would cost her another five. She'd already thrown away seventy of her four-hundred-dollar take. Good thing tonight was her last night. Because Claire was seriously losing her touch.

The Patek's metal wristband dug into her thigh and Claire shifted in her seat, stretching out her legs so she could dig it out of her pocket. She shouldn't have brought it. Should have left it under her mattress or stuffed it in a Ziploc and floated it in the toilet tank for safekeeping like she had her other treasures. For some reason, though, she couldn't part from it. She traced her fingers along the ridges of the wristband, brushed her thumb across the crystal face.

What in the actual hell was wrong with her?

Claire's life was supposed to be about breaking away from what she'd grown up with, breaking the cycle of dysfunction, and all that uplifting healthy psyche crap. Going after someone who obviously had a laundry list of his own problems wasn't a good idea. He was probably an addict. A liar. And god only knew what else.

Aren't you a liar and a con artist? Way to rock that double standard.

But she wasn't an addict. She'd never popped a pill or smoked so much as a cigarette. She'd never stuck a needle in her arm or snorted a damned thing up her nose. And it wasn't like she'd never had the opportunity. Even alcohol was a touchy subject with Claire. She rarely drank and most of the time she used alcohol as a distraction, liquoring up her mark while she pretended to imbibe. She never wanted anything less than a clear and level head at all times.

And somehow, in the course of one brief, amazing encounter, this man—this *stranger*—had unraveled her. How?

The cab dropped her off at the corner of Miller just as the bus pulled up to the stop. Claire tossed the driver five bucks and hoofed it across the street, barely making the bus before it pulled back out into traffic. She made her way to the back of the bus—*great, not a single seat*—and grabbed onto the metal bar in the aisle to keep from falling on her ass as they negotiated the late-night traffic. L.A. really was a city that never slept. Not to mention a city of a million cars. Did no one care about the environment?

Oh, who was she kidding? If she could afford a car, she'd be cruising all over the city just like everyone else. In her defense, though, she'd totally spring for a hybrid. Claire's stomach soured as the scenery transformed from the fancy storefronts and luxurious clubs and became the run-down, neglected, poor part of L.A. that she knew but certainly didn't love.

As though a switch had been flipped inside of her, Claire's chest swelled with a surge of strong emotion. A sense of elation that stole her breath and blurred her vision. *Michael.* The uncanny instinct that never steered her wrong told Claire in an instant that he was close. *How? Why?* But most important, *where?* She leaned to her left over the seat and two very annoyed passengers and caught sight of a sleek jet-black sports car in the opposite lane of traffic. *There.* She caught sight of Michael seated in the passenger seat and their eyes met for the briefest moment. The car drove past the bus and Claire shifted, pressing her palms flat against the back window. Michael turned in his seat, his gaze locked on hers. In a flash of red brake lights, the car skidded, the squealing of tires followed up by angry horns as the vehicle came to a dead stop right in the middle of the street.

Holy shit. What in the hell was going on?

The bus continued on its track, the driver oblivious to Claire's distress. Michael was in that car. She'd felt his presence as surely as if he were standing beside her. A shout built up in her chest, the urge to order the driver to let her off too strong to resist. He was there, just a football field's length away . . . two lengths . . . three.

"Stop!" The word burst, unbidden, from Claire's lips. "Stop the bus!"

All eyes turned to Claire, but she didn't care. She needed to get off the bus. She couldn't explain it, but the urge was beyond reason. His need stretched out in the space between them, reaching deep into her soul and latching on with sharp teeth that wouldn't let go.

"Is this an emergency?" the driver asked over the intercom. "I'll have to call nine-one-one if this is an emergency."

"Um, no!" Claire called back. She definitely didn't need a visit from L.A.P.D. A rule of the hustle that needed no explanation: Avoid the cops at all costs.

"Then you can get off at the next stop," the bus driver replied. "Because I've got a schedule to keep."

"Stop! Stop the car. Now, Ronan!"

At first, Michael thought he'd imagined it. How could it be possible to feel her so strongly amidst a steady stream of traffic and bodies? But her presence burned in his soul, an inextinguishable fire that seared him from the inside out moments before he'd caught sight of her through the bus window. Michael's fangs ripped down from his gums, tearing the flesh with the force. He cradled his head in his palms as the Collective assaulted him, the memories awakening centuries-old instinct that he was helpless to fight.

Mine.

Without question, Ronan slammed on the brakes, sending the car fishtailing on the city street, the low-profile tires of his Aston Martin screaming. Around them, motorists honked their horns, leaning out of their windows to shout obscenities. Michael gritted his teeth against the press of the Collective, his fangs delivering two sets of punctures to his lower lip from the strain. Blood welled inside of his mouth, the sweet tang combined with his mate's proximity igniting his thirst.

The distance between them grew, stretching out within him until every tendon pulled taut, each muscle trembling under the strain. Michael shoved open the door, the metal groaning from the force. Ronan grabbed on to Michael's collar to keep him inside and he turned to his friend, fangs bared as a feral snarl tore from his throat.

"Take it easy, Mikhail. Let me get off the fucking street before someone rear-ends us, or runs over your ass." Clearly agitated, Ronan's pupils flashed silver. As with any animal, it took only a small act of aggression to put a vampire—or dhampir—on the defensive. This would end badly if Michael didn't get a grip, and he needed his wits about him if he was going to find his mate. Already the bus had traveled the length of a block . . . and another. Too far for his peace of mind, and growing.

Michael forced himself back into the seat and took a breath that was neither deep nor calming as Ronan put the car into gear and pulled into the first available parking space before coming to a stop. Ronan killed the engine and Michael pinched the bridge of his nose as he took several more deep breaths in a futile effort to calm the fuck down.

"Okay, *now* you can get out."

Michael tore out of the car, taking a stumbling step, the hum of sudden lust coursing through him. "I can still feel her," he rasped.

Michael let out a quick burst of breath. Though he craved the human's blood, longed for her body, and wanted the strength she could give him, he'd tried to convince himself that his base desires were the end of where his obsession led. After tonight, however, he knew with certainty that he'd been lying to himself. *"Rodstvennaya dusha,"* Michael whispered. "The human truly is my mate."

And she was close.

CHAPTER
7

Claire rushed to the front of the bus, all but bouncing with nervous energy. The next stop was five blocks away, but that was two too far. The sense that Michael was still near twisted her insides into a knot of anxious energy. A sense of euphoria swelled in her chest and it was all she could do to keep from stomping on the driver's foot to get him to speed it up to the next stop. She was down the stairs and waiting at the door before the bus could come to a stop, and the second the door opened she hopped out onto the sidewalk. She headed back toward where the bus had passed the black car that she'd seen Michael inside. What in the hell was she doing? This was insane! But even as crazy as the idea of tracking down a ghost felt, she kept putting one foot in front of the other.

As she hustled down the sidewalk, Claire dug through her purse for the small canister of pepper spray and the pocketknife she carried with her at all times. She tucked the pepper spray into her left palm and the knife into her right. The blade was only about four inches long, not really enough to do serious damage, but it would work in a clinch.

She was still seriously on edge from her conversation with the priest who'd come into the diner tonight. It had been a long time since she'd felt so unsafe.

In this part of the city there were more dark corners than brightly lit streets and every shady alley was an opportunity for disaster. Claire's tennis shoes whispered over the sidewalk with each step, and it took a real effort not to sprint away from every cast shadow. In the jungles of Los Angeles predators frothed at the prospect of fleeing prey, just like beasts did in the forests. She'd be asking for trouble if she ran. And so, despite the urge to pick up her pace, she kept it nice and steady. Just an innocent stroll through the worn and neglected neighborhoods of L.A.

"You shouldn't be out at night alone, Claire. Demons hide in the shadows."

From the very shadows he spoke of the priest stepped from an alley thirty or so feet in front of her. Though she'd been prepared for a second encounter with him, it didn't make his appearance any less unsettling. Had he been following her? In the dark of night, the whites of his eyes disappeared entirely, appearing to be nothing more than glistening obsidian orbs. The inky locks of his hair seemed to sway in a non-existent breeze, undulating like myriad serpents atop his head. Had his features been so angular and sharp before? Fear pooled hot in Claire's stomach, the acid churning and burning its way up her throat.

She opened her mouth to speak, but nothing came out. As if small talk were even necessary at this point. This man meant to do her harm and that was the only thing Claire needed to concern herself with. Her hand curled around the canister of pepper spray, her finger poised at the trigger. The pocketknife was a last resort and she eased the blade out with her thumb, ready to put it to use if need be.

The priest started toward her slowly, his calm, rolling gait reminding Claire of an animal on the hunt. His black patent-leather shoes didn't make a sound as his feet struck the sidewalk, as though the concrete conspired to mute his presence. "You're not running from me, Claire. Why not?"

Yeah, Claire, why the hell not? She took one deep steadying breath and then another, digging the balls of her feet into her shoes, prepared to stand her ground. He wanted her to run. Wanted to chase her down. Claire refused to give him the satisfaction. From a young age she'd learned that she needed to be scrappy if she wanted to survive the life she'd been given. No way was she running from some creepy-ass dude just because he gave her the willies. "Believe me, buddy, I've seen my share of scary things. I don't frighten easily."

He paused. "Indeed?"

In the blink of an eye he was in front of her. Claire took a stumbling step backward, jamming her spine into a parking meter. How in the hell had he done that? One second three car lengths separated them, and the next he was standing right in front of her. He canted his head to one side, studying her as one animal took stock of another. A deep musky scent permeated the air and Claire stifled a gag as the priest leaned in toward her, sniffing the air like a dog.

"He's had your blood," the priest hissed with a hungry smile. "No doubt he'll be tracking you."

Claire stepped to the side and put several needed feet between her and the priest. Not only was he creepy; the dude also was obviously six eggs short of a dozen. "Look, I don't want any trouble. I didn't mean to filch on your territory. I won't hit the club district again. In fact, I'm not planning to hit any districts ever again. Lesson learned. So let's just go our separate ways and call it a night, okay?"

His sick smile grew and he bared his teeth, making him look even more like an animal. Claire's pulse jumped in her veins as a trickle of fear seeped into her bloodstream. *Jesus.* What was she looking at here? One strong hand snapped up toward her and Claire brought the canister of pepper spray up, aiming it at the priest's eyes as she depressed the trigger.

He shook his head, sending droplets of pepper spray flying. Aside from that singular action, he gave no sign that it even affected him. Claire stared, dumbstruck. In a flash of motion the priest reached out and seized her by the throat. His flesh was searing hot against hers, his thumb and fingers digging in just below either side of her jawbone, and she cried out in pain.

Her voice was nothing more than a hoarse rasp as she forced it past the restriction of his fingers on her throat. "Let me go . . . you son of a bitch!" With her right hand she struck out with the pocketknife, catching her assailant between his neck and shoulder. He drew in a sharp breath, seizing her wrist in his opposite hand and wrenching it backward until she had no choice but to drop the knife or suffer a broken hand.

"You've been soiled, Claire." His fetid breath caressed her face, and her stomach heaved, threatening to empty the contents of her stomach. "Tainted. Marked by the beast himself."

"I don't know what you're talking about." Her voice was a hoarse rasp as she struggled against him, but he held her in an unrelenting iron grip. The guy could give any MMA champ a run for his money and that was saying something considering he was maybe five-five and a hundred and forty pounds. "Please . . ." Any bravado she might have felt was long gone. Streetwise or not, Claire was way over her head and she knew it. "Please, just let me go."

"I can't do that, Claire. Fate must be realigned."

Tendrils of black crept back into the whites of his eyes, spreading out in dark veins throughout the delicate skin of his eyelids. The heady, musky smell intensified and Claire gagged, swallowing down the bile that rose in her throat.

She took in shallow gulps of breath as the priest's grip on her throat tightened and he slowly raised her up off of the ground until only the tips of her toes made contact with the sidewalk beneath her.

He released her wrist and Claire clawed at the hand holding her. With a swift kick she connected with his shin, but she might as well have been kicking at a brick wall for all the good it did her.

"I won't kill you, Claire," the priest said almost conversationally. He kept her suspended in the air as though he could support her weight for the rest of the night without tiring. "Not yet, anyway. I can't promise not to hurt you in the meantime, though. I do so love to exact pain."

He released his grip on her throat and Claire tumbled to the ground in a heap. A sharp pang radiated from her hip bone upon contact with the concrete, but she didn't have time to acknowledge it. She scrambled for freedom, her nails scraping against the sidewalk as she fought for traction with the slick soles of her tennis shoes. Behind her the sound of metal scraping against concrete drew her attention, and Claire's heart jumped up into her throat.

She got to her feet not a moment too soon. Taking off as fast as her wobbly legs would carry her, she ran. The eerie silence behind her did little to assuage her fear, because she knew the priest was close behind.

With inhuman speed he overtook her, his body an immovable wall that appeared before her. Claire's body made contact and she bounced back, her head smacking with a sick crack on the sidewalk as she landed. White lights twinkled in her vision. Addled, she tried to get up, but her limbs were heavy and her head spun. The priest settled down on top of her, straddling her waist. A perverse anticipation twinkled in his eyes and the inky blackness returned to swallow the whites of his eyes entirely. How could any of this possibly be real? His dark pink tongue darted out to lick his lips as he brought the flat of the pocketknife's blade against Claire's right cheek.

"It's time to draw a little blood." He angled the blade so that the sharp edge rested against the hollow of Claire's cheek. "And coax the vampire out of hiding."

His mate's scream of pain reached Michael and heat seared through his chest, her presence calling to him in a way that no other's could. Without a word he propelled himself forward and headed in the direction of her screams.

He pushed himself faster, the buildings a blur in his vision as he dashed the length of the city block. He came to a stop mere feet from the female he'd been searching for only to find her held securely in the embrace of a priest. But this was no ordinary clergyman, nor was he human. The beast held Michael's mate tight against his body, one hand wrapped securely around her throat, the other clutching a small knife that he held against her jugular. Blood trickled down one of her cheeks, the scent igniting Michael's thirst as much as it fueled his rage. The priest leaned in and, with his gaze locked with Michael's, dragged his tongue up the length of Michael's mate's cheek, taking her blood on his tongue.

A snarl tore through Michael's throat. He took a step forward and the priest pressed the blade into the delicate flesh of his mate's throat. "Take another step, vampire, and I'll spill this precious blood of hers. I'll flood the street with it and you can watch her die."

"Shit." Ronan's voice behind Michael was tentative, full of confusion. "This sure as hell doesn't look good."

"No," Michael replied, his eyes still fixed on the priest who held his prize. "It isn't. The slayers have found us, Ronan."

The Sortiari had come to Los Angeles and this one meant to kill his mate.

CHAPTER
8

A red haze of unrestrained rage clouded Michael's vision. His single obsessive thought was to bring a painful, bloody death to the creature that dared to harm his mate. Her fear permeated the air, the acrid scent like scorched plastic. Ronan tensed beside him and took two tentative steps back. A violent snarl pierced the quiet, and the sidewalk trembled beneath Michael's feet.

"Easy, vampire." The slayer's eyes gleamed like obsidian. He drew her deeper into the shadows of the alley. "My hold on her is tenuous."

Easy? Michael was going to rip the bastard's throat out.

The slayer dragged his tongue across her cheek once again, taking her blood into his mouth. Michael's lip curled at the affront as the slayer taunted him. "Sweet," the beast hissed. "No wonder you want her so badly."

Michael took a lunging step forward and the slayer choked up on the tiny knife, nicking her skin. A rivulet of blood trickled down her neck, and Michael's thirst flared hot in his throat, distracting him from the urge to commit violence.

"Come forward and drink of her."

Like a moth drawn inexorably to a flame, Michael took a slow step forward and then another. The sweetness of her blood overrode the sharp tang of her fear, the need to taste the crimson drops sending him into a state of mindlessness and utter loss of control.

Michael's gaze narrowed on the ribbon of red that flashed across the pale column of his mate's throat. She struggled against the slayer's grip, her eyes wide and shining with fear. Her voice was nothing more than a whisper, her mouth barely moving with the word "Mikhail."

A battle cry erupted from Michael's lips, the shout charging the air with his residual rage. The slayer's black eyes flickered with trepidation even as his lips thinned into an arrogant smirk. His actions were a dark smudge in the shadows as he shoved Michael's mate forward. A distraction, to be sure, but Michael wasn't about to take any chances with her delicate human body. He cradled her in his arms, catching her before she sprawled to the sidewalk. He kept his gaze locked on the slayer as the false priest produced a silver dagger and a wicked wooden stake from a wide belt slung around his waist.

"Protect her, Ronan." As the slayer lunged, Michael spun away, handing his mate into Ronan's capable arms. The dagger glinted in a flash of silver and caught Michael high on his biceps, searing his flesh as the blade cut through his shirt and grazed his skin.

The Sortiari had done their due diligence, training their berserkers and creating fine-tuned killing machines. With inhuman speed the slayer struck out again, this time catching Michael in the torso. He hissed in a sharp breath, forced the pain to the back of his mind as he pulled his daggers from their sheaths. No longer on the defensive, Michael lashed out, cutting and stabbing, his movements a blur as he sent the slayer into retreat.

With each swing of his arms Michael felt invigorated, every connection with his enemy's body a thrill that spread through him like wildfire. The slayer was fast, every action precise. Well trained and as deadly an opponent as ever Michael had faced; but he refused to let the slayer win. They'd failed to kill him two centuries ago; it wouldn't happen now. He blocked a downward cut of the dagger, and the slayer used the opportunity to come at him from the left, grasping the silver-tipped stake tightly. Michael kicked out, catching his attacker in the gut, and the slayer flew backward, landing on the pavement with a crunch of broken bones.

Still the bastard came at Michael with no outward expression that he felt an ounce of pain. In the grip of battle lust, a berserker was nearly invincible. They healed almost instantly from their injuries. Bred for war, they were killing machines. Perfect assassins.

The slayer moved as though through time, his speed astounding even to Michael. In the blink of an eye the slayer was beside him and a white hot-bolt of pain shot from his shoulder, down his left arm as the silver blade sank into his flesh. His hand went numb, his fingers releasing their grip, and one dagger fell to the pavement with a ring of metal.

Michael went down on a knee and behind him Claire cried out, the sound of her distress cutting him deeper than any Sortiari blade. The slayer brought his left arm up, the stake held high as he said, "We are Fate." He struck with a quick downward stab and froze, the stake poised just above Michael's chest.

The slayer's dark eyes stared, disbelieving as his voice gurgled in his throat. Blood welled from his mouth as Michael sank the other blade into his enemy's flesh, tearing through skin, sinew, and tendon. Michael opened the slayer's throat in a forceful jerk, and dark crimson spilled from the wound, over the black fabric of his priest's façade.

Blood had indeed flooded the streets tonight, but it wasn't Michael's mate's. A low growl rumbled in his throat as he let the slayer fall to the ground like a puppet whose strings had been cut. The sounds of a struggle drew Michael's attention. He whipped around to see his frantic female kicking and fighting against Ronan, desperate to free herself from the man's hold.

"Let me go, asshole!"

"Mikhail? A little help here?"

Ronan looked as shocked as the slayer had over the course of events. He held on to the female, barely registering her struggles or cries. Her eyes were wide with fear and the frantic beat of her heart, the blood rushing through her veins, echoed in Michael's ears. "Be calm," he said as he approached her. The slayer's blood stained Michael's hands and shirt, no doubt making him look like a monster. He retrieved his fallen dagger from the ground and sheathed them both. Mercy was not afforded to slayers. Neither was an honorable death.

"Don't touch me. Get away from me!"

Her chest rose and fell with her quickened breath, and despite Ronan's hold on her, she swayed on her feet.

"Amy—"

"That'snotmyname!" The words were strung together, little more than a frantic blubber. "Let. Me. Go!" She kicked at Ronan once again and managed to free herself from his grasp. She tripped on her own feet, sprawling face-first onto the unyielding sidewalk. A snarl built in Michael's chest that she'd take so little care with herself. She scrambled away, clawing up to her feet only to stumble again as she fell back against the brick of the building behind her.

"Y-you killed that man!"

Stating the obvious must have been a human defense mechanism. Something to help her reconcile what she'd just witnessed. Her distress caused Michael pain, but until she allowed him to comfort her, to reassure her of her safety, there was nothing he could do to assuage her fears. "He intended to kill you. I will not suffer any creature to live that means to do you harm."

Michael took a step toward her and she scurried back like a mouse caught in a fox's sight, using the alley wall as leverage to hold her upright. He took another step toward her and she whimpered with fear, a sound that cut him deeper than any slayer's blade ever could.

"Try to calm down." Michael took a slow step forward and approached his female with arms outstretched in supplication. She pressed her body against the unyielding bricks as though hoping they'd swallow her up. The fear that leached from her pores burned his nostrils and masked the sweet scent of her blood. "I'm not going to hurt you."

"Bullshit."

Ronan smiled. "Come on, we, well, he"—he jutted his chin toward Michael—"just saved your life. Do you really think we want to hurt you?"

Her pulse slowed and she studied Ronan with an intensity that caused a pang of jealousy to flare in Michael's chest. He let out a low growl that vibrated in his throat.

"Down, boy." Ronan cut Michael a look.

Michael swallowed down the residual aggression that caused his fangs to pulse in his gums. He lowered his voice, solely for her. "Take a deep breath. Gather your thoughts. You *know* I won't harm you."

His mate eased herself away from the wall, no longer trying to become one with the bricks. She took a stuttering breath and then another. "Maybe not." Her gaze locked with Michael's. "But I still don't trust you."

Despite the fear that shook her right down to her bone marrow, Claire's heart soared in her chest at the sight of

Michael standing not five feet away. This was crazy. Completely bat-shit insane. The star of her nightly sex dreams had just brutally killed someone. With a freaking knife! Granted, the bastard had been about to carve her up like a Thanksgiving turkey, but it was murder just the same. Her mind refused to wrap itself around what had just happened. Never in her life had she seen anyone move so fast, yet both men had been nothing more than a blur in her vision as they fought. The entire scuffle seemed to pass in the blink of an eye. Shit like that just didn't happen.

She studied the man who approached her like she was the dangerous one. Ha! If that wasn't the joke of the century. He was slightly smaller than Michael, though no less imposing. His use of the name Claire had spoken in her dream—Mikhail—sparked her curiosity. And despite her very dangerous, very precarious situation, her instinct did in fact tell her that she had nothing to fear from these men.

The other man—Ronan she thought his name was—smiled and Claire blinked, craned forward to get a better look, and blinked again. Were those fangs poking down from his gums? *Jesus.* She'd heard of people getting body modifications done, forking their tongues like lizards' and having cat whiskers implanted into their faces, but she'd never seen it firsthand. *Seriously,* fangs. The priest had used the word "vampire." Claire thought back to her dream. . . . *What. In. The. Hell?* Maybe these guys were part of some deranged cosplay group? She'd witnessed some pretty effed-up shit in L.A. but this took the cake.

"It isn't safe here. We need to leave. Immediately."

Mister Tall, Dark, and Overprotective was a little on edge. "What's the matter?" Accusation flared in her tone. "Worried about the cops?"

His turquoise eyes bore straight through her. "Hardly.

Where there is one slayer, more will be close behind. I need to get you to safety before the vermin crawl from their holes."

"I'll be fine on my own. Thanks."

His gaze darkened and his lip curled into a sardonic smirk. "You're coming with me."

Claire's eyes widened with incredulity. Unlike his buddy's, Michael's upper jaw sported two sets of fangs. Who in the hell had money to throw around on unnecessary dental work like that? Maybe for once her instincts were steering her wrong. "Look, buddy, I was born at night, but it wasn't last night." His gaze slid over her, protective and predatory, and she shivered. "No way am I jumping out of the frying pan and into the fire just because you say I should." Holy crap, even bloodied and looking like an axe murderer, he stirred her desire. *Sick!* But no matter how badly she wanted to touch him, kiss him, and do naughty, *naughty* things to him, Claire wasn't going to fall for his spoon-fed bullshit.

Michael brushed past his crony and Claire bristled. Each individual nerve ending in her body was aware of him, igniting with a heat that left her flushed and sweating. Her body was a sex-starved traitor, responding to his massive body and dark, broody expression that all but stripped her bare to his gaze. That same low, delicious rumble that had driven her crazy at the club vibrated in his chest and it was all she could do not to tackle him to the sidewalk. Her mind was starting to think that her body might be on the right track. *Damn it, Claire, focus!*

No matter how much she wanted him, he was still dangerous. Panic swelled within her like water at high tide and Michael's step faltered as though he felt the shift as well. "Sorry, but there's no way in hell I'm going anywhere with you." No one conned a con artist.

"I'm afraid this isn't up for discussion." His voice vibrated through her, and Claire's bones went soft. "You're coming with me. End of discussion."

Claire snorted. Michael was sporting a pair, wasn't he? She looked to Ronan. "Is he always this pushy?"

Ronan folded his shoulders across his wide chest. "I'm afraid so."

"Too bad for you, *Michael,* because I'm just as stubborn as you are pushy. First of all, you lied to me. I don't appreciate that. Second, I don't let perfect strangers—not to mention guys who think every day is Halloween—haul me off to god knows where. And third, whether it was self-defense or not, you just killed a man." Panic flared within her once again, drowning out the sense of elation that had swelled in her chest. She kept her gaze from wandering to the spot on the sidewalk where her assailant lay in a pool of his own blood, and swallowed down the bile that rose in her throat. She had to get away from here. Now. Alone. "Do you what you want, but I'm getting the hell out of here before the police show up and throw us all in jail."

Michael flashed a superior grin and Claire couldn't help but notice that his fangs were longer than Ronan's. He took a step toward her and her body went rigid.

"Easy," he said as he put the pad of his thumb to the sharp point of one of those fangs, breaking the skin. Blood welled from the wound and Michael reached out, brushing it over the cut that bastard had made on her cheek. Delicious heat suffused her skin and she felt a tug. Her breath hitched and when he pulled away she put her own fingertips to the place he'd just touched to find the skin smooth, the wound instantaneously healed. "Jesus Christ," she breathed. "What did you just do to me?"

A rush of smug pleasure radiated from Claire's center and she was struck with the realization that it wasn't her pleasure she was feeling. Could this night get any more surreal?

"I'm not concerned about the authorities," Michael simply replied.

Claire's jaw hung slack and she gave herself a mental shake. She was losing her edge and needed to get the upper hand. Now. "You should be. When they get an eyeful of your bloody clothes and the dead body over there, you might as well embrace the orange jumpsuit, if you know what I mean."

Again that look of smug superiority crossed his features and Claire braced her knees to keep them from buckling. Seriously, what was *wrong* with her? "His brethren will be along shortly to remove any evidence of his death. Which is why we need to leave. No more trifling, no more excuses. You're coming with me. *Now.*"

CHAPTER
9

Stubborn female!

Her emotions swung on a pendulum, at once frightened and panicked and a moment later angry and suspicious. In the days since Michael had taken her blood, his heart had begun to slow. It would cease beating altogether in a matter of hours, his internal organs returning to dormancy until he fed again. He refused to drink from any other than this female, which meant he would need to take her blood again. Soon.

"Ronan, get the car. We're leaving."

The soft sounds of Ronan's footsteps faded into the distance as he left to get the car, but Michael kept his gaze locked on his female. As long as his heart still beat and her blood coursed through his veins, he'd be stronger. More capable to protect her. But if he didn't get her to the safety of his home soon there would be a crowd of slayers they'd have no choice but to fight. Ronan was capable but still only a dhampir. They'd be easily overtaken, and what the Sortiari had failed to do a century ago would be finished once and for all, tonight.

There were so many questions to be answered. She'd called him a liar, though she'd admitted in the midst of her frantic fear that Amy wasn't her name. What sort of woman was this female whom Michael found himself helplessly drawn to? He'd always assumed that his mate would be strong, intelligent, and honorable. Not to mention a creature of his own ilk. If she was none of these things, how could he possibly love her? To be trapped in a mate bond with a female he found unworthy would be a fate worse than any the Sortiari could conceive of.

He knew her soul, though. And it burned with a bright, pure light. Uncorrupted no matter what she tried to make him believe to the contrary. Perhaps they both had their secrets. So many questions were unanswered, but they'd run out of time.

Her body twitched, the slightest tell that she was preparing to bolt.

"Do not think of running from me, female. It will do you little good. I'd catch you before you took even three steps."

Her cheeks puffed as she blew out a quick breath. "Do me a favor. *Don't* call me 'female.'"

So full of fire, this one. Her outward show of defiance did nothing to hide the sweet, fragrant bloom of her desire, however. She wanted him. Craved him as surely as he craved her. A human would neither sense nor understand the connection forged between them, but Michael did. "What should I call you then, my pretty little liar?"

In the distance, the quiet purr of Ronan's Aston Martin's engine approached. *Thank the gods.* Michael felt too exposed on the street, time ticking by much too quickly. The slayers were excellent trackers. He needed to put as much distance between them and their enemies as soon as possible.

"We're leaving."

Indecision flashed over the female's features and Michel let out a sigh. She pushed off from the brick wall and took off at a sprint. True to his word, he overtook her in three quick strides, seized her by the wrist, and hauled her back against his body. "Let me go!" The words were forced from between her teeth as she kicked her legs out and gripped his hand in an effort to pry his fingers away.

Ronan came to a stop a few feet away and Michael lifted her up into his arms, her weight as insubstantial as a feather in his grasp. Ronan came around and opened the rear passenger side door for Michael. Her protests mattered little to him at this point. Whether she realized it or not, she belonged to him now. "Fighting me will do you no good," he said close to her ear. "You'll simply exhaust yourself trying."

"You can't snatch me off the street and force me to go with you, you jerk!" She clawed at his arm, but her struggles got her nowhere. "If you put me in that car, I swear to god I'll bail the first chance I get."

Michael pulled away and flashed her a cold smile. Her golden eyes locked on his mouth and a flicker of fear brushed against his senses. "You are mine to protect. *Mine.* But I won't hesitate to punish you if need be." The words rumbled on a low growl in his chest. "If you attempt to do anything to harm yourself, the consequences will be dire."

"This is kidnapping." The pleading words left her mouth in a rush. "You've already killed someone tonight; do you really want to add a federal charge to your list of crimes? Let me go. I won't say anything; I promise. The guy was going to kill me. You totally saved my ass and I appreciate it. I won't talk to the cops; I swear."

Michael deposited his prize in the backseat. The air left her lungs in a *woof* of breath and she let out an enraged shriek. "Can you lock her in?" he said to Ronan. Michael's eyes met hers. "In case she decides to *bail.*"

Ronan rolled his eyes and flipped a switch on the inside of the door panel and then went around and repeated the process on the other door. "Never thought I'd need to engage the child locks."

"If she insists on behaving like a child, we'll have to treat her as one," Michael replied.

"Be still, my heart," Ronan replied over the roof of the car before he opened his own door. "All of this romance is choking me up."

"We might be followed," Michael said. "A direct route home might not be a good idea."

"You act like this is my first rodeo." Ronan buckled his seat belt and pulled out onto the street. "You just worry about protecting our cargo. I'll worry about getting it where it needs to go."

That's what she was, it seemed. Cargo. A rare and valuable treasure entrusted in his safekeeping—

A barrage of images assaulted Michael's mind and he went to his knees, cracking the sidewalk beneath him from the impact. He'd shouldered the whole of the Collective for far too long and he was breaking under the strain of memories.

The empty void where his soul had once been became full, almost to bursting . The tether spurred him past reason and the female's scent drove him into a frenzy. Her impact upon him was unfathomable, changing him in an instant. He couldn't keep himself from her no matter what she was or how fervently he might try to deny their bond. Their souls were tethered. She felt it as surely as he did. A sweetness permeated the air, the female's arousal hardening his cock and elongating his fangs.

Michael gave his head a violent shake, as though he could dislodge the memory. It was too much for him to bear alone, and the images were nothing more than flashes he could make no sense of. He cradled his head in his palms, gritting his teeth against the pounding in his skull.

"She is strong enough," he said to the council of vampires seated before him. *"I beg you, allow me to turn her."*

"It is forbidden." That bastard Alexei Aristov looked at him with cruel disdain. As the ruler of the entire Russian territory and its many covens, Aristov spoke for the council and his word was law. *"She is not your mate, nor could she be. You cannot be tethered by a human. It's impossible and you are mistaken. She will not survive the transformation. Keep her as your lover if you must. But that is as far as you are permitted to go. Enjoy the human's body. Drink of her blood. But do not seek to turn her. If you act against the mandate of this council, the punishment is death."*

Michael gasped as though coming up for air after being too long under the water. He'd seen his father's face through the vampire's memories, stern, proud. Another collage of images assaulted Michael, and his breath stalled as he was plunged under the surface again.

The female went limp in his arms, her flesh so pale and cold that for a moment he was afraid he'd killed her. He'd drained her to the precipice of death, but he'd prove those fools wrong. The council didn't know his mate like he did. She was strong enough. She would survive. He scored his wrist with one sharp fang and pressed the wound to his lover's mouth. When the crimson drops ceased to flow, he scored his wrist again, forcing her to take his blood. At first she didn't respond and his heart beat a frantic rhythm as fear took hold. But soon she roused, sealing her lips around the wound as she took deep pulls. Her hands came up to hold his wrist as she drank, and the flat edges of her teeth broke the skin as the frenzy of feeding took hold.

Elation soared in his chest. He knew she'd survive. Knew *it.* She *was* his.

*Hope turned to terror as she pulled violently away,
thrashing in his embrace. She broke free, tearing at her
hair and pulling long tufts from her scalp in a bloodied
mass. Silver flashed in her pupils, and dainty fangs protruded from her gums. But the soul of the female he loved
was gone and, likewise, the string that tied them together,
tethered his soul to his body, was cut. In her wild, empty
gaze he sensed nothing but a mindless creature writhing
in pain.*

*A violent scream ripped from her throat. Tears streamed
down her once-flushed cheeks. Her back bowed off the
ground and with the sound of her spine snapping from the
strain he swore that her pain was his own. Bruises appeared on her pale arms, her legs and torso, across her
jawline, and over her shoulders as her body rejected the
blood he'd given her. Her scream pierced the night air,
echoing eerily into silence as her body stilled before him.*

*Blood trickled from her nose, her delicate ears, and her
beautiful eyes like crimson tears. Her mouth was frozen in
a silent cry that at once destroyed him. "No!" he shouted
as he threw his body over hers as though to protect her
from what had already taken her from him. "Collette!" He
cradled her in his arms, rocking her. "Collette, don't leave
me."*

*But it was past the time for beseeching words. Impos-
sible to reverse the damage he'd done. He should have
heeded the council's words and now it was too late.*

His love was dead at his own hand.

An agonized roar burst from Michael's chest, the pain
of the vampire's memory so real he might as well have
killed the woman himself. The sound echoed off the walls
of the alley beside them and rattled the windows of a
nearby retail space. Was this the fate that awaited him? To
live without truly claiming his mate or run the risk of killing her in the process of turning her?

"Mikhail?" Ronan jumped out of the car and raced to Michael, his gaze fearful.

Michael looked up to find Claire stretched across the seat. A deep crease marred her smooth brow and her golden eyes shone with concern. Gods, the emotion etched on her face was enough to lay him low.

As well it should. "I'm fine." He held up a staying hand and pushed himself to stand. A despair unlike anything he'd ever felt before ripped through him, shredding his composure.

"Are you sure? Mikhail"—Ronan's voice dropped for his ears alone—"you should feed."

"No. We need to leave. Now." He slid into the seat beside Claire, who continued to study him quietly. Not even the annihilation of his race had affected him so deeply. This had become a suicide mission. How could he deny his own instinct, his own mating drive? The taking and giving of blood was essential to solidifying the mate bond, and yet, if the memories he'd witnessed were correct, she could never drink of him. Being with her while restraining himself from claiming her would kill him as surely as doing so would kill her.

Ronan gave Michael a last searching look before he settled in behind the wheel. "All right, we're out of here," he said as he pulled out onto the street.

Michael couldn't allow himself to form an attachment to this female. Not after what he'd just witnessed in the dead vampire's memory. Perhaps it was for the best that she'd resisted him. He could take her blood, let her life essence feed his power and nothing more if she despised him. Her hatred would keep him from doing something he would surely regret.

Wind rushed through an open window beside him, and by the time Michael could react the female was already hanging over the door, the top half of her body dangling over the street rushing by beneath her. Ronan chanced a glance back and the car swerved. "Shit!" He jerked the wheel and they lurched back into their lane.

Michael hooked his finger through her belt loop before she toppled headfirst out of the car. He jerked her back inside, none too gently pulling her against his body, and she shot him a glare that should have melted the flesh from his bones. "You didn't think to lock the windows, Ronan?"

He gave Michael an apologetic shrug. "I didn't think she'd actually try to jump."

Obviously this female didn't want for courage. An admirable trait but no less annoying considering their situation. "I told you the consequences would be dire if you tried to harm yourself. Would you test me, female?"

"I told you not to call me that." In the dark interior of the car, her eyes sparked with golden fire, her cheeks flushed with anger. Michael's body responded, and he cursed his weakness. How could he possibly keep her at arm's length when he craved her body as much as he craved her blood?

"What should I call you, then?"

She bucked her chin. "Don't call me anything, *Mikhail*."

From the driver's seat Ronan gave an amused snort.

Her use of Michael's given name rang with accusation, and yet he yearned to hear it spoken from her lips again. "Until you give me a name by which to address you, I will call you female."

"Then call me Amy."

Michael turned and faced forward once again. "No. Since you've already admitted that's not your true name, I will not call you Amy."

"Sort of hypocritical for a guy who told me his name was *Michael*."

Ronan turned and cut him a look as if to say, "Well, she

has a point." "Michael is the Americanized version of my name. Hardly a lie."

She gave a humorless laugh. "Hardly the truth, either."

What should have been a relatively quick drive to the outskirts of the city became a long, winding path as Ronan traversed side streets and back roads, doubling back toward the south end of the city before merging with the heavily trafficked main streets. "I think we've covered our tracks well enough." Ronan shifted into a higher gear as he wove a path through the throng of late-night traffic. "Time to get the hell out of Dodge."

"Tell me, female, how did the slayer find you?" Despite Ronan's confidence, Michael kept a vigilant eye on the surrounding vehicles, expecting an attack at any moment. The Collective still weighed on his mind and his strength was flagging. Ronan was right. Michael would need to feed soon and he wouldn't feel completely safe until they were back home.

"Slayer?" She repeated the word as though it were foreign. "I have no idea what you're talking about." A slow, resigned sigh escaped her chest. "And my name is Claire."

At this point, what would it matter if they knew her real name? Besides, if he called her female one more time she was going to go ballistic. Claire had met some charmers in her life, but Michael took the cake. The bossy attitude he was sporting was just a notch above caveman. Totally unattractive.

So why did her body hum like a tuning fork at the dark, commanding tenor of his voice? Why had she been so worried when he'd collapsed to the ground, his head cradled in his large palms? And why—despite her trepidation—did she know that Michael would die before he let any harm come to her?

"The slayer that attacked you. How did he find you?"

As if adding a couple of extra words would make any of this easier for Claire to comprehend. "The priest? He came into the diner earlier tonight. And I don't know how he found me." She'd abandoned her theory that the priest was another hustler trying to scare her away from his property. Now she was leaning toward some sort of Mafia war. Obviously the priest had seen her with Michael at Diablo and thought they were a lot closer than they really were. The mistake wouldn't have been too tough to make considering the fact she'd been wrapped around him like a second skin. "Whoever the guy was, he was fucking nuts."

"What did he say to you?" Michael's warm tone vibrated through her. How could she possibly keep the upper hand when just a few words from him turned her body traitor?

Claire shrugged. "A bunch of crazy shit that made no sense."

Claire suppressed a shiver as she recalled the endless black depths of the priest's irises, the dark tendrils that fanned out from his eyes and bled into his skin. His strength and speed. Totally unreal. And the words that caused her stomach to tie itself into knots: *It's time to draw a little blood. And coax the vampire out of hiding.* No way had she imagined any of it. She had no idea what these guys were involved in, but she wanted no part of it.

"Please," she said in a last-ditch effort to save her skin, "I promise I won't talk. Just pull over and let me out."

"Try to relax, Claire." Michael spoke as if trying to talk her off a ledge. "You're among friends. And you're safe."

She wanted to call bullshit, but his words rang true. Damn it. Could the night get any crazier? Did she really want to find out?

The rest of the drive passed in silence. Though she couldn't see him well in the dark interior of the car, Claire felt the tension Michael was throwing off. Energy that buffeted her skin like waves crashing on the shore. The sense that something connected them, like an invisible length of rope, unnerved her. She tried to push the sensation to the back of her mind, but as she settled into the plush leather seat the invisible tether that connected her to him tugged at her center. She wondered, did he feel it, too?

"So . . . what did this car set you back?" She needed something to distract her from the strange connection vibrating through every cell in her body. Claire had never owned a junker car, let alone ridden in one that cost more than ten years' worth of her rent. When would she get the opportunity again to talk about luxury cars with someone able to afford one?

"About three-seventy-five with all the extras." Ronan spoke about the price of an Aston Martin Vanquish like some people talked about buying a case of soda.

Beneath the long sleeve of Claire's shirt, the Patek's cool metal caressed her skin, reminding her of how she'd gotten into this mess in the first place. She'd held on to that damned watch like the spoils of war, too covetous to even sell it off to her fence. Michael was doing that with her now. He'd all but declared her his property, killed a man to take possession of her. And now Michael was carting her off to god knew where with a warning that he wouldn't hesitate to punish her if she stepped a toe out of line.

Jesus Christ, Claire, have you lost your mind? She should be forming an escape plan, not worrying about the welfare of one captor while exchanging small talk with the other about the price tag of his sweet ride. Not once had she ever doubted her instincts to steer her wrong, but there was a first time for everything. She might have felt at ease with these guys, but they were dangerous. Deadly. And obviously insane considering the fact that they'd tipped their teeth with fake vampire fangs. She hadn't been able to get out of the car before they'd locked her inside. Didn't matter, though. They'd have to stop soon, and when they did she'd make a break for it.

Forty-five minutes later, Claire found herself staring out of the window at the twinkling lights of L.A. from the top of a tall hill. This far from the city, it looked like a vast universe, stars shining through the endless darkness. So this was how the 1 percent lived. Looking down from the clouds like the gods of Olympus at the world below. It was just her luck that she'd be kidnapped by wealthy psychopaths. She'd have to endure the added torture of being taunted by luxury she didn't have a snowball's chance in hell of ever knowing.

And to top it all off, it appeared they were planning on holding her prisoner inside of a freaking castle. Guards sat in a little building beside a wrought-iron gate waiting to let the car through. Who in the hell was this Michael that he needed a small army's worth of protection? She didn't doubt that they were well armed and even better trained. Deranged cosplayer was taking a backseat to drug czar at the moment. *Holy. Shit.*

"I don't envy your power bill," Claire remarked wryly as Ronan pulled into a paved circular driveway complete with a massive marble fountain. Beside the six-car garage, the main house stretched on for what seemed like miles. Hell, Claire had seen a hotel or three smaller than this house. In fact, she had a hard time wrapping her head around why anyone would need a house this big. A small village could have taken up residence here and the chances of running into any of your housemates would still be slim. Claire was fairly sure she could live her entire life off of the money Michael—or Ronan, or whoever—had paid for this place.

Just . . . wow.

Right on cue the front door opened and a man stepped

out from the house, his shadow outlined in the swath of light cutting through the darkened portico. He stepped up to the car and opened Michael's door for him. *Huh.* A castle, complete with a servant. Was he loyal, though? With any luck, Claire would be able to buy her freedom and the guy currently offering up a polite greeting might be her ticket out of there.

A few presumably polite words were exchanged between the two, too low for Claire to hear. She muttered under her breath in a dark and broody voice, "Get the dungeon ready, Jeeves. Extraheavy shackles for our prisoner."

From the front seat Ronan burst out in a round of robust laughter. "It's about time we had someone around here with a sense of humor."

She shifted in her seat and leaned over the center console. "You think I'm kidding?"

Before Ronan could respond, her door was pulled open and Michael leaned down, his arm outstretched. Nothing like extending a gentlemanly hand after forcing a woman bodily into a car and kidnapping her. "Claire," he said in that insufferably commanding tone. "Come inside."

"I'm good where I am."

His eyes flashed silver and Claire's heart jumped into her throat. "Come inside, or I'll throw you over my shoulder and carry you inside."

She folded her arms across her chest and relaxed back into the seat. No way was she going to make this easy for him. He could try to intimidate her all he wanted. Not even his crazy Riddick eyes were going to coax her out of the car. Fake fangs, weird contact lenses. *Jesus, who are these guys?*

Michael reached into the backseat and Claire wished for a moment that she hadn't called his bluff. He latched on to her legs and spun her around until she was laid out on the seat. As slick as going down a waterslide, she was pulled across the leather upholstery and hefted in the air again as though she weighed nothing. A squeal of protest erupted from her throat as he deposited her on top of one massive shoulder, leaving her head to dangle over his back, her hair cascading almost to the ground.

"Put me down!"

"I warned you." With each step, her breath was forced from her chest and she had no choice but to dangle there like a sack of potatoes or else rest her hands on his ass to brace herself. "I always follow through, Claire. If you insist on testing me, be prepared for the consequences." She tried to ignore the solid mass of muscle carting her through the front door, the way his high-priced slacks hugged the very ass she'd just considered latching on to.

"Yeah," she said through a huff of breath. "Well . . . if you don't . . . put me . . . down . . ."—holy crap, she was going to pass out from all the blood currently rushing into her brain—"we're going to have a *very* serious problem."

"The slayers have found you. They won't stop until you're dead. I'd say we already have a very serious problem. Wouldn't you agree?"

If this was a dream, Claire was more than ready to wake up.

CHAPTER
10

"I know it's been a while, Mikhail, but you really need a refresher on how to deal with the fairer sex."

Michael narrowed his gaze but didn't bother to look at Ronan. No, his eyes were fixed on Claire, sitting ramrod straight on the plush, never-used sofa in the formal living room. She stared straight ahead, her golden eyes focused on nothing. Her arms hugged her body and her left hand fiddled with something bulky against her skin, hidden by the long sleeve of her shirt. Michael's fingers twitched as he took in the sight of her hair, a glimmering cascade of gold that fell over her shoulder in silky sheets. Gods, how he wanted to run his fingers through that length.

"Ronan is right." Alex bent close to Michael as though worried Claire might overhear. "This isn't her world. This isn't an adjustment that can be made in a matter of minutes. For all she knows, you're a psychopath."

Michael cast a sidelong glance at the human and arched a brow.

Alex shrugged and averted his gaze. "Of course *we* know you're not a psychopath. All I'm saying is that you should try to be patient with her. Ease her into the situation."

Michael let out a slow breath. As though tethering his soul had been a slow and gradual thing. Hadn't he been thrown into this situation as well? Blindsided with the immediacy of Claire's effect on him. Beside him, Ronan was perched at the bar, helping himself to the bottle of sixty-year-old Macallan. How could he be so cavalier after everything that had happened tonight? How could Alex? The Sortiari would be looking for them, adding another layer to an already-complicated situation. And rather than worry about their meager defenses, the two of them wanted to school him on chivalry?

"I haven't mistreated her."

"You haven't lavished her with tender affection, either," Ronan pointed out. "I hate to break it to you, my friend, but as a general rule, women's hearts aren't won through kidnapping and violence."

Alex pursed his lips, his eyes widening a fraction as though he agreed with Ronan. But rather than speak his mind, Alex busied himself elsewhere, leaving them to their discussion as Ronan poured another Scotch and slid the squat glass toward Michael. *Thank gods.* He drank deeply, letting the liquor wash away the resurging thirst that burned in his throat. "I'm not interested in winning her heart. Only taking her vein."

They spoke in hushed tones, though Claire kept her gaze straight ahead, effectively ignoring them. Where was the fiery female who'd begged for his attentions at the nightclub? The woman who'd tried to defy him not an hour ago on the darkened street? Why did he even care? She was here for one reason and one reason only: to provide him with blood and the strength he needed to resurrect his race.

Vampires and dhampirs alike possessed many traits that would be considered primal by human standards.

They were predators after all, hunters. They fought like animals, protected their loved ones like animals. Coveted their mates with the fierceness of wild beasts. And there were some who coveted their own souls above all else. The soulless existence of a vampire was seen as an abomination to them, despite the prospect of a tether. Michael's mate would be seen as a threat. Any creature who sought to do his mate harm would meet a violent end. "Steps will need to be taken to ensure her continued protection."

"Time to circle the wagons," Ronan replied with a smirk. "Amass our allies and all that?"

The human had awakened Michael. Her soul had roused his from endless slumber and her blood had given him strength the likes of which he'd never thought possible. "It is time to amass an army," he replied.

Claire stood from the couch and crossed the expanse of the living room to where Michael and Ronan stood at the bar. Michael straightened, set his glass down on the granite countertop. Her gaze pinned him in place, the intensity of those bright eyes and the stubborn set of her delicate jaw lending her a fierceness that stole his breath. "How long do you think you can keep me here?"

Ronan cleared his throat and set his glass down. "This is my cue to take my leave." Michael expected Ronan to help him build an army of vampires and the male was ready to tuck tail at the sight of an enraged human female. "I'll need you here after the sun rises. Alex will be here but—"

"Don't worry. I'll be back after sunrise." Ronan flashed a cocky grin. "I'm counting on you to hold up your end of the agreement."

Michael inclined his head. "Be careful, Ronan. The Sortiari will be out in force from now on."

He turned to Claire and winked. "Such a worrier. Take it easy on him until I get back. His ego is delicate."

The quip earned a sweet smile from Claire, and Michael's jealousy flared hot in his chest. Ronan shook his head and clapped Michael on the back. "I can see that detachment is working well for you. Good luck, Mikhail."

All the while acutely aware of Claire's gaze, Michael watched Ronan leave the room. She placed a hand on her hip as she waited for Michael to look at her. How could three nights' time make such a difference? She'd been so willing in his arms at the nightclub. And then, when he saw her on the bus, her hands pressed against the glass, he'd felt the bond ignite between them, her need just as powerful as his.

He'd proved himself capable of protecting her tonight. Killed for her. Brought her here in order to ensure her safety, and yet he felt her disdain like myriad daggers piercing his flesh. "Would you like a drink, Claire? Something to eat?" He could be gentle with her. Hospitable.

"What I want is for you answer my question. How long do you plan to keep me here, *Mikhail*?"

He let out a long sigh and poured himself another finger of scotch. Might as well enjoy it while his heart still beat and blood flowed. "You're in my care and you'll stay here for as long as I say you'll stay here."

Claire snorted. "I'm out of here."

"You're not going anywhere."

Her eyes sparked with fire. "Oh no? Watch me."

She spun around and stalked toward the door, not even bothering to run this time. Rather than go after her, Michael was entranced by the curve of her waist, the sway of her hips and her pert, round ass that all but invited his touch. Though her current petulance made him think that a good spanking might be in order. And that thought did nothing to tame the erection throbbing behind his fly. *Good gods*. How could he even think about keeping his distance from her when all he wanted was to get closer? To do lewd and desperate things to her?

He let her put distance between them. The predator in him rose to the surface, ready to give chase, and Michael reveled in that thrill. His throat burned with thirst and her scent enveloped him. Her soul called to him, pulling the tether between them taut. A growl of pure hunger vibrated in his chest and he overtook her in a blur of motion, slamming the heavy front door closed before she even had a chance to fully open it.

"Back off," she snapped without turning to face him.

He leaned in to her, breathed deeply of the sweet scent that clung to her. She wasn't afraid of him but excited. Her arousal perfumed the air, intoxicated him, and robbed him of his senses. "You don't want that, Claire, and you know it."

She snorted. "The hell I don't."

Her hands dropped to her sides, palms laid flat against her thighs. Michael tilted his head toward hers, so close to the delicate skin of her throat that he trembled with restraint. "Then tell me again." His voice was little more than a harsh whisper. "Tell me to back away, to let you walk out that door. Tell me you don't want to be here and I'll let you leave. Say you don't feel me in every single particle of your being and I'll let you go right now."

Claire's breath came in quick little pants and she pressed her palms tight against her thighs to keep them from shaking. The words formed on her tongue, but she couldn't push them past her lips. His body loomed over hers, the wall of muscle that was his chest pressed tight against her back. The heat of his mouth brushed the skin of her throat and her lower abdomen clenched. Instead of saying the words she wanted to say, all she could do was think, *Do it. Put your mouth on me. Just like that night in the club. In my dreams. Do it!* As though she had no control over her own body, her head tilted to the right, sending her hair off of her shoulder to spill down her back, exposing her neck to him. A low rumble vibrated in Michael's chest and he let out a shuddering breath.

"Gods, Claire. You're a cruel female."

His dark, smoky tone stirred her desire and from the center of her being she felt the invisible tug of whatever unexplainable force connected them. He was right, damn it. She didn't want to leave. Didn't think she could force her feet to take her out that door if she wanted to.

The urge to lean back, to let his big body support hers, was almost too great to resist. Claire swayed on her feet. His very presence made her light-headed. Giddy. Standing behind her, his body touching hers in more places than was appropriate, was a stranger. A cold-blooded killer. And who knew what else. And god help her, she *wanted him*. Wanted him like she wanted food, water, her next damned breath. She reached out with her right hand and clutched her left wrist, sliding her fingers along the ridges of the Patek's wristband through the long sleeve of her shirt. Jesus, there was something seriously wrong with her. Was it too soon to blame her reaction to him on Stockholm syndrome?

"I want some answers," she said. "And if you don't give them to me, I'm going to go out and find them on my own."

Again that sense of connection flared between them, sending a rush of anxious energy through Claire's bloodstream. She felt his disappointment, as though he'd hoped to continue their power struggle. Who in the hell was this man who had such a visceral effect on her? And why could she not bring herself to leave his side?

The heat of his body left hers and Claire hugged her arms around her middle. Only a few feet separated them, but she was overcome with a profound awareness of his absence. She turned, her body whipping around much faster than she'd intended, to find him heading back into the massive living room, his stride long and purposeful.

"Come and take a seat, Claire," he said without turning to face her. "I'll try not to bite."

A shiver raced across her skin at the innuendo. The heat in his words was unmistakable, and though she couldn't see his face, she had a feeling that a very male, very satisfied smile accented his full mouth. It was like he could climb right inside her head and read her thoughts. Did he know that she wanted him to do just that? Seriously, she needed professional help.

He took a seat, facing her, on one of the wide, overstuffed sofas. There was a regality to his posture as he stretched his arms out over the back, his torso ramrod straight as he crossed an ankle over his knee. Relaxed. Confident. He commanded attention and would have owned the room had there been a hundred and fifty people crowding the space and not simply Claire.

"Ask your questions," he said in that smooth, seductive voice. "I'm at your disposal."

Who talked like that? Seriously, it was like he'd stepped right out of a time machine.

"Are you a member of some sort of cult?"

He quirked a brow. "No."

"Mafia?"

A slow smile spread on his handsome face, revealing the glistening tips of his fangs. "No."

"Deranged cosplayer?"

His brow furrowed. "I have no idea what that is, but I'm going to go out on limb and say no, I'm not a deranged cosplayer."

A burst of adrenaline shot through her bloodstream. She pressed her lips together to suppress the smile that threatened as she walked slowly toward the couch and pointed a finger toward his mouth. "Are those real?"

With that sinful smile still affixed to his face, he replied, "Yes."

"What about Ronan?"

The cocksure expression faded and a low growl permeated the silence. "What about him?"

"Is he like you?"

His expression clouded and silver chased across his gaze. "More or less. Ronan is a dhampir."

Claire studied the reflection in his eyes, anxiety tying her in knots as she began to doubt that he was in fact wearing contact lenses. She sensed his mood shift from cocky playfulness to something darker and decided to leave her questions about Ronan to the wayside. *Crap.* Was she really going to buy into this? "The priest who attacked me tonight . . . he wasn't human, was he?"

"No."

Ho-ly shit. Not an ounce of deception in the word. She swallowed. "And neither are you."

The smile returned, this time feral. "No. Neither am I."

Truth.

"Jesus," she said on an exhalation of breath.

Claire found herself collapsing into the nearest chair. She hadn't truly believed it until this moment. Had spent the past hours convincing herself that none of this was real. Michael's strange behavior at the club, the fangs, the silver flash in his eyes, the way he made her feel. And the priest. His black eyes and even blacker heart. *It's time to . . . coax the vampire out of hiding.*

"You really did bite me that night at the club, didn't you?"

His expression became hungry and Claire felt a rush of warmth between her thighs. It was like her body was hardwired to respond to him. She had not an ounce of control over herself. "I did. Your blood is a heady nectar. The sweetest thing I've *ever* tasted."

Claire swallowed against the dryness in her throat even as a deep throb of desire settled between her thighs. "I think I'm going crazy," she murmured. "I feel things that I don't understand. I'm having the most"—a bark of laughter escaped her lips—"insane dreams. What did you do to me that night?"

His gaze was no less heated as he leaned forward on the couch. He rested his elbows on his knees and regarded her for a moment. "We are tethered, Claire. Your soul and mine. I've done nothing to you that you haven't done to me. You are . . . my mate."

Mate? Was he out of his fucking mind? "You might as well be speaking German to me right now, because I don't understand a single word that's coming out of your mouth."

Was it too late to hightail it for the door? Granted, he'd catch her before she could set a foot onto the driveway, but still.

"I don't understand it, either." He let out a slow sigh and raked his fingers through his hair. Her eyes followed the motion and her own fingers twitched. "You're human and it shouldn't be possible. And yet, here you sit."

"How can you be sure?" The question seemed trite, even to her. She'd felt an inextricable, instant connection with him that night at Diablo. Not so easy to dismiss as an error in judgment. "I mean, you could have made a mistake."

"There is no mistake." He stood and crossed the room to where she sat, settling down beside her. Electricity charged the air between them, a pleasant tingle over Claire's skin. He smelled like heaven: dark chocolate and cinnamon topped off with a crispness like the air after a hard rain. He reached out and smoothed her hair back from her face, studying her with an intensity that caused her to tremble.

"Until that night, I was untethered. Soulless. The scent of your blood called to me, and in that moment my soul was returned. You are mine, Claire, and you know this. You feel it just as surely as I do. Or have you forgotten the way you begged for me to touch you that night?"

She opened her mouth, ready to protest. She'd been caught up in the moment, sure, but that didn't mean— He seized her mouth in a ravenous kiss that left her breathless and her lips bruised from the punishment. Hard, unyielding, he slanted his mouth across hers, deepening the kiss as he thrust his tongue in her mouth. Possessed with an almost savage need, Claire answered, cleaving to him as she fisted his shirt and pulled him closer.

He gripped her upper arm in one strong hand and the other he used to cup the back of her neck. He eased her head to one side and Claire's head spun in a dizzying blur. *Yes. Yes, yes, yes.* Anticipation coiled tight in her stomach at the prospect of what he was about to do. Just like that night. Like in her dream. His mouth left hers and she let go of his shirt to coil her fingers through his hair. Mindless, she pressed him to her throat, her breath racing in desperate gasps.

In an instant he took her down, laying her out on the couch as he settled between her thighs. Claire thrust her hips up, grinding into the length of his erection straining against the fly of his pants. On the heels of the sharp sting of his bite pleasure seized her, pulsing through her body in a warm rush that made her cry out. *Oh, god.* She could come like this. Just from a single sharp bite. A low, satisfied groan rumbled in his throat, accompanied by a slow, deep suction. Claire became light-headed; the room seemed to drop out from beneath her as she floated on a cloud of pure bliss.

"More." The word passed slow and lazy from her lips. "Don't stop."

Michael pulled back with a roar, his mouth stained crimson. Panic lit his handsome features and the bright silver fled from his gaze, leaving nothing more than clear turquoise. His breath sawed in and out of his chest and his hand was shaking as he put his thumb in his mouth and bit down with his fangs. Two drops of blood welled from the punctures and he brushed the pad of his thumb over the skin on Claire's throat, causing her to shudder.

She couldn't speak, couldn't keep her world from careening. Her own breath sped in her chest and her body ached with the need to pull him back to her. No man had ever driven her to such a reckless state.

"You cannot leave." Michael wiped at his mouth as he pushed himself away and off the couch. Claire was stunned, hurt slicing through her at his sudden coldness. "You're not a prisoner, Claire, but don't make me turn you into one. There are guards stationed throughout the property. Alex knows to watch over you, and if you trick him or try to leave under his watch I won't hesitate to punish him. And it will be dire."

He turned and left the room in a blur of motion. Alone, Claire clutched at her chest as she willed the lump of emotion that had risen in her throat to go away. His rejection cut through her with a razor-sharp edge and she hated him for making her feel so vulnerable.

CHAPTER
11

"I didn't expect to see you tonight, Ronan," a smooth female voice purred from the darkness. "I thought your king had warned you away from me."

Ronan stepped out of the shadows and braced a shoulder against the doorjamb. "He's your king, too, Siobhan. Your disdain is what has caused him to form an . . . unsavory opinion of you."

"Do you think I care what Mikhail Aristov thinks of me?" The dhampir female strode across the room, her black hair cascading over one shoulder and her green eyes alight with heat. The sway of her hips held Ronan in thrall. Her black leather pants left nothing to the imagination and her breasts nearly spilled from her corseted top. The female oozed sex. "Why are you here?"

"You know why I'm here."

Her lips brushed his ear as her hand reached down to cup his cock through his slacks. "Maybe I just want to hear you say it."

It showed how badly he needed to take the edge off that he'd come here tonight. His reasons weren't entirely selfish, however. Siobhan had something he wanted and he wasn't leaving until he got it. Mikhail needed all the help he could get. He needed answers as to why he'd been tethered by a human and he needed an army with which to hold the Sortiari at bay. And so here Ronan was, right in the lion's den ready to serve himself up as a main course in order to ensure he could do those things for his king. He seized Siobhan roughly by the wrist and brought her hand up between them. "Your constant and foolish attempts at a power grab have been ill conceived. It's time to stop this nonsense. You've made an enemy of your king when what you should have done was align yourself with Mikhail as soon as possible."

She jerked her hand from Ronan's grasp and a feral hiss slipped from between her bared fangs. "I'm not interested in aligning myself with him."

"Not even now that he's no longer one of the soulless?"

Siobhan's eyes narrowed to emerald slits that glittered in the darkness. "You're a liar."

A corner of Ronan's mouth quirked. "He's been tethered. You'd recognize it if you had a scrap of sense. His power has been awakened by this female and Mikhail's throne will be once and for all solidified in the resurrection of the vampire race. He will rule *both of our races*."

Siobhan began to pace, the click of her stilettos echoing across the nearly empty room. "Who is the female?"

He chuckled. "Like I'd tell you." Though Siobhan offered certain distractions that he appreciated, Ronan's loyalty to Mikhail was unquestionable.

She rounded on him, her pupils flashing silver. "Why tell me anything then?"

"Don't be a fool, Siobhan. His allies will be rewarded for their loyalty, and all you've managed to prove to him is that you're a bigoted, power-hungry bitch who'd just as soon see him dead."

"Such compliments, Ronan," she said with a smirk. "You're making me wet."

It was spoken with her trademark sarcasm, but the heady scent of her desire thickened the air with a rich perfume. Ronan's body responded in kind. There'd be time enough for sport later, though. Right now he needed something from her, and he wasn't going to leave until he got it.

"I came here for the *kodeks krovi*. And you're going to give it to me."

Siobhan stared, eyes wide, before bursting out into a round of incredulous laughter, wind chimes in a hurricane that rang in Ronan's ears. "The blood codex. You're joking, right?"

Gods, he wished he were. Mikhail had all but proclaimed that he would never take Claire as his mate. Ronan suspected that it had more to do with her delicate human state than Mikhail's desire to claim her as his. He could drink of her, but he could easily kill her if he wasn't careful. And likewise, she could never drink of him, fortify her strength, if Mikhail suspected that the transition would kill her. Withholding himself from her, denying that base instinct, would send him into madness. He couldn't rule, couldn't resurrect the race to its former glory, unless he was fully mated to Claire. And Ronan was determined to find a way to make it happen.

"Do I look like I'm joking?" He was about to make a deal with the devil, and already Ronan could feel his soul slipping away before Mikhail would even have an opportunity to send it into oblivion. Siobhan was good for a toss when the mood struck, but the female was as deadly as a viper. This was no trifling thing Ronan did here tonight.

"You won't reveal anything about Mikhail's female, and you show up out of the blue, asking for a relic of vampire lore his own father put to record. . . ." A smile stretched across Siobhan's full crimson lips. "Am I sensing trouble in paradise for your king?"

The female was not only heartless but also vicious. If she had even an inkling that Mikhail might be weak she wouldn't waste a moment to take him down. "Hardly."

"Is she a shifter? Werewolf? Perhaps a lowly white witch?" Siobhan clasped her hands together gleefully, reveling in the possibilities.

"She's a female worthy of your admiration and fear, Siobhan. Take care." Ronan didn't doubt that Claire would make a fearsome vampire. She had the spirit, the survival instinct, and more than enough fight in her. He just had to convince Mikhail of it. "I came here tonight not only for the codex but to urge you to form your alliances carefully. Your coven is strong. You could serve Mikhail well."

"What makes you think I'm interested in serving any male?" Siobhan seethed. "Let alone one who would take away my soul. You didn't come here tonight to urge me to ally myself with Mikhail. You came here for the codex." Her lips stretched into an indulgent smile. "And to fuck me."

Ronan hiked a shoulder. He wouldn't deny it. It had been one hell of a night and he was hoping she'd help him to take the edge off. "Give me the codex. You have no need of it." Siobhan had a cache of vampire relics stashed away. Sort of ironic, since the female had no interest in being turned.

"No." She flicked her wrist. "But *you* do. That makes it valuable to me."

"So rather than give it to me because we're friends, you'll use the codex as leverage?"

"Friends?" Her voice was a seductive purr that vibrated down Ronan's spine. "Is that all that we are?"

A corner of his mouth tugged into a reluctant smile. "We're very, *very* good friends."

Siobhan crossed the room toward him and Ronan swore her hips had a magical quality that could hypnotize anyone who dared to watch them sway. She ran her nose along his throat, inhaling deeply. "Swear your fealty to me, Ronan, and I'll give you the codex."

She palmed his cock again and the bastard was already hard as stone. If his dick could swear fealty, it would be as good as hers. "I can't do that. I'm sworn to Mikhail and no one else."

An aggrieved sigh slipped from her lips. "Such a waste. Then swear your body to me. Pledge to me here and now that you'll give yourself to no other female and I'll give the codex to you."

It wasn't a mate bond, but swearing himself to her in such a way could be dangerous. Still, he enjoyed Siobhan's body regularly enough as it was. He'd simply be giving her something that she already had. "For how long?"

She crossed to the king-size mattress at the far corner of the room and Ronan followed as though he had no choice. He'd never understood why she chose to live this way, like a squatter without the means to put a decent roof over her head. It suited her wild personality, though. The female was far from housebroken; that's probably why he came to her time and again with no other thought but using her for his pleasure.

"For as long as I see fit." She kicked off her boots, peeled the tight leather pants down the length of her thighs, and shoved them somewhere to the side. Her tight corseted top went next and her breasts spilled free, the dusky nipples already erect and straining toward him as though in need of his touch. Desire swelled inside of him, coursing through his veins with a heat that caused Ronan to sweat. "Come now, Ronan. It's a small price to pay for what you want, is it not?"

Siobhan stretched out on the bed, her body a pale pearl

nestled amidst the rumpled black sheets. The scent of her arousal caused his fangs to throb in his gums, and though he had no need to feed, the urge to sink his fangs—as well as his cock—into her was too strong to resist. If he took her vein it would seal their agreement with a blood troth, and Siobhan knew it. She'd enticed him with her body, knowing that he wouldn't turn her down.

There were worse things than pledging his body to this female. Convincing Mikhail to turn Claire would guarantee that Ronan would be gifted with the transformation he'd yearned for over centuries. A blood troth was the least of his concerns at this point. "I want the codex tonight." He fumbled with the buttons of his shirt in his haste to get it off and kicked off his shoes and slacks. Siobhan's eyes flashed silver as she spread her legs in invitation and Ronan's cock pulsed hard and hot as he shoved his boxer briefs down over his ass.

"Tonight," Siobhan agreed. He covered her body with his and jerked her lacy thong aside, shoving into her in a single hard thrust. She arched up to meet him and Ronan hissed at the sharp sting of her fangs as they punctured his throat. A low rumble gathered in his chest as Siobhan drank deeply, her sex clenching around his erection with every pull of her mouth.

Since Mikhail's awakening, Ronan had felt stronger with each passing day, his own urges and desires intensifying a hundredfold. He thrust hard into the female beneath him, gripped her soft thighs, and guided her legs around him. Siobhan wound her fists in his hair, her fangs still engaged as she drank from him. With a shout Ronan stood, cupping her ass as he pounded unmercifully into her. She disengaged from his throat with an impassioned cry and Ronan turned to sit on the mattress. He caught a fistful of her silky raven hair and jerked her head to the side. Her pussy clenched him tight as she came and Ronan bit down hard on Siobhan's throat, eliciting a cry from her lips that only caused him to thrust harder and deeper. Her blood flowed over his tongue, sweet and heady. Ronan sucked as hard as he fucked her, effectively sealing their agreement with the exchange of blood. His orgasm ripped through him and Ronan pulled away from her throat with a shout, his cock twitching inside of her as she continued to ride him with abandon.

"Fuck! Ah, *gods,* that feels good."

Siobhan's throaty laughter caressed his ear moments before her tongue flicked out at his throat, closing the wounds she'd made. He returned the favor, closing the punctures and lapping lazily at the blood that trickled down the pale column of her throat and between her lush breasts.

"Carrig, *dewch â'r codex mi!*" Siobhan's voice echoed through the ruins of the abandoned building in the old Welsh dialect she used to speak to her coven. Moments later, a male entered her private floor with a large leather-bound book tucked under his arm.

Ronan shifted on the bed, very aware that he was still buried to the hilt inside of her. Siobhan didn't seem to share in his modesty, though the other male's eyes lit with desire when he took in the sight of them still flushed with passion and breathing heavily.

Their pact made, Siobhan kept to her word, though Ronan would have liked the opportunity to put his damned pants back on first. "The book," Carrig said with a low bow, setting the codex down on the bed beside them. Silver glinted in his dark gaze and his mouth parted to reveal the tips of his fangs. "Would you like me for anything else, mistress?" The male did nothing to hide his anticipation, and he gave Ronan a slow, seductive smile that revealed the full length of his fangs along the row of straight white teeth.

"What do you say, Ronan?" Siobhan purred in his ear. "Should we ask Carrig to join us?" She kept her eyes on the other male as her fingers caressed over Ronan's shoulders and down his forearms. Their agreement did not include the other members of Siobhan's coven, however, and Ronan had no intention of allowing her to pass him around.

"No." The word was spoken with a finality that caused Carrig's expression to fall like a poorly baked soufflé.

Siobhan hiked a shoulder. "Apparently Ronan is shy. That will be all, Carrig. For now."

Carrig gave a nod of his head and disappeared into the shadows. Ronan thrust Siobhan from his body, no longer interested in playing her games, and she stretched out on the bed, watching through the narrowed slits of her eyes as he retrieved his shirt and slacks from the floor.

"I made my troth to you and no one else." He shoved his arms into the sleeves of his shirt with enough force to rip the seams. "If you think to play games with me, Siobhan, you'll be disappointed."

Siobhan licked a drop of his blood from the corner of her mouth. "Oh, Ronan. I haven't begun to play with you. Take the codex. I hope you find whatever answers you seek from it. But in exchange for my generosity, your body is *mine*. To use as I see fit, whenever and however I want. Break your oath to me, and I will be . . . upset."

Her innocent tone belied the fire in her emerald gaze. Ronan cursed his own foolishness at letting his cock make decisions for him. He could have found another way to get the codex from her. The truth of the matter was, his libido had been raging out of control for days. He'd needed a release, and clearly, there hadn't been enough blood in his brain to make a logical decision. "I wouldn't think of upsetting you, Siobhan." He could argue his point with her later. Right now he needed to get the codex out of there before she changed her mind.

"Good." She stretched out on the bed, all willowy limbs and creamy skin. "Then take your clothes off and join me. I'm not even close to being done with you yet."

Her command chafed, but Ronan made sure not to let her see him bristle. Instead, he shucked his shirt and let his slacks fall beside his discarded shoes and socks. He eased down beside her on the bed, reaching out to fondle the heavy weight of her breast, plucking at the hardened nipple as though taking succulent fruit from the vine.

"Harder," she commanded, and Ronan gave her tender flesh a tight pinch. She rolled her hips, her back arching off the bed, and let out a low moan. "I find it flattering that you don't want to share, Ronan. You must know that I'm very generous with the members of my coven, though. I'll give you your way tonight, but in the future, you will deny me *nothing*. Do you understand?"

Yep. He'd sold his soul. And this devil was a cruel mistress indeed. "I understand." That didn't mean he'd supplicate to her in the future, however. Blood troth or not.

"Good." She reached for his cock and it hardened in her palm. *Traitorous bastard.* He'd give the female what she wanted. Fuck her until she was too exhausted to speak his name, let alone issue another command. By then the sun would be up and Ronan had a responsibility to Mikhail to watch over his mate. No rest for the wicked, he supposed. Not if he wanted his due reward for his loyalty.

He stretched out on his back and rolled Siobhan onto his chest. A low purr vibrated in her throat as she settled herself on top of him, the slick heat of her sex gliding over his erection, causing a rumble of appreciation to grow in his own chest. If he'd condemned himself to hell, Ronan supposed that there were worse ways to burn.

By dawn, Siobhan would be tucked under her black sheets, her breathing soft and even in the aftermath of their hours-long tryst. The female was insatiable, fierce. And Ronan had the claw marks on his back to prove it. Not that he was complaining too much. He'd needed the release—as well as the workout—and he enjoyed rough sex with her. She'd taken more blood from him tonight than she'd need to sustain her for a year or longer. And even though a part of him despised her for manipulating him, Ronan respected her. Maybe even feared her, a little. Perhaps it was a good thing that she reviled the idea of being turned. She would be a fearsome vampire indeed. One that, if left unchecked, could be a serious contender for Mikhail's throne.

No matter her politics, of one thing Ronan was certain. Mikhail needed Siobhan as an ally. He had enough enemies as it was, especially with confirmation of the Sortiari's reemergence in the city. It was more important than ever that Mikhail show the dhampir covens that he was a king worth following. A benevolent leader who would raise them up, and they would share in his strength. None of that would happen, however, if Mikhail remained a stubborn ass and refused to turn Claire.

Ronan stroked the aged and worn leather that covered the codex. With any luck, the answers to all of their problems lay within the pages.

CHAPTER
12

Claire stared at the empty hallway that Mikhail—she refused to think of him as Michael anymore—had passed down, a hole the size of Texas opening up inside of her. She felt his absence so acutely, as if some vital part of her was missing. A phantom pain from a limb no longer intact. And it bothered the holy living crap out of her. His rejection still stung, embarrassment a bitter pill to swallow after she'd all but tackled him only to have him pull away. If he didn't want her, what was the point in keeping her there? Surely the other man, Ronan, would keep Mikhail from doing anything *dire* to Alex if she chose to bolt. Could she do it? Despite the connection that she felt, could she leave him?

Good hustlers weren't stupid. The best con artists never made a move without gathering as much intel as possible when working an angle. And Claire wasn't willing to do anything until she knew everything she needed to. That priest had tried to kill her tonight. And he wasn't any more human than Mikhail was. Where was she safer? Here, with a man—no, a *vampire*—she barely knew, or out there on her own? For the first time in a long time, Claire feared the prospect of going it alone.

Let the mark think he's in charge. Mikhail was reluctant to talk, but she could loosen him up. She put her own hurt on the back burner and dragged her gaze from that empty spot, instead turning her attention to the rumble of protest coming from her gut. If Claire had learned anything over the course of her life, it was that any obstacle could be surmounted as long as you had a full stomach.

"I'm cooking!" she announced to no one, hoping that Mikhail's temper would cool and he'd come back to join her. He'd yet to give her any answers that weren't monosyllabic, and she wasn't going to make a decision about leaving until she had more information. "Pancakes sound good." Four a.m. was totally a breakfast hour. Pushing herself from the couch, she wandered through the living room and down a hallway in search of the kitchen. "And coffee. Lots of coffee."

Even after being there most of the night, Claire was still baffled by the sheer size of the house. The kitchen was bigger than the entire diner, stocked with high-end appliances that had to cost more than she made in a year. Hell, the formal dining room alone was set up to accommodate thirty or so people and Claire doubted that Mikhail had ever sat at the mahogany length one time, let alone entertained a roomful of dinner guests. Such a waste of money. She hopped up on the counter to snatch a fancy stainless-steel fry pan from a pot rack hanging above the island and set it on the stovetop.

"Don't let Alex catch you using his Demeyere pans," Mikhail remarked as he strode into the kitchen. His expression was pinched, his brows drawn over his bright eyes, his lips a hard line. "He thinks he's the king of this castle. He doesn't even let me use those."

Claire chuckled. Though Mikhail's expression was still

pretty fierce, she sensed that his temper had cooled somewhat. She was totally the mistress of manipulation. Maybe she hadn't lost her touch for the con after all. "Noted." She continued to root around the kitchen, digging through cupboards. In a few short strides he was beside her, opening cupboards, gathering up bowls, utensils, flour, milk, and eggs. Had she managed to tame the savage beast with the prospect of pancakes? *Point: Claire.*

She kept her smug satisfaction hidden as she peeked into the clear glass doors of the humongous refrigerator, stunned at the amount of food inside. "You wouldn't figure a vampire's fridge to be so well stocked."

Mikhail flashed a reluctant smile. His dual sets of fangs were more pronounced in relation to his other teeth. "And what do you know of a vampire's eating habits, my little human?"

Claire's stomach clenched at the word "my." She'd never been anyone's anything before. "Not much thanks to you." Aside from Mikhail attacking her like he was a starving man and she was a cheeseburger and then setting her aside like she'd ruined his diet, he worked the mysterious, cryptic *I'll tell you as much as you need to know* angle well. "I've got to say, I'm still not wrapping my head around any of it. Seriously. Vampires?"

"I am the last of the Ancient Ones." His voice was low and somber as Mikhail whisked a couple of eggs and added them to the flour and other dry ingredients he'd put in a clear glass bowl. "The last true vampire. The rest are only dhampirs, waiting to be turned."

A wave of sadness stole over Claire and she swallowed against the emotion rising in her throat. Talk about surreal. This wasn't a conversation she ever thought she'd have with another person—er, uh, sort of person. Well, a sane one, anyway. "You're seriously the only vampire on the entire planet? I mean, there's not even the slightest possibility there's one that you don't know about? Like a tribe of them in the rain forest or something?"

His mouth quirked in a half smile, but the expression didn't reach his eyes. "I would know. There are no others."

Mikhail was orphaned, just like Claire. True, they were adults, hardly waiting for the magical day they'd be adopted, but still. She'd always felt such a profound loneliness that the burden of it was almost too much to bear. To know that Mikhail might've experienced that same sense of detachment forged an even stronger sense of connection to him. "I'm not exactly an endangered species, but I've been alone for as long as I can remember. And my mom took off when I was sixteen, so I've been on my own for a while now. It's a horrible thing not to have someone—anyone who *knows* you. Not like people who see you every day, but people who share your past and history. You can be surrounded by people and be utterly alone. Know what I mean?"

Mikhail's gaze met hers, his expression so full of unspoken emotion that it caused Claire's heart to stutter in her chest. "I do know." His rich voice reached out with twining fingers that penetrated past skin and bone, burrowing into her soul. "There is nothing so crippling in this world as isolation."

A quiet moment passed between them and Claire tried to center her racing thoughts. She was supposed to be working him for information, not sharing her innermost emotions. But she couldn't help but trust him, couldn't quell the feeling of rightness that seized her when she was close to him. Or the urge to get a hell of a lot closer.

"Ronan is a dhampir, is that right?" Claire steered the conversation back to the gathering of information. She couldn't afford an emotional attachment. Not when she wasn't sure whether she was staying or not. "What is that exactly?"

A territorial growl erupted in Michael's chest and Claire took note of the sudden change in his demeanor. "He is, though not for long. Now that you're here, I will turn him and the vampire race will finally be replenished after two centuries of near extinction." He set the pan on the burner and the gas flame jumped to life. As it heated he mixed a little melted butter and milk into the pancake batter, whisking it until it was smooth.

"I still don't understand what any of this has to do with me."

"I see the doubt in your eyes, Claire. You tethered my soul and your blood awakened my power. You are inexorably mine. What has been forged between us cannot be broken. You are *rodstvennaya dusha*. My mate."

Mikhail's explanation was brief and to the point. Abrupt. Just like him. But this business about her being his . . . "*Mate?* Animals mate. Humans, not so much."

Mikhail poured a ladleful of batter onto the buttered pan and it sizzled. "Humans mate."

"Humans *date*. They get married. They divorce. What you're talking about sounds a hell of a lot more permanent than what humans do."

"We're all animals, Claire. Some of are simply closer to our more primal instincts than others."

A chill shivered down Claire's spine. Hadn't she attacked him like a feline in heat right on his living room couch? And hadn't she wanted him to bite her? To sink his fangs into her like some wild thing? There was no doubt in her mind that Mikhail was a dangerous predator. Every bit the animal he professed himself to be. One that wouldn't think twice before ripping out his enemy's throat. "Tell me about the priest." No way was she ready to think about this whole "mate" business. That little tidbit was going to have to go on the back burner for now.

Mikhail kept his back to her, his attention fixed on the

pancakes. He transferred one from the pan to a plate and poured another ladleful of batter on the hot surface. "What's the matter, worried I can't handle it?" At this point, nothing could shock her. "Was he a werewolf? Zombie? Or maybe a disgruntled hellhound?" Mikhail let out a soft snort of amusement. She was tempted to pat herself on the back, chipping at his stone exterior for however brief a moment. Instead, Claire decided to put herself to good use and ventured around the island in search of coffee. "If these guys supposedly want to kill me, don't you think it's only fair I know who they are and why?"

Mikhail sighed. *Resignation. Woot! Claire: two. Vampire: zip.* He was probably rolling his eyes and weighing his options. It was too late for him to play coy with her, though. They'd shared a moment of solidarity. Keeping anything from her now would negate that, and Claire was banking on it.

"The less you know, the better. I'm only trying to protect you, Claire."

"I don't need protection. I've been taking care of myself since I was six and my mom decided that being an addict was more fun than being a parent. What I need is some goddamned information."

Mikhail flipped his pancake and crossed to the far end of the kitchen. He retrieved a stainless-steel canister that he handed to her. "Coffee."

Was mind reading a supernatural trait? Claire wondered. Or maybe her vampire just had Sherlockian powers of deduction. Claire paused. *Hers?* No matter the connection between them, he wasn't her anything, and she needed to remind herself of that. She filled the mesh basket in the fancy Cuisinart coffeemaker and filled the reservoir with water. It was still hard to believe that she was standing in a house that would probably make Donald Trump green with envy. This place was a burglar's dream.

"Hey, where is Alex anyway? I don't want to hurt his feelings, by violating the sacred space of his kitchen and eating food that he didn't cook, but I got the impression that you wanted him to stick around." If Mikhail wasn't going to pony up any more information, could she really stay here in blissful ignorance? No. If she chose to trust him, he'd have to trust her in return. Otherwise there was no point in staying. Though, if she decided to run, she'd feel a hell of a lot better about leaving if she knew Alex wasn't around to be on the receiving end of Mikhail's wrath.

"He's been up all night. I told him to go home. Besides, I'm pretty sure we can manage without him."

Interesting. Had Mikhail been bluffing when he threatened to hurt Alex if Claire took off? *I always follow through . . .* The promise in his earlier words caused a wave of trepidation to roll through her. His eyes shone with heat, locked on hers. A thrum settled low in her abdomen and Claire swore under her breath. With just a look he could banish her anxiety and have her ready to climb him like a tree. "Are you sure about that? Shouldn't he be the one making coffee and pancakes while dabbing our mouths with napkins, or whatever it is rich people expect of the hired help?"

So much sass. He liked it. Michael placed two plates of pancakes on the kitchen island along with a bottle of syrup and a dish of butter. He set down forks and a butter knife before taking a seat. "Alex works for me, but I doubt he'll be dabbing any mouths anytime soon. He'll be back at sunrise. For the time being, I'm your servant."

Claire regarded him from beneath lowered lashes, her full lips twitching as she fought a smile. Michael leaned toward her as though his body and not just his soul had been tethered to her. How could he possibly hold himself from her—let her sustain him with nothing more than her blood—when all he could think about was kissing her again? Touching her soft flesh? Gods, he wanted her. Wanted her to be *his*. Perhaps he could enjoy her company—her body—without the complication of a mate bond. Without sharing his blood with her. He was a selfish enough bastard to consider the possibility of doing just that.

When the coffee was done brewing, Claire brought the pot over and set it on the counter while Michael supplied the cups, sugar, and cream. They both settled down onto their chairs and into their meals.

"The slayers," she said without making eye contact. "Tell me about them."

Likewise, Michael paid way too much attention to his pancakes. "Claire, it's my intention to ease you into this life. I'm sure the past few hours have been a shock to your system and—"

"Look, the past seventeen years of my life have been sink or swim. I'm not some delicate, fragile flower that you need to shelter. Give it to me straight or you can forget me hanging around, because I'm not going to sit here for god knows how long without any information to back up why I'm safer here than I am at my own apartment."

Gods, the way she spoke. So unabashed. Her fire only made him want her more. Michael met her gaze knowing that his own reflected silver. She brought out the animal in him as no other ever had, and fighting his impulse to strip her and take her right there on the kitchen counter was akin to fighting his thirst for blood. He was quickly discovering that he couldn't deny her wishes any more than he could deny his own desire for her. "We call them slayers. They are berserker assassins, brutal beasts bred for killing and sent by the Sortiari to exterminate the vampire race."

She quirked a brow. "And the Sortiari are . . . ?"

"They are the influencers of Fate, or so they claim. A secret society that has infiltrated every aspect of the world as we know it and whose assassins have been known to hide behind the cloister. For millennia the Sortiari have taken it upon themselves to fulfill what they believe is a divine purpose: changing the course of Fate. The supernatural community isn't their only target. Politicians, religious figures, humanitarians, criminals . . . Anyone or anything that goes against their agenda is a potential target."

"Holy shit," Claire said with a disbelieving laugh. "Is this a Dan Brown novel come to life or what?" Her expression became serious as she studied Michael with an intensity that heated his blood. "So why do they want me dead? I'm not rich. Not powerful. I've got about ten bucks to my name and I'm a waitress. Aside from my blood, which you seem to think is pretty dynamite, there's nothing special about me."

"Claire, I don't think you understand your importance." How could she? Michael pinched the bridge of his nose and let out a slow breath. "I am the *last* vampire. If I should die, the race dies with me." How could he possibly explain to her how much she meant to him? To all of them? "You are my mate. The female who has returned my *soul* to me and awakened the seat of my power. Because of this, I can turn dhampirs. They can finally become what they're meant to be. The Sortiari spent centuries trying to eradicate the vampire race. You are the only thing standing between them and success."

Claire focused her attention on her plate, her brow furrowed. "How is a dhampir made?"

Michael took a monster bite of pancake and chewed for a quiet moment. "Dhampirs are born. Either from a vampire mating or a vampire/human coupling."

"What about a dhampir coupling?" Her curiosity was a

boon to his confidence. Perhaps if he did as she asked and armed her with information he could convince her to stay.

"Dhampir males are sterile," he replied. "Until we're made vampires, we are unable to reproduce."

"Wait." Her dubious smile caused his abdomen to tighten. Gods, how he wanted her. "How is that even possible? Vampires are dead. Or undead. Aren't you?"

Michael gave an amused snort. "Our physiology is much more complex than even modern science could comprehend. When a dhampir is made into a vampire, his soul is sent into oblivion. It's the price that's paid for becoming stronger and developing keener senses. In a way, a vampire's body does essentially become undead. Our hearts cease beating; the breath stalls in our chests. Blood no longer flows through our veins and we no longer need food to sustain us. But there is a hunger. A thirst for blood that must be sated. And when a vampire drinks from a living vein, our bodies awaken, resume their normal functions until the lifeblood cycles through our system. In most cases, a vampire needs to drink from either his mate or a dhampir to thrive. Human blood isn't enough to sustain us. After the blood works through our systems, the vampire's body returns to dormancy until the thirst returns and the cycle starts anew."

Claire's answering smile dazzled him. "Creepy. And sort of cool. I'm pretty sure any scientist would shit a brick to get his hands on you." Her playful tone tied Michael into knots, sent a rush of desire through his veins. "You said human blood isn't enough. I'm human. But you seem to think mine is like the Red Bull of blood."

Michael laughed. "It is. To me. It's the mate bond that makes it so. Claire, when a soul is sent into oblivion, it doesn't simply float away. It attaches itself to another soul. In this case, yours. Through the centuries your soul anchored mine, and when you were born you took it with you. When I saw you, you returned my soul to me. You *tethered* me. We are two halves of a whole. It's a bond that can't *ever* be broken."

Claire pushed her plate away as though she'd lost her appetite. A wave of anxiety crested over Michael. He'd hoped his honesty would draw her closer to him, invite her trust, not push her away. "To think of my soul as some infinite thing, hanging out in the universe until I was born, goes a little deeper than I usually like to think. I mean, that my *soul* would have reached out and grabbed on to yours? Sort of a fairy tale, don't you think? I've got to be honest with you, I stopped believing in fairy tales a long time ago." A moment of silence stretched out between them and Michael's chest ached with her sorrow. His fangs throbbed in his gums as he was possessed with an urge to rip the throat from anyone who would do her harm. "So"—she cleared the thick emotion from her throat—"does becoming a vampire mark some sort of uh . . . sexual maturity?"

Pancake lodged in his throat and he washed it down with coffee. So brazen, so curious, his female was. Lust burned his gut, hardened his cock, but Michael pushed his desire to the back of his mind. For now, he'd sate her desire for knowledge and nothing else. "I'd love to hear Ronan's response to that," he said with a laugh. "I'm sure he'd be unnecessarily outraged at the notion that he was unable to bed every female that caught his eye. But to answer your question, becoming a vampire initiates our fertility."

"It seems like a contradiction to nature, don't you think? You're only able to reproduce after your soul leaves and your body dies."

"Whose nature?" Michael countered. "Yours? Perhaps. But in my world, it *is* natural."

"What would happen if Ronan drank my blood?"

"He would die a slow and painful death," Michael responded as he suppressed a territorial growl.

Claire covered her mouth, nearly choking on her coffee. "My blood would kill him?"

"No," Michael said with a humorless laugh, "but the two-hundred-and-fifty-pound vampire sitting beside you would get the job done. Claire, I told you that we're closer to our animal natures than humans. Vampires are incredibly territorial. I wouldn't hesitate to kill anyone who tried to take what belongs to me. You need to be very aware of that aspect of my nature."

"Well," she said on a breath. "Overprotective with a violent streak." She looked away and a ripple of discomfort vibrated through Michael. Perhaps he should have been more delicate on the subject of his territoriality, but he no longer wished to hide his true nature from her. Doubt gnawed at him. Her doubt. And the sensation left him feeling too raw. "Sunlight bothers you?"

"Yes." Michael studied her. He'd seen the look before; she was trying to get a read on him. If she'd simply open up to him, she'd realize that their tether left him bare to her. He could hide nothing. "Dhampirs can tolerate sunlight as well as humans, but exposure would kill me."

"Wow," Claire said with a laugh. "L.A. really isn't the best city for you to be living in, you know. How often do you need blood?"

He popped the last bite of pancake into his mouth. "In the past, I could sustain myself by taking blood once every three or four months." His gaze leveled on her. "But I've found that when it comes to you, I am *insatiable*."

Claire's beautiful mouth parted with a breath and her lips formed a silent *oh*. A thrill chased through him and his thirst blazed hot in his throat.

"Your eyes are silver." Her voice was little more than a whisper, her eyes shining with heat. Her pulse raced, the vein in her throat throbbing against her tender flesh. The sound of her heart as it pounded in her chest caused a surge of lust to dizzy him. How could he have ever thought to hold himself from her?

Michael's skin prickled with the coming sunrise, and a stone of disappointment settled in his gut. Their time together had come to an end much too soon, and within minutes the blinds would come down to lock them both in this wretched tomb. Gods, how he hated the sun.

"What's the matter?" Her expression softened with concern and Michael swore it tore the muscles of his heart.

"The sun is about to rise." Already his limbs felt weighed down, his body preparing for the sleep that would soon overtake him. If only he could have one more hour with her. *Hell, another minute.* He wasn't ready to leave her side. "Alex should be here soon. Ronan as well. They'll watch over you while I sleep."

She regarded him with narrowed eyes. *So suspicious.* "Just gonna hit the hay, huh? Just like that."

"I'm afraid it's an unfortunate necessity." How much should he divulge to her about his weakness once the sun rose? "I have no choice but to sleep. Another quirk of physiology."

She flashed a mischievous smile that tightened his chest. "So you're saying if you don't go lie down now, you'll just crumple to the floor?"

He smiled in turn. "More or less."

"Well then." Claire continued to study him as though she could climb into his very soul. "I guess you'd better get to bed. I doubt I could carry you up the stairs if you passed out on the kitchen floor."

No, but he could carry her without any exertion whatsoever. She was a feather in his arms and he ached to take her upstairs, lay her down in his bed, and feel the warmth of her body tucked against his. Leaving her for even a few hours seemed too great a feat. He'd meant what he'd said about easing her into this life, though. Michael knew that if he pushed too hard she'd run.

He crossed the kitchen to where she stood by the sink, rinsing her plate. She faced him, her eyes large and luminous. "Behave yourself, Claire." He kissed her forehead and she leaned in to his touch, her body melting against his. Gods, if he didn't leave now he'd never part from her. "Have a good day, my little human." Michael turned and walked away, and the effort was like prying two magnets apart. In a few short hours, Claire had managed to embed herself further into his heart. His soul.

And now that she was here, he was going to do everything in his power to ensure that she stayed.

they'd shared a bed and blood, Michael had known that she wasn't truly his. Hers was not the soul that made his whole. Only through the collective memory had Michael experienced the magic of a true mating bond. That is, until three nights ago when his soul had rushed back to him, filling the void that had consumed him for centuries.

The sun had yet to set; he felt it in every cell that constructed him. And yet he was awake. His body and mind alert. The death-like sleep of the daylight hours no longer held him in its grip. But he hungered.

For Claire.

His fangs throbbed in his gums, painfully so, and his throat burned with an unquenchable fire. Could it be that the remnants of his dream ignited his thirst? His urgent want of Ilya that crossed over centuries and fixated on a human? Or was he simply making excuses, anything to explain away the soul-deep need he felt for Claire.

In the inky darkness, the walls closed in on him, the air became stagnant. The smell of death was still fresh in his mind and panic surged in Michael's chest, burning as hot as his thirst. He pushed himself from the mattress, tripped on the thick Persian rug, and stumbled to the ground. With a low growl he shot up from the floor and dressed, racing for the door, cracking the hinges free of the jamb as he threw it open. He ran, taking deep gulps of air into his lungs.

Want. Need. Desire. Thirst.

His emotions ran the gamut, cycling through him like boiling storm clouds. The house was dark, pockets of artificial light illuminating the long hallway to the staircase. Michael stumbled as he rushed down the hallway, his desperation rising to a fevered pitch. He couldn't stand being locked up in this fucking tomb, shut out from the world. Each step down the staircase was rushed, his fingers cracking the wooden banister from his unyielding grip.

CHAPTER
13

Freshly spilled blood perfumed the air and Mikhail's throat burned with thirst. The need to drink was strong, despite the fact that he'd had his fill before going into battle. Accursed bloodlust. His secondary fangs throbbed in time with the beat of his heart. Some of the Sortiari had voluntarily slit their own throats in an effort to distract the vampire forces from the battle and weaken their defenses. Mikhail would not be deterred, however. The bastards had taken Ilya, and he would not rest until he found her.

With his heavy broadsword he struck out, cutting down his enemies like crisp autumn wheat. All around him was death: the bodies of the Sortiari soldiers and their slayers, more vampires than he could count. His stomach turned as rage clouded Mikhail's vision. With all that had been lost, he wouldn't survive losing her, too.

"Ilya!"

Michael came awake with a start, the name burstin
from his lips in a tortured shout that echoed off the wall
Before the Sortiari had obliterated the vampires, he'd h
a female. A newly turned vampire named Ilya. Thou

Her scent drove him mad, the thought of once again sinking his fangs into the tender flesh of her throat sending him past reason. On the second-story landing Michael paused before he rushed down the stairs and headed in the direction of that tantalizing scent.

"Claire."

She stood at the front door, one hand frozen on the brass knob. The sheets of her hair cascaded down one shoulder and spilled over her bare arm, wheat on a snowy field. Her cheeks were flushed with blood, her lips dark pink and inviting. Michael shook the remnants of his dream from his mind, as well as the desire that surged within him, hardening his cock to the point of near pain. Gods, he wanted her, wanted to bury himself so deep inside of her that he no longer knew where his body ended and hers began.

"What are you doing?" Panic infused his tone as he pushed his palm against the still-closed door. Did she think to leave him? "I told you what would happen if you thought to walk out that door."

"Mikhail." She hid her nerves well under a façade of calm, but the sound of her rushing pulse echoed in his ears like thunder. A little mouse caught in the jaws of a hungry cat. "What are you doing up? I thought you'd be down for the count." She gave a nervous laugh. "I was just going out for some fresh air. You know, feeling a little shut up."

"Don't attempt to manage me, Claire." Her cheeks further bloomed with a crimson stain and the scent of her blood sent him reeling. His true name on her lips was heaven, the sound a slow caress. Too much for him to bear. "And don't call me Mikhail. That male no longer exists."

She canted her head to one side. Studied him as though trying to deconstruct him as she took a tentative step away from the door. "Ronan calls you Mikhail."

"Ronan is presumptuous." He took a step toward her. And another. Claire didn't back away. Rather, she squared her shoulders and knocked her chin defiantly into the air. *Such bravery in this female. Such strength.*

"I heard you shout. Are you all right?"

Was that concern or suspicion in her tone? "Where were you going?"

She looked him dead in the eye without an ounce of guile. She tucked her left hand behind her back as though hiding something. *Crafty female.* "I told you. Out for fresh air."

Where was Alex? And where in the hell was Ronan? He'd promised to return at sunrise. "Ronan!" Michael's voice boomed through the house, but his feisty female didn't so much as cringe at the sound. She stood stalwart against the coming storm, shoulders squared as though prepared to go to battle.

"He's busy." Claire folded her arms in front of her chest, pushing her breasts up to swell above the deep V of her shirt. Michael suppressed the urge to snatch her up and sink his fangs into that tantalizing mound of flesh. "And Alex isn't here, so don't bother shouting for him, either."

Ronan stepped into the room not a moment later, his expression etched with concern and not a little shock. "The sun is still up."

"Thank you, Ronan. I wouldn't have known had you not informed me." Michael let out a long sigh. "Where's Alex?"

Ronan looked around as though he had no idea who Michael was talking about. *Good gods.* "I called and told him not to bother coming back. Everything's under control here. There was no need for him to be here."

"Oh really?" Michael snatched Claire's left hand from its folded position, an expensive leather wallet clutched in her grip. She tried to pull away and the long sleeve of her shirt slipped up her arm, revealing his Patek circling her wrist. Her gaze met his and her cheeks flushed before she looked away, guilty. How long had she had it? Since that night at Diablo, no doubt. She'd lured him to the back of the club with the intention of robbing him. His mate had quite the skill set, it seemed.

Ronan stared at Claire, his jaw a little slack, before he checked his jacket. "You picked my pocket?"

Michael rolled his eyes at Ronan's appreciative tone. He plucked the wallet from her grasp and tossed it back to its owner but left his watch on her wrist.

Claire's mouth puckered and she crossed her arms back across her chest, making her look like a petulant child. Michael kept his fingers curled around her arm, and his thumb acted of its own volition, brushing over her creamy skin. "Just a breath of fresh air?" he asked, cocking a dubious brow.

She looked away, her jaw locked down tight. Her emotions shifted from shock and embarrassment to a deep hurt that reached through their tether and stabbed Michael's heart. He'd caused that pain, and shame welled up hot and thick in his throat. He'd taken her vein, all but using her before he cast her aside as though she were nothing. Meant nothing to him. Then, he'd coaxed her in gentle conversation only to leave her in another male's care once the sun rose. Could she not sense the indecision warring within him? The need he felt to make her truly his? And the fear that it could never, ever be.

"Since you're up," Ronan said, angling his body so that his back was turned to Claire, "there's something I need to discuss with you. Something *important*."

Michael's gaze slid toward Claire. If he left her alone again, she'd run.

"I think we can trust her to behave. And not to pick any more pockets today, can't we, Claire?"

She ignored Michael and focused her attention on Ronan. "Sure. Whatever. I don't need fresh air. I'll just watch TV."

Claire turned and hooked her thumbs into her back pockets, the casual gesture causing her pert breasts to jut and strain against the flimsy fabric of her T-shirt. Michael swallowed down the lust that swelled within him like a tide. The need for both her body and her blood once again sent him teetering on the edge of logical thought. She eased away from the door, a movement meant to be casual. Tension vibrated through her; her pulse had picked up the moment he'd come upon her and the frantic beat of her heart was enough to tell him that had he woken a moment later she would have been gone. She'd stolen Ronan's wallet and planned to leave, of that Michael had no doubt.

"I thought vampires couldn't be awake during the day?" She shot an accusing glance his way as though she'd caught him in a lie. She was a cunning female. Using deflection to hide her own guilt.

He turned slowly to face her, his brow arched.

"I have to say, Mikhail, I'm curious as well."

From over Michael's shoulder Claire's gaze met Ronan's, and a reluctant smile crept onto her lips. What had they talked about while he slept? What bonds had they formed? He didn't like the ease with which she bestowed her favor upon the other male. The quick expression of good humor that caused Michael's body to warm and his cock to grow hard. A pang of jealousy shot through his chest and he rubbed through his shirt at the star-shaped scar that hovered over his heart. Ronan might have been his friend, but Michael couldn't help the feral growl that boiled up his throat.

"Wait for me in the study, Ronan." Michael's eyes never left Claire's, the shimmering golden depths evaporating everything around him.

"This concerns Claire, too," Ronan remarked.

Michael didn't bother to face his friend. If he did he might be tempted to tear out the other male's throat. His tone chilled with each word: "Does it?"

Claire looked from Ronan to him and back, her brow puckered. She'd be wise to avert her gaze from the other male, especially when Michael's emotions were so volatile. The Collective tugged at the threads of his memory. A primal, instinctual urge to take Claire upstairs, sink his teeth into her throat and his cock into her soft flesh, overriding any sense of decorum or his own self-imposed abstinence. He wanted to bite her. Drink from her. Fuck her until there was no doubt in her mind to whom she belonged. She would never look at another male again with even a hint of affection when he was done with her.

"You and I will discuss whatever business you have, Ronan. Alone."

Claire took a step toward Michael. "There's no way you're going to have a conversation about me behind my back, buddy." Claire poked her finger into his chest. He looked down at that slender digit and locked his jaw down tight. The pad of her finger rested on his scar, and the rumbling in his chest intensified to a snarl.

The pain from that damned scar was soul deep and Claire had just poked an already-agitated animal. She met his eyes with defiance and showed not an ounce of fear. *Admirable.* Michael held her gaze and drew on his power—power that, ironically, she'd helped to restore—and her hand dropped to her side, limp.

"Claire," he intoned. "Sleep."

Her eyes drifted shut and she crumpled like tissue paper into his arms.

"That's one way to get a woman out of your hair," Ronan quipped in his insufferably snarky way. "Really, Mikhail, could you be more high-handed?"

"In my study," he instructed from between clenched teeth. "I'll meet you there shortly."

Ronan let out a long-suffering sigh and turned on a heel. "Suit yourself," he said as he left the room. "But heed my warning, Mikhail: If you continue to treat her as a kept thing, she'll flee her cage and slip right through your fingers. And if that happens, we might as well hand ourselves over to the Sortiari slayers. Or run the stakes through our hearts with our own hands."

Quiet indignation simmered under the surface of Michael's barely checked temper. *High-handed?* He was the reluctant king of an orphaned race whose future depended on the very fragile, very *human,* female in his arms. A female who could never truly be his mate. He had no choice *but* to be high-handed. And how he treated Claire was for her own protection. She might have seemed to be made of steel, but once the scope of her situation sank in her weak human psyche would crack. Ronan thought she would flee? Michael would hunt her to the ends of the earth.

He marched up the stairs to the second-story landing, passing the hallway lined with guest rooms. Whether she could be his mate or not, Claire belonged to him. He refused to put her anywhere but in his bed. No one ventured past the second story. Not even Alex. The third story of the house belonged to Michael alone. He'd freed himself from one prison only to entomb himself in another. It was dark at the top of the landing. Quiet. The re-creation of a century's worth of hellish loneliness. Was it wrong to want to keep Claire for himself, a prisoner here just as surely as he was?

Did what either of them wanted matter in the larger scope of what was needed for the continuation of the race?

He set her on the mattress as though she were nothing more than a hollowed-out eggshell. Too delicate to suffer even the slightest mishandling. Her hair fanned out on the navy blue pillowcase like gold shimmering under deep water. Michael reached down to brush the stray locks from her face and Claire sighed, a sound so pure and sweet it caused his heart to clench in his chest.

She was a kept thing. A beautiful, exotic animal, delicate and rare. She had awakened his power, would be the mother of a long-dead race, and she had no idea how important she was to all of them.

The scent of her blood filled the enclosed space of his bedroom with a sweetness that made his mouth water. Michael's fangs throbbed in his gums, and fiery heat scorched a path up his throat. He'd fed from her just hours ago, and yet he hungered for her with the intensity of the newly turned. His heart beat with a vigorous rhythm in his chest, and at his core power surged within him. He felt invigorated. Alive. And still it wasn't enough. He wanted more, to glut himself on her blood. As long as she was human, the greatest danger to her life was Michael himself.

He jerked upright, only now realizing that he was bent over her, his mouth sealed over her throat. The bloodlust had seized him with a totality that weakened not only his mind but also his will. He would have taken her. Sunk his fangs into her neck and ravished her while she slept soundly under the influence of his command. Gods, not even twenty-four hours had passed and already he found himself helpless to resist her siren song. The hold she had over him was instant. Powerful.

And dangerous.

"Mikhail?" Ronan's voice filtered up the stairway from the bottom floor. "Are you going to make me wait all day? Put Sleeping Beauty to bed and let's get on with it!"

Michael pushed himself away from Claire, every inch of him trembling. He balled his hands into fists as he strode toward the doorway, all the while his body screaming for him to turn around and do what he'd yearned to do. Though he resented the other male's constant presence, as Michael eased the door shut behind him he realized that Ronan might be all that stood between him and utter ruin. Perhaps it wasn't just the Sortiari Claire needed protection from. Michael was beginning to think that someone ought to protect her from him as well.

Ronan paced the confines of the study, looking a bit like a caged animal himself when Michael walked through the open doors. His hair sat atop his head in a wild tangle as he gnawed on his thumbnail like it might be his last meal. "What happened between the two of you while I slept?"

Ronan turned to face him, his expression that of a disappointed parent. "Really, Mikhail? Not even a full day with your mate and you're already jealous."

"What happened?" That Ronan was deflecting caused Michael's ire to mount, jealous or not. Something had woken him from his sleep. A feat that had never been accomplished in all of the many centuries of his existence. He'd felt a sense of urgency upon waking. Panic. Had Ronan scared Claire? Threatened her? Made an unwanted advance? Michael's bloodlust raged. It wouldn't matter at this point whose blood he feasted upon. If Ronan had offended Claire in some way, Michael would sate his thirst right here and now.

"If becoming a tethered vampire turns one into a mindless animal ruled by his base emotions, perhaps I should reconsider accepting your generous gift." Ronan took a seat at Michael's desk, opened an old leather-bound book, and focused his attention on whatever was written there. Michael knew that book. He'd seen it somewhere before . . . many years ago.

"Where did you get that codex?" His jealousy took a backseat to his curiosity. Many of the vampire race's relics had been scattered to the winds after the Sortiari attacks. He'd recovered a few of them over the past decades, but this particular tome he'd thought lost.

"You're not the only one with connections," Ronan replied. "Or influence."

Smug. Michael had time enough to grill Ronan on just how and from whom he got the book, but the appearance of the relic was currently the least of his worries. "What does the book have to do with Claire?"

"I'm not entirely sure." As he continued to flip through the pages, Ronan cast a sidelong glance Michael's way. "I haven't found exactly what I'm looking for yet, but if my assumptions are correct, I think I've saved you a lifetime's worth of worry, my friend."

Michael quirked a brow. "How so?"

"I think that Claire is a Vessel."

He let out a disbelieving bark of laughter. "And here I thought you'd come to me with something that wasn't founded on myth and legend." Michael paced the room, his brain buzzing with need. Until Claire, he'd kept his thirst at bay for months at a time without even a hint of mindless bloodlust. But now taking her vein had become his obsession, the thirst mounting to the point that only an act of violence would keep him from her. *Claire, a Vessel.* Michael let out a derisive snort. She might as well be a unicorn.

"Why is it so hard to believe?" Ronan kept his nose buried in the pages, his attention focused on the ancient text.

"Because there is no such thing." The hope that had dared to soar in Michael's chest fell from the sky with broken wings. "It is a romantic story passed down through the ages. Something to give foolish lovers hope." He thought back to the memory of the vampire who'd killed his human lover. Surely he'd been convinced the woman was a Vessel as well.

"No. You're wrong."

Gods, Ronan infuriated Michael with the way he refused to raise his eyes from the yellowed vellum pages. His fingertip skimmed the lines as he read, his lips moving without sound. "And how is it, Ronan, that you have seemed to have found something that no vampire has ever encountered?"

"I didn't find her, Mikhail. You did."

Michael let out a long sigh. "If you're trying to anger me, it's working."

Ronan ignored Michael's tightly spoken words. "I haven't had long to read. An hour or so. It'll take days for me to get through it all. But from what I can tell, a Vessel carries a certain . . . spark. A strength of mind and spirit. An inner light or aura of power that calls to a vampire. Sort of like supernatural catnip."

Michael raised a brow and fixed Ronan with a stern stare. "Are you saying that Claire calls to you?" Ronan was enough of a vampire to feel an instinctual pull if what he said about her was correct. Would Michael soon be fighting a horde of males for possession of Claire? He'd kill anyone—including Ronan—who sought to take her from him.

Ronan looked up from the codex. "You might want to do something about your persistent growling. It's off-putting."

The feral rumble died in Michael's chest, though his annoyance failed to dissipate. "Why is it you refuse to answer my questions, Ronan? I ask you from where you acquired the codex, you deflect. I ask what you discussed with Claire, you deflect." Michael's teeth clamped down tight and he ground out, "I ask if you feel drawn to her, and you *deflect*. I'm tired of you dodging my questions."

"Yeah? Well, I'm tired of you acting like an uncivilized fool with the sort of base urges a caveman would cringe at.

Claire and I exchanged polite conversation while you slept. Nothing more than that. Do I feel drawn to her? No. Do I sense the power of her life force? Of course I do. We *all* do. But I also sense an otherness in her that is . . . unsettling. As for the codex," Ronan said on a sigh. "I acquired it from Siobhan. At what price is none of your gods-damned business. Now, can we please get back on track?"

Siobhan. Gods, that female was a thorn in Michael's side. She thought herself a queen and ruled her coven with an iron fist, not to mention a supremacy and disdain for the vampire race. She reviled the idea of being turned. Of sacrificing her soul, despite the prospect of a tether. That Ronan chose to consort with her was yet another annoyance that Michael had no choice but to suffer. Who the male bedded was none of Michael's business. But if Ronan had breathed a word of Claire's existence to the cagey female he wouldn't hesitate to demand that Ronan end their affair. Siobhan was wild. Dangerous. A variable he didn't have time to address.

Dry heat licked at his throat and Michael continued to pace, focusing his energy on placing one foot in front of the other. Anything to keep his mind from his damnable thirst. No matter how he'd gotten the codex, Ronan was offering Michael a glimmer of hope, dim though it might be. But even a glimmer was a dangerous thing after centuries of darkness. "Tell me everything you know so far," he said. "We'll start from there."

CHAPTER
14

Claire woke feeling downright hungover. She'd slept like
the dead, sort of funny considering her current circumstances. It took a few minutes for her eyes to adjust to the
dark gray twilight, and her surroundings slowly came
sharper into focus, the shadowy outlines of the bedroom
more defined. She lay in a virtual island of a bed, the large
California king dwarfed by the sheer size of the bedroom.
The heavy metal window coverings had retracted and a
light evening breeze stirred the curtains as the sound of
birds settling down for the night filled the air.

She stretched her arms high above her head, wondering
at the stiffness she felt. The priest had roughed her up
pretty good last night, but she felt as though she hadn't
flexed her muscles in at least a month. The fog that settled
in her brain seemed reluctant to lift, and remnants of
dreams clung like cobwebs in her memory: Mikhail coming to her again and again and instructing her to sleep in
that deliciously deep voice of his. And in her dream Claire
had fallen into his arms, helpless to deny the command.
Weird. Especially since she couldn't remember ever going

to bed. The last thing she remembered, she was about to blow out of this place, hand on the damned doorknob before Mikhail had put the kibosh on that plan. They'd been standing in the foyer and then . . . *nothing*. Everything after that moment was a total blank.

"Aw, crap!" Claire shot up to a sitting position, immediately regretting it. Her head pounded and the room swam. *Wow.* She really did feel hungover. She'd missed her shift at the diner and Lance was going to kill her. She couldn't afford to get fired, death threats from secret societies or not. And if her new babysitter thought he could just keep her locked up in his spiffy mansion like some sort of stray cat at the pound, well, he had another think coming.

From the center of the bed she crawled toward the nightstand. Holy crap, the mattress was enormous. An entire family could sleep on the damned thing. A sigh of relief escaped her chest at the sight of the telephone, and she eased it from the cradle, dialing the diner's number as she held her breath and said a silent prayer that she still had a job.

"Pancake Palace," Lance answered with way too much cheer for someone who stood at a hot stove for sixteen-plus hours a day.

"Hey, Lance. It's Claire. I'm so sorry I missed my shift—"

"Holy shit, Claire! Where are you? Are you okay? I've been worried sick!" The panic that infused Lance's words put her on high alert. Way too much concern for someone who'd just barely missed a shift. "I was getting ready to file a missing-persons report."

"I missed you, too." Claire cleared her throat, her voice thick and lazy with sleep. What was going on with her? "Look at us. One shift apart and we're pining for each other like an old married couple."

A pregnant pause followed and her stomach twisted into an anxious knot. "Claire . . . it's been three days."

What?! "Um, yeah. Right." A good hustler was always quick on her feet. "That's what I meant. I've been pretty much out of it. I think it might be mono."

"Shit." Lance groaned. "You washed your hands religiously on your last shift, didn't you?"

The last thing he'd want was a potential health scare at the diner. "Oh yeah. I always overdo it in the hand-washing department. But I think I'd better keep my distance until I can get into an urgent-care clinic for tests. If you have to hire someone to replace me, I'll understand." Claire swallowed down the lump in her throat. She needed that job, damn it. *Please, please don't fire me.*

"You should have called me sooner, Claire. But I had mono in high school so I know it can lay you low. I might have to hire someone temporarily, but don't worry. Your job is yours as soon as you're certified germ-free. But until then, I don't want to see your face. Understand?"

She let out an audible sigh of relief. "Gotcha."

"Feel better, Claire."

"Thanks, Lance. I'll see you later."

"Let me know if you need anything," he said.

"I will. Bye."

For a long moment Claire sat on the edge of bed, the phone clutched in her grip. Three days? How? On wobbly legs she stumbled across the vast bedroom, her vision failing as night slowly swallowed the last remaining gray of twilight. "Damn it!" She sucked in a sharp breath as her knee smacked against the polished wood of an antique couch, and she skirted the sitting area, her bare feet sinking into the thick pile of the expensive carpeting. When had she taken off her shoes? What in the hell was going on?

Fiery indignation swelled up inside of her, burning

through the oxygen in her lungs until all that was left was a raging inferno. Mikhail had done something to her. She recalled the glint of silver flash in his eyes moments before he spoke the command "sleep." He'd worked some sort of freaky vampire mojo on her! "Bastard," Claire said from between clenched teeth. "I'm going to kick his ass!"

She tripped in her rush for the door, throwing it open too quickly, only to bang up her opposite knee. "Shit. Mikhail!" His name burst from her lips in an angry shout as she limped down the hallway toward the third-story landing. "Mikhail!" She was going to kill him. Kill. Him. No one hustled a hustler, and Claire's pride had taken a serious hit. He'd stacked the deck in his favor, using whatever supernatural power he had to keep her in an unconscious state. It was one way to keep a houseguest, she supposed. *What. A. Jerk.*

Good lord, this place was a freaking museum. Down one flight of stairs, onto the second-floor landing, Claire felt if she took a wrong turn she might end up in Narnia or some shit. Both of her knees were throbbing and she was still so groggy that putting one foot in front of the other seemed like too great a feat to surmount. Fueled by anger, she continued on her track. She might well pass out by the time she made it to the bottom floor, but damn it, she was going to give that high-handed bloodsucker a piece of her mind before she did.

She flew down the second flight of stairs, tripping on the last three in a graceless slide that nearly deposited her on her ass when she hit the first floor. Mikhail came around the corner, looking as drop-dead gorgeous and put together as ever, one sardonic brow cocked curiously. "Claire." How was it possible for him to sound totally calm and collected? It made her even angrier. *And how dare he be so damned gorgeous!* It was totally an unfair advantage. "You should be resting."

"Oh no, you don't." God, he smelled good. A waft of dark chocolate and warm summer gardens hit her nostrils, and Claire's step faltered. His effect on her was instant and visceral. She wanted to strip him naked and lick him from head to toe. *Damn him.* "Three days!" she railed. "I've been asleep for *three days*?"

He took a slow step toward her, and another. The rolling gait was hypnotic, predatory. Each individual muscle in his body flexed and released, an artistic display partially hidden by the expertly tailored dress shirt and slacks. A shirt and slacks she wanted to tear off of him—

Focus, Claire. Get it together. Don't let him hustle you again.

She froze at the bottom of the stairs, her body temperature rising the closer he got. His gaze drifted to her cheeks that she knew were flushed with color. It didn't take much for him to rattle her, and he was well aware that he had the upper hand. *Well, not for long.*

"Claire." He rested his hands on her shoulders and she bristled. He'd done this to her before. At the doorway. His pupils flashed silver and Claire's limbs became heavy. Tired. "Sleep."

No! The command screamed through her mind as she latched on to the necessary will to fight whatever power he used to make her compliant. She felt a push, as though rejecting the intrusion into her psyche, and Claire straightened, her limbs no longer heavy and her mind clear of the fog that had weighed her down. "Don't you dare try to work your mind-control magic on me ever again, Mikhail! Seriously, what in the hell were you thinking? I've been asleep for days?" Claire took a cleansing breath, but it did little to assuage her anger. "You're lucky you're bigger than me because if you weren't I would lay you *out*!"

Mikhail pulled back, his brow furrowed as shock

dawned on his handsome features. "Claire," he said again as quicksilver chased over his gaze. "*Sleep*."

"No."

She'd never seen him so taken aback. Not the calm, bossy, überbadass vampire. The furrow in his brow deepened. A crease that cut just above the bridge of his nose. "I can't compel you."

"Noway, nohow." Her stomach growled with all of the ferocity of an agitated bear and Claire hugged her torso to mute the sound. Pretty hard to act like a tough girl when her gut was shouting for a cheeseburger. "Now, you listen to me. I'm not some doll you can tuck under the covers and disregard. I'm starving. Dirty. I ache everywhere. And I need a damned glass of water! Do you not have any idea how to take care of someone?" She marched past him toward the kitchen. "I'm serious, Mikhail. If you don't feed me in about five seconds, I am going to go *off*."

Michael stared after Claire, dumbstruck.

She'd shaken off his attempt to compel her as water ran from a duck's back. It was impossible. A feat he'd never seen accomplished by a human. And yet she'd stood tall, her eyes sparking with gold fire as she resisted his influence. Fierce. Strong. Powerful. He turned and followed after her, helpless. He'd failed to control her, but her hold on him was undeniable. She accused him of starving her, but it was he who was starved. For her. For her blood. Her body.

For the first time, Michael was beginning to believe in Ronan's insistence that Claire was indeed a Vessel. How else could she have withstood his power? He followed her into the kitchen, unable to resist her pull. The tables had turned, it seemed. For she had surely compelled him.

For days, he'd kept her in a state of oblivion. Ronan had condemned him for it, and Alex . . . he'd taken his leave with a disapproving glare and a vow not to return until Michael had regained his wits. It had seemed the only option at the time. They'd found little more information on Vessels than when they'd begun. Just useless mythology and conjecture. How could it be that no vampire in the race's history had ever encountered one? If they had, Michael would have knowledge of it through the Collective. Of course, just because no one had encountered a Vessel didn't mean that one didn't exist.

It was dangerous to hope at this point. Michael couldn't allow himself any optimistic sentiment. Claire had a strong will, of that he had no doubt. Her mind was sharp; her wit, quick. That did not, however, make her a magical human creature able to survive the transition. Nor did it guarantee she could withstand the burden of the Collective. It didn't solidify her status as his mate.

"You're lucky I'm starving." Michael entered the kitchen to find Claire rummaging through the refrigerator, stacking piles of food on the counter. "Otherwise, I'd have been out the door five minutes ago."

She reached for the hanging pot rack, her fingers barely skimming the edge of a frying pan. Her brow furrowed in concentration as she rose on her tiptoes, still too short to reach. "Allow me." Michael closed the space between them and reached up, plucking the pan from its hook. Her shoulder brushed his torso and a tremor ran the length of his body that settled low in his gut and tightened his balls. The last remnants of her blood were cycling through his system, and it wouldn't be long before his body returned to dormancy. Which only caused him to hunger for her that much more.

She snatched the pan from his grasp, her eyes hooded as she took a tentative step away. "Thanks. I'd say it's the least you could do, considering."

The venom in her tone burned through him. All of them

were right, though. Ronan, Alex, Claire. He'd done a foolish thing in keeping her complacent against her will. It
was not the sort of behavior that would foster any trust—
or affection—between them. "Sit." She gave him an aston-
ished look that said, *You're seriously going to order me
around?* Michael sighed and pinched the bridge of his
nose. He'd denied himself the company of others for far
too long. A century in a tomb and another century's worth
of solitude had done nothing to strengthen his social
graces. "Please, Claire." He held out a hand to indicate the
tall bar stool. "Sit. I'll cook for you."

She raised a dubious brow. "No games?"

A rush of excitement chased through him as his palm
found the small of her back. Michael gently urged her
toward the high stool and she reluctantly let him. "No pretense. I give you my word."

"All right." Claire hopped up on the stool, her expression that of a wary animal ready to bolt at a moment's
notice.

In taking her, keeping her, Michael had failed her. How
could he expect her to be what he needed her to be—his
strength, power, and purpose—when he treated her as
though she were nothing but a vase meant to rest on a shelf
until he found need of it? She would never be willing to
help raise them all up if he did nothing more than drag her
down. Claire was as vital to the race as Michael was. Her
destruction would be his. Whether she realized it or not,
they were already one. Inexorably connected. And yet he
knew so little about her.

"Why did you get off the bus that night?" It seemed the
best place to start a conversation with her. Michael turned
his attention toward the pile of food Claire had taken from
the refrigerator and he sorted through it, gathering the ingredients he'd need to make the chicken piccata Alex had
planned for dinner before taking his sabbatical.

"You mean *three days ago,* when you and Ronan found me?"

Michael cringed at the accusation in her tone. "Yes. Where were you going, and alone in such a dangerous part of the city?"

"This might surprise you, Mikhail, but in the twenty-first century a woman can be out whenever and wherever she wants. Without an escort."

Gods, the way she said his name. He wanted to be that male again. Mikhail Aristov. Vampire. Warrior. Obliterator of his enemies. Michael Aristov was a harmless venture capitalist. A persona created to hide who and what he truly was. Michael was weak in comparison. And the Sortiari would prey on that weakness.

Her voice was as smooth and rich as cream when she said, "I was looking for you."

Michael focused his attention on the task at hand, dredging the chicken cutlets in flour before putting them in the heated pan. But his heart soared. To hear her give words to what he'd already felt that night—the connection and need that sparked between them—was more than he could have hoped for.

"I don't know how the priest found me," she added. "I wasn't even close to the diner."

"It's likely the Sortiari have been tracking you." Michael didn't want to frighten her, but it was important that she realized the scope of the Sortiari's power. "They've probably known about you for as long as I have." Or longer. A fact that burned in his gut like a hot cinder. "Diner?" Keeping the conversation light was key to putting her at ease.

"I'm a waitress." Her voice dropped an octave as though she was embarrassed to utter the words.

"And a thief," Michael remarked. He turned to face her and cocked a brow, his mouth curving into a smile.

Claire returned his smile, hers brilliant as well as mischievous. "I prefer the term 'hustler.'" She caressed the wristband of his watch and Michael's chest swelled with satisfaction to see something of his on her body. "Do you think Ronan's mad at me for stealing his wallet?" she asked with chagrin. "I took it in case I needed some cash. I wouldn't have used his credit cards or anything. That'll get you thrown in prison, fast."

Clever female. Beyond his admiration, Michael could only imagine the hit Ronan's pride had taken at how easily Claire had managed to steal the wallet. "Why would you need cash?"

"For a cab."

She'd planned to leave him. A sense of urgency and loss had brought him from the death-like grip of his daytime sleep. Some inner instinct had prompted him to seek her out. The tether was strong. Unbreakable. Even apart he felt her. Sensed her emotions. Despair sucked the air from his lungs. If Ronan was wrong and she couldn't be turned, her short human life would be nothing more than hours compared to Michael's. He would die without her. And so far he'd managed to show how much she meant to him by making her his prisoner. No wonder she'd attempted to leave.

"You're afraid of me." It wasn't a question. Her fear sharpened her scent, soured the floral sweetness of her blood.

"I'm afraid of the situation." She spun the watchband on her wrist. "And maybe a little of you."

"You have nothing to fear from me, Claire." Michael returned to his task, worried that if he kept his eyes on her he'd throw caution to the wind and take her, sink his fangs into her throat again. "I will never harm you."

"I know that." The words drifted to his ears on a whisper. "And that's what scares me."

Silence descended and Michael resisted the urge to turn and look at her. To reassure himself that she was still there. He found the concept of their tethering difficult to wrap his mind around even though it was commonplace for vampires. If all of this was hard for him to understand, he could only imagine how difficult it was for Claire.

Thirty quiet minutes passed and Michael plated two chicken cutlets and a pile of pasta drowned in marinara sauce for Claire. He set the plate in front of her and poured her a glass of red wine, all the while watching her from the corner of his eye.

She leaned over the plate and inhaled, her eyes drifting shut in bliss. "I don't think I've ever smelled anything so good in my entire life."

A sense of pride overtook Michael, that he could please her, and he slid the glass toward her. "I didn't take into consideration how hungry you'd be." He added a tall glass of water next to the wine. "I'm sorry."

Claire fixed him with a stern eye and pursed her lips. He found her ire adorable. "You should be. I'm still mad at you, Mikhail. I'm just too hungry to worry about it right now."

He didn't respond, simply busied himself with his own plate. His heart was barely beating, he wasn't even sure his body could process food at this point, but he wanted to sit beside her. Partake of a meal with her. Share some sort of domestic moment that might endear him to her even some small amount. At this point, he'd eat a bucket of nails to gain her favor if that's what it took.

A moan worked its way up her throat as she dug into her meal with gusto. "Oh dear god, that's delicious," she said through a mouthful of pasta. "I'd apologize in advance for the unladylike way I'm about to inhale this pasta, but that would take time away from eating."

She ate like a soldier in the field, bite after bite, her eyes never leaving her plate. Michael's own fork hovered near his mouth as he watched her, amusement tugging at his lips. "You weren't joking when you said you were hungry."

Her gaze slid to the side and she paused midbite. "*Three days,* Mikhail."

The rebuke didn't go unnoticed and her point was taken. He'd have to make amends somehow. "Why do you call me Mikhail?" He knew what the answer would be, but it pleased him to hear it.

"Because it's your name." Claire didn't look at him but gave her full attention to the plate in front of her.

"My name is Michael."

"No, it isn't." Her matter-of-fact tone coaxed a smile to his face. He enjoyed her argumentative nature. "I can feel the lie, taste it on my tongue, when I call you Michael, so I won't call you that. No matter how much you want me to."

Extraordinary. If what she said was true, her instincts were more akin to a vampire's than a human's. Just one more oddity that tempted to steer him to believe that Claire was in fact a mysterious Vessel. "I like the way it sounds when you say it. No one has called me Mikhail in a very long time."

"Ronan calls you Mikhail," Claire pointed out yet again.

"True. But it doesn't sound half as sweet when he says it."

Claire paused, turned to him, and a brilliant smile spread across her face. "Did you just pay me a compliment, Mikhail?"

Gods. It was torture to be so close to her and not reach out and touch. Claire was beautiful and intelligent; her wit was quick and sharp. "I did," he replied, forcing his attention to the pasta he pushed around his plate with the fork. "Does it please you?"

He gave her a sidelong glance and his gut clenched as crimson bloomed on her cheeks. "Maybe," she said, popping a bite of chicken into her mouth.

Did it matter whether she was a Vessel or not? Michael knew without a doubt that his want of her would not diminish, either way. Likewise, he was certain that this mindless desire would most assuredly doom them both.

CHAPTER
15

"Do you have any fours?"

"No. Go fish."

If Ronan could see him now, camped out on the living-room floor, the male would suffocate from bouts of laughter. But Michael didn't care. Every moment spent with Claire was precious; each new day, a gift he couldn't wait to unwrap.

Another three days had passed. Three days shut up in his tomb of a house while Ronan acted as his envoy, reaching out to the strongest dhampir covens and bringing them into their fold, allies who were capable of sustaining the change. An army of vampire warriors to fight the Sortiari. So he could protect Claire.

His mate. The Vessel and mother of the vampire race. Or so he hoped.

"It's your turn."

Michael looked up at Claire's expectant face, a sweet smile curving her full pink lips. Gods, how he wanted to touch her again. Taste her. Feel the petal softness of her mouth against his. "Sorry. Do you have any aces?"

Claire screwed her mouth into a petulant pout a[nd] handed over a card. The distance that separated them no[w] was mere inches, though it felt like a cavernous expanse that stretched on for miles. He didn't know how to close the gap. What to do, to say, that would make her fully trust him. His heart had ceased beating two days ago and never had he felt the absence as acutely as he did now. Claire's blood no longer sustained him, and if he didn't feed again soon he would lose himself to the bloodlust and take her vein whether she wanted him to or not.

"Your eyes are silver."

Michael sorted out four aces and set the cards aside. "Are they." He didn't need confirmation. His emotions teetered on the edge. Volatile. Each passing moment spent with Claire was heaven and hell all at once. Or, perhaps more to the point, purgatory.

"Something's upsetting you," she remarked in the matter-of-fact way that he admired. "Or you're thinking about working some of your mind-control mojo on me."

As if that would work. Michael let out a chuff of breath. "I'm . . ." Words escaped him. Clogged his mind like slush trying to pass down a frozen stream. "Frustrated."

"I don't know why." Claire's tone was light, but her eyes were hooded. Dark gold in a midnight sky. "You're winning."

"I'd hoped the distance between us would close, but it seems with each passing day it grows wider." The frustration he'd tried to squash built inside of him, boiling and churning like a river current. "You still don't trust me."

"No." Claire set her cards aside and drew her knees up to her chest, hugging them close. "I don't."

"Why?"

"Because you still want me to call you Michael for starters."

Again with this foolishness? Michael pushed himself up

from the floor and blew out a gust of breath. "It shouldn't matter to you what name I choose to go by."

"It matters if it's a lie."

Infuriating female. "It's only a lie if you choose to see it as one. It doesn't change who I am."

"Exactly!" Claire stood as well, scattering cards in her wake. Her hair cascaded over one shoulder in a golden sheet and her cheeks flushed with anger that sparked his bloodlust further. "So why lie about it? It doesn't change who you are, *Mikhail*."

His secondary fangs punched down in his gums and a growl built in his chest. "You lied. Gave me a false name the first night we met."

"No kidding!" Claire spat. "Because I was hustling you. I lied to you, but I wasn't lying to myself. Which is what you do every single day. You lie to yourself about who you really are and there's no way I can trust you—*at all*—as long as you continue to do that."

How could he explain to her the pain he felt? The guilt? The responsibility that wearing that name weighed him down with? It was a mantle he'd cast off for a reason, and she insisted on draping it over him again and again without thought.

"Ronan says—"

"I don't give a fuck-all what Ronan says!" Michael railed, the words scorching a path up his throat. "He oversteps just as you do." He stalked toward her but Claire stood her ground, her chin raised defiantly. "You don't know the pain you cause me every single time you speak that name." Pain, yes. But pleasure, too. A pleasure so intense it cut through him like a well-honed blade and burned him with a heat that rivaled the Sortiari's cleansing fire. He didn't want her to call him Mikhail because it only made him want her more. Crave her with an intensity that he didn't understand and couldn't stop. Unless they could find proof that Claire was indeed a Vessel, she could never be anything more to him than a blood source. And that fact made him want to shout his ire at the gods and cut a bloody swath that left nothing but destruction in his path. Anything to dull the heartache and inexplicable sense of loss he felt each and every time she spoke his name.

"No, I suppose I don't know the pain I cause you." Claire fixed him with a caustic glare as her jaw took a stubborn set. "Because you haven't told me anything about you! I've been a prisoner in this house for almost a week with no explanation besides that it's for my own protection. I've stayed. Even after you *rejected* me. And it's not even because I didn't have a choice, but because every instinct in my body is screaming at me to trust you. How can I, though, when you keep so much from me? Trust isn't a one-way street, Mikhail. If you want my trust, you have to give me yours. So until you decide to pull your heavy-handed, stubborn head out of your ass, don't talk to me. And since you don't seem to respond to anything other than anger, I'm giving you an ultimatum. You've got exactly twenty-four hours to give me a good reason why I should stay here with you. If you can't, then I'm out of here. For good."

"Rejected you?" Gods, it took a sheer act of will to keep himself from her. "What are you talking about?"

"That night!" Her jaw clenched tight and she let out a strained breath. "You want my trust? I let you bite me, Mikhail! Practically handed myself over to you on a silver platter like some fancy dinner special! And what did you do? You pulled away, acted as though I'd done something wrong. I trusted you, Mikhail. And you didn't trust me back." She laughed without emotion. "Hell, you didn't even want me."

She turned and headed toward the foyer. Michael felt her slipping away like water through a sieve. "Claire, do not leave this house." He stalked after her, his fists balled at his sides. He couldn't explain his irrational fear any more than he could control it. He had no reason to believe that the Sortiari—or anyone besides Ronan, for that matter—knew where she was, and his property was well protected. But his gut clenched at the thought of her stepping out the door and into the night.

"Go to hell, Mikhail," she spat as she jerked open the front door. "You don't get to tell me what to do anymore."

The door slammed behind her with a finality that Michael felt in his very bone marrow. If she left now, he'd have no chance of finding her. Not a drop of her blood remained in his body. Ronan had warned him, but he'd chosen not to heed the male's warnings. In treating Claire as though she were nothing more than a possession—a fancy dinner special—Michael had pushed her away. He was a foolish, stubborn ass and if he didn't open up to her, let her in, he'd lose her and any hope of rebuilding his race. Forever.

He had little experience with tender emotions such as patience, understanding, or even love. Centuries of soullessness and apathy had done him well in battle, and though he'd cared for Ilya, their relationship had little to do with tender emotions and more with raw lust. The pain he'd felt when he lost her reflected the destruction of his race more than her specifically. And over the past century, his rarely beating heart had hardened to stone. Michael Aristov had no need of emotions.

Until now.

Careful not to alert her to his presence, Michael eased open the front door and stepped out into the warm night air. He caught her scent on the breeze, sweeter than any of the flowers that graced his vast garden. Solar lights illuminated a path through the hedges and flower beds to the large fountain in the center of the three-thousand-square-foot

space. Each inch of it was carefully manicured and planted
with night-blooming species. Moonflowers and jasmine,
night queen and Casablanca lilies. Michael would never
see the roses in the light of day or the vibrant orange of
the birds-of-paradise against a blue sky, but he didn't care.
He saw as well at night as anyone else did in full light. And
the flowers were just as fragrant under a cloak of darkness
as they were under the punishing rays of the sun. Perhaps
more so. But none of the beauty his garden possessed could
hold a candle to the woman sitting at the edge of the fountain, caressing the water with her fingertips.

"I can feel you." Claire didn't turn to face him, simply
kept her attention focused on the pool of water that rippled
under her touch. He walked slowly toward her as though
afraid that she'd take flight at the slightest movement. "It's
like you're under my skin. Embedded in a part of my brain
that I never knew existed. You're my sixth sense, Mikhail."
She gave a rueful laugh. "Whatever that means. I know I
don't have any right to be so mad. It's not like I've been an
open book. I don't talk about my life because I'm embarrassed. I'm a hustler. A liar. My mom was a drug addict
and a thief and I don't even know who my father is. I barely
graduated high school and I have nothing to show for my
life. What about you, Mikhail? What do you have to be
ashamed of that you won't share anything about your life
with me? You're frustrated by the distance between us, but
it's you that's causing it. Why make me stay if you're not
interested in anything but my blood? We could fix that issue with a plastic bag and some IV tubing. What am I to
you? You know, besides meals on wheels."

It shouldn't have mattered what he thought or felt about
her. He was little more than a stranger. A self-appointed
babysitter. Her jailer. And yet the way he shut her out, refused to talk about himself at all, cut her to the quick.

Like you've been so forthcoming about your life, Claire?
This entire situation was bat-shit insane. Vampires? Dhampirs? Secret societies and supernatural assassins? *Good
god.* Maybe she'd died on the sidewalk a week ago and all
of this was some strange purgatory. Her punishment for
being a liar and a thief. Insanity, the penance she'd have to
pay before she was allowed to go to heaven. Because there
wasn't a damned thing about what was going on right now
that could be classified as sane.

A ripple chased over her skin with each step Mikhail
took toward her. Her acute awareness of his presence unnerved her. Excited her. Awakened something deep inside
of her that had remained dormant until now.

"What are you to me?" His voice coiled around her in
a velvet caress, as dark and warm as the night sky. "Claire.
You are *everything.*"

Tears sprang to her eyes and she willed the traitorous
flow to cease. No one had ever needed her. Cared enough
about her to worry whether she was alive or dead. She
barely knew him, yet Mikhail's words meant more to her
than he could know. The honesty of those words vibrated
through every molecule that constructed her. How was it
possible to feel such a strong connection to someone she'd
only known for a week?

Cool water slipped through her fingers. It wasn't good
for her to stay here, living like a princess in a castle. Sooner
or later the fantasy would have to come to an end. She'd
return to her crappy run-down apartment with no food in
the fridge and pulling bills out of a hat as she tried to decide whether the power or water bill would get paid that
month. No more servants, no more fancy sports cars. No
more *GQ* handsome man to keep watch over her. Because
just like all good things, this would eventually have to
come to an end.

He sat behind her on the ledge of the fountain, so close

that a tingle vibrated over her skin from the almost contact. So far from the city, the only sound was that of crickets chirping as Mikhail took a deep breath and held it in his lungs. "You smell like the forest in summer," he said on a breath. "Flowers in full bloom. Your blood is the headiest scent of all, though. It goes straight to my head, like an aged brandy. I could become drunk from nothing more than a sip."

Pretty words. And just like the brandy he spoke of, those words heated her body to the boiling point. But that wasn't what she wanted to hear. Not really. "Tell me something real, Mikhail. Something about *you*." She didn't dare look at him, didn't trust herself when he was close enough to touch. "Give me something, any reason at all to trust you."

He swept her hair away from her shoulder and she shivered when his fingertips brushed where her shoulder met her neck. His breath was warm as his lips hovered near her ear. "I was born in Kiev in the year 1622. My father was a warrior and a king; my mother came from an Irish coven and was a princess in her own right. I was raised to fight alongside my father. To beat back the slayers who sought to wipe us from the face of the earth. I fought, fed, fucked my way through centuries of existence. I took a female as my consort and we lived in relative content. I didn't trouble myself with mates or bonds. I cared little for the return of my soul. My only concern was the obliteration of my enemies. In turn, my enemies obliterated everything I knew. And now I am the last of the Ancient Ones and the entirety of my race's collective memories lives within me."

Truth. It rang through her with the clarity of a church bell. A low rumble vibrated in Mikhail's chest, a contented purr that turned Claire's bones to mush. "Who was the woman?" Jealousy flared hot in her veins, but why? She couldn't understand the sharp pang any more than she could the inexplicable connection she felt to the man sitting behind her.

"Ilya. Daughter of Viktor Delov. He was the warlord of our coven."

Claire let her fingers drift through the water, back and forth, back and forth. Mikhail leaned in toward her and his hands curled around her hips, gripping her tight. "A slayer killed Ilya. Pulled the womb from her body while she still lived. And when none remained but me, he taunted me with the knowledge. Burned and tortured me. Flayed the skin from my body and threw it into the flames. And when I thought I'd go mad from the need for revenge and from my own helplessness, the slayer pierced my chest with a silver-tipped stake and left me for dead at the bottom of a tomb."

Truth.

Claire's breath caught in her chest and she eased herself toward him until her back rested against the unyielding wall of Mikhail's muscled chest. His hands snaked around her waist and he pulled her closer. Such a natural place to be, held in his embrace. Claire trembled, fearful of her reaction to him and the ease at which he put her. "How did you survive?"

Mikhail's lips came to rest at her ear and he inhaled deeply, holding his breath in his lungs for a long moment. "I was weak. Starved. Hopeless and helpless. Alone. I lay in that dank, dark, cramped black hole for a century feeding on rodents and whatever small creature found its way inside. One hundred years before I could gather the strength necessary to slide the heavy stone lid aside and set myself free."

Claire's hands snaked around his and she squeezed him tight. "One hundred years?" she breathed. The span of time was incomprehensible to her. "Mikhail . . ." Her heart ached for him. For everything he'd lost. Suffered. Survived.

His lips found the juncture of her jaw and throat. Claire shuddered at the wet heat of his tongue and tilted her head to the side to give him better access. He opened his mouth wide, the scrape of his fangs across her skin causing Claire's abdomen to tighten and her sex to throb. She reached back and threaded her fingers through the hair at his nape as her head fell back to rest on his shoulder.

"Why did you turn me away like that? I thought that you wanted me, but . . ."

"I've never wanted *anything* as much as I want you." His fingers traced a path along the shell of her ear and she shivered. "I wasn't turning you away, Claire. I was protecting you."

"From what?" she murmured.

"From me."

"Mikhail, I think it's time you let me decide what I need protection from." She reached up, dragged the tips of her fingers across his jaw, her nails catching on the short stubble. "Because it sure as hell isn't you."

"I'll never take sustenance from another for the remainder of my existence. Never put my hands upon another female. You belong to me as surely as I am bound to you. And that knowledge will be my undoing as surely as any stake driven into my heart."

Claire shivered at his words. "Why?"

"Ronan thinks you a Vessel." Mikhail's voice was almost a palpable thing, vibrating along her flesh. "A human made for a vampire. Strong enough to survive the transformation and able to bear the weight of the Collective." He let out a soft snort. "A hopeful fairy tale."

She didn't dare turn to face him, just focused on the

sound of his voice and the way his fingers gripped "What's the Collective?"

"It is our memory. Vampires are connected through blood. The single source that created us. Our memories are one and it can be a heavy burden to bear." He paused. "It . . . weighs on the mind."

No kidding. Claire couldn't imagine what it would be like to experience memories that weren't hers, not to mention the obvious violation of privacy. She'd never thought about Mikhail's endgame in all of this until tonight. He wanted to make her a *vampire*? "Why can't I just stay me?" Was she really so bad as a human? "You said my blood is what's important. That and the whole tethering thing." Which she still didn't fully understand. "Do I have to be a vampire, too?"

"Yes." He gripped her tighter with the emphatic word. "I yearn for you. Every single fucking day. I want you unlike anything I've ever wanted in centuries of existence. You ask why I've put distance between us. Why I've shut you out. It's because I can't bear the thought of not having you. *All of you."*

Every word from his mouth rang with truth. An intimacy forged between them that hadn't been there before. If it was possible, it seemed to anchor them even closer together than they already were. He could have her. All of her just like he wanted. She would gladly give herself to him if it meant she could keep feeling this way.

"What if I am a Vessel?" Stranger things had happened.

"It is a myth. There has never been record of one, nor have I found memory of one in the Collective."

"There's a first time for everything, Mikhail."

"I've taken your blood twice. More than I should have, and your strength didn't flag. You learned to resist my power and can't be compelled. Your life essence is an elixir

, you returned my soul to me. I want to believe and
. . What if I'm wrong?"

Claire wrapped her hands around his much larger ones
d squeezed. "But what if you're right?"

He stiffened behind her and she let her head fall back on
his shoulder once again. His fingers curled tight around her
hips. "I can't withhold myself any longer. I won't. Give
yourself to me, Claire. Submit."

A rush of warmth spread between her thighs and Claire
took Mikhail's hand to guide it toward the waistband of her
jeans. It didn't take much to lose herself to him. A touch.
The brand of his mouth on her skin. The heat in his whispered words. Her fingers fumbled with the button and
shook as she worked the zipper of her jeans down. "Touch
me." Sweet lord, her lips could barely form the words, she
was so mindless with want. "God, Mikhail, I need you to
put your hands on me."

She couldn't explain it, couldn't identify the need that
licked at her flesh and burned from the inside out. The connection that fused between them flared bright, arching
and binding them in a way that Claire didn't fully understand. She was helpless to fight it.

His hand plunged past the elastic waistband of her underwear and he cupped her heated and throbbing sex in his
cool palm. Claire gasped at the sensation and he covered
her mouth with his, swallowing the sound. Her nails dug
into the back of his neck, and he groaned, his tongue lapping at hers, thrusting in a wild tangle that left Claire
breathless and mad with desire. His finger found her clit,
lightly circling the tight knot of nerves, and he pulled away,
holding Claire's face steady with his free hand while he
continued to stroke her. "No male save me will ever touch
you, taste you, enjoy the pleasure of your body. You are
mine, Claire. *My mate.*" He flicked his finger over her clit
and she cried out, her gaze locked on his. Silver flashed in

his pupils and the intensity of his expression both frightened and excited her. "Say the words, Claire. Tell me you're mine and no other's."

She could barely form a coherent thought, let alone speak. He slid his fingers through her slick, swollen lips and teased her opening. A desperate whimper escaped her as her hips thrust up to meet him. He pulled away, feathered the pad of his finger over her clit once again. A cruel, sensual torture devised to coax the words he wanted to hear from her lips. Was it a vow freely given if Claire was helpless to deny him anything?

"I'm yours." The words pushed past her lips with little effort. "Whatever you want, Mikhail, you can have it. My body. My blood." He already had her soul. "Anything."

He guided one leg over the lip of the fountain and her jeans soaked through as she sank calf deep into the chilly water. Thighs spread wide, he urged her to lean back fully against him as his mouth forged a fiery path down her throat to her pulse point. *Do it!* The thought screamed through her mind with the scrape of his fangs. She shivered. *Bite me.*

She'd never wanted anything more. Her cries echoed into the night as Mikhail increased the pressure, circling her clit while he sucked the tender flesh of her throat. Claire bucked her hips into his touch, clawed at his arm as his free hand ventured up her shirt and pulled away the cup of her bra. He fondled her breast as two strong fingers plunged deep into her pussy, and just when Claire didn't think she could take another moment of blinding pleasure his fangs broke through her skin, the delicious sting accompanied by a soft pop.

"Oh! God!"

The words tore from her throat in a ragged shout that shook through her body with the magnitude of a 7.0 earthquake. A low growl rumbled in Mikhail's chest as he thrust his fingers deep inside of her, plucked at her aching nipple, and took draw after powerful draw from her throat.

Claire squeezed her eyes shut as the orgasm seized her. Riots of color and twinkling stars burst behind her lids. Every inch of her shook violently, her body clenching and releasing with each delicious pulse, wave after wave of pleasure that stole her breath, her voice, every thought in her head, until there was nothing left to sustain her but the man who held her in his embrace. Mikhail became the center of her universe, and as she came down from the euphoric high she realized that the words offered to him were the truest she'd ever spoken. There would never be another man. Ever.

CHAPTER
16

Mikhail Aristov had been resurrected by the female in his arms. He never felt it more completely than in this moment. No longer would he cower behind another's name, hide in the cover of shadows from his enemies. Claire belonged to *him*. Never had he believed it more than he did in this moment. The Vessel. Mother of the vampire race. And he would be a male worthy of the honor of being her mate.

His heart stuttered in his chest. *Thrump . . . th-thrump . . .* coming slowly to life until it pulsed with a vitality that sent a surge of strength coursing through his veins. He gathered Claire into his arms and cradled her body against his as he turned and took her from the hard concrete surface of the fountain down into the cool, manicured carpeting of grass that blanketed the vast lawn. He stripped her shirt and in his impatience to see her body gripped the center of her bra and ripped it free, rending the fabric as though it were made of crepe paper. Moonlight filtered down through the sky, gleaming on her pale breasts, the rosy pink nipples puckered into stiff peaks from the cool kiss of air.

Mikhail shook with the restraint it took to keep from plunging his cock to the root in her slick, tight heat. His strength was immense, unrestrained as he ripped the denim of her jeans, tearing the seam down the center in his haste to see her bare.

"Hurry, Mikhail."

Claire's breathy plea rippled along his flesh, resonating inside of him until he swore her need was his own. Bare feet dug into the grass as she thrust her hips up, allowing him to remove the tattered remains of her jeans and underwear.

Almighty gods—

Mikhail sucked in a sharp breath as his gaze landed between Claire's thighs. The nest of curls was trimmed short, almost shorn completely, allowing him an unfettered view of her glistening sex. From between the swollen lips her stiff bud protruded proudly, as though begging for more of his touch. The scent of her arousal enveloped him, drove him mad with need, thirst, and lust. He tore his own shirt from his body, popping the buttons in his haste to feel his bare skin against hers. His slacks were next, and Claire leaned up, her hands shaking as she reached for him and helped to free his cock from the restraining fabric.

"I can smell you." Wonder accented the words spoken between pants of breath, and her eyes shone in the dark like gold coins. "That scent . . . spicy and sweet. It's driving me crazy."

Human senses weren't acute enough to pick up on the subtle scents that a vampire's could. She smelled his desire, the mating urge that he could do nothing to hide. His body was sending out pheromones that a human might register on an unconscious level, but Claire recognized them. Responded to them. Further evidence that she was so much more than a mere human.

Though he wanted to savor her, taste every inch of her,

acquaint himself with her body, urgency dictated that Mikhail take her, hard and deep. Sink his fangs into her flesh and join their bodies while he took her blood.

He gripped her hips in his hands and angled her up as he lowered his body to the cool grass. He was starved for her. Mindless with want. A low moan vibrated in his throat as his mouth met her sex and he lapped at her greedily, tasting the sweetness of her arousal on his tongue. Claire rolled her hips, grinding against his mouth. Her back arched up from the grass and she wound her fists in the strands of his hair, holding him fast against her.

"Don't stop." The words left Claire's mouth in a low, drawn-out moan that caused Mikhail's balls to grow tight. It had been so long . . . *centuries* since he'd sunk his cock into a female's flesh. He was about to take her outside on the lawn like an animal, yet he couldn't be bothered to care. Wild as any beast roaming the forest, he was guided by something larger than himself. The need to couple with this female—*possess* her—steered his singular thought. He behaved like an animal because he was one.

Claire writhed beneath him, her cries of passion filling his ears and sending him further past reason. His fangs throbbed in his gums; his throat burned as his thirst remained unsated. Mikhail's breath sawed in and out of his chest as he pulled away, dragging his open mouth along her inner thigh. With a low moan, she spread her legs wide. "Do it. Bite me, Mikhail."

At the moment his fangs punctured her skin Mikhail slid two fingers into the slick heat of her pussy. Claire cried out, her back bowing as she threw her arms out beside her as though to anchor herself to the ground.

Her blood flowed over his tongue, the sweetest ambrosia that intoxicated him in an instant. He'd taken the vein at her throat not a moment ago, yet he was starved for her, each swallow only igniting his thirst rather than quenching it. As Claire continued to writhe beneath him, he feathered his thumb over her stiff and swollen nub. Her inner walls clenched around his fingers as her hips bucked and his name burst from her lips on a ragged scream.

"Mikhail!"

Gods, the power. It surged within him, ignited every nerve in his body. It took an effort of sheer will to disengage and close the wounds. He wanted to drain her. Drink from her until her heart ceased its beating. Feed her from his vein and watch as she was reborn and made his forever. Mikhail needed to tread lightly. He couldn't allow himself this fantasy of turning her until he was certain. Already his tenuous hold on her balanced on a razor's edge. One misstep could send her running and it would be his ruination.

Mikhail's cock throbbed between his legs, so hard that it caused him pain. He ached for release, to spend his seed inside of her, to join their bodies as one. A low moan of pleasure answered him as he came up on his knees and grabbed Claire's hips, jerking her toward him. He fisted his cock, guided the engorged head to her entrance, and sucked in a hiss of breath with the shock of wet heat that welcomed him.

"Yes." Claire thrust her hips up to meet him, a frustrated groan escaping from between her clenched teeth. "I need you inside of me, Mikhail. Now. Please. God, now!"

She raked her hands through the long tangles of her hair, her eyes wild with passion. Every bit the animal he was, she worked her slick flesh over his cock, pleasuring herself with each thrust of her hips. Mikhail's body went taut, the sensation so intense, he didn't want her to stop. When her cries became more desperate, impassioned, he knew she was close to orgasm, and he refused to let her come until he was buried to the hilt inside of her.

"You will wait for me, Claire." Mikhail pulled away despite her protests, bracing one arm beside her while he cupped the back of her neck with the other. He lowered his lips to hers, kissing her with a furious desperation that she answered as she slanted her mouth over his. One fang nicked her bottom lip, and he groaned into her mouth as he savored the taste of her blood on his tongue. He probed at her opening, easing in inch by torturous inch. She was so tight, she squeezed him like a fist and his body trembled with restraint.

Claire's impatience won out over his caution. She impaled herself on him with a desperate thrust of her hips and Mikhail held her steady as she panted through a moment of stillness, a low whimper of pain pushing past her parted lips.

Her eyes drifted shut and he stroked his thumb over the pounding vein of her jugular. "Look at me."

Mikhail refused to move until she met his gaze. Her lids fluttered open and he lost himself in the dark glittering gold. How lovely she'd look with silver flashing in contrast. With a rumbling purr he pulled out to the tip, shuddering as her tight heat sought to hold on to him. A sharp thrust and he buried himself to the root. Claire cried out, but she didn't look away.

"Again."

The command was spoken in a sultry, smoky tone that heated the blood in Mikhail's veins. He pulled out again, reveling in the satin glide, and pounded into her, hard and deep.

"Ohhhhh." That sound. The drawn-out "oh" that ended on a moan spurred him on and Mikhail increased his pace, moving above her in a hard rhythm that left them both breathless and panting. Claire hooked her legs around his thighs, her heels digging into his ass as she tilted her hips upward to give him even deeper access.

Teeth clenched, a satisfied growl vibrated in his chest.

"Mine." Guttural. A feral claim of ownership that Claire's body responded to as her pussy clenched tight around his shaft. He wanted to fuck her senseless, until that hot, tight channel milked him dry.

Her fingers curled around his shoulders, her nails biting into the flesh. "Mine." She repeated the word with such possessiveness that Mikhail thought it would take little else to bring him release.

This woman was his mate. *His.* She *was* strong enough to receive the gift he would give her. And it was time to take them one step closer to the mating that would bind them together forever.

Claire would have died before using words like "unparalleled passion," "soul mate," or "destiny." But with each passing moment she realized that what was happening between them now was bigger than her. Bigger than both of them. And she was helpless to fight it.

God, the way he made her feel! Without a thought to the fact that she was stretched out on his front lawn, fucking him like some sort of crazed exhibitionist didn't even register. She wanted to scream. To cry out with each powerful thrust of his hips. To take him deeper, harder. What he gave her wasn't enough and she didn't know how to get more. Mikhail overwhelmed her, dominated her, held her in orbit as though he were the sun and she was nothing more than a planet caught in his gravity. She'd lost herself to him and still she wished there were more of herself to give.

There would never be *enough*.

Something was absent from this moment. As he ground his hips into hers again and again a hollowness opened up inside of Claire. A cavern so deep and dark that she despaired of ever finding her way out of it. Instinct tugged at the back of her mind, her senses sharpening, smell, sound, sight, seeming to heighten with each passing second. Something was required of her—of them—in order for their union to be complete.

"Drink from me, Mikhail." The words left her as though on autopilot. "Take my blood."

A sound that was purely male rumbled in his chest as he dipped his head to her throat. It's not like he hadn't already buried his fangs in her skin, but Claire wanted it—no, *needed* it—again. Now. In this moment while he fucked her. His mouth sealed over her throat and anticipation coiled low in her abdomen, sending a renewed rush of wetness to her core. The sound of their bodies meeting and parting as he increased his pace and intensity only heightened her pleasure, and Claire rolled her head to the side in order to give him full access to the column of her throat.

His mouth was a brand. Fiery heat that seared in the moment before his fangs punctured her skin. Yet another orgasm seized her, this one more intense and gripping than any of the others. Claire lost herself to the sensation, floated away not on a cloud of bliss but a violent storm. One that tossed her on wild waves and broke her apart on the shore of Mikhail's onslaught. His arms held her tight, his lips sealed over her throat as each pull of his mouth matched the thrust of his cock.

Harder. Faster. Deeper. More. The words ran a loop in Claire's mind, but they refused to form on her tongue. Just when her pleasure began to ebb, another wave crested, this one just as powerful as the first. She threw her head back and screamed, a long, loud exclamation of pleasure that left her throat raw and aching. Her hands came around Mikhail's back and she held his head against her, desperate for him to drink from her, to take every last drop of blood she had to offer. Self-preservation didn't exist as she began to float away, her limbs heavy and her mind soft and cottony. He could drain her, drink her to the point of death, and yet it was what she wanted. Somehow, she knew that this was supposed to happen.

Mikhail pulled away from her neck with a shout that echoed off the high Hollywood Hills. His body went rigid and Claire writhed beneath him as his cock jerked inside of her and filled her with a decadent heat that left her weak, shaking, breathless. And wanting *more*.

A trickle of fear entered her bloodstream as Mikhail's thrusts became shallow and gentle. She'd never been possessed with such mindless lust for a man before. Had never gone to that place where nothing—not life, death, or anything else—mattered but *him*.

Something had happened in that moment between his teeth sinking into her throat and the moment he came inside of her. As though some cosmic force had fused them together, welded their halves into an inseparable whole. Was this the tether? Had her soul finally recognized his?

"What is it, Claire?" Mikhail's voice floated to her ears with feather softness, a slow caress that caused chills to dance over her flesh. "Why are you frightened?"

"How do you know?" He stroked her hair with gentle care, braced up on one arm as he studied her. Still seated deep inside of her, Mikhail gave a shallow roll of his hips, and she let out a slow sigh, the gentle motion rekindling her desire.

"Your scent. The tang of your fear sours the sweetness of your pleasure."

"The way you talk"—she let out a nervous laugh—"it makes my stomach do backflips." His brow furrowed as though he couldn't decide whether her statement was meant as a compliment or not. "I like it, Mikhail." His body relaxed and she sensed that she'd reassured him.

"That doesn't explain why you're afraid." He kissed a lazy path down her throat and she sighed as the heat of his tongue laved at the puncture wounds he'd made with his fangs. The roll of his hips increased in pace and pressure and Claire opened up to him, her body responding and ready for more.

"I'm afraid of what I feel." Her back arched off the cool grass as she came up to meet him in a slow, sensual kiss. "I've never experienced anything like what just happened between us." Another kiss, this one deeper as her tongue slid against his. "It's scary."

"This is just the beginning." Mikhail rolled onto his back, his dark features enveloped by the shadows. His blue-green eyes flashed with silver as he settled Claire on his lap and took her hips in his strong hands. In the shadows, his features sharpened, making him look like the predator he was. His hawkish gaze pinned her and for a moment everything but him melted into darkness. "Each time we couple, the mating bond will intensify. Soon I will nourish you, give you my blood, and your transformation will be complete. You'll be able to sense my emotions. You'll feel my presence even from the distance of many miles. You are a Vessel, Claire. I believe it now."

A ripple of trepidation raced through her and Claire shoved her worry to the back of her mind. Now that she knew he was so in tune to what she felt, she'd have to be careful to guard her heart—as well as her mind. He was so confident. So sure that the course they found themselves on was the right one. Claire wished she could share in that optimism. But she knew better.

Mikhail levered himself up and wrapped his arms around her, pulling her body down hard on top of him. Claire gasped at the shock of sensation, a renewed rush of wetness spreading between her thighs. She might have been unsure, but of one thing she was certain: Her body craved his like a drug and once would never be enough.

She rode him with abandon, letting her head fall back on her shoulders. A strong fist wound in her hair and tugged to expose her throat to him. Her limbs were heavy, her mind slow to react. Claire was drunk on Mikhail, intoxicated by his body, his heady words, the thick length of his erection that stretched and filled her completely.

As though of their own volition, her arms snaked around him, her nails biting into his shoulders. He let out a slow hiss, his hips bucking as he fucked her with abandon. Her breasts bounced against him, his chest teasing her nipples into stiff, aching points.

"I'm going to fuck you until the sun rises." His breath was hot in her ear, his voice a low rumble that ignited a fire inside of her. "Bury my face between your thighs and lap idly at your pussy until I've had my fill."

Holy shit. No one had ever said such dirty, wanton things to her. Flushed with heat, need, a hunger that she didn't understand, Claire ground her hips against his, drawing him in as deep as she could.

"I'm going to take your vein." His voice rasped in her ear. "Over and again. Glut myself on the sweet nectar of your blood. Your voice will be ragged from your screams and you will come for me, Claire. For me alone. No other male. For eternity."

As though he sensed the orgasm about to seize her, Mikhail buried his face in her throat and bit down. A cold rush, like someone had shot her up with some grade-A shit, zinged through her veins and Claire sobbed her pleasure, each cresting wave more powerful than the last. He let go of her and braced his arms behind him, using the ground as leverage as he pounded into her, almost violently, until a shout tore from his throat and she was flooded with warmth as he came deep inside of her.

She was light-headed and dizzy, the world careening around her in a drunken haze that left her feeling a little too giddy. Mikhail's tongue passed over her throat and he nuzzled into her. "You are mine, Claire," he said through ragged pants of breath. "From this moment until the gods decide otherwise."

She swallowed down the fear that welled up fresh inside of her. *Holy crap, Claire. What have you gotten yourself into?*

Mikhail had tucked her into bed just before sunrise. He slept peacefully beside her, the slumber of the undead, she supposed. Claire had learned something about Mikhail Aristov over the course of the night: He kept his promises.

He'd made love to her for *hours*. He'd spent that idle time between her legs, lazy passes of his tongue that sent her into a state of ecstasy so intense that she'd sworn she was having an out-of-body experience. He'd made love to her slowly and gently. Fucked her hard and with a rough edge that excited her and made her beg him for more. He'd taken the vein at her throat, her thigh, and her wrist, greedily devoured her until Claire once again reached that point where she was more than willing to offer up her life to him. Only to have him pull away and lave her wounds once the high of their orgasms ebbed.

Mikhail had made many, *many* promises to her tonight. One of them being that he'd turn her before the week was out.

A vampire by Friday. She snorted. *Sounds like the name of a hot new band.*

She'd barely dipped a toe past the surface of his world and now he wanted her to jump right into the deep end, headfirst. To Mikhail, there was no longer a question. No more doubts. He was convinced she would survive the transition. She belonged to him, and in order for her to truly be his she had to become a vampire. He didn't even ask her opinion on the matter, just made the proclamation.

Ronan had called Mikhail a king. And not for the first time, Claire recognized that regal high-handedness in him. There was only one option: Obey.

She didn't know if she was ready for this life.

For days she'd been shut up in this house, closed off to the world after dawn, living in a sunless state and only allowed to see the world through night's cloak. She missed her job, interacting with other people. Hell, she even missed her sore feet and achy back at the end of the day. She missed Vanessa. Was she okay? Eating? How was school going? Was her mother even *trying* to stay sober?

Panic surged in Claire's chest. She threw the covers from her body and launched herself from the bed. Her breath raced in her chest and her heart beat so frantically, she thought it might burst through her rib cage at any second. "Jesus Christ." Barely a whisper and yet as good as a shout when keeping company with creatures like Mikhail. He stirred in the bed, the blankets falling away to reveal the muscled perfection of his chest. Her panic ebbed by small degrees and Claire tiptoed to his side of the bed and stood over him, her curiosity piqued when her gaze landed on a star-shaped scar that puckered the skin above his heart. She hadn't noticed it earlier, so blinded by her passion.

She reached out and traced the rough edge of skin. His brow furrowed in sleep and his lip curled into a feral snarl. The man sleeping before her was as much a wild animal as a tiger roaming the jungle. Just because he looked domesticated didn't mean he was tame. No, he was a killer, ruthless and fierce. He took what he wanted without apology. And he'd made it quite plainly known that he wanted her. For eternity.

Eternity!

Another bout of hyperventilation overcame her and

Claire leaned over, putting her head between her knees. It was impossible to think clearly when he was near. His presence commanded her attention, drew her to him. When he was in the room—*hell, just in the house*—Claire felt his presence so acutely that he might as well have been under her skin. How could she possibly make a logical decision when she already felt fused to the man lying still as death beneath her touch?

I have to get out of here.

It was all too much. She didn't trust her mind, her feelings. She didn't trust herself to make a rational decision when he put his hands on her. His mouth . . . Claire shivered at the memory of his touch and found that she was leaning toward him, reaching out as though helplessly drawn to do so. She'd give him anything he asked without thinking twice about it. So much for the street-smart, savvy hustler. All it took to bring her down was one gorgeous, commanding vampire.

Go figure.

Claire retrieved one of Mikhail's discarded shirts from the floor. It hung almost to her knees and the sleeves fell far past her hands. She was never more aware of his size than she was right now, swimming in the garment like a toddler dressed up in an adult's shirt. He'd ripped her bra in half. Her jeans, too. Obliterated in his haste to take her. A rush of warmth spread between her thighs at the memory. *Jesus, Claire. Get it together!* The mere thought of Mikhail turned her to mush. Which was why she needed to get the hell out of there so she could think straight.

She buttoned up the shirt and found a belt in the closet that she wound around her waist to make the too-long shirt look more like a dress. This was L.A., no one would bat a lash at her attempt at a fashion statement. Gray light infused the darkened room, the first signs of dawn on the horizon. She needed to leave while it was still dark enough to slip under the radar of the guards posted outside and before the heavy blinds shut down over the windows. If she didn't get out of there before sunrise, he'd never let her leave.

And honestly, she probably wouldn't want to.

The Patek watch that had started it all sat on a mahogany dresser and Claire snatched it up and put it on her wrist. She had no idea if she was coming back, and if she wasn't she couldn't leave without some part of him to keep close to her heart. With her shoes in hand, she padded from the room, careful to ease the door open with barely a sound, her footsteps were heavy, reluctant. Her own body betrayed her, urging her to stay put.

I'm so sorry, Mikhail. Guilt burned at the back of her throat. Sat heavy on her heart like a stone. Maybe she'd come to terms with forever. Maybe leaving her humanity behind to be with him would become something she could accept once she removed herself from the situation long enough to give it the serious thought it deserved. But until she put some distance between them she'd never know for sure if the decisions she made—her feelings—were her own or something fabricated by the inexplicable connection between them.

She tiptoed down the two flights of stairs and through the house like the thief she was. Miles from the city, she'd have to walk until she could hitch a ride. Thanks to the fact that she'd left her purse on the sidewalk when Mikhail had saved her from the priest, catching a cab was out of the question. Out the front door and into the driveway, Claire averted her gaze from the gardens and vast lawn. The lush carpet of grass that Mikhail had laid her down in as he'd made love to her again and again in the fragrant night air.

In the eastern sky, the first orange hints of dawn made their appearance. Mikhail would be a prisoner in his own home, and it caused a sick pang of regret to flare in her stomach. He'd be alone. Angry. Hurt. God, she was a horrible person. A coward. She probably wasn't deserving of the affection he wanted to bestow on her.

She definitely wasn't deserving of his forgiveness.

CHAPTER
17

Of all the dhampirs Ronan knew, Eric Jenner was the only male more ruthless than himself. Jenner was a true warrior down to the marrow of his bones, fierce and stalwart. A big son of a bitch, too. Even for a dhampir. Once Mikhail turned Jenner, he'd be a force to be reckoned with. A vampire worthy of the position Ronan was about to give him. And he'd be up to his neck in bullshit before he had a chance to adjust to his new existence.

"Siobhan won't be pleased." Jenner's voice boomed without any effort to project, deep and gruff. "She'll have your balls when she finds out."

She's already got them. Ronan pushed the details of his arrangement with Siobhan to the back of his mind and focused his attention on the task at hand. "You let me worry about her."

Ronan had known Jenner for almost as long as he'd known Mikhail. It was blind chance that Ronan had stumbled upon the orphaned vampire mere days after he'd escaped from the hell the slayer had left him to die in. Knowing that the future of the race depended on Mikhail's survival, Ronan hadn't wasted a second in getting him out of Europe. America had seemed like a world away. Hell, it had been more than two hundred years ago. Jenner had been living in the country for a few months and Ronan had befriended him. So much history. Ronan had thought to take Mikhail far from the Sortiari's reach. And now that anonymity Ronan had hoped to give his friend was long gone.

"There might be others in the coven who would want to be turned," Jenner said, thoughtful. "Though Siobhan's sowed the seeds of her hatred well. She could convince a snake it could fly if it suited her mood."

True. Hadn't she convinced Ronan to trade his body for the codex? "I'm not interested in making an enemy out of her, and stealing her people from under her nose isn't the way to keep her placated."

"Hers isn't the only coven in the city. Who else have you reached out to?"

As Ronan's sole employee, Jenner could be counted on in any situation. He was one of very few Ronan trusted, and beyond capable. But the male was no diplomat. He broke bones first and asked questions later. "I've contacted Samuel and Juliana. Their covens are second largest to Siobhan's." Of the thirteen dhampir covens scattered throughout the city, none were as powerful as Siobhan's. Petty squabbles broke out occasionally, but no one seemed interested in testing the female's mettle. "Three more have contacted me in the past week. As you can guess, they're all jumping at the chance to transition."

Jenner snorted. "And tip the scales of power, no doubt."

That's what Mikhail and Ronan were afraid of. "They'll have to be vetted. Their allegiances made." A price would have to be paid for Mikhail's blood and it wasn't simply their souls. "We can't have vampires running amok all over the city. Boundaries will have to be drawn. Some will probably be asked to move further from the city." It would be possible once their numbers increased and they could share in their combined power. "Gods, we're building a society from the ground up. I have no fucking idea where to start."

Jenner leaned forward in his chair, his dark eyes fixed on Ronan. "Start with me. And go from there."

"That's the plan," Ronan said on an exhausted sigh. "All I want to know from you, Jenner, is are you sure you're ready?"

"Fuck yeah, I'm ready." The male rolled his massive shoulders and cracked his neck from side to side. "I've been ready for decades."

So many of them had. Mikhail had been the bane of their existence for so long. The last of the Ancient Ones and not powerful enough to raise his people to glory. But since he'd taken Claire's blood things were moving quickly. Almost too quickly. Details had to be worked out, alliances broken and made. An army amassed in the span of days when it should take weeks—months—to see it done. And the politics of it all made Ronan's head spin. In his line of work, when there was a problem he took care of it. You've got a sex tape that needs squashing? No problem. Girlfriend's pregnant by your co-star? No one will ever find out. Your coke dealer is threatening to out you in *Star* magazine? Not with the right incentive not to. But this . . . Ronan raked his fingers through his hair. If they didn't get Mikhail's future kingdom in order, fast, they'd be an easy mark for the Sortiari. And that couldn't happen.

The bureaucracy of building a kingdom and protecting its king did little for Ronan's patience, and likewise, he was expected to have it all worked out before Mikhail would even consider turning him. There was nothing more important to Mikhail than securing their safety, but that security balanced on a razor's edge. It wouldn't take much to tip the balance and ruin everything they sought to build.

Siobhan was just the female to do the tipping.

"If a tentative peace can't be reached between Siobhan and Mikhail, there's no point in any of this, you know."

Aside from being a big, scary motherfucker, Jenner was also quite brilliant. He might have talked like an extra from *Sons of Anarchy,* but his mind was quicker than those of most of the Nobel Prize winners put together. Another reason Ronan had picked him to be the second dhampir for Mikhail to turn.

"Do you think she'll declare war?" The question was rhetorical. Of course she would. The female craved blood and carnage the way others craved chocolate.

"She'll make her demands—and expect them to be met without question," Jenner remarked. "And when Mikhail tells her to fuck off, she'll draw first blood. Of that I have no doubt."

Nor did Ronan. "What do you think she'll demand? I mean, besides an oath from Mikhail not to turn a single member of her coven."

"Maybe a throne of her very own?" Jenner gave a rueful laugh. "The possibilities are endless."

Exhaustion weighed heavily on Ronan as he slumped back in the plush leather armchair in his office. The skyscraper looked out over downtown Los Angeles, but he couldn't be bothered to appreciate the view or anything else right now. He doubted that continuing to fuck her senseless would do much to distract Siobhan from her ambitions. Rather, he suspected that she'd use her arrangement with him as a tool against Mikhail to plant a seed of doubt in the male's mind as to Ronan's loyalty. And trying to convince her that swearing allegiance to Mikhail was in her best interest was proving to be a daunting task, to say the least.

"An accord must be reached, no matter how tenuous." Even veiled peace was better than outright aggression. At any rate, it would buy Ronan some much-needed time. "It's achieving it that's the problem."

"Agreed." Jenner's voice scraped over Ronan's ears like sandpaper. "What we need is a distraction."

"How do you distract a female with a one-track mind?" She'd been relentless over the past week, demanding Ronan's presence in her bed nightly. Which made it nearly impossible to focus his attention on reaching out to Mikhail's allies as his king had requested.

"Give her what she wants." Jenner hiked a heavily muscled shoulder.

Ronan let out a derisive snort. The female only wanted two things: to be fucked and to fight. A kernel of an idea took root in his mind and he could have kicked himself for not thinking of it sooner. "Jenner, you clever bastard. Are you suggesting that I incite an uprising or two?"

A feral grin spread across the male's mouth. "Why not?"

It could work. Dissention between the covens was a common enough occurrence. She'd be so busy putting out smaller fires that she'd not only put her suspicions about Mikhail's mate and the resurrection of his power on the backburner, but she might give Ronan a little space as well. "Of course, it could all backfire and then we'll be seriously fucked."

Jenner laughed. A truly menacing sound without humor. "I thought you could fix anything, Ronan."

Up until a couple of weeks ago, so did he. "I'll need help." He knew more than a few dhampirs who enjoyed stirring shit up, but he had to keep his eye on the long game. A week's worth of distraction wouldn't be enough to derail Siobhan's ambition. He'd need a solid month, maybe more, before he could be assured of Mikhail's—and Claire's—protection. And he wasn't even taking into account that it would be days after his transition before he would be back to 100 percent. "I have to know I can count on you as well. Because if Siobhan figures out what we're up to, she'll have both of our asses."

Jenner's eyes narrowed to dark slits, making him appear even more deadly, his pupils flashing with quicksilver. "I might be a member of her coven, but she doesn't *own* me. I plan on declaring my independence from her tonight. She'll be pissed, but what the fuck do I care? Once I'm turned, I'd like to see her try to wreak havoc on me. When she sees the evidence of Mikhail's ascension to power, she'll be begging for a male to bite her and drink her dry."

By far the truest words spoken today. She talked a good game, but what Siobhan truly craved was power. She'd throw her convictions to the side in an instant if being turned helped to elevate her status. Ronan's gut clenched at the realization. After Mikhail turned him, he'd be stronger. More powerful than he could imagine. Finally becoming the creature he was born to be. That strength and power would be more seductive to Siobhan than ever and breaking his agreement with her would be nigh impossible. He'd pledged his body to her like a common whore. For Mikhail. His king. And his friend.

Not even a vampire king could break the troth once it was given. It had been made with blood and only though blood could it be broken. Ronan was officially fucked for all eternity.

Fan-fucking-tastic.

"There's something you're not telling me." Jenner did nothing to hide the accusation in his tone. "And until you tell me all there is to know, I'm not helping you do shit."

Ronan pinched the bridge of his nose and leaned back in his chair. Trust was essential if any of this was going to work, and there was no use in demanding Jenner's trust if Ronan wasn't willing to return it. There was too much history between them for him to doubt his friend's loyalty. "Claire is gone."

Jenner let out a bark of disbelieving laughter. "Gone. How is that even possible? If she's tethered him and she's had his blood—"

"Mikhail's mate is human. Sort of makes tracking her down problematic."

Jenner leaned back in his chair and howled. "Jesus fucking Christ, Ronan. Mikhail's got bigger problems than Siobhan if that's the case. How do either of you possibly hope to resurrect the race if his mate is not only a human but not even present for him to feed from?"

Ronan had tried to remain optimistic, but when Jenner laid it all out like that, he had to admit, their situation was pretty gods-damned bleak. "She'll come back. And when she does, Mikhail will turn her."

Jenner arched a brow. "Oh, so she's a magic human, then."

Ronan chose to ignore the male's sarcasm. "You let me worry about Mikhail's problems while you focus on *mine*. I want Siobhan distracted. Can you do that or not?"

Jenner pulled his cell phone out of his pocket, his brow furrowed as he quickly scanned whatever message was on the screen. "I don't think you'll have to worry about keeping her busy." His eyes met Ronan's, his expression grave. "Slayers attacked two covens today. In broad daylight. Hers and Saeed's in the Valley. They don't care about discretion, and more attacks will come."

"Fuck!" The expletive shot from Ronan's mouth as he pushed himself from his chair. Too many variables stood in their way, the most important being Claire's whereabouts. And now he had random attacks to worry about? "Mikhail will need to be notified. We'll help however we can, but gods, we're totally unprepared." It was time to bump up the timetable. Mikhail wanted to wait for his mate to come back to him before Ronan was turned, but they couldn't wait. "Let's get moving before there isn't a gods-damned race to save."

Jenner levered himself out of the chair and followed Ronan out the door. "I'll give it to you, Ronan. You're earning your reward from Mikhail."

Wasn't that the fucking truth?

CHAPTER
18

Claire collapsed over the toilet and emptied her guts into the bowl, her stomach heaving again and again until there was nothing left but aching dry heaves that burned her throat and left her raw from the inside out. She felt like death. Worse than death. Like death run over seventeen times by a commuter bus, flipped over, reheated, and then run over again. And she was *tired*. So damned tired she could barely put one foot in front of the other, let alone serve plate after plate of food all day.

She gripped the little plastic stick in her fist so tightly she'd cut off the circulation to her fingers. This wasn't the stomach flu. And since she hadn't been able to stomach food for over a week, it wasn't a tainted batch of ramen noodles, either. No, her ailment was far, *far* more complicated than simple food poisoning. She stared at the red plus sign staring back at her from the little window. It was the fifth stick she'd peed on in the past three days. This wasn't a false positive, and it wasn't karma biting her in the ass for telling Lance that she had mono, either.

Pregnant!

The word echoed in her mind as though shouted down
a long corridor, ending with a silent finality that left her
shaking and on the verge of tears. Since leaving Mikhail's
house twelve days ago, she'd focused all of her energy on
blocking whatever connection it was they shared. Anything to keep him from finding her. Bringing her back to
him. Because once that happened Claire was certain that
she'd never leave his side again.

She belonged to him as surely as he belonged to her.

Even apart, her body vibrated with awareness of him, as
though some part of him was embedded within her. The
sense of rightness that resonated through her scared Claire
more than anything else in her entire messed-up life. Every
minute of every day her thoughts wandered to her vampire.
The man who was supposed to be hers for all eternity. The
man who'd been determined to make sure that she was
given that eternity.

Nothing had ever spooked Claire, the unflappable hustler, the way Mikhail had that night after they'd made love.
He'd been so full of joy, so positive that she was this Vessel, he'd been prepared to sink his teeth into her throat
again and again, draining her of her lifeblood so that he
could replenish her with his own and thus turn her into a
vampire.

Strong. Powerful. Immortal.

A shudder danced over her skin as she brought her fingers to her throat and felt the slow throb of her pulse. The
ecstasy she'd felt the moment he sank his fangs into her
flesh was unparalleled. The memory of each deep thrust
inside of her, coupled with the strong pull of his mouth,
made her inner thighs slick with desire. Claire's stomach
cramped violently and she lurched over the toilet bowl
once again. God, how ridiculous was it that she was literally losing her lunch in the midst of a sexual fantasy?

Mikhail might have been convinced that she was this

Vessel. In the heat of the moment she had been, too. But now Claire wasn't so sure. Wouldn't a human with the capability to survive being turned into a vampire be able to withstand a little morning sickness? Not to mention she'd had the speed and vitality of a tortoise lately. Ever since meeting Mikhail she'd felt a strange draw, and it had only gotten worse over the past several days. If anything, she was below average on the superpower scale.

A wave of nausea hit her and Claire suffered through another bout of dry heaves. She was tempted to force-feed herself a plate of pancakes and guzzle a gallon of water just so her stomach would have something to throw up next time. Mikhail's vampire sperm must have possessed some seriously supernatural swimmers. Who in the hell got morning sickness a couple of weeks after getting pregnant?

"Claire, you okay?" Lance's voice accompanied the soft knock on the bathroom door, and she slowly pushed herself up from the floor.

"I'm fine. I'll be out in a second." She turned on the faucet and splashed cold water on her face after washing her hands. She looked like hell. There wasn't enough concealer on the planet to hide the dark circles under her eyes, and her skin was so pale it was practically transparent. Just the sort of image people want to see as they're being served a meal. Good lord. She looked like a patient from some viral apocalypse flick.

When she emerged from the bathroom, Lance was waiting by the door, his arms folded across his chest. "I thought you said you were over the mono."

"Me too." Of course her current malady had mono trumped by about a hundred million. "I'm probably just not back to one hundred percent is all."

"Go home. You can't be here if you're still sick, Claire, and you've been dragging around for the past week like you're on your last leg. I'm trying to bring customers in, not send them screaming for the door."

She let out a tired groan and leaned against the wall for support. "I know. You're right. But I promise I'm not contagious." Unless vampire sperm could magically impregnate not just her but anyone who got too close to her. "I can't afford to miss any more shifts and I'd never come to work if I was sick; you know that. It's just exhaustion, that's all." Rent was due next week and she was already going to be short thanks to her little vacation with Mikhail. "I need to be here."

"You so much as sneeze and you're out the door," Lance warned.

"No sneezes, no coughing, not even a sniffle. I swear." She couldn't guarantee that she wouldn't have to sprint to the bathroom again, though. Especially if someone came in and ordered the corned-beef hash. *Blech.*

"All right." Lance gave her a sympathetic pat on the shoulder. "But I'm switching your morning shift tomorrow with Kerri's afternoon one so you can sleep in. You look like you could use a little rest."

God bless him. "Thanks." Claire was certain she'd collapse into bed as soon as she got home and sleep until tomorrow afternoon. She'd never known such bone-deep exhaustion.

Lance winked as he headed back toward the kitchen. "Get back to work."

"Yes, sir." Claire winked back and took off to check on her tables.

The remainder of her shift passed quickly thanks to a steady stream of customers and the twenty packets of saltines that no longer made her feel like she was going to upchuck her stomach lining. She kept one eye on the door at all times, her nerves getting the better of her every time a man walked in wearing a dark-colored shirt. She'd fled the safety of Mikhail's fortress of a house, but she wasn't stupid. Claire knew that it wouldn't take long for the Sortiari to realize that she was no longer under the vampire's protection. And when they did they'd come for her. And they wouldn't play nice.

When she'd grilled Mikhail for information on the secret society that had it out for him and apparently everyone he'd ever met, she'd been less concerned with the foot soldiers and more interested with who was pulling the strings. The puppets had been inconsequential. As a hustler, Claire never bothered with lackeys. If she couldn't do business with the number one guy—be it to fence something she'd lifted or to play the shill—she didn't waste her time. She'd needed to understand what these Sortiari were before she could get a bead on their guard dogs. In hindsight, she should have learned everything she could about the slayers. Including their weaknesses. Because if she had another late-night run-in with the freakishly strong black-eyed monsters she doubted she'd come out of it on top.

As Claire busied herself with filling salt and pepper shakers and replenishing ketchup bottles for the next day, her thoughts drifted inevitably to Mikhail. Was he upset? Distraught that she'd left? Angry? Did he miss her with the same bone-deep ache that she felt? Most important, would he find her or had Claire managed to successfully block their connection and mask her whereabouts from him? He'd glutted himself on her blood the last night they'd been together. She could still hear the steady beat of his heart in her ears, feel the gentle pulse against her cheek. He could try to track her now, hunt her down like he had before. And a part of her yearned for it. Hoped against all hope that he'd come and find her once again.

Surely he'd show up eventually. Then again, she'd run out on him when she knew he couldn't go after her. That sort of morning-after dash tended to send a pretty straightforward message. He could have decided to wash his hands of her. Not to mention that she was doing everything in her power to disrupt the tether that connected his soul to hers. So yeah. Could she really be surprised that he hadn't shown up ready to whisk her off her feet?

Deep down, she hoped he hadn't written her off. She just needed some space. Time away to think. But if she went back to him would he insist on turning her? What would he think about the prospect of becoming a father? Maybe vampire baby daddies didn't like to be strapped down by kids, either. In which case, maybe all of this worrying was moot?

Claire wrapped her arms around her torso tightly, as though trying to hold the halves of her body together. She missed him so much that she hurt. Would it be so awful to let him turn her? To go back to him and beg him to forgive her for leaving?

Would he even want her back or had she burned the one bridge she couldn't bear to set fire to?

Not since the slayer had left him to die had Mikhail felt such despair. The Collective assaulted his mind, memories that bled into his reality until he couldn't separate the two. His throat burned with thirst and his heartbeat had begun to slow until he could no longer bear the sound of its strangled rhythm within his chest. He wanted to claw at his flesh, reach through muscle and bone, and rip the damned thing out once and for all.

The pain of losing her was unbearable.

"Five dead. Another twelve wounded."

Ronan's words faded to the back of Mikhail's mind, incomprehensible and inseparable from the memory of a war long since fought and lost. Where was she? Why had she left? He couldn't feel her presence, not even a hint of where she might be. As when she'd resisted his attempt to compel her, she was somehow blocking the bond created by their tether. It was obvious she didn't want him to find her, and so for days he hadn't even tried.

Anger at the way she'd left him welled fresh and hot in his chest. He had neither the time nor the patience for her games. If she wanted to go, fine. Wanted to shun the protection he'd offered, so be it. Mikhail had lived for centuries, survived a slayer's killing blow and decades at the bottom of a tomb. He would not let her succeed where the others had failed. She would *not* be the end of him.

"Mikhail, did you hear me?"

He raked his hands through his hair as an enraged snarl worked its way up his throat. His fangs punched down from his gums as rage and despair settled on him like a heavy mantle he was helpless to cast off. *Claire . . . Claire, Claire, Claire . . .* Her name in his mind attacked his sense of sanity. The memory of her, willing in his arms, was the most unspeakable torture. She'd run away, hidden herself from him, and he had no doubt that somewhere the Sortiari lay in wait, their slayers poised to take her life, and he would be helpless to stop it.

"Mikhail!" Ronan's shout rang in his ears. "Gods damn it, listen to me. We're under siege and unless you do something about it we're all going to die!"

Mikhail gave a violent shake of his head in a hopeless effort to dislodge his lingering thoughts of Claire. His emotional compass swung from north to south. At once he was enraged, vowing never to give her a second thought, and the next moment mourning her loss as though she'd died. He had to face the reality that she was gone. Hidden from him. Her presence no longer burned in his soul; it was nothing more than a pinpoint of light in vast darkness. And there wasn't anything he could do about it. But standing before him, Ronan and a majority of the dhampir race beseeched him for leadership. He needed to focus on the crisis he could manage instead of the one that was out of his control.

"I'm sorry that Claire is gone." Mikhail's back was turned to his friend, but the words were like a slap to his face. "We found her once; we'll find her again. Perhaps she's safer on her own. If she's hidden herself from you, then she's hidden from them as well. Until we can contain the slayers' attacks to a manageable level, she's in less danger the farther away from you she is." Ronan took a deep breath and threw his shoulders back. "But right now, Mikhail, you have to keep your word to me. Before you're too gods-damned weak to do the deed. Our people need protection. We need to stand against the guardians of Fate and let them know that we will not be put down like feral dogs. Show your people that you're deserving of their allegiance."

It was a speech worthy of any general heading onto the battlefield. One Mikhail had given himself many times over the course of his long life. But without Claire by his side, all of it felt futile. A cause lost before it could ever be saved. She'd given him a gift of strength, however. And to let it go to waste would be blasphemy.

"Tell me more about this Jenner." Mikhail kept his gaze locked on the garden, shrouded by night but no less vibrant to his gaze. Moonlight glistened in the fountain, the sound of the rushing water as clear to Mikhail's ears as if he were standing beside the boiling geyser. He'd spent every night near the fountain since Claire had left. Reliving their moments together as his body yearned for more. One night had bound him to her. Eight glorious hours that her body had belonged to him and him alone. He *would* go after her. And when he found her he would do everything in his power to ensure that she never had reason to leave him again.

"He's strong. Fierce. A certifiable badass. He'll endure the change; I'm sure of it."

Mikhail wished he shared Ronan's sunny outlook. "He was one of Siobhan's?"

"He was, but not anymore. He knows which horse to put his money on."

Mikhael turned to face Ronan, unable to hide the disdainful sneer that curled his lip. "So you're saying Jenner has hedged his bets and assumes that swearing fealty to me will not only garner him what he wants, but keep him alive?" He didn't want or need any male to come to him for the sole purpose of meeting his own selfish agenda. Siobhan was still dhampir and unable to turn anyone. Her power lay in her hatred. Prejudice of any kind was unwelcome in Mikhail's inner circle. He would never think to turn any dhampir against his will, and yet if Siobhan had it her way Mikhail would be painted as a monster, ravaging his people for the single-minded purpose of banishing their souls.

"What I'm saying, you stubborn pain in the ass, is that Jenner wants what's best for the race. He wants to put the Sortiari in their place once and for all. And he wants to serve his king."

"King." Mikhail let out a derisive snort. "I've been laid low by a female. I'm losing my mind. It won't be long before you're all blindly following a madman. Is that what you want?"

"I want what you promised me," Ronan said. "I want you to keep your word. As for your mind, I'm not concerned. Any male without his mate would suffer as you do. Claire doesn't understand. She doesn't know this life the way we know it. Give her time. She'll come around. In fact, I'll wager she comes back to you before we even have the chance to find her."

Hopeful, optimistic bastard. "And if she doesn't?"

Ronan's gaze met Mikhail's and a silent moment passed between them. "She's the Vessel," he simply said.

As though Claire's free will had been taken away simply because she was special. But that wasn't the case at all. She'd given herself to him freely and not because she was a Vessel. Mikhail refused to believe that their connection was forged as a result of the tethering and nothing else. Something had sparked between them that went beyond simple biology. *Then why did she leave you, you stupid bastard?*

"We need Jenner," Ronan continued. "We're recruiting by the day, searching the city, putting the word out to all of the thirteen covens. It won't be long before the candidates are lined up and begging to be turned."

Mikhail couldn't do it all on his own. Especially if Claire chose to remain hidden from him. His strength would flag, and until he fed from her again his blood wouldn't be potent enough to bring other dhampirs through the transition. If he didn't turn Ronan soon, everything they'd fought for until now would be for naught.

"The Collective will overwhelm you," Mikhail warned. "If you don't rein in control, you'll drown in the memories." Even now he felt it hard to breathe under the onslaught. "Your senses will become even more acute. Your strength, immeasurable. Your bloodlust will increase by a thousandfold and mastering it will be almost impossible. Are you ready for all of that, Ronan? Are you ready to surrender your soul?"

"I've been ready for centuries," Ronan said with a passion that Mikhail knew all too well. "We all have. Surely you feel the pull, the desperation, of your people. You can't sustain us all forever. I'm ready to be what our race needs. Let me help to shoulder the burden, Mikhail."

Mikhail knew of no better male than the one standing before him. Nor one more worthy of the honor of his bite.

"Where is Jenner now?" If Ronan underwent the transition, Mikhail would need the service of a capable male. Especially since the Sortiari had grown bold in their attacks on dhampir covens.

"In the kitchen. I had Alex make him a few sandwiches while we talked. It takes a shitload of calories to feed someone as big as him."

At least Mikhail could always be assured a moment of levity while in Ronan's company. "Bring him in. I want to talk to him—alone." Mikhail would be better able to gauge the dhampir's intentions without Ronan present. Soon, his once quiet house would be bustling with activity as Ronan brought more dhampirs into their fold. Despite the crushing disappointment Mikhail felt at Claire's absence, there was a spark of hope igniting deep within him. The vampire race would be born again and looking to him for guidance.

It was time for Mikhail to ready himself for war.

He remained standing, too gods-damned on edge to sit for even a second. Ronan returned a few moments later with the dhampir in tow, a male worthy of the title warrior. Hair cut so close to his scalp that it was nearly bald, and covered in archaic tattoos, Jenner projected an aura of intimidation that Mikhail appreciated. Jenner didn't take a knee, or bow, or anything dramatic like that, but he did incline his head for the barest moment in a show of respect to Mikhail. When Jenner brought his head up silver chased across his dark gaze as he studied Mikhail with open—though not hostile—curiosity. White teeth flashed in a feral smile, the contrast to Jenner's darker skin giving him the appearance of someone who spent his fair share of time dazzling others under the heat of the California sun.

"You're not what I expected," Mikhail admitted. Siobhan had amassed a good company of fighters, there was no doubt.

"I'm not what a lot of people expect." Beneath his rough

exterior there was a charm to Jenner's personality. Mischief shone in his eyes and in the curve of his grin. Mischief and a fair share of malice as well.

"You've left Siobhan's coven?"

Jenner hiked an unconcerned shoulder. "More or less. Ronan and I agree that she needs to be coddled to a certain extent."

Siobhan could certainly be an ally. It would just take time to wear her down. Time that Mikhail didn't think he could spare. "What of the slayers? Have they attacked her coven?"

Jenner's voice was as gruff as his appearance. "Three times in the past two weeks. Your ascension to power is a thorn in her side. She blames the attacks on you and is using the rhetoric to turn others against you."

This male was more than sheer brawn. He had a sound mind and a good head on his shoulders. Ronan's judgment couldn't be questioned. He certainly knew what he'd been doing when he selected Jenner as the next to be turned. "And what do you think of my ascension, Jenner? Do you share your mistress's opinion?"

The male's gaze darkened as a low growl rumbled in his chest. "I do not belong to Siobhan."

Mikhail cocked a brow. "To whom do you belong, then?"

Jenner's lip curled. "To no male. And no female. I belong to myself." Mikhail opened his mouth to respond, but Jenner cut him off. "But I will serve you as my king. Swear my fealty to you for as long as you'll have it. And should you choose to honor me with your bite, I'll serve you well."

"And should I ask you to kill Siobhan . . . ?"

Jenner fixed Mikhail with a narrowed stare. "I would not advise it, but I would carry out the deed, nonetheless."

"You'll stay here." Mikhail turned back toward the garden. "The transition will keep Ronan from service for at least three days. You'll be my second until his transition is complete."

"As you say." The rough tenor of Jenner's voice did not quaver with even an ounce of doubt.

"Send Ronan in."

"Yes, my liege." The title, the very formality with which Jenner spoke to him both unnerved and energized him. *My liege.* Could he be a king worth following?

Silence descended with Jenner's stealthy retreat. The male would become a formidable vampire. One that would make the Sortiari tremble with fear. The scent of Ronan's blood indicated his entrance into the room. Mikhail's thirst burned his throat, and though he'd promised never to drink from another but Claire, it was his vow to Ronan and to the entirety of his race that prompted his actions.

"Jenner said you wanted to see me? How did it go between the two of you?"

Mikhail attacked in a flash of motion, taking Ronan to the floor like any starved predator would. Without a word, Mikhail sank his fangs into his friend's throat, tearing at the vein to open it fully. He glutted himself on the warm, thick blood until it no longer flowed willingly over his tongue but rather required long, deep draws at the vein to drain it from Ronan's body. The male's heartbeat slowed as the male clawed at Mikhail's arm, his eyes wide with fear.

Thump, thump. Thump, thump. Thump. Thump . . . thump.

Ronan's heart beat its last as a dhampir, and Mikhail released his jaw from the male's throat, sinking his fangs into his own wrist to open the vein. Mikhail pressed it to Ronan's mouth and let the blood trickle down his throat, coaxing him to drink. Soon the sting of his fangs bit into Mikhail's wrist as Ronan latched on and fed greedily, pull after powerful pull until the myriad voices of the Collective quieted in Mikhail's mind and he swayed from the rush of power that left him as it fused with Ronan.

The dhampir pulled violently away, a shout of pain bursting from his lips as his back bowed off the floor. Mikhail called for Jenner and he burst through the doors, his brow furrowed at the scene unraveling before him. *"Fuck."*

"Take him upstairs," Mikhail said through pants of breath. "And stay clear of his fangs. I'll be up in a moment."

Jenner didn't ask a single question, didn't utter a sound. He simply nodded in acknowledgment and did as instructed. *A fine male indeed.*

Mikhail collapsed on the floor, his strength that of a child in comparison to what it was moments ago. He needed Claire. Needed her to replenish him, to give him strength. *Where are you?* his soul called out to hers in desperation as his eyes drifted shut.

The last of the Ancient Ones no longer. That was, if Ronan managed to survive the transition.

CHAPTER
19

Fire raced through Ronan's veins. Blistering heat scorched his skin and his throat was a raging inferno that no amount of water could quench. Pain radiated through every inch of his body as his muscles seized. His jaw locked down tight and his fangs punctured his bottom lip, the heady scent of his own blood sending him into a frenzy of thirst and lust. Something held him down, bound his wrists and ankles. A familiar panic surged, and he thrashed against the restraints, a low, dangerous hiss issuing from between his teeth.

At the center of his being, a great cavern opened up. Everything he was, everything he had been, rushed into the darkened void, sucked away from him like water down a drain. The emptiness was all consuming, the hollowness more than he could bear. His sense of self evaporated, and try as he might to hold on to that part of himself, it slipped away until there was nothing left but a husk. He was now one of the soulless. Untethered. *Vampire*.

Ronan fought to free his hands: There were few things that enraged him more the being bound. Blood pooled in the seam of his lips and his tongue flicked out as he lapped desperately at his self-inflicted wound.

"Calm yourself, Ronan." Mikhail's voice was like a beacon of light in an endless night, calling to him down the length of a tunnel. "If you let yourself succumb to the bloodlust, you'll go mad."

He ran through the darkened streets, desperate. The thirst was too much, the transition too violent. He could think of only two things: feeding and fucking, and it didn't matter which came first as long as he was sated. In the distance, the scent of blood called to him, maddened him. Drove him to a place of need that extinguished reason. Like an animal, he lifted his nose to the air, inhaled the sweet aroma, and changed his course. At the end of a dark alley he found her, huddled, shivering on the cold cobbles, covered with nothing more than a tattered blanket to shield her from the elements.

Her eyes grew wide when she spotted him, and the tang of fear sullied the delicious aroma of her blood. He pounced on her in a blur of motion, his fangs buried in her throat before she could build up a scream. The first gush of blood was a cool salve, banishing the dry heat that licked up his throat. He bit down harder, crushing her windpipe in his powerful jaws, the air choked from her lungs before her heart even had a chance to stop beating—

"No!"

Ronan thrashed, arched his back high, and pulled at his restraints. Eyes wide, he took in his surroundings, his disorientation only heightened by the memories that assaulted his mind. The colors were almost blinding despite the darkness of the room, and every particle of dust in the air created an individual scent that melded into an olfactory overload that both confused and infuriated him. The sounds—louder, sharper, with dimensions he'd never noticed before—buffeted his ears and he wanted nothing more than to clasp his hands over his head to block out the offending noise. He'd thought his senses were keen before . . . but gods, this was *unbearable*.

"You can feed. But only if you can control your frenzy!"

Mikhail's voice boomed in Ronan's ears as he talked to him like he was three years old—or the family pet. "Stop fucking shouting at me." Ronan's own voice seemed amplified, roughened by the fire in his throat. "Untie me. Now, damn it."

"That's not going to happen. You're still too volatile."

He wanted to look Mikhail in the eye, but his own refused to focus, darting from one focal point to another until he became dizzy. His stomach heaved and Ronan swallowed against the dry spasms working in his throat. Fuck, he didn't even have an ounce of bile to choke up or a bit of saliva to swallow his sickness down.

"Ahhhhhhhh!" The shout burned all the way up his throat as he began to thrash anew. The heat, the sound, the sharpness of *everything,* coupled with the panic caused by his restraints was slowly causing him to unravel.

"Ronan!" Mikhail's command was white noise in the back of Ronan's mind. Another wave of memories crested in his consciousness and Ronan was swallowed by the undertow. The room faded away and he was transported into the past, into the memory of an Ancient One, reliving a life that wasn't his.

"Ronan!"

He couldn't breathe. Fear seized him and he broke the surface of the memory, coming back into the present. The familiar expansion of his lungs failed no matter how much air he took in through his nose.

"Your body is dying, Ronan. The transition is nearly complete." Mikhail leaned over Ronan, holding the male's body down as he thrashed against his bonds. "Don't fight it. I'll release you soon, I swear. Let it happen and the pain won't be as severe. Once you feed, your lungs will begin to function again, but until then, you don't need oxygen to survive. Try not to panic."

Transition.

His own memories came back to him in a rush. He'd walked into Mikhail's study, expecting to continue their discussion. But the male had attacked, taking Ronan down to the floor to drink him dry. His world faded around him and he floated. Mikhail pressed his wrist to Ronan's mouth and Ronan drank. Drank and drank until he thought he'd burst. And then everything had gone dark.

"How long?" He closed his eyes, focused past the restraints, and picked through the myriad sounds for that of Mikhail's heartbeat. The too-slow, sporadic thrum centered Ronan and at the same time caused his thirst to flare hot in his throat. "How long have I been in transition?"

"Almost three days," Mikhail said. Ronan kept his eyes closed and his focus centered. As his body stilled, his friend relaxed his grip and slowly pulled away. "You're nearing the end. All that's left is for you to feed."

The memories of the Collective scratched at the back of his mind, forcing themselves to the forefront of his thoughts, but he refused to succumb to its pull. Rather, he listened to the sound of Mikhail's pulse, let the sound calm him. If he could just settle the fuck down, he could sate the burning thirst that was no doubt sending him quickly toward insanity and Mikhail would free him.

"I'm under control," he said through clenched teeth. In his mind the words were a murmur, though to his ears as good as an angry shout. He dropped down to the equivalent of a panting whisper. "I can do this, Mikhail. Unbind my wrists and let me feed."

To prove his point he lay still as death, which wasn't a far cry from his current physical state, on the mattress. The absence of regular bodily function—his mouth not producing saliva, his still lungs and almost non-existent heartbeat—threatened to send him back toward panic. The emptiness he felt at his core, endless and dark, made him want to scream with fear, but Ronan took control of his thoughts. This was all part of the transition. Feeding would reawaken his body. Though he was technically dying, he was also reborn. This was what he had wanted for so long. He'd willingly sacrificed his soul.

Finally, he was vampire.

"You'll adjust in time." Mikhail unlocked one of the manacles that secured Ronan to the bed, and Ronan rolled his wrist to alleviate the stiffness. He squinted. Even in the darkened room the brightness permeated his eyes like needles spearing the sockets. "All of your senses are more acute. You'll learn to differentiate between scents and sounds. Without sunlight, your already-keen eyesight will allow you to see plainly in the darkest of nights. And there is something else. . . ."

What was coming was no surprise to Ronan. After all, he'd drawn on Mikhail's strength for decades. "The dhampirs will sense that I've been turned and they'll draw on my power."

"It will be different than you're used to. You've been on the receiving end for decades. Now, you'll be giving. The draw feels like . . ." Mikhail paused as though searching for the right word.

"A violation?" Ronan ventured as he tried futilely to swallow.

"In a way." Without another word Mikhail released Ronan's other wrist. "You'll forgive me for not freeing your ankles just yet. I have to be sure."

Ronan shot upright and the room blurred with his speed. "Sure of what?"

"Jenner!" Mikhail called. Ronan cringed from the volume but forced his mind to adjust to the discomfort.

A moment later the bedroom door swung open and Jenner walked in, escorting a female Ronan didn't recognize. He cocked his head and looked askance at Mikhail. Her heart fluttered with nerves, jacking up her pulse rate along with a rich bloom of scent that made Ronan's mouth water. Or at least it would have if it weren't so gods-damned dry. The female was excited and a little scared, too. Her reaction called to the predator in him and a secondary set of fangs punched violently down from his gums, throbbing. If he didn't sink them into her throat, *now,* he'd go mad.

"If you harm her, Ronan, I'll beat you bloody. Do you understand me?"

Mikhail's protective tone was admirable. "I understand." The bloodlust gripped Ronan and he forced himself to focus on his promise to take care with the female who'd volunteered to feed him. He wanted her. Wanted her blood to gush down his throat. The dhampir took a seat on the edge of the bed and brushed her hair to one side, baring her throat to him.

Ronan seized her in a blur of motion and sank his fangs into her flesh.

Bliss.

"You look tired, Claire."

She gave Vanessa a wan smile as she paused near the open door. "Tired" was an understatement. More than ready to collapse, Claire wanted nothing more than to fall face-first into bed. "I'm beat. Still getting over the mono." If by "mono" she meant "morning sickness." "How's school going? You need anything? Notebooks? Pencils? A binder?"

"No, I'm okay." She leaned her little body against the doorframe and folded her arms across her chest. "I was wondering, though . . . I mean, if you're not still too sick . . ."

Claire waited patiently for Vanessa to ask her question. She knew better than anyone how embarrassing it could be to ask for help. Even from a friend. When they'd been down-and-out, her mother never had a problem with the whole beg, borrow, and steal mentality. Claire could never stomach the begging or borrowing. Obviously, she hadn't minded stealing.

"I want to buy a bra and Mom isn't exactly, well, you know."

She didn't have to say any more. Claire knew exactly what Vanessa's mom was. But seriously, a bra? Vanessa was in the fifth grade for crying out loud. "Well, if you think you really need one, we could go tomorrow. I'm closing at the diner. We can go shopping before I have to be at work." She might have enough energy to take Vanessa shopping if they went early. With each passing day Claire was so exhausted by sundown that she could barely keep her eyes open.

"That would be great!" Vanessa's expression brightened and she leaned toward Claire. "Corra McKenna says that every girl in the fifth grade owns at least a sports bra." Vanessa's gaze dropped to her chest and she shrugged. "It's not like I've got much to worry about down there, but I don't want to be the only girl in the school who doesn't wear a bra, you know?"

"Be ready by nine, okay? We'll get donuts before we hit the store." Well, Claire would get Vanessa donuts, anyway. She doubted she'd be able to stomach a glass of water, let alone a deep-fried pastry. Her stomach heaved just at the thought and she took a step away from the door. "I'm going to go lie down and get some rest. I'll see you in the morning, though. Okay?"

"I'll be ready." Vanessa was practically bouncing with excitement. "See you tomorrow!"

"See ya."

Claire shut the door to her apartment behind her and turned the dead bolt. Lord, she was exhausted. Step by step, one foot dragged after the other as she lost focus of everything around her in the course of her trek to the bedroom. Her hands wandered to her lower abdomen, palms splayed over her womb. There was a child growing inside of her. An actual little . . . person? Were vampires considered people? And in her case, would the baby be a dhampir? Mikhail said that vampire/human pairings resulted in dhampir babies. What did vampire hybrid babies look like, anyway? Were they born with little bitty fangs? If that was the case, breast-feeding was out of the question.

Whether her baby would have mini-fangs came second to the fact that in nine months Claire was going to be responsible for a helpless little life. Someone was going to depend on her. Look to her for guidance. Hell, for food and shelter. She'd have to clothe him and feed him, put him to bed, and make sure he was clean—

He.

A secret smile curved Claire's lips. She didn't know how, but she was certain the baby was going to be a boy. With Mikhail's dark hair and aqua blue eyes. The thought of her vampire made her chest ache as tears sprang to her eyes. *Stupid hormones.* Running out on him had been a total dick move. And continuing to focus all of her energy on blocking their connection was even worse. Maybe that was why she'd been so exhausted lately. Her body was already trying to funnel everything she had to the baby; by blocking Mikhail she was expending energy she didn't have.

Another week. She needed one more week to think things through. Decide what she really wanted. Could he even turn her now that she was pregnant? She had no idea how this whole vampire thing worked. Even more reason to go back to him. Claire didn't like to fly blind. It went against her nature. Mikhail could arm her with knowledge, help her to form the best plan of attack.

Above all of that, though, she missed him. He was with her whether he realized it or not. She felt his presence as though he were standing right beside her, and there were moments when she would turn around convinced he'd be at her back. How was it possible to yearn so deeply for someone she'd spent so little time with?

Claire collapsed on the bed, too tired even to take her shoes off. Outside, the sound of a police siren grew louder and louder, rushing past the apartment building with a flash of red and blue lights before fading off into the distance. She missed Mikhail's house, far away from the lights and sounds of the city. She longed for the quiet and the soft peacefulness. She longed for *him*.

I'll try to be the mom you deserve, baby. Her thoughts drifted as sleep descended. *And maybe, if we're lucky, you'll get the dad you deserve, too.*

CHAPTER
20

Ian Gregor lounged against the hard back of the cheap office chair in Tristan McAlister's tidy office. He missed the days of keeps and castles, dark and foreboding mead halls illuminated by torchlight. He missed the gods-damned mystery of it all. Waiting around for the director in a brightly lit office with silk greenery decorating the bookcase was a far cry from the Sortiari's former glory.

Whatever happened to a little pomp and fucking circumstance?

After another ten minutes of mind-melting boredom, Tristan decided to grace the room with his presence, strolling through the door as though the world waited to do his bidding. The Sortiari had always been a group of smug, egotistical bastards. At least one thing hadn't changed over the centuries since their inception. And since you couldn't get higher up in the ranks than the position Tristan now held, there was nothing left but to sit and listen to what the bastard had to say.

"I'm afraid the situation has changed, Gregor."

"The hell it has." They were still fighting the same

battles they always had. Were still acting on the whispered orders of mysterious seers who steered the council's directives. And Tristan was still a suspicious son of a bitch who was so out of touch his office sported decorating accents that had died out in the eighties. He needed to get rid of the Rubik's Cube and step into the twenty-first century.

And now Gregor was supposed to sit here and listen to this secretive, sanctimonious son of a bitch tell him that things had changed? That a centuries'-long need for vengeance should simply be cast aside. Disregarded and tucked away into their sordid history? Gregor squared his shoulders. His bloodline could be traced back to the earliest Scottish royalty. A bloodline that had been all but squashed by the treachery of a power-hungry laird and his filthy coven. For Gregor, nothing had changed.

"Tell me, Tristan. What have your seers seen now, after so many centuries of certainty that what we're doing isn't in Fate's best interest any longer?"

Tristan let out a long sigh and raked a hand through his tawny hair that was beginning to show signs of gray at the temples. Nothing was infallible, not even the director of the guardians of Fate, it seemed. Gregor tried to stem the smug sense of satisfaction that tugged at his lips. In shutting himself away from the world, becoming a veritable hermit, Tristan had accomplished nothing but to sign his own death warrant.

"If you go after him, you'll set things in motion that can't be undone," Tristan said. "Is that what you want, Gregor? Is your sense of vengeance so strong that you would malign Fate in the process of seeing it through?"

He didn't even have to consider his response. "Yes."

"You have no quarrel with Mikhail Aristov," Tristan replied. "You merely seek to destroy what he represents."

Exactly! Wasn't that the point? "Two hundred and fifty years ago, you set me loose upon them with instructions to kill every last one. What has changed that suddenly Mikhail Aristov gets to cheat death not once, but twice in the same millennium?"

"I don't expect you to understand, Gregor. You can't see past your own blind hatred."

As though the directive to eradicate an entire species was a decision borne of compassion. "Explain it to me." His tone cooled to freezing. "Indulge me."

"It's Fate's decree," Tristan simply said. "That's all you need to know."

Gregor shot forward and brought his fist down on the desktop, sending a pot of silk violets to the floor. The air in Tristan's office became static with the residual charge of magic. Magic Tristan was too damned weak or too damned cowardly to wield. "What about your promise to me?" he railed. "I've served you faithfully!"

His accent thickened, the long-lost brogue of his ancestral tongue returning with his anger. He'd turned his curse into a blessing of sorts, letting the Sortiari use him and his brethren to their benefit. But it was apparent now that he and his were nothing more than the lapdogs the vampires thought them to be. Kept on too short a leash.

No longer.

"You've killed them all, Gregor. What more do you want? There is a change on the horizon. A change we hadn't foreseen until now. It's time to let the scales balance. This has to end."

"It's not over until I say it is." Gregor pushed himself up from the chair and stalked toward the door. Not all of them were dead. There was still one more vampire walking the earth, and once Gregor wiped Mikhail Aristov from existence he'd begin the task of wiping out Mikhail's kin. And perhaps as Gregor strangled the life from every last dhampir he'd finally find the one he was looking for.

"There is a girl." Tristan's urgent tone gave Gregor

pause and he stopped halfway out the door. "Blond, still a child. She's under the protection of the vampire's mate. Not a hair on her head is to be harmed, Gregor. Do you understand me?"

He turned a caustic eye to Tristan. "She's important, is she?"

Tristan's somber words struck a chord. "You have no idea how important."

Looked like the director had his priorities in order. Gregor decided to read between the lines on this one: *Kill the vampire and his mate if you must, but spare the girl.* Of course, Gregor made no guarantees.

"You should think about redecorating," he said upon leaving. "Try Crate and Barrel. I'm sure you can order online without even having to leave the safety of your office." And with that, he closed the door behind him, having likely exchanged the last words he would ever speak with any member of the Sortiari.

"Well? What did the bastard say?"

The Sortiari's leashed pet no longer, Gregor fell into step beside his second, Alec. "Nothing that matters," Gregor answered as he gathered his weapons from the security desk. McAlister was so gods-damned paranoid he wouldn't even let his own people into his office armed. "Did you find her?"

"Aye," Alec replied. "Right where we left her. Mikhail must have cut her loose. That or she's decided keeping company with a vampire isn't in her best interest."

Gregor let out a derisive snort. Was that the reason McAlister had shut him down? Had Aristov's little pet experienced a change of heart? "He'll come after her." They stopped in front of a bank of elevators and stepped inside the first available car. Gregor pushed the button for the ground floor. "And we can ambush him."

"It'll have to be soon. If we wait long enough, the son of a bitch will have amassed an army of his own. No use giving him the upper hand."

"No, there isn't. That's why you're going to take a detachment of men and wait for him at that diner." If the bitch was stupid enough to carry on with her life as though it had never changed, you could damn well bet that Gregor would capitalize on it. "And I want her followed. Find out where she lives." If they failed to capture Mikhail at the diner, odds were good he'd scent her out at her home. Maybe then Gregor could set his eyes on the human girl as well. The one who was so gods-damned important to the Sortiari. If he played his cards right, the girl could be a useful bargaining chip in the future.

"How many men do you want me to bring along?"

Gregor stepped out of the elevator into the parking garage and headed toward his car. The number of berserkers employed by the Sortiari totaled a little over four hundred. Two hundred of those were in Los Angeles right now to deal with Mikhail's ascension to power. *Gods. Two hundred berserkers to take down one vampire. Shameful.*

Though hadn't Gregor been the one who'd failed to kill Mikhail in the first place? They wouldn't be here now had it not been for his mistake. "Take thirty. I don't want the odds tipped in his favor."

"You'd think if Fate wanted the vampire dead it wouldn't be so hard to accomplish," Alec remarked. "If it's Fate's will, then the fucker should die whether we take three or thirty men along."

Gregor bristled. Sound logic from his cousin. Wonders never ceased. "That's why you're taking thirty." He hit the key fob and disengaged the alarm on his BMW. "To make sure that Fate gets it right this time." It had been a long gods-damned time since he'd bought into the Sortiari's views on Fate. He didn't give a single fuck about their grand mission—or their seers. He cared about one thing and one thing only: that every last vampire and dhampir on the planet was dead.

He stared over the hood of the car at Alec. "You won't be answering to Tristan or the council anymore. To me and me alone."

Alec smirked. "It's about fucking time."

Aye. It was.

CHAPTER
21

When the war had escalated and the vampires could no longer keep the upper hand against Sortiari attacks, Mikhail had prowled outlying villages, farms tucked away from prying eyes under the cover of darkness, in search of slayers and Sortiari sympathizers. Then the church's hold had been absolute. The slayers used the cloister in order to manipulate hapless humans into sheltering them and, in some cases, giving aid to their cause. Superstition ran rampant and they feared the *vampyres* of legend: unholy, soulless demons that ravaged villages, killing indiscriminately in their quest for blood. Well, at least the legends had gotten something right. Their soulless states made them no more evil than any creature that roamed the earth, but perhaps it was that state of emptiness that had prompted the Sortiari to eradicate them. Ignorance bred nothing but mindless violence. The Fate they'd claimed to serve was nothing more than a reflection of their own misguided fears.

Tonight he'd hunted back alleys and neighborhoods across L.A., but not for the influencers of Fate or their berserker lapdogs. The resurgence of his enemies was the least of Mikhail's worries right now. He'd sworn that he'd let Claire be. That he would not be mastered by the tether that secured his soul to hers. He'd been lying to himself of course. He could no more keep himself from her than he could stop the sun from rising every morning.

If he didn't find Claire soon, he'd go out of his fucking mind.

Dressed for battle, Mikhail had never felt more like himself. Like the male he used to be. Abandoning the high-priced suits and designer business attire, he'd outfitted himself in the combat gear of a modern-day warrior. A thick nylon belt held throwing knives, daggers, and a .40-caliber Ruger. And his black long-sleeved shirt and fatigues were woven with a lightweight body armor that would deflect a blade with ease. He might not have had the advantage of the magic that the Sortiari used to infuse their weapons, but he had his speed, strength, and stealth. He could break an enemy's neck with a simple turn of his hand. His thick-soled boots pounded the pavement as he walked, a rhythm that helped to center his thoughts. A centuries-long war was about to be fought in Los Angeles, and he couldn't help but wonder how many slayers would swarm the city as the Sortiari unleashed the berserkers, fully consumed with battle lust.

How many more dhampirs would die before he regained the strength to turn them?

Turning Ronan had weakened Mikhail considerably. The Collective wore on his mind, his ability to bury the memories in his subconscious diminished without the strength Claire's blood and life force gave him. He was lost without her.

Arrogant decisions never produced favorable outcomes. He'd pushed Claire too hard, too soon. Interactions with humans were rare. In the Collective, only a few memories of vampire/human relationships stood out, one of which being the torturous vision of the male who'd inadvertently killed his lover in the hopes of turning her. Mikhail had taken Claire like she was some paltry bauble he'd found on the street. Given her no choice in her present or future, only demanded obedience under the guise of protection. Despite his treatment of her, she'd surrendered her body to him. A gift he hadn't deserved. He'd repaid her by proclaiming that her life as she knew it was over. That she belonged to him and would give up her humanity without a second thought.

None of his regrets or plans for amends would matter if he couldn't find her, though.

In the eastern sky, the first streaks of gray washed across the horizon. Another night wasted. He revisited the street where the slayer had attacked her. Claire's scent lingered, barely noticeable under the layers of filth and pollution and myriad creatures who'd traversed the same path in the past two weeks. Gods, the city was so vast. She could be *anywhere*.

For all he knew, she'd taken a plane and flown as far away from him as possible. Though her blood no longer coursed through his veins, Mikhail should have been able to track her through their tether. He'd joined their bodies, taken her blood again and again. The only thing that would have solidified an unbreakable connection between them would have been if she'd taken his vein as well. Once that was done, he would have been able to track her location no matter the distance. But until then, he was lost. Swimming in a sea so deep and endless, he despaired of ever reaching the shore.

Claire's presence fluttered across his senses, almost too faint to be real. Mikhail turned, his pace brisk as he rushed down the sidewalk toward a run-down diner tucked between an abandoned building and a pawnshop. A breeze kicked up dust and debris and her scent slammed into him, nearly bringing him to his knees.

Through the large picture window of the storefront he spied her and a wave of intense need seized him. A sign on the entrance indicated that the diner wasn't yet open for the day as she busied herself with brewing coffee and setting pastries out on a large serving platter that she covered with a clear plastic dome. Dark shadows formed half-moons beneath her eyes and the hollows of her cheeks sank slightly into her face. The bright spark was absent from her golden eyes, and in its place was a bone-deep exhaustion that permeated Mikhail's pores and drew on his already-weakened stores of energy.

Was she ill? Hurt? *Dying?*

Panic surged in his chest as he recalled the memory of the human woman as she died from her lover's bite. Though Mikhail hadn't fed Claire from his vein, he hadn't considered the possibility that by taking so much of her blood he could have done irreparable damage to her.

He rushed toward the door, determined to get her to safety. He'd pore over the pages of the blood codex, send Ronan to the far ends of the earth in search of a cure for whatever ailed her. Anything to ensure that she could remain by his side, healthy and thriving—

The scent of blood reached his nostrils and Mikhail stopped dead in his tracks. A creature dressed from head to toe in black approached slowly, a steady ribbon of crimson trickling from his outstretched fist.

"We assumed you'd crawl out of your hole again."

Icy rage slid down Mikhail's spine. The slayer's voice was as dark and cold as a tomb. Mikhail cast a furtive glance toward the diner, desperate to pull the slayer's focus from where Claire stood, completely defenseless.

The assassin followed Mikhail's gaze, a sinister smirk

pulling at his lips. "Don't worry; we'll deal with her soon enough."

Mikhail flew into action. He rounded on the slayer, fangs bared. The Sortiari must have learned their lesson from their last attempt to kill him because the assassin standing before him now was a mountain of a creature, bulging with muscle and armed for battle.

He flashed a wide grin that showcased his elongated incisors. Inky black swallowed the whites of his eyes and he moved with the fluidity of a seasoned warrior. From a sheath at his back he produced a long dagger. Blue steel winked under the streetlight and he struck out with the speed of a cobra, catching Mikhail's right biceps with the blade. The physical pain was nothing compared to the sharp jab to his ego. Without Claire's blood to sustain him, he was weaker, slower, his mind less sharp than it should have been.

Alone on the streets without additional defense, he'd left Jenner to watch over Ronan. Mikhail was one weakened vampire against a Goliath of a slayer—a berserker warlord who undoubtedly had reinforcements close. A few weeks ago Mikhail might have allowed the slayer to run a stake through his heart, just to be done with this existence once and for all. But no longer. He had something to live for. A mate to seek out and a race to replenish. And he'd be damned if he let this—or any other of the Sortiari's hellish creatures—end him.

A battle shout erupted from Mikhail's lips as he charged his opponent. The slayer braced for the attack and met him head-on, his razor-sharp teeth bared and ready to shred. A loud crack echoed off of the building facades as Mikhail took the slayer to the ground, slamming his considerable frame on the sidewalk that broke from the impact.

"I was told you were formidable." Blood spewed from

the slayer's mouth with his laughter. "But that was barely a love tap." He rolled before Mikhail could stomp down on his head and sprang back to his feet. "The great Mikhail Aristov, *neubivayemyy*. You're not even worth my time."

The slayer spat at Mikhail's feet as he slowly circled him. The assassin called him *the unkillable*. He could only hope that the title held true and instilled his opponent with a healthy dose of fear. "Then be on your way, and I'll spare you," he suggested with a slow smile. His fangs elongated at the onset of battle lust, his need to tear his enemy to shreds only second to his need for blood.

"The sun is about to rise, vampire. If you're going to kill me, better make it quick. Otherwise, I might just let the sunlight do the job for me. I'll watch you burn and give your ashes to your mate before I break her neck."

Already Mikhail's skin prickled with the coming morning light, but he'd be damned if he burned this or any other morning. He pulled twin daggers from their sheaths and spun them in his fists, prepared for an attack. The slayer lashed out and Mikhail dodged a wild swing and missed the cut of the slayer's dagger by inches. Mikhail used the misstep to his advantage and caught the bastard in the jaw with the pommel of his weapon in a solid right hook. When his opponent stumbled, Mikhail lurched forward and brought his arm around in a downward sweep, stabbing lightning quick at the juncture of the slayer's neck and shoulder.

The blade sank to the hilt. Blood gushed over Mikhail's fist, the scent setting his throat ablaze with thirst. Pulling away, the slayer took a lilting step to the right, laughter gurgling in his chest as he yanked the blade free and tossed it to the sidewalk with a clatter.

Smug bastard couldn't even die with quiet dignity. He clapped a hand over the wound, blood pulsing from between his fingers with every beat of his heart. Onyx swallowed his gaze, the inky black tendrils spreading out through his eyelids and the high bones of his cheeks. In the grip of battle lust it would take severing his head from his shoulders to kill the berserker. Eerie laughter grated on Mikhail's ears and he reached for the dagger so he could finish the slayer off once and for all.

From the corner of his eye he caught sight of several bodies racing down the sidewalk toward him. Where there was one slayer more were sure to follow. A wounded slayer in front of him, more up ahead, and probably several at his back. He'd faced worse odds. Mikhail braced himself for the attack, the black, soulless eyes of the creatures advancing on him as dark as the tomb he'd been forced to live a century in.

"You think you can kill me?" he screamed over the din of city sounds that buffeted his ears. "I am *neubivayemyy*!"

In thirty minutes' time, he'd either vanquish his enemies, die at their hands, or burn in the accursed sunrise. Either way, he'd fight as though this was his last battle. A shout from an alleyway at his left drew Mikhail's attention and he turned. *Gods.* What more could possibly try to kill him this morning?

A female emerged from the shadows like a vengeful wraith. Clad from head to toe in black leather, only the pale skin of her cheeks shone from under the cover of her raven hair. Green eyes flashed silver in the gray dawn, and behind her a small escort of dhampirs followed, every last one of them decked out for full-out war. *Siobhan*. The female had impeccable timing. No swords or daggers for this gruesome assembly. They carried an arsenal of modern-day weaponry at their disposal.

"To your right!" Siobhan barked the order to the males behind her and shots rang out. Apparently, the female was intent on killing their shared enemies first, so perhaps she could kill him herself later.

In this case, the enemy of his enemy was his friend. He could fight Siobhan later. All that mattered right now was decimating the slayers before they could get their hands on Claire. He took several steps back, as though in retreat, drawing the fight as far from her as he could.

Slayers converged on the street, seeming to appear from thin air, a swarm of dark shapes in the gray dawn. Mikhail choked up on his daggers, loosening his fingers from around the grips as he shifted his weight on the balls of his feet, readying himself for the oncoming attack. The berserker warlord was wounded but no less enraged for the injury done to him. A sneer stretched his upper lip, accompanied by a smug look of satisfaction. Mikhail let the battle behind him fade to the back of his mind, instead focusing on the threat in front of him. Another slayer joined the big bastard trying to put a stake in Mikhail's heart, armed with some of the same modern-day tactical gear Siobhan's dhampirs were armed with.

Mikhail sheathed one of his daggers, opting instead for a throwing knife. Almost as fast as a shot he drew the blade from his belt and let it fly, burying the blade to the short hilt in the second slayer's neck. He plucked the blade from the slayer's skin like it was nothing more than a sliver, but Mikhail's aim had been true and blood spurted from the nicked vein. Gods, how his throat burned with thirst.

His attention was drawn to the crimson stream flowing from the slayer's neck, but Mikhail shook off the command of bloodlust, rushing at the bigger slayer with a snarl. Dagger play called for close quarters, but Mikhail's fangs were just as deadly as the dagger in his hand. He stabbed, cut, his arm moving in a blur as he snapped down with his powerful jaws, tearing flesh as he went.

Mikhail fought like a male possessed, slashing, cutting, kicking out, and throwing punches with a lifetime's worth of anger and vengeance behind every blow. Mikhail beat the slayer bloody, pummeling him until he swayed on his feet, nothing more than a mass of broken bones.

In his blind rage Mikhail took a step too close, and the berserker swept his feet out from under him. He hit the pavement hard and propelled himself up just before the second slayer could ram the silver-tipped stake through his chest.

Enough of this bullshit.

He rushed the weaker of the two, taking the slayer down in a full-body tackle. With both daggers gripped firmly in his fists, he slashed the berserker's throat through to the spine. With Mikhail's attention diverted, a solid kick connected with his jaw and he flew backward, skidding several feet over rough pavement before coming to a stop. The berserker warlord pulled a pistol from his holster and leveled it with Mikhail's face.

"We are Fate."

Before he could pull the trigger, the slayer collapsed to his knees. A long blade protruded from his throat and his breath gurgled in his chest as he was shoved forward. Siobhan towered over him, her booted foot planted firmly on the slayer's back as she cut down again, severing his spine at the back of his neck. She wiped her blade clean on her thigh and sauntered over to Mikhail, her spiked heels clicking on the sidewalk.

"Well, Mikhail," Siobhan purred. She cut a glance toward the first yellow rays of sunlight and turned back to him with a triumphant smile. "It looks as though I've saved your life. I think for such a favor you owe me a debt, no?"

After half a day with Vanessa, a full shift, and a few hours' sleep yesterday, Claire wasn't ready to start all over again with a long morning shift. Who in the hell wanted breakfast at 5:00 a.m. anyway? The past twenty-four hours blurred together as she set several cheese Danishes onto a platter and put the plastic lid back in place. The scent of brewing coffee did wonders for her nausea. Maybe dhampir babies liked Colombian roast.

Warmth bloomed in the center of her chest and Claire froze in her tracks. It spread outward to her limbs, a radiant heat that infused her with strength and vitality. Banished all traces of the nausea and crippling exhaustion. Made her feel more alive than she had since leaving Mikhail alone in his bed.

Mikhail.

Her vampire was close. She sensed him in the core of her soul. The need to go to him overwhelmed her, sent one foot in front of the other as though she had no control over her own limbs. A heavy weight lifted from Claire as she opened the connection between them, allowing his strength to flood her, replenish everything she'd given to the tiny life growing inside of her.

Pop! Pop! Pop!

Gunfire echoed in her ears and she forced her body away from the glass door. She took refuge behind the tall counter, crouching down and cradling her abdomen to shield her unborn child from impending danger. *Oh, god. Mikhail is out there!*

He was strong. Infallible. An immortal vampire who tore his enemies' throats out with his bare hands. Surely he could hold his own in any situation, but as the sound of angry shouts melded with the clash of metal the first traitorous signs of doubt shredded her confidence.

She had to help him.

All she could hope to do, weaponless, defenseless, was distract any attackers long enough for Mikhail to gain the upper hand. She threw open the door with enough force to take it off the hinges and sprinted out onto the street just as the first morning rays of sunlight crested the cityscape beyond. *Holy shit!* The street looked like a war zone.

Bodies littered the ground and Claire raced toward the carnage in search of him, praying that he wasn't among the fallen. A blur of motion caught her attention from her periphery and Claire turned in time to see a tall, thin woman dressed from head to toe in black, her dark hair flying out behind her like curls of satin ribbon as she ran. To her left, a company of rough-looking brawlers hauled a body in their wake, forcing him toward a side alley as he fought to free himself.

"Mikhail!"

Claire's strangled shout echoed in her ears, drowning out the sound of approaching sirens. Sunlight filtered through the tall buildings, cutting a swath down the darkened sidewalk, but still Mikhail fought against his captors. The golden rays caressed his skin, and his back arched as his face contorted with pain. Claire doubled over; his pain was hers and the scorching heat seared her flesh and brought the blood in her veins to the boiling point.

The men dragging him away used Mikhail's weakness to their advantage as they hauled him into the shadows of the alley. Claire's own pain subsided and she sprinted down the sidewalk, desperate to get to him. Muscles aching, lungs burning, she pushed herself as fast as she could go, rounding the corner at a full sprint only to find the alleyway empty.

He was *gone*.

No! Her soul called out for him, a soundless yet keening cry that resounded in her mind and left her weak and shaking. Someone might as well have ripped Claire's beating heart from her chest, the separation was so acute. She collapsed to her knees, her chest heaving with each labored breath as white lights danced in her vision. The whine of sirens grew closer, a cacophony to drown out her own screaming thoughts as L.A.P.D. and emergency services personnel arrived on the scene.

God, please let him be okay. She sent a silent plea out into the universe as a horde of police converged on her. "Turn around slowly! Hands above your head!"

It would figure that the one time she got pinched would be the one time she was actually innocent. Claire did as she was told, pivoting on one foot toward the authoritative tone. The breath stalled in her chest as she took in the empty sidewalk, all but two of the bodies that had littered the side of the street gone.

What in the hell . . .

"Okay, Miss Thompson. Tell me one more time what you saw."

Claire sat in one of the booths of the diner, recounting the morning for the detective for what felt like the millionth time. There wasn't any way the L.A.P.D. could consider her a suspect thanks to Lance vouching for the fact that she'd been inside the diner when the shots were fired. The detective's tactics were admirable, though. Obviously trying to shake her down in the hopes that she knew something more than she was telling them. She'd run out into the thick of it, after all. No one with even a scrap of self-preservation instinct did anything that stupid.

"Lance was in the back doing prep work for the breakfast rush and I was getting ready to open. I heard a fight outside, followed by gunshots." The detective—Rourke, according to his badge—eyed her with an intensity that made Claire's insides quiver. It was the cold stare of an animal, emotionless and calculating, as though he was sizing up a potential threat. She swallowed against the dryness in her throat and bolstered the confidence she needed to sell her story. "There were two men lying facedown on the sidewalk and three more dragging another man toward the alley. I ran out and shouted for them to stop because it was obvious the other guy was being kidnapped or something, but by the time I caught up to them they were gone."

Detective Rourke rapped his pencil on the tabletop, the *tap, tap, tap* drilling straight into Claire's skull. "And you didn't know the man who was being apprehended?" Rourke fixed her with a stare that sent an icy chill through her soul. "You have no idea who he was?"

She shook her head. "Do you think this was gang related?" Not that it mattered. Claire just wanted him to answer one of her questions to create a baseline for his responses. She didn't trust him, or the shadow that passed over his gaze. It was time to put her internal lie detector to work.

"Not necessarily."

Truth. Or at least a vague enough response to make her think he was being truthful.

"What we're concerned about is an act of violence perpetrated by a very unstable man who might be tempted to lash out again. Next time, it could be in the middle of a mall or at an elementary school. Anything you can remember would be helpful, Claire. We want to find the person responsible before any more lives are lost."

Again Rourke spoke with just enough truth to the lie that it was hard for Claire to get a clear read on him. Too soon to call bullshit. His familiarity with her sent a tremor through her. First "Miss Thompson" and now "Claire." As though he was trying to foster some sort of intimacy and trust between them. It was going to take a hell of a lot more than the use of her first name to put her at ease. "I told you, the man I saw was being taken against his will. I don't think he was the one who killed those men."

Rourke's eyes narrowed as he studied her. "How can you be sure if you didn't see anything that happened prior to leaving the diner?"

Worry ate away at her and Claire swallowed down the

fear that congealed in her stomach like a stone. "What precinct did you say you were with, Detective?"

His indulgent smile didn't reach his cold eyes. "Metropolitan Division."

Lie.

"Oh." Claire pinned him with her gaze. "My friend Leah works as a dispatcher there. Do you know her?"

"Sure, I know Leah. She's a great girl."

Lie. Claire didn't know anyone who worked for the L.A.P.D. and neither did Detective Rourke. "Well, you'll have to tell her I say hello the next time you see her." Claire rose from the booth and he followed suit, the way he mirrored her action with fluid precision sending up another red flag. It was an intimidation tactic she'd used a few times herself. "I wish I could be of more help, but that's all I know. I hope you find the guy. This neighborhood doesn't see much excitement and I'm sure a lot of people would like to keep it that way."

Rourke stared at her for just a beat too long, his lips a thin, hard line. She recalled what Mikhail had told her about the Sortiari infiltrating every facet of society and a shiver raced from the base of her neck all the way to her toes. Her only consolation was that if this guy was in fact with the Sortiari, then it meant that the guys who'd dragged Mikhail away weren't members. She hoped in this case Mikhail would be safer with the devils he didn't know.

"I'll call you if I remember anything, though."

Rourke blinked as though remembering he had an act to keep up and smiled. "That would be great. And we might send someone over for a follow-up. Will you be here all day?"

Not if she could help it. Every internal alarm in her body blared and Claire had never wanted to run as badly as she did now. "Yep." It took every ounce of will she possessed to appear calm. "I work until five."

"Great. Thank you for your time, Claire. I'll be in touch."

A dangerous aura surrounded Detective Rourke. One that made Claire think she wouldn't want to tangle with him a second time. She needed to get out of there. And she needed to find Mikhail. God, she'd been stupid to so easily shun his protection. The connection blazed between them, whatever cosmic force that had bound their souls. In that moment the decision had been made for her. Whatever came from here on out, they'd have to be in it together. Claire was through with going it alone. She needed Mikhail. And she wasn't going to live another moment without him.

CHAPTER
22

Mikhail paced the confines of Siobhan's lair, all the while cursing the reviled sun that kept him from going to Claire. He'd fought against the crafty female's stalwart guards in an effort to get to her, only to feel the searing heat of the sun lick at his body while blisters formed on his flesh moments before they'd pulled him into the protection of the shadowed alley.

"You're making me dizzy," Siobhan complained. She lounged on a makeshift throne, one shapely leg bouncing over the arm. "You're here until sundown, Mikhail. Why worry about what you can't change?"

For thirteen hours he'd been cooped up in the ramshackle building Siobhan claimed as her own. He'd awakened well before sunset, his body fighting against daylight's hold in his need to get to his mate. Honestly, he was surprised they hadn't killed him the moment daylight had put him down. It was unsafe for a vampire to be away from the protection of his home during the day and this was why. Gods, Siobhan been talking for hours and already Mikhail was sick of her. He rounded on the dhampir, fangs bared. "And just what do you expect me to do?"

Her emerald eyes flashed with silver as a half smile tugged at her full lips to reveal the delicate point of one fang. "I think we should talk, don't you?"

He snorted. "I have *nothing* to say to you."

"Nothing?" Her mocking laughter echoed in the empty building. "Not even for the female who saved your life?"

"Dragging me away like a hostage is hardly saving my life."

"True," Siobhan agreed. "Though I could have let the slayers have you. Or I could have watched you burn in the sunlight. But since I was feeling benevolent, I chose to help you." She paused, a calculating smile spreading across her face. "And to look after your mate."

Mikhail stiffened, a growl building in his chest. He forced the words from between clenched teeth. "If any harm comes to her—"

"Relax, Mikhail." Siobhan gave a dismissive wave of her hand. "I couldn't be bothered to give a single shit about who you've chosen to bed. She's safe. Carrig followed her from that rathole diner to an apartment building on South Westlake. I've got to say, I never took you for the type that would slum it."

Anger churned in his gut and rumbled in his chest. "Mind your tongue, female. You're speaking of my mate."

Siobhan gave a superior smirk. "For such a favor— protecting what's yours—I think I deserve a boon. Don't you, *Your Highness*?"

Mikhail chose to ignore the sneer in her tone. If he didn't rein in his temper, he'd rip open her throat and start a war he didn't have time to fight. "I gave you my thanks. Is that not enough?"

Another round of amused laughter answered him. "Not by a long shot."

Of course not. Not for someone as devious and calculating as she appeared to be. "What do you want then?"

"I want Ronan."

Mikhail quirked a brow. *Ronan?* No, Siobhan wanted *power.* A higher rank than that of her current existence. How could Ronan possibly elevate her, unless she knew that the male had been turned and sought to exploit that power somehow? "Ronan isn't mine to give any more than he's yours to possess."

"He's sworn allegiance to you. Release him of his troth."

Not likely. "Why?" With Ronan in her court, Siobhan could turn her entire coven, create a force to be reckoned with. But she'd made no secret of her disdain for vampire-kind and wanted no part of being soulless and untethered. So why, then, would she want a vampire in her folds? "Perhaps your disdain of being turned is simple pretense? Do you want to be turned, dhampir? Do you secretly yearn for the strength *your king* could give you?" She sat up straighter, baring her teeth as a warning hiss gathered in her throat. "Whatever your plans, Siobhan, I will not release Ronan from his troth. Only he can do that. If he wants to break his allegiance with me, then so be it."

Siobhan's emerald eyes narrowed. "You're as arrogant as you are foolish, Mikhail. I have absolutely *no* interest whatsoever in leaving the light—*or my soul*—behind. Keep your strength and oblivion. I want none of it."

He rounded on her with blinding speed, hands braced on the arms of her so-called throne as he snarled in her face. "Then what do you want? Stop posturing and casting threats, and *wasting my time!*"

She bucked her chin defiantly and swung her legs over the arm of the chair, knocking his arms aside. The pointed heels of her stiletto boots struck the floor with a snap as she settled back and faced him fully. "I'm not a fool, so do me the courtesy of not treating me like one. I know all about your mate, Mikhail. She's human." Siobhan's statement, coupled with her superior smirk, caused a rumble of anger to erupt in Mikhail's chest. "Tsk-tsk, Mikhail. If I were you, I'd watch my temper."

He pushed himself away from the chair, lest he be tempted to sink his fangs as far as they'd go into the female's throat. Nothing would please him more than silencing her once and for all and the only thing keeping him from doing the deed was the army of dhampir soldiers she'd amassed to watch her back.

Between rotting underground in a foul, dark tomb and spending his daylight hours with this female he'd gladly take the tomb. "Whatever my mate might be, she is not your concern." He pushed the words through his teeth. "And a threat against her, no matter how veiled, will result in your death, female."

A satisfied smirk tugged at her thin lips. "Worthier males than you have tried. And failed. It's not me or mine that you need concern yourself with, Mikhail. I couldn't give a shit about your mate's shortcomings."

"Then why cast threats?"

"Because I can be a bitch when I don't get what I want." She dusted a fleck of invisible lint from her upper arm. "Give Ronan to me and I'll keep her identity secret. Otherwise . . ." Silver flashed in her eyes and she bared her fangs. "I'll help incite an uprising that will make the Sortiari raids that wiped out your kind look pathetic in comparison."

With every passing day this female was becoming more of a thorn in his side. "I told you, he's not mine to give."

"Of the thirteen covens, how many do you think will be faithful to you? And what of the covens outside the city? There's a coven in Seattle that despises humans." Her light, conversational tone grated on Mikhail's ears. "They hunt them like wild game once a month and glut themselves on blood. I can only imagine what they'll think when they discover the queen of the vampires is a creature they hold in as high regard as a doe in the forest."

Mikhail's temper flared. His fangs dug into his bottom lip and the taste of blood only spurred him toward violence. "Say another word and I'll flay the skin from your body."

From the shadows Siobhan's guards made their presence known, the silver of their eyes reflecting like those of a pack of wolves. This was intolerable. The sun would be setting in a matter of minutes and he was tired of putting up a calm, defenseless front for her benefit.

"You'd die before you could even think of laying a finger on me."

It was time that Siobhan realized just who she was up against. In a blink he grabbed her by the collar and took her down to the floor. She struggled against him, reached for the dagger sheathed at her side, but he was faster and snatched it before she could wrap her palm around the hilt.

The steel sang as he ripped the dagger free from the scabbard and straddled her body. He held the sharp edge to her throat. It nicked the skin, and blood welled from the wound, a crimson teardrop that ran in a dark rivulet down the pale column of her throat. "I've more than a finger on you, Siobhan," he growled next to her ear. "So you'll forgive me if I find your threats . . . idle."

A feral hiss escaped from between her bared fangs as she struggled against him. He shot upright, bringing her with him just as her force of bodyguards attacked. The flash of steel caught his attention and Mikhail spun away. He released his grip on Siobhan and she flew across the room, sliding over the neglected tile floor before her body crashed into the wall.

Surrounded by a formidable force of dhampir warriors, it took every ounce of his concentration to keep from feeling the bite of metal on his skin. He parried several downward stabs, one of their sweeping cuts equal to three of his. They fought with ferocity and he admired their valor. Siobhan's dhampirs were warriors worthy of their station and so much more.

It didn't mean he wouldn't put them down if need be.

He caught one of Siobhan's guards in the ribs with the dagger, cutting just deep enough to immobilize him. Another Mikhail took down with a kick to his knee. The third went down in a blur of motion as he snatched the male in his grasp and lifted the male's body high over his head, bringing the guard to the floor with enough momentum to create a fissure in the old tiles.

That left one lone opponent, and he was a burly son of a bitch.

Mikhail spun the dagger in his palm, choking up on the hilt. He hadn't felt so alive in centuries as he circled the dhampir whose hawkish gaze assessed his every move. "Your affront to my queen will not go unpunished, vampire."

Cocky. And a little misguided. Siobhan was no more a queen than the slayers were human, but Mikhail wasn't about to mince words at this point. "And her affront to me will not be *tolerated*." He attacked with blinding speed, sending the dhampir immediately into retreat. The male fought like an animal, snarling, swinging out with wild thrusts, the dagger held tight in his right hand while he parried Mikhail's attack with the dagger in his left. A surge of strength shot through Mikhail as the sun finally dipped below the horizon. It was time to go to Claire and end this nonsense between them once and for all.

Mikhail spun, catching the dhampir on the backswing, and the male went sprawling to the floor like a felled tree. The male flipped onto his back and rolled his legs up, propelling his body from the floor in a graceful arch. With a wide sweep of his leg Mikhail caught the dhampir before the male could get his footing and sent him back to the floor. Mikhail brought his fist up high and rammed it into his opponent's gut, knocking the air from his lungs.

The male rolled onto his stomach, scrambling to his knees as he fought for breath. Mikhail's lungs didn't require oxygen and perhaps he'd shown the dhampirs in the course of their fight that they could benefit from the transition. Truth be told, he didn't want any of them—including Siobhan—as enemies. But until they came to their senses and cast off their prejudice and sense of entitlement he had no choice but to consider this coven hostile.

He stalked across the vast room to where Siobhan lay against the far wall. Still dazed, she stared up at Mikhail, her eyes flashing with angry fire. "I took you in," she seethed. "Sheltered you from the sun and watched over your mate. And this is how you show your gratitude?"

"My gratitude is shown by the fact that you're still alive, Siobhan." Mikhail tucked the procured dagger into the empty sheath at his thigh. "Don't forget it is I whom you answer to, not the other way around. Pray I continue to show you *my* benevolence. I'll send someone to retrieve my confiscated weapons, and in the meantime I suggest you think long and hard about your future."

She pushed herself up to sit and graced him with a sweet smile. "And perhaps you should do the same, Mikhail."

He inclined his head and turned his back to her, strolling slowly from her presence and that of her guards. It was time for Mikhail, the last true vampire no longer, to show those who thought him weak just how powerful he was. And in order to truly do so, he needed his mate by his side.

Claire paced her tiny living room as her stomach tied itself into an unyielding knot. Mikhail was likely being tortured right now by Sortiari assassins and she had no idea who to turn to for help. Despair pooled in her gut until her entire body ached from the worry she felt. Since dropping the mental and emotional barrier she'd constructed to block her connection to Mikhail she'd hoped that if he could get free from his captors he'd find her easily. The detective who'd questioned her had Claire freaked the fuck out. She wasn't safe. None of them were. And it was time to circle the wagons if they had any hope of surviving Mikhail's enemies. If she'd had only herself to worry about, Claire doubted she'd be quite so worried. But the little guy growing inside of her deserved all of the protection he could get. And she couldn't keep him safe without Mikhail's help.

Not for the first time, Claire cursed her lack of a phone. Even if she did manage to find the number to Mikhail's house in the hopes of tracking Alex or Ronan down, how in the hell was she supposed to get ahold of them? Using the pay phone down the street would leave her too exposed. If the Sortiari knew where she worked, it wasn't a far cry to assume that they knew where she lived.

God, Claire. How could you be so stupid? An unspoken rule of the hustle: *Always* cover your tracks.

A change in tactics was in order. Odds were, if Mikhail was missing, Ronan was already at his house, rallying the troops or whatever. She didn't know if someone who valued his privacy as much as her vampire did would actually list his number in the phone book, but at this point she could only hope for a little luck to be thrown her way. She left her apartment and crossed the hall to Vanessa's unit.

"Hey, Claire!" Vanessa greeted her brightly. Her posture was ramrod straight, her shoulders squared and tilted slightly back. "Bet you can't guess what I'm wearing right now."

Claire laughed. "I bet I can. And I have to say, it makes you look at least twelve." Vanessa's expression lit up, her proud grin more radiant than the sun. "Just remember, it's okay to be ten. And do ten-year-old things. Don't let that bra go to your head, young lady." Claire gave herself a mental pat on the back for her matronly words. Despite her upbringing, maybe there was hope that she'd be an okay mom.

Vanessa giggled. "As if. And Claire, I'm almost eleven. So, what's up?"

Claire shook herself from the nostalgia of Vanessa's *Clueless* moment. "I need to use your phone and a phone book. Do you think your mom would mind?"

Vanessa's expression deflated like an old balloon. "Mom's sleeping. I doubt anything would wake her up right now."

Translation: She'd swallowed a handful of pills and was down for the count. "Oh." An awkward silence passed and Claire gave Vanessa a reassuring smile. "It'll be okay, kiddo. *You're* okay. That's all that matters." It was the sort of reassurance that didn't require further explanation. Having lived through it herself, Claire knew that Vanessa was the type of girl who'd come out on the other side relatively unscathed.

"The phone's on the kitchen counter. Phone book, too." Vanessa didn't respond to Claire's reassurance, but she didn't have to. They had an unspoken bond. Sort of like the one between Claire and Mikhail. A connection fused by something that she didn't understand. But maybe she wasn't meant to.

"Thanks." She thumbed through the white pages, her finger tracing down the list of *A* names, *Argyle . . . Arinson . . . Aristov! Anya, Dimitri, John, Marcus . . . Mitchell. God damn it.* Switching to the yellow pages, she resumed her search, through listings for private security firms, talent agents, lawyers, investment bankers, doctors . . . anything that struck her as the sort of job that would support Mikhail's lavish lifestyle. She let out a groan of frustration and ripped one of the pages in half, midturn. It was like looking for a needle in a stack of needles, covered by a haystack engulfed in flames.

God damn it. Despair unlike anything she'd ever felt stabbed at her heart and Claire swallowed down the lump that rose in her throat. She *never* should have left him, and now she might never see Mikhail again.

CHAPTER
23

Mikhail flew through the dark alleys and empty streets to the address that Siobhan claimed Carrig had followed Claire to. It was a race against his enemies to find her and they'd had the advantage of daylight on their sides. He had to find her.

The connection between them burned bright, radiating from his chest outward like a beacon that called to him from the darkest abyss. He'd never felt it with such clarity and intensity, which meant that either Claire was in trouble or she'd finally quit blocking him. Which both excited and terrified him. He let it lead him, gave himself completely over to the instinct, and in a matter of seconds he was standing before an apartment building that made Siobhan's abandoned and condemned building look like a palace in comparison.

His mate lived in such poverty?

His worry warred with the indignation that she would leave him to return to this life. No security. No protection. The very building looked like it might fall down around her head at any moment. Sounds reached his ears in a sensory overload that made Mikhail want to clutch at his skull. A party within, music blaring. The voices of too many humans living together in a single space mingled into one. White noise that assaulted him. Chaos to his superhuman senses. A surge of emotion crashed into him, nearly bringing Mikhail to his knees. Claire was inside. She was upset. Scared. He drew the dagger from its sheath and sped through the entrance and up the stairs to the second floor.

Her scent reached his nostrils and it only served to send him into a state of bloodlust that stole his ability to think clearly. There was something different . . . the bloom of fragrance somehow richer, more intense. His fangs throbbed in his gums as Mikhail stopped dead in front of a door marked 216. Claire was on the other side, and before he could lay his fist to the aged and battered wood it swung open to reveal the one thing he coveted. Longed for. Couldn't live without.

"Mikhail."

Her bemused expression belied the rush of relief that bathed him in warmth. She kept the door close to her body, blocking his view of the apartment. *Why?* Who was with her? Mikhail would kill any creature who dared to stand between them.

"Claire? Is everything okay?"

From behind her a quiet voice spoke, and Mikhail pushed against the door to reveal tucked behind Claire a young girl, her face a study in both bravery and fear. The juxtaposition made her appear feral. A tiny fox caught in a snare. Their eyes locked and a spasm of energy snapped out at Mikhail like a whip before drawing back. An extraordinary child born of an extraordinary mother?

The realization that he knew so little about his mate stabbed straight through his heart. Two helpless creatures to protect. Claire must have known that her daughter couldn't be turned. That was why she'd left him. And where, Mikhail wondered, was the child's father? Who else would he have to fight to ensure that Claire remained by his side?

She turned and whispered words of reassurance to the girl before slipping into the hallway and closing the door behind her. For a long moment, they stared at each other. Then Claire let out a strangled sob and threw herself into his arms. "Oh my god, Mikhail. I thought the Sortiari had you. When I saw them dragging you off into that alley . . ." Her words trailed off, muffled by his shirt.

There was much to discuss and not nearly enough time for everything that needed to be said. "We need to get inside." He reached for the doorknob behind her and she stiffened.

"No. Not here." She grabbed his hand and led him down the hallway, entering the apartment two doors down. Mikhail's confusion increased with every passing moment. Who lived with her daughter in the other apartment? The girl's father perhaps? Her scent was unlike Claire's. Another curiosity. At the back of his mind the Collective pressed against his consciousness and he pushed back. He couldn't afford to lose even an ounce of mental clarity right now.

Mikhail stepped into the apartment and his chest ached at what he saw. The entire living space was no bigger than his foyer. The walls were bare and the paint peeled from the drywall. Her furniture consisted of one battered couch and a threadbare recliner that reeked with layer upon layer of scents as though each had seen the use of multiple owners.

The refrigerator in the dilapidated kitchen made a knocking sound that grated on his ears and the faucet dripped in a steady rhythm. The carpeting was old and ragged, the cheap linoleum covering the floor stained and cut with deep grooves. He finished his assessment to find her gaze cast downward as though ashamed. "Not quite as swanky as your digs, huh?"

Gods, how he'd failed her. He'd thought only to satisfy his own selfish needs without a thought to hers. He would take care of Claire from this moment on. Her and her child. He'd take them both away from this existence. Claire was a queen. His queen. And it was high time she started living like one.

"You left because of the child." A thought struck him. One that ignited his anger to flare brighter than his concern. "What of the father?"

Claire's jaw slackened and a crease cut into her forehead. "The father?"

Gods, this was unbearable. Jealousy swelled inside of Mikhail, raging like an inferno at the thought of another man touching her. Burying his face between her silky thighs. Claire belonged to *him*. "The child's father!" he railed. Fiery heat licked up his spine, and his fangs throbbed at they punched down from his gums. A haze of red clouded his vision as he advanced on Claire. She fell into retreat, her eyes wide, but he could do nothing to control the jealous rage that seized him. "Is he the reason you left me? Sneaking out of my bed as though what happened between us was a shameful thing you couldn't wait to escape?" His voice boomed in the quiet apartment and Claire cringed. She stopped only when her back met the far wall and Mikhail crowded her until his nose was mere inches from her upturned face.

"The child's father is an asshole!" Claire shouted back.

"Tell me, Claire." Mikhail put his mouth to her ear. Her scent drove him mad and he wanted nothing more than to take her vein and fuck her until she never thought of another male save him ever again. "Why you choose to live in this hovel, work in that pathetic diner, over being with me?"

He'd come here tonight to make amends, to let her know that he wouldn't pressure her into the transition. To bring her home where he could *protect* her. But all of his good intentions evaporated under the thought that she would cast him aside for another male. For this life of poverty and hardship. The Collective scratched at his mind, myriad voices that threatened to drown out his own thoughts. He wasn't thinking straight. Couldn't. Not when he needed to feed so desperately. Not when she was so close—

"If you'd shut up long enough to let me explain!" Claire's eyes lit with an indignant spark and she clamped her jaw down tight. She let out a long sigh and knocked her head back against the wall with a frustrated groan. "You're such a fool, Mikhail."

His anger shattered with the sweet sorrow of her voice, the sight of her cheeks, flushed and warm, and the lush fullness of her lips that rested in a perpetual pout. Despite the anger that consumed them, the danger that pressed upon them, and despite the child down the hall and the male who might come between them, Mikhail's need for Claire surpassed even common sense. He took her in his arms, kissing her, starved for the contact.

Claire cleaved to him, molding her body tight against his. He slanted his mouth over hers, deepening the kiss, and his fangs scraped against her bottom lip, coaxing drops of blood to the surface of her delicate skin. Mikhail groaned as the bloodlust held him in its grip, and he sank his fangs deeper into her bottom lip. The drops increased to four small trickles and he lapped at her mouth, ravenous as he kissed and fed from her.

"Oh, god, Mikhail." Claire pulled away and clawed at his pants, tearing the button free before jerking down the zipper. "Take my throat. I want your bite."

She was just as mindless with desire as he was and his cock jerked as she took it firmly in her grip. Like an animal he sank his fangs into the flesh that concealed her throbbing vein, and the bliss of feeding from her overtook him as the sweet nectar of Claire's blood flowed freely over his tongue. Her back arched and she cried out as she stroked him from the base of his cock all the way up to the engorged head. With her free hand she shoved his pants down over his ass and dug her nails in as she squeezed his flesh. Mikhail pulled away with a low growl and laved the wounds he'd made. He stripped her shirt from her body and jerked the cups of her bra down off her breasts before burying his face against the satiny flesh.

"Yes!"

He sank his fangs into the swell of her breast and covered the pearled nipple with his mouth. Claire sobbed her pleasure and wound her fists into his hair as she held him against her. With a low growl Mikhail tore her bra away, discarding the fabric, and shoved the elastic waistband of her pants down over her ass as he suckled her. Her underwear came next and she kicked the restricting garments from her ankles. Mikhail cupped the globes of her ass in his palms and lifted her up against the wall. She wrapped her legs around his waist, hooking her ankles together as she thrust her hips toward him. A rich bloom of her floral scent swirled in his senses, the evidence of her arousal and need to couple with him as delicious and maddening as the blood he suckled from her breast.

"I need you to fuck me, Mikhail," Claire said from between panting breaths. "Now."

He pulled away without closing his bites. Blood trickled from the wounds, collecting at her nipple before forming a heavy crimson drop that he licked away with a flick of his tongue. Claire cried out, squirming in his grasp, and he watched again with fascination until another drop formed. This time he covered the stiff peak with his lips and sucked deeply.

"Oh, god." Claire's head thrashed from side to side as her hips undulated against him in a desperate frenzy. "Take me, Mikhail. Please."

He took the heavy weight of his cock in his hand and guided it to her entrance. Her pussy was swollen, dripping with arousal, and he dragged the engorged head through her soaking lips. Claire let out a low moan and he repeated the action, lingering on her tight little clit. The sensation caused a shiver to ripple over him and Mikhail gnashed his teeth as he pressed into her with a forceful thrust.

"Ohhhhh . . ." The sound slid from between Claire's lips with her breath as she came. Mikhail thrust hard with every deep contraction, intensifying her pleasure until her body became limp and liquid in his embrace. A couple of weeks apart from him had felt like an eternity and their argument, his crazy demands—not to mention that he'd known she was pregnant—vanished under the instinctual urge to join her body with his.

Through the blinding assault of ecstasy Claire's gaze found Mikhail. His eyes flashed with silver, locked on her breasts. She looked down at the rivulet of blood that ran over her breast and dripped off of her nipple and her body clenched with renewed passion. He was fixated, seemingly entranced by the sight of it, and his obsession only spurred Claire to a higher state of mindless need.

"I want to taste my blood on your tongue, Mikhail." His eyes met hers, wide and wild. "Do it," she urged as another wave of intense pleasure threated to crest and take her under.

He dragged the flat of his tongue across her breast and Claire let out a desperate gasp. Anticipation coiled in her stomach as he slanted his mouth across hers, his tongue thrusting in time with his hips. The coppery tang of her blood shouldn't have made her want more, but it did. And this time it was Mikhail's blood that she wanted to taste. To drink. The instinct to gorge herself on his blood wound itself into her very DNA until she thought she might go mad in want of it.

He broke their kiss and pulled back as though to gauge her reaction. Claire licked her lips and his eyes flashed, riveted to the motion. "You're mine, Claire." He thrust deep, knocking her head against the wall, and she let out a low moan. *"Mine."* Harder. Deeper. "And I'll make sure that *any* male who thinks to lay claim to you knows that fact."

"Yes!" How could she possibly think of any other man, ever? Mikhail was the center of her universe, a force too powerful to resist. His muscles rippled beneath her touch, flexing and releasing. The veins stood out on his neck as he fucked her with furious abandon. "I want to taste you, Mikhail. Drink from you. I *have* to!"

She couldn't explain the urge, but neither could she do anything to fight it. Mikhail let out a triumphant purr as he brought his wrist to his mouth and bit down hard. He pressed his wrist to her mouth and Claire latched on, digging the blunt ends of her teeth into his flesh as she sucked. His hips bucked wildly, and at the first warm gush of salty copper that filled her mouth Claire's body coiled tight on the verge of another mind-shattering orgasm.

Hands wrapped tightly around his arm, she held his wrist to her mouth, drawing on his scored flesh with deep, hungry sucks. Mikhail's lips pulled back to reveal the sharp points of his elongated fangs moments before his jaw clamped down. A shock of heat flooded her as his cock pulsed with every wave of his orgasm. Every muscle, every vein, that corded his body stood out in stark relief as a deep, satisfied roar erupted from his throat.

Claire came with him, her second orgasm more powerful than the first. Her body quaked with the force and

Mikhail's skin popped under her teeth as she bit down on his wrist to increase the flow of blood.

She floated away with each powerful spasm of her inner walls. Left her body completely behind as she floated on a cloud of sheer ecstasy. She was nothing more than a tangle of nerves and sensation, a gossamer thing without form.

For what seemed like years, the only sound in the tiny apartment was that of their mingled breaths. She looked down at Mikhail's wrist, and the open wounds shrunk before her eyes until they healed completely, the skin as smooth and flawless as it had been moments ago. She dragged her eyes upward to find his almost completely silver now, only a trace of vibrant blue ringing the irises.

"Your mouth is so lovely stained with my blood." The guttural quality to his voice made her core contract, squeezing his still-erect cock inside of her. He lowered his mouth to hers and kissed her slowly. Gently. Lapping at her lips and tongue in a satiny glide that filled her with a renewed rush of heat.

"Mikhail," she said against his mouth. Her words weren't her own but rather spurred by something deep inside of her that she didn't understand. "I want *more*."

CHAPTER
24

Claire had taken his vein, completing their blood bond. It was something he never would have expected, not until after her transition, and that she was begging for more challenged his tenuous self-control. It would be a simple thing to drain her while his cock was still buried in the slick heat of her pussy. And when her heart ceased its beating he'd offer her his vein once again, triggering her transition while he filled her with his seed.

The animal in him surged to the surface of his psyche, demanding that he ravage her. Extinguish the flame of her human existence so he could spark something new and wild, giving life to the vampire she would become. "Claire, don't ask this of me." His fangs tingled in his gums and he was overcome with the urge to bite her. To drink her dry while he fucked her. "Not when your daughter is so close and there is so much unresolved between us."

Claire pulled back so quickly that her head smacked against the wall. Her brow furrowed as she searched his face. "What are you talking about?"

He held her close, the heat of her body a soothing balm

on his skin. "Your child. The one in the apartment down the hall." He smoothed Claire's hair back and let his fingers thread through the silky strands. Perhaps the small amount of blood she'd taken from him had addled her mind. A ribbon of panic unfurled in his gut and he withdrew from her body, the profound sense of loss he felt only heightening his distress.

The same confused frown puckered her brow as Claire unwound her legs from his waist. He set her gently on her feet and she leaned back against the wall, her arms still slung over his shoulders. "You think Vanessa is my *daughter*?" She choked out a disbelieving laugh. "I would have been fourteen when she was born!"

Now it was Mikhail's turn to be confused. "You didn't deny you had a child. And you said yourself that your child's father was an asshole."

Claire's cheeks flushed with color. "I was talking about *you*. That caveman attitude of yours drives me up a wall sometimes!"

He was her child's father? But the girl wasn't her daughter. . . . The gears turned in Mikhail's mind, slow to move. He took a stumbling step back and then another. The Collective stirred in his mind, coupled with the unidentifiable scent that clung to Claire. His gaze raked down the length of her body, pausing at the almost indiscernible curve to her lower abdomen. That fullness hadn't been there before. Her breasts, though perfectly round, were in fact heavier than they'd been just two weeks ago.

"For someone with centuries under his belt, you're a little slow to catch on, aren't you?"

A bright smile lit her features as her hands wandered to her belly. Mikhail dropped to his knees before her, wrapped his arms around her torso, and pressed his cheek to her womb. "My child," he murmured against her skin. "You're carrying my child?"

Claire threaded her fingers through his hair as though to soothe him. "It's a boy," she whispered. "Don't ask me how I know."

His child. His *son*.

Emotion swelled in Mikhail's chest to the point that he thought he'd burst. Claire had never belonged more to him than she did in this moment. "You hid yourself from me. . . ."

Her voice was rich with emotion as she curved her body over his. "I was scared. Confused. I still am. I don't understand how I feel or why. Nothing makes sense except for the fact that I want you, Mikhail. I've never felt anything more true or right in my entire life."

"I've lived for centuries. Fought. Bled. Sought pleasure when I wanted it. Watched the eradication of my people and lay helpless, entombed, unable to do a gods-damned thing about it. I've suffered. But never have I loved. Not until now, not until this moment, have I known what it is to truly love something." He covered the curve of her stomach with his palm. "I love this child. I love *you*."

Claire slid from his grasp, her soft skin brushing against him as she padded past him into the tiny living room. His gaze followed her, like a magnet pulling metal, as he admired her narrow waist that flared out at her hips and rounded the perfect globes of her ass. "You can't be in love with someone that you don't even know. You think it's love, but it's just the tether that makes you feel that way."

Each syllable spoken was laced with a soft sadness that sliced through Mikhail's heart, leaving nothing but bloodied tatters behind. He turned toward her and rose from his knees. "Have you ever loved, Claire?"

The delicate features of her face hardened to stone. "No."

"Then how do you know I can't love you and that you in turn can't love me?"

Mikhail took in the sight of her, skin still flushed, her right breast and throat still showing signs of the marks he'd given her. She was sex personified. Glorious, sensual, and unashamed. The pregnancy had given her a roundness that she hadn't possessed before. A softness that he yearned to stretch his naked body along.

She turned her back to him. He crossed the room to where she stood and molded his body to hers, cradling his still-stiff cock into the crease of her ass. At his gentle thrust she let out a shuddering sigh, and he reached around to take the weight of her breasts in his palms.

"You are made for me," he whispered against her ear. "The gods have laid out our path and we have no choice but to follow it. How could I not love you? We are two halves of a whole. Now joined, we will never be parted."

"I don't understand any of it."

With gentle strokes, Mikhail caressed the tight points of her nipples, plucking at them before working his way back over the puckered dusky pink flesh to the creamy porcelain swell that filled his palms. Claire let her head fall back on his shoulder as her eyelids drifted shut, the dark lashes fluttering against her cheeks.

"I wish I could make you understand how important you are, Claire." He ventured downward, one palm sliding between her breasts, over the flat of her stomach and the slight swell of her lower abdomen. He slipped his fingers between her thighs and her swollen lips. A low whimper made its way to his ears, and Mikhail's sac tightened at the sweet sound. "Your blood called to me. A siren song I was helpless to resist. And when I first took your vein that night, you awakened the seat of my power, strengthened me so that I might strengthen the whole of my people and replenish my race."

He circled her clit and Claire's legs gave out. With his free hand he encircled her waist, holding her against him.

"You are a Vessel, Claire. Unique. You can bear the weight of the Collective. Your blood is the only thing I need to sustain me. To sustain us all. You're meant to be the mother of the vampire race. They can feel you. They know your strength, and even from great distances they can feed upon your life force."

She rolled her head against his shoulder and a sheet of her silken hair cascaded over his arm. "Who?"

"The dhampirs," he murmured against her ear. "Concentrate, Claire. Can you feel their pull?"

Claire shuddered in his embrace. His long fingers stroked her with artful precision while his voice, dark and decadent, served only to seduce her further. As if she could ever deny him anything.

"Concentrate, Claire. Can you feel their pull?"

The days of exhaustion. Constant, gnawing hunger that she'd been too nauseous to satisfy. Falling into bed fully clothed, only to pass into a deep, dreamless sleep until she had no choice but to drag herself out of bed for her shift at the diner. All this time she'd thought it had been the pregnancy. The baby taking what he needed from her.

"I feel it," she whispered. "They're taking more than I have to give."

"They need you." Mikhail slipped one finger and then another into her pussy and Claire cried out. "*I* need you. Your blood will save us all."

Claire came in a violent spasm that rocked her from the tip of her head and rippled to the base of her toes. "Oh, god, Mikhail!"

"You might not think that I can love you, but I'm going to prove you wrong, Claire. And you're going to love me, too."

He sealed his mouth over her throat and bit down. Another orgasm came immediately on the heels of the first and Claire bucked in his grasp, holding on to him as though her life depended on it. Wave after wave of pleasure crested over her as he fed from her vein, and Mikhail brought her down slowly, each pull of his mouth thrumming through her while he stroked her with soft, languid passes of his fingers.

Years sped by in the span of seconds and Claire remained still in his embrace until he'd had his fill. The heat of his tongue soothed his bite and his lips brushed the sensitive skin at her jawline, under her ear, and at the hairline at her temple. "You will love me, Claire. I promise you that."

She couldn't help but think that with his many gifts— supernatural speed, good looks, and the ability to bend others to his will—Mikhail Aristov would've made one hell of a hustler.

Claire stuffed the rest of her clothes into a duffel bag and took a last look around her bedroom. Her next-door neighbor was throwing another rager that was just a notch below blow-your-eardrums-out loud. She definitely wouldn't miss having to put up with that bullshit.

Sunrise was only a few hours off, and Mikhail was pacing the confines of the apartment like a caged beast. The thought of returning home with him was bittersweet and filled her with a crippling guilt. There was a name for that feeling. Survivor's remorse?

How could she possibly run away with Mikhail to live in his castle and leave Vanessa behind to fend for herself? Who would make sure there was food in the fridge and that she had everything she needed for school? Leaving like this, just packing a bag and walking out on the life Claire'd carved out for herself, made her feel like a total asshole. She didn't have any obligations to Vanessa. She wasn't Claire's daughter. But didn't the kid deserve an explanation and a proper good-bye?

Claire deposited her bag on the couch and crossed the room to where Mikhail continued to pace, a dagger clutched tight in his right hand. His brow furrowed as he searched her face. "What's wrong?"

The fact that he could sense her emotions was going to take some getting used to. Claire offered him a reassuring smile and let out a measured breath. "I need to go say good-bye to Vanessa before I go." Unless Carlene was having a bad night, as Vanessa called them, she'd more than likely be asleep. Still, Claire couldn't disappear without a word. Even if she had to wake the kiddo up, she was going to give Vanessa a proper good-bye.

"All right, love." Mikhail spun the dagger in his large hand, a blur of motion that ended in a flash of steel. "We'll go together."

Overprotective with a violent streak. Her first impression of Mikhail had been spot-on. "I don't think I need an armed guard to go across the hall with me. Do you?"

His tone brooked no argument. "Yes."

"All right. Fine. Has anyone ever told you that you're very pushy?"

Mikhail flashed a confident smile that showcased the wicked points of his fangs. Dear god, he was magnificent. He sheathed the dagger and took her hand just as his cell rang. With a grunt of annoyance he dug the phone from his pocket and answered. "What is it, Jenner?"

Mikhail's eyes widened a fraction, enough to tell Claire that whatever was going on, it wasn't good. She released his hand and he plunged his fingers through the length of his hair and let out a frustrated breath. "I should have known better than to unshackle him. Do you know where he's gone?" A pause followed and Mikhail's eyes flashed silver. "To Siobhan no doubt."

Whoever was gone, from the sound of Mikhail's tone he was in big trouble. The conversation continued on and

Claire had a feeling that this was going to take a while. Her vampire paced the confines of her apartment, his conversation fading to the back of Claire's mind. The sun was about to rise and he'd drag her out of there before she had a chance to talk to Vanessa.

She left his conversation undisturbed and snuck out the door and went across the hall. Her stomach clenched and her vision blurred from a rush of adrenaline as she took in the sight of the girl's apartment door hanging open, the jamb splintered.

"Vanessa?" Claire's voice broke on the word, her lungs burning with the need to take a breath. The sparse apartment had been completely destroyed: furniture upturned, cupboards ransacked, and drawers emptied and discarded.

A low moan caught her attention and Claire's heart beat a frantic rhythm against her rib cage as she rushed down the narrow hallway. Carlene lay facedown on the carpet, her body halfway out of the bedroom. Blood soaked into the cheap carpeting, a deep crimson stain that caused Claire's stomach to heave.

She dropped to her knees beside Vanessa's mother. She was breathing, but just barely. Blood oozed from a wide gash in her head.

Claire rushed for the kitchen and grabbed the phone. Her fingers shaking, she dialed 9-1-1. The dispatcher answered, "Los Angeles County Dispatch—"

The phone dropped from Claire's grip as a hand came around her mouth. She was hauled against the solid form of a body, every inch a wall of unyielding muscle and strength. Shock punched through her chest and she fought against the iron hold. She should have expected this. Should have been prepared! *Cowardly bastards!*

How long had the slayers been watching her? Waiting for the opportunity to lure her from Mikhail's protection rather than fight the vampire here? They would set a another trap, lure *him* in. And they'd baited Claire with Vanessa as surely as they'd bait Mikhail with her.

From the corner of her eye Claire caught sight of Vanessa being hauled out the door by a monster of a man. Helpless, her eyes wide and fearful, she struggled against her captor. Claire fought for all she was worth, kicking and swinging her arms. She sank her teeth into the hand covering her mouth, a grim sense of satisfaction spurring her on as she broke the skin and tasted blood. The slayer cursed, pulling his hand away with a hiss of breath.

She opened her mouth to scream for Mikhail, but the slayer's hand came back to Claire's mouth, this time covering her face with a rag that smelled sickly sweet and sucked the air from her lungs. Her head swam and her vision blurred. And though she tried to fight, her limbs became heavy and her arms hung limp. They were going to take her, take Vanessa, and there wasn't a goddamned thing she could do to stop it.

She tried to form the words as darkness descended, but she couldn't get her lips to move. Her mind screamed his name; her soul reached out for his. *Mikhail!* But he couldn't hear her. Couldn't do a damned thing to help her.

It was already too late.

Gods, how could Claire live in this place? From the sound of it, there was a rave going in full force in the apartment next door. The sound of the music, coupled with myriad voices penetrating the walls, made it difficult to focus on his conversation with Jenner. Or anything else.

"He seemed like he had his shit straight when he left, but who knows." That Ronan would leave the house wasn't surprising. Vampires fresh from their transition were restless and hard to control. Once Mikhail got Claire home and behind the safety of his walls he'd deal with Ronan's disappearance. Until then, the male was on his own.

"Don't go out looking for him. I need you at the house."
The slayers had become more brazen in their attacks, their
numbers increasing. "I'm bringing Claire back with me
and I want the property well protected."

The air left Mikhail's lungs in a forceful rush. He
crashed to his knees, his vision blurring at the periphery.
Raw panic seeped into his bloodstream, contracting his
chest to the point of pain, and the room swam in and out
of focus as he tried to gain his bearings.

Claire.

The phone fell from his grasp, crashing to the floor as
he pulled the dagger from its sheath, his pace steady and
slow as he fought against every instinct to rush into the
hallway. Both the doors to the child's apartment and
Claire's were wide-open. *Damn it,* she'd gone to see the
girl without him. Through the raucous music and chatter
next door the only sound to reach Mikhail's ears was that
of ragged, wet breaths that chilled the blood in his veins.

Inside the apartment, a woman lay unconscious on the
floor. A large gash in her skull oozed blood and her breathing was shallow. Furniture had been overturned and broken in the struggle, and Mikhail cursed the chaotic noise
and Jenner's phone call that had distracted him. He bent
over the woman, scored his thumb, and pressed it to the
wound. A small kindness but all he could do. "Claire?"
His vision refused to focus as he searched the cramped
space. "Claire?" His illogical mind refused to acknowledge
what he already knew. "Claire?" His voice ripped from
his throat in a ragged shout.

Taken.

A roar of unfettered rage shook the walls of the apartment. Mikhail's fingers curled around the dagger's hilt
until the guard bit into his flesh, drawing blood. Despair
welled within him, threatening to bring him to his knees.
Mere feet had separated them and the slayers had taken her

right from under his nose. They'd used the child, knowing of Claire's affection for her, staging the perfect ambush. Had they been aware of Mikhail's presence in the building? Or was it just cruel chance that he'd been close enough to keep Claire safe and yet she'd fallen into their hands with ease? His soul cried out for hers, the loss almost too much to bear. It would be a race against the sunrise if he had any hopes of finding her, and even then—

He'd had her blood, and she'd taken his.

Relief washed over him as his panic began to ebb. He could track her. Find her with ease. Mikhail sheathed his dagger and rushed from the apartment. He retrieved his phone and just as quickly fled from the apartment building, nothing more than another fleeting shadow in the darkened cityscape.

He would find his mate. And he would kill every last soul who had a hand in her kidnapping.

CHAPTER
25

Ronan'd been given no opportunity to say good-bye to the sun.

Though he had wanted this, yearned for the transition for as long as he could remember, it still stung that Mikhail had given him no choice in how and when it would be done. However, his choice in the matter was a small price to pay for the power that swirled within him.

His first order of business, post-transition, had been to feed. And Ronan had glutted himself on blood. The dhampir female had been a willing participant, giving him as much as she could before she'd become too weak to further nourish him. While Jenner tended to her well-being, another hunger had grown inside of Ronan. One that had him climbing the fucking walls with unparalleled need. And he knew exactly where he could go to get the necessary satisfaction.

He entered Siobhan's stronghold, unconcerned with the looks he received from the dhampirs lining the corridors of the ramshackle building. One of them no longer, he saw them through new eyes, ones that could discern even the slightest weakness. And in a beat he was able to calculate how to exploit those weaknesses. Knew what course of action to take should the situation escalate to violence. It was no wonder Mikhail had been such a famed warrior. But it also prompted Ronan to wonder just how formidable the Sortiari slayers were to have managed to nearly exterminate the entire race of vampires.

Because right now he felt like a fucking *god*.

"You have to be announced," a frantic female said as Ronan approached Siobhan's private rooms. "My mistress is otherwise engaged at the moment."

"Well, that's too damned bad, isn't it?" Ronan flashed Siobhan's attendant a wicked grin and her eyes grew wide as she backed away. His tongue flicked out at the tip of one of his elongated fangs. Already he couldn't wait to sink them into Siobhan's creamy porcelain flesh.

He burst through the doors to find her spread out on top of her bed, wrists and ankles bound to the headboard and footboard as two males attended her. From the looks of it they'd barely started, and he was about to send them both packing. If he didn't bury his cock inside of her soon, he'd go out of his fucking mind. The transition had brought with it such intense sensations and urges that Ronan was finding it difficult to cope. "Get out," he growled at the surprised dhampirs. "Before I throw you out."

They deferred to their would-be queen, who gave a slight nod of her head. The males walked past Ronan with scowls on their faces and he took in the sight of their naked bodies, cocks upright and straining with the need for release. He almost felt sorry for them. And also aroused. He'd refused Siobhan's offer to bring another male into their trysts, but Ronan was so wound up that the idea of a full-on orgy made his own cock hard as fucking marble inside of his jeans.

He'd have to fuck her until sunrise before he felt any relief.

From across the room Siobhan studied him, her emerald gaze keen and sparkling with desire. Her thighs and swollen lips glistened with her arousal and the scent caused a low growl to build in Ronan's chest. Always the dominant one, he'd never seen Siobhan in such a submissive position, her legs spread wide and bound to the footboard at the ankles. Her wrists were bound as well, held taut to either side of her. She arched her back and her breasts rolled with the motion as though begging for his touch.

"What makes you think you can walk in here unbidden?" Her tone hinted at rebuke, but her expression begged for him to come closer. "You should be punished for your arrogance."

Ronan smirked as he approached the bed. Her scent bloomed around him, settling on the air in a heavy haze that damn near drove him mad with desire. "I don't think you're in any position to punish anyone, Siobhan." He reached out to test the steadfastness of her bonds and her hips rolled up, exposing the petal pink flesh of her sex. Ronan's gut clenched and he stripped bare, tossing his clothes behind him in a flurry of motion.

"What's he done to you?" Siobhan's scent changed. Her anxiety spiked with a tangy citrus edge. "He's turned you?" Angry silver flashed in her eyes. "That bastard made you one of the *soulless*."

Ronan flashed his dual sets of fangs and another burst of citrus hit his nostrils. He liked to see her squirm for a change. The female who'd been ballsy enough to extort his body as payment for a simple book struggling against her bonds. "Are you afraid?" The predator in him surged to the surface, exulting in her fear. But the male in him couldn't wait to take her, to fuck her so deep and so hard that she'd be too exhausted to worry about what he'd become or how.

"Of course not." Her tiny fang nicked her full bottom lip, where a drop of blood welled. A strategic move if ever he'd seen one. "I'm disgusted. Not to mention disappointed."

Ronan scoffed at her scandalized tone as he stalked to the bed. She tilted her head up defiantly, her pouty bottom lip begging to be sucked. Ronan braced one arm on either side of her head and bent down. With a slow flick, he caught the ruby droplet on his tongue. Siobhan's breath came in shallow pants and her heart beat a mad rhythm in her chest, music to Ronan's ears.

He reached down between her thighs and caught her pussy in his palm as he slathered her mound and thighs with her own wetness. "Are you ready to be fucked without mercy, female?"

Siobhan arched her back and drew her arms and legs in tight, breaking her bonds with snaps of the nylon. The cords dangled from her wrists and ankles, the sight almost as arousing as that of her trussed up to the bed. She launched herself at him, wrapping one of the cords around his throat. In a graceful maneuver she settled on his back, her legs wrapped around his waist as she tightened the cord.

"You've betrayed me, Ronan." She choked up tighter, but he didn't need to breathe anymore. "You pledged your body to *me*. You are *mine*. And I did not give you leave to allow Mikhail Aristov to turn you."

Ronan tossed her from his back as one brushed off an inconsequential fly. She landed on the bed with a bounce and he took a moment to enjoy the view before he joined her on the mattress and pinned her down. Emerald fire lit her eyes as a corner of her mouth hinted at a smirk. She might have pretended as though his transformation disgusted her, but the scent of her renewed arousal told another story.

He lowered his mouth to hers and Siobhan snapped her jaw at him. Her defiance only made him want her more, and he risked the nip of her tiny fangs, pressing his parted lips to hers. She bit down and the sweet tang of blood ignited his lust for both her body and her vein. He had to be careful, though. His thirst was still unmanageable, and the slightest slip would see her body drained. Likewise, if he fed her from his vein she'd turn, and he doubted that either Siobhan or Mikhail would be too happy about it.

She bit again, this time tearing the delicate flesh of his lower lip. His tongue flicked out at the wound and it healed instantly. Pulling away, he locked his gaze with hers. "You're full of fire tonight."

"I'm full of rage," she seethed. "And that bastard Mikhail is going to pay for what he's done to you." Ronan guided the weight of his cock to her slick entrance and slid home. Siobhan cried out as she thrust her hips up to meet him. "I'm going to punish you for what you've done. You'll beg me for mercy by the time I'm through."

He dragged his fangs up the slim column of her throat and Siobhan shuddered. "Punish me?" He pulled out to the hood of his cock and plunged in again, deep and hard. Her legs came around to encircle his waist, her heels digging into his ass. He rocked his hips, stroking along the tight channel of her sex, and she let out a low moan. "Maybe I'll let you try. Just to show you what you're up against now."

"Harder," she commanded.

He pulled out and entered her with slow, shallow thrusts instead. She gritted her teeth, a growl of frustration vibrating in her throat. "I'm going to give you to my attendants as a plaything." She ground her hips into his in an effort to deepen his penetration, but he held her down on the mattress. "I'm going to let them use you. Bind you and fuck *you* without mercy. They'll show you such pleasure that you'll hate yourself, begging for more while you kneel at my feet in thanks."

He let out a low chuckle. "It'll be you that's begging before I'm done with you, Siobhan."

His bloodlust mounted as his gaze fixed on the pulsing vein at her throat. He wound his fist into the length of her raven hair and forced her head to the side, giving him unhindered access to her vein. With a roar he sank his fangs deep into her throat, and as he did her pussy clenched around his cock. "You're a bastard, Ronan!" she called out as she came. Her body twitched with each deep pulse, and as Ronan fed his own release came crashing over him in a violent wave. Siobhan clutched on to him, her long nails drawing blood as they dug into his back. "And if you think I'll ever release you of your troth because you've been turned, you're nothing more than a fool."

"Claire, wake up, please! You have to stay awake!"

She was slipping. Whatever those bastards had drugged her with was taking her down for the count. Weak, barely holding on to consciousness, she lay on a hard, cold surface, her wrists and ankles bound. She fought against the restraints, yanking as she tried to reach the cords with her mouth. A frustrated groan worked its way up her throat as another wave of bone-deep exhaustion seized her. If she was going to be of any use at all to Vanessa, she needed to shake off whatever fog still clung to her brain and get it together. God, she needed Mikhail. There was no way she'd get out of this mess without him. Claire had no idea how the tether between them worked, but she had to at least try to reach out to him.

Vanessa wept silently and it enraged Claire to think that someone so young had to endure so much. She'd taken care of herself for so long, and now she was little more than a captive, caught up in something she had no knowledge or control over. And Carlene. Was she even still alive? If the slayers had managed to kill her mother, Vanessa would be even more on her own now than she had been.

What would happen to her if they made it out of this?

Who would take care of Vanessa? The thought of her being thrown into the foster-care system made Claire sick. *Concentrate, damn it. Focus on what you can affect right now and don't worry about the future.* Odds were, her worry for Vanessa was pointless. If the slayers had it their way, Claire and Vanessa would both be dead before sunrise anyway.

Claire focused on her surroundings. The basement was large, with too many dark corners. A single light illuminated the space, casting shadows that seemed to shift and re-form in a sinister dance. Claire blinked as she tried to banish the fatigue that weighted her lids. One of the shadows grew larger as it drew close. The soft layers of darkness became sharper, denser, and a man emerged. Dark, deadly black eyes and even blacker soul. If Claire had been a more faithful woman, she would have sworn that the devil himself stood beside them.

Vanessa whimpered at the sight of him, a sound that caused a superior smile to spread across the slayer's face. *Sick bastard, getting off on scaring a kid.* Claire tried her best to soothe Vanessa. "It's okay, Vanessa. You're going to be okay, honey."

"Of course," the slayer purred. "I would never murder an innocent child."

Claire glared her hatred at her captor. Several dark forms moved from the shadows to join him. *Jesus.* There was an army's worth of them. Claire swallowed down the fear that choked her. "If that's true, then I want your word," she said through the thickness in her throat. "Don't hurt her."

"And you have it." The slayer's eyes were no longer black but a shade of deep forest green. If she'd passed him on the street Claire might have thought him attractive with his strong jaw, sharp cheekbones, and full lips. He raked his hand through his sandy blond hair, pushing it back from his forehead, and his brows drew sharply down. "I honor

my word, Claire. Besides, she's important. It is Fate's decree that she should live."

Claire cast a furtive glance Vanessa's way. What did
these so-called guardians of Fate know about her? "What
are you going to do with her, then?" She doubted they'd
just let Vanessa go. Not after what she'd been a witness to.

"That's not up to me." The slayer leveled his gaze on
Claire. Not cold or even murderous. But, rather, curious. "I
have to admit, you're not what I expected, Claire."

What in the hell was that supposed to mean?

"Mikhail's coming, you know." A good hustler could
talk her way out of any situation, and Claire was more than
ready to put a healthy dose of fear into her captor. "And he
won't show you an ounce of mercy for what you've done."
She brought her head up from the table she was tied to and
leveled her gaze on the slayer. She kept her tone mild and
sweet. "I won't even flinch when he rips your throat out.
And if you touch one hair on that girl's head, I'm going to
help him make you suffer."

She was answered with cold, emotionless laughter that
chilled the blood in her veins. "It's too bad I have to kill
you." He exchanged a quiet word with one of his comrades
as one by one they filed out of the basement. "I think I
could like you."

"You still could, you know." Claire projected the trustworthy vibe that had helped her to become a master at her
craft. "Why not let us go and leave us alone to make our
own fate?"

His gaze hardened at her words, the forest green of his
eyes going deathly black. "If only." It was obvious that the
slayer didn't harbor the tiniest bit of remorse over his actions. "But even if the gods themselves stood before me
and commanded me to let you go, it wouldn't happen."

"Gregor, what do you want done with the girl?" one of

his cronies interrupted, and the slayer pinned Vanessa with a contemplative stare.

"She's in Fate's hands now." His cryptic response seemed to be adequate enough for the muscle he'd brought along. "Take her upstairs and lock her in one of the rooms." He cast his attention back to Claire. "You see, Claire, I'm not a complete monster."

"Wh-what?" Vanessa finally looked up from her stupor and fixed Claire with wide, panicked eyes. "No! You can't take me! Don't let them take me, Claire!"

Claire's chest ached as her heart seemed to shatter into myriad pieces. She'd tried so hard to help take care of Vanessa. To shelter her. Provide for her when no one else would. And in the long run, none of it meant a goddamned thing.

Before Claire could respond Gregor ripped Vanessa from her spot on the floor. She thrashed and fought against his hold, screaming and kicking as he set her forcefully down on her feet. He brought the barrel of a monster handgun to her face and Vanessa went still. "Fate has decided to spare you, little girl. Don't make me regret saving your life."

Vanessa glared at him, her little lips drawn in a defiant pucker.

"You will go with Alec, and if you make so much as a peep I'll come upstairs and put a bullet in your head."

Gregor spoke to her in a soft, lilting tone that sent a shiver down Claire's spine. Vanessa's eyes slid to the right and Claire nodded her head, giving her permission to agree to the slayer's demand.

"I understand," she replied through a fresh bout of tears.

"Good." He gave her a fatherly peck to the top of her head and Claire's rage boiled anew. How dare that piece of shit treat Vanessa with any sort of kindness after what he'd put her through!

"It's going to be okay, Vanessa!" Claire called out as the girl was handed over to Alec, who cradled her in his arms as he packed her up the narrow staircase. "I promise!"

Gregor followed his friend up the stairs and turned when he reached the top. "Now, you be a good girl and stay put." The bastard had the nerve to snicker. "And try not to wear yourself out." He opened the door, letting in a swath of light. "Enjoy your moment of peace, Claire. It's the last bit of it you're going to get." He closed the door behind him, leaving Claire once again in relative darkness.

"You bastard!"

Her voice echoed off the basement walls and ended with a silent finality that chilled her to her marrow.

With an effort that left her breathless she tried to remember the feeling of all of those dhampirs drawing on her energy, and when she found it, like a reverse vacuum, she tried to take back everything she'd given. A burst of strength and vitality rushed through her, the high so intense she thought she might pass out, but instead she projected that energy at Mikhail, willing him to take every bit of it. The draw left her shaking and panting for breath, her surroundings blurring in and out of focus.

Please, please find us, Mikhail.

CHAPTER
26

Thank gods he'd given Claire his blood.

Relief swamped him, though short-lived. Mikhail went to his knees as he was overtaken with a rush of energy so intense that it robbed him of his senses. He was formless, a soul without a body floating in the dark abyss. Foreboding crested over him as though some unknown force had reached out to him. Imploring.

Claire.

Her pain was his, her fear and panic choking the air from him. The connection that arced between them burned white-hot once again and Mikhail's jaw clamped down, his fangs puncturing his bottom lip. *Pain.* So much pain it made his stomach heave. And he knew that what he felt was a mere shadow of the pain that seized Claire in its grip.

The sun would rise soon enough. He couldn't waste another second. He kept to the back alleys, stealthy, a shadow gliding through darkness. His blood in her veins called to him, guiding him through the city and beyond, the houses growing larger, the landscape more rural. His

gaze narrowed on an inconspicuous ranch-style house
tucked deep in a cul-de-sac. The houses flanking it were
still under construction, with no neighbors to bother with.

Mikhail's hands shook with unrestrained rage as he dug
his phone from his pocket. Unwilling to alert anyone to his
presence, he fired off a quick text message to Jenner with
the address and an order to find Ronan and meet him there
as soon as possible. Without knowing how many slayers
occupied the nearly finished house, it had been best to err
on the side of caution and call for backup. That didn't mean
he was going to sit around and wait for them to show up,
however.

Like a wraith, he slipped through the temporary front
door, nothing more than a sheet of chipboard with a cheap
knob affixed to it. Claire's heart beat wildly in her chest;
the sound carried to his ears through the walls. Panic and
fear soured the air and Mikhail's lip curled. Whoever
deigned to hurt his mate was about to meet a brutal and
bloody end.

A small group of slayers stood on the other side of the
door. An animal scent clung to them, musky and earthy. So
potent that it sickened him. The Collective flooded his
mind, memories of the eradication of his kind drowning
him in anger and sorrow until the present was nothing but
a reflection of his past.

He was stronger than this. Stronger than these memories of vampires long dead. All because of Claire.

Mikhail's warrior's instinct kicked in with a ferocity
that left his enemies laboring to gain the upper hand as he
attacked. Four berserkers against a single vampire. Mikhail
funneled every ounce of his hatred and sorrow into his actions as he kicked, hacked at limbs, and stabbed. He buried his dagger to the hilt in one slayer's chest. He went
down, disabled but not dead. Another fell from his own
folly as he ventured too close to Mikhail's face. He sank

his fangs into the berserker's throat and tore out his jugular with a jerk of his head. Two enemies down. Two to go.

The world careened around him in a riot of color as he spun, parrying a sword thrust with the short dagger as he landed a solid kick to his attacker's gut. With his left hand he snatched a slayer by the shirt collar and flung the slayer on top of the dining-room table. It splintered into myriad bits of wood and laminate. Mikhail brought down his dagger, severing the slayer's head with a single forceful cut.

Another attacked, the whites of his eyes completely swallowed with endless black. The berserker's inner beast had the slayer completely in its grasp and he fought with mindless ferocity, hacking away with a short sword while he tried to corner Mikhail at the far end of the kitchen. Mikhail reached out and grabbed the berserker's head and gave it a hard turn. The bones cracked under the pressure and the slayer slumped to the floor. With the head still intact, the body would soon regenerate, but Mikhail's grab bought him enough breathing room to prepare for the coming onslaught. He followed the sound of Claire's heartbeat, throwing open a door near the kitchen that led to the cold basement below.

"You're certainly a hard male to kill, Aristov."

He stared into the eyes of his worst nightmare. The beast that had haunted even his waking hours for the past two centuries. As though taunting him, the scar on his chest sent a pang of renewed pain through him, so intense he could've sworn it penetrated the muscles of his beating heart.

"I'm going to kill you," he snarled at his most hated enemy. "And it won't be quick."

Another intense pulse of pain consumed Mikhail and his body curled in on itself as he tried to protect himself from an inescapable foe.

"As though Fate would allow that to happen. I'm going

to finish what I started centuries ago," the berserker said with a sinister leer. "And then I'm going to bury you in a hole so deep and so dark, you'll pray for death to release you from the hell I've created for you!"

Obsidian swallowed his irises, as empty and fathomless as his black soul. A slow smirk spread across his face as he knelt beside Claire and took her face roughly in his hand. Her eyes slid to the side, but she didn't make so much as a whimper of sound. Rather, she turned away from Mikhail, squared her face with the slayer's, and spat in his face.

The slayer's humorless laughter filled Mikhail with dread. "Your new female is braver than your last one." The slayer ran his nose along her jaw, into her hair, and inhaled deeply before winding his fist in the length of her hair. With a hard jerk he forced her head back, and Claire gritted her teeth as though trying to keep from crying out. "Her threshold for pain is remarkable. . . ." He twisted his fist tighter and a single tear slid down Claire's cheek. The slayer smirked and before he ran the flat of his tongue across her cheek, he turned to look at Mikhail. "She's pregnant," he said with wonder.

A shot rang out and pain seared through Mikhail's shoulder. Like the burn of sunlight on his skin, it penetrated his veins, blazing a path to his heart. *Pop! Pop! Pop!* Three more shots hit him in quick succession and his back arched as Mikhail fell to his knees. Dear gods, it felt as though the very sun has risen within him and was burning him from the inside out.

Slayers converged, three of the berserkers he'd fought upstairs and two more he hadn't seen upon entering. Mikhail panted through the pain, determined to keep a level head through the sensation that the blood in his veins boiled. Like a whip his arm reached out, snagging one of his attackers by the ankle. Mikhail brought him to the floor and climbed on top of him, burying a dagger to the hilt in the slayer's chest. He refused to go down without a fight.

"No!" Claire screamed as another shot rang out. Mikhail's back bowed and he toppled over the injured berserker to the floor.

Mikhail was injured. Outnumbered. But he fought with deadly determination, hacking, stabbing, and swinging out with his fist. He took a fist to the gut and another to the face. His vision blurred as his blood burned and the slayers converged, too many to fight in his weakened state.

"Mikhail!" Claire cried out, her voice nearly hoarse and rough with emotion. "I'm going to help him kill you!" she screamed at the slayer. "You're going to suffer!"

"She's a warrior, this one," the slayer remarked as Mikhail was hauled up and bound with heavy lengths of silver chains. "It'll almost be a shame to kill her."

A roar of pure anguish tore from his chest, shaking the building on its foundation. Mikhail renewed his efforts, fighting against the blinding pain from the silver that nearly paralyzed him. The circle of berserkers closed ranks, blow after bloody blow landing on his body, his head and limbs. He fought for consciousness, but the darkness pulled him under like a riptide.

Mikhail snapped awake at the sound of a tortured scream that ripped through him body and soul. It weighted down his heart like a stone sinking to the bottom of the ocean and stabbed with serrated edges into his consciousness. How long had he been out? The scent of blood, heady and inviting, filled his nostrils as bloodlust mingled with his confusion. He shook the fog from his mind as he waded through hazy memory to find something solid to grasp on to. A deep ache still throbbed under his skin, the remnants of whatever sorcery those berserker fucks had infused their bullets with.

Another scream pierced the air, echoing in the enclosed space. Mikhail came fully into consciousness as Claire's pain clawed a path through him. *No. No. No. No!* He lurched forward, ready to rush to her aid, but he found his arms bound and suspended high above him. Legs spread wide and secured to the floor with silver cuffs and a heavy length of silver chain. Confusion clouded his thoughts as he fought against his bonds. This was a memory. The ghosts of his past come to haunt him. Present and past clashed before his eyes, Claire's tortured screams bouncing off the stone walls of the accursed tomb the slayer had left him to die in.

Soft, wracking sobs reached his ears and Mikhail gave a violent shake of his head. The walls that closed him in weren't stone but concrete. And though he might have been underground, this was no tomb, but a basement. The events of the past hours trickled into his consciousness and his anger burned fresh, returning his clarity like a breeze banishing autumn leaves.

"You're awake. Good."

Mikhail's head whipped around to the sound of the slayer's voice as a vicious snarl tore from his throat. He pulled on the silver chains, the metal searing as it dug into his flesh. "Still claiming your chains are woven with the hair of archangels, slayer?"

The slayer gave a soft chuff of laughter. "That story doesn't quite pack the same punch as it did a few hundred years ago. Besides, you're arrogant enough to believe that you're above the reproach of a human god."

Now it was Mikhail's turn to laugh. "Aren't you, berserker?"

His gods were just as old as Mikhail's, and none of them had anything to do with a human notion of deity. Their kind had walked the earth for eons, remnants of magic and superstition long gone from the human lexicon.

From the shadows Claire sobbed quietly. Mikhail forced his gaze to remain locked on the slayer. The longer Mikhail kept him engaged, the better. Until he could free himself, he'd offer Claire any sort of respite he could. On the surface, he was calm, nothing like the mindless animal he'd been the last time he'd been trussed up by this particular slayer. But under the surface an inferno of rage blazed within him and he vowed that for every ounce of pain Claire felt the slayer would experience it a hundredfold.

The slayer didn't answer, just fixed Mikhail with his emotionless black stare. The soft soles of his boots were soundless as he crossed the concrete floor. He turned, every line of his face accented with hatred and his lip drawn into a disdainful sneer as he flipped on a light.

Mikhail's gut bottomed out at the sight of Claire, tied to the long table with lengths of rough braided rope, blood coating nearly every inch of exposed skin. Her pants had been stripped from her body, leaving her clothed in little more than her underwear and a strappy shirt that barely covered her torso. Her eyes were squeezed tightly shut, as though blocking out the outside world would somehow free her of her torture. The calm that Mikhail had fought so hard to maintain shattered at the sight of her and the mindless, rabid animal clawed to the surface of his psyche.

"You will suffer the pain of a million deaths!" Mikhail railed. A wordless sound of pure anguish exploded from him as he fought against his bonds. "Your torture will span centuries, slayer!"

"You know *nothing* of suffering," the berserker seethed.

While Mikhail fell victim to his rage, the slayer remained calm. He retrieved a silver dagger from the foot of the table and returned to Claire's side, leaning in close to her ear. His gaze, black and fathomless as his soul, locked on Mikhail, as he spoke to Claire. "Your mate is angry over his helplessness, I think. Though he should be proud of the strength you've exhibited. I'm afraid the mother of the vampire race cannot be suffered to live, however. *I* will not allow it."

He sank the blade into the flesh at Claire's collarbone, tracing a bloody path from the hollow of her throat to her shoulder as he cut. Mikhail thrashed as her back bowed off the table, a scream of pure terror and pain ripping from her and ending on a strangled sob. *"Claire!"* His own voice boomed in the vast basement, pinging off the walls as though down the length of an endless cave. She refused to open her eyes, but he needed her to see him. So she would *know* that he would gladly die before he let her endure any more pain.

The scent of her blood called to him and Mikhail's fangs throbbed in his gums as the bloodlust rooted deeper, his throat aching with a dry fire. Her wounds were extensive. She'd lost pints of blood on the slayer's table and she didn't have much more to give.

"I'm going to feed you to the newly turned, you berserker fuck!" Mikhail shouted. A smile that was pure madness lit the slayer's features as he drove the blade deep into Claire's upper arm. She tried to scream again, but either her voice was gone or her vocal cords were too damaged to produce a sound. The hoarse rasp was worse than any scream, though. It lacked the force of her earlier protests, and Mikhail knew that if he didn't do something Claire would not be long for this world.

He could try to filter what little strength he had back to her, to help her withstand the slayer's torture. But if he did, there would be nothing left for him and escape would be impossible. His captor was right about one thing: Mikhail's helplessness had laid him low.

The slayer wandered down the length of Claire's body, tracing her lacerated flesh with the bloody tip of his dagger. A pained whimper filled Mikhail's ears and Claire's body reacted to the contact with grotesque twitches that turned his gut. The slayer circled Claire's belly with the tip of the blade, an almost gentle, loving gesture. His eyes met Mikhail's and he quirked a brow. "Do you think it's a boy?"

The Sortiari have killed your females, ripped the wombs from their wretched bodies, and burned the abominations growing inside of them in sacred flames.

Words from his past took root in Mikhail's mind and once again in he was in that tomb, centuries ago, with nothing more than the knowledge that his race had been eradicated to keep him company. The tightly reined control he held over his emotions snapped, and with it the length of silver chain that bound his right arm to the crossbeam above him.

His left arm came next, the large metal eyelet pinging on the concrete along with the chain. History would not repeat itself. He refused to relive the loss that had nearly killed him. The Sortiari might have thought themselves the guardians of Fate, but Mikhail was about to show them that he refused to bow to their visions of a future where his kind did not exist.

Where Claire did not exist.

His battle cry shook the walls that surrounded him. The sounds of heavy footsteps on the stairway behind him troubled him very little in his single-minded purpose to free Claire and murder her captor. The slayer abandoned his post, giving Claire the moment of respite Mikhail had prayed for. Though weakened by the silver, he used its weight to his advantage, hauling up the heavy metal chains in his grip and swinging them high above his head. It was an effort of sheer will to bear their weight, but there wasn't a force upon this earth that could prevent Mikhail from protecting his mate or the life of his unborn son.

With a hop backward the slayer barely missed the length

of chain as Mikhail swung it toward the berserker. He tried to keep his focus centered on the impending battle and not on his mate, who'd become still as death on the surface of the table. Their connection arced, though admittedly not blazing in his soul as it once had. Claire's fire was quickly dying, and if he didn't do something soon to save her he had no doubt that he wouldn't survive the loss.

The four remaining berserkers entered the fray. Mikhail let out a guttural shout from the effort, concentrating his force at the males who'd yet to find the strength of their battle rage that would lend them invincibility. He took them out with a wide sweep of the chain, and they fell on top of one another in a heap of tangled limbs. Another managed to duck beneath the chain and Mikhail caught him, wrapping a section around the beast's neck and pulling tight to choke the air from the berserker's lungs. "Are you a coward, slayer?" Mikhail snarled at his ancient enemy. "You'll let your comrades suffer to save your pathetic flesh?"

The slayer drew a second dagger from a sheath at his side. "Hold!" The barked command gained their attention in an instant and the whole of his forces went still. A warning growl, like that of an enraged bear, rumbled in his chest and black swallowed the whites of his eyes. The slayer snarled, revealing his elongated incisors. "I didn't get to kill your bastard of a father," he said with regret. "Or your whore of a mother. You think you're noble, but you're nothing more than shit on my boots!" His accent thickened and spittle flew from the slayer's mouth with each emphatic word. He paused as his attention was drawn to the blood dripping from his dagger. Claire's blood. His next words were low, nearly inaudible, as he raised his eyes to Mikhail: "And I won't suffer a single one of you to live."

CHAPTER
27

Mikhail fought like a male possessed, but he was flagging. The silver had weakened him considerably, and he found its weight harder and harder to lift. His enemy was fast. Strong. Possessed of the strength and infallibility of the berserker. A more vicious creature Mikhail had not met, and by the way his opponent fought it was obvious that the slayer had been—and still was—a formidable warlord worthy of the title.

At the root of it all, his hatred for the Sortiari fueled him forward past the pain and exhaustion. That these supposed guardians of Fate would hide behind their foot soldiers only served to prove that in their hearts they were nothing more than faceless cowards.

The rallying shouts of the slayer's comrades grated on Mikhail's ears. While Claire bled to death on that table the berserkers stood by and watched the spectacle before them, eagerly riveted to the blood sport on display. Raw burns marred his wrists and ankles, sweat trickled down his brow and soaked his shirt through. His pants were tattered and hung from his hips, tripping him up more times than he could count. But Mikhail fought for the life of his mate. The life of his child. For his very future. And he would not stop until one of the berserkers managed to run a stake through his fucking heart.

The slayer's silver blade caught Mikhail in the ribs and he hissed in a sharp breath. He lashed out, striking the bastard in the side of the head, and the slayer reeled backward, blood pouring from the newly made gash. Bloodlust clouded his vision, but he pushed the thirst to the back of his mind. He lashed out again, sweeping the slayer's legs out from underneath him, his skull striking the concrete floor with a satisfying crack.

"Kill the bastard, Gregor!"

The name gave Mikhail pause and his misstep earned him a slash of the blade across his torso. His back bowed with pain and he swung the heavy length of chain at the slayer's face, missing him by mere inches. "Gregor the Black?" Mikhail ventured with another wild swing of the chain as he pushed himself to his feet.

Now it was the slayer's turn to lose a step. His eyes narrowed at Mikhail's words and his lips pulled back in a snarl. The Sortiari had been crafty indeed in enlisting this particular slayer into their service. Centuries of hatred fueled his actions. Revenge was a wound that never healed, and Gregor's had been festering for quite some time.

An eye for an eye. A clan for a clan. "You petty bastard," Mikhail ground out. He stomped down on Gregor's midsection. The slayer caught the chain secured to Mikhail's ankle and yanked, sending him sprawling to the ground. Gregor might have been down but was not bested yet.

Gregor rolled over to his stomach, another misstep. Mikhail threw himself on top of the other male and looped the chain around the slayer's throat. Whether he killed Gregor before his men swooped in to help didn't concern

Mikhail, only that he caused his enemy as much pain as possible in the interim.

Chaos broke out as he squeezed the breath from Gregor's lungs. Mikhail looked up to find Ronan, Jenner, and a small army of dhampirs pouring down the stairs into the bowels of the basement. Mikhail's attention wandered and Gregor seized the opportunity to throw Mikhail from his back. The berserker's strength was massive as he pitched Mikhail high in the air. He flipped, landing on his back with enough force to create a fissure in the concrete floor.

Like the coward he was, Gregor wasted no time in securing his own safety. He ducked and wove through the fighters, heading for the stairs, which he climbed three at a time. At the top of the landing, he paused, his eyes locked with Mikhail's. Gregor's gaze narrowed as he bared his teeth and in the blink of an eye was gone.

Mikhail stomped down on the chain dangling from his right wrist and pulled. His muscles strained, veins rising to the surface of his skin with the effort he exerted, increasing the tension until the links gave way of the wrist cuff. He repeated the actions on his left wrist and each of his feet, panting through the pain as the cuffs bit into his skin, the silver burning and blistering him in the process. When the final link snapped, he cast his bonds aside and rushed to Claire's side.

"Claire. Claire!" Fear congealed in Mikhail's stomach, cold and unyielding. He tore at the rope that tied her down, snapping the bonds as though they were simple strands of thread. "Stay with me. Do you hear me, Claire?" He gave her a shake. "Don't you dare leave me!"

Claire floated in a realm of dark nothingness. Mikhail's voice came to her as though across the width of a canyon, faint and breathy. She didn't want to leave this painless place of cool comfort. Why would he want her to leave? Maybe instead of coaxing her out, he should join her. Wasn't he tired of fighting? She was.

Formless hands hovered over where her womb would be. Where her son floated in the same dark comfort, unaware of what went on in the outside world. He was safe. Protected. If she stayed in this place, no evil could touch him. . . .

A disconcerting thought scratched at the back of Claire's mind. The safety that she'd sought, locked herself away in, wasn't a shelter at all, was it? No. She was *dying*. Sure, the pain was gone. The worry. But no matter how much she wanted to hide from the anguish of Gregor's sick torture, she had to go back. She had to give her baby a chance to live. Hell, she had to give herself a chance! How could she possibly stay in this soft, dark oblivion when her soul was tethered to Mikhail's on the other side?

She couldn't leave that piece of herself behind.

As if she were swimming from the bottom of a deep lake, Claire's lungs burned as she paddled and kicked through the dark abyss toward a muted light far above her. Mikhail's pleading tone grew louder, more urgent, as she made her way closer, but the murky depths didn't glide over her skin like water. It held on like sludge, pulling her down a foot for every two she gained.

The prospect of being thrown unwillingly into this life that seemed so commonplace to Mikhail had spurred her to leave the safety of his protection and it had cost them both dearly. She'd thought she was doing what was best, until she could think things through, decide for herself where she belonged. Now, though, she knew that the only place she'd ever belonged was at his side.

No matter where she lived, no matter the distance between them, his enemies would be waiting to take her. Use her as leverage, destroy her in hopes of securing some crazy preconceived notion of the future. She wouldn't survive Mikhail's world in this state. She wasn't surviving it now. The only way she'd be able to live was to allow him to do what he'd wanted all along.

Only as a vampire would she endure this.

For as long as she could remember, Claire had relied solely on herself. Living with a junkie had a tendency to give a person a pretty jaded outlook on humanity. Trust didn't exist in the world of lies, selfishness, and abuse she'd been brought up in. It was as foreign a concept to her as love itself. But Mikhail made her want to trust. To make a sacrifice for someone else's sake and not because she was simply working an angle. The light above her grew brighter and she put every ounce of energy left in her body into breaching the surface. She couldn't allow Mikhail to continue to insert himself into the path of danger because she was simply human and too weak. If she could just survive this moment, she'd gladly let him turn her. There was no pain on this earth worse than the thought of living without him. Of not being able to see the face of her baby boy staring up at her.

She breached the surface with a gasp, the bright light above her head an exposed lightbulb that glared down on her, swinging to and fro in a lazy circle. "Claire? Claire!" Another shuddering breath filled her lungs as his face came clearer into focus. "Stay with me. Do you hear me, Claire?" He gave her a shake. "Don't you dare leave me!"

"Did you make him suffer?"

Her voice was foreign in her ears, raspy and weak. A sharp pain radiated up the length of her throat and she swallowed at the dryness that coated her tongue, unable to generate the saliva necessary to keep it from sticking to her mouth. As she came more fully into awareness, Claire began to regret trying so hard to leave oblivion.

The pain was paralyzing. Blinding in its intensity. She

wanted to empty her lungs on a violent scream, but she didn't have the energy for even that tiny thing. Burning up and freezing all at once, every nerve ending on her body raw and exposed. That bastard Gregor had cut into her again and again, slicing, stabbing, eliciting scream after tortured scream from her in order to make Mikhail suffer. He'd brought the knife to her belly, traced her womb with the sharp tip—

"The baby!" she rasped. Her arms flailed, as useless as cooked noodles beside her, as she tried to clutch at her abdomen. A sob lodged itself in her throat. "Oh my god!"

"Shhh." Mikhail brushed her hair back from her forehead, the only place on her body that she didn't feel pain. "The baby's fine, Claire. Try not to move."

She took in his expression, doubt and worry marring his handsome face. He'd given her assurance, but he wasn't confident. A tear leaked from the corner of her eye and rolled down her temple. "Vanessa." Worry sliced through Claire like Gregor's blade. "She's here. Locked in a room somewhere. Please, Mikhail, don't let her—"

"Shh. Don't worry, love; we'll find her. And we'll keep her safe."

Relief was a balm on her overheated skin. "I'm going to die, aren't I?"

The words brought Mikhail to his knees beside her. "No." He choked on the word.

She gave him a wan smile. "Liar." Claire tried to lift her arms, move her legs, but they wouldn't budge. "Or maybe not." The smell of blood surrounded her; she was bathed in it, sticky with the evidence of her torture. How was there any left in her body? "Not if you turn me."

CHAPTER
28

It was the only way to save her and they both knew it. Around him, the melee had come to a bloody conclusion, the bodies of Gregor's men the only evidence of a battle that he'd long abandoned to save his own skin. Mikhail was hauled up bodily and he grabbed his assailant by the throat, slamming him against the wall with enough force to put the bastard straight through it.

"It's me!" Though Mikhail had him by the throat, Jenner put his hands up in surrender. It took sheer strength of will to release the other male. Ally or not, Mikhail was still an animal, threatened. His mate was threatened. Dying. And if he didn't act soon, feeding Claire gallons of his blood would do nothing to save her.

Jenner shook out his shoulders as though he too resisted the urge to fight back. In a battle, their animal natures became more prevalent. Instinct overrode common sense, and logical decisions were overlooked in favor of rash violence. His eyes flashed silver and his lip pulled back to reveal his short fangs. But as the battle fog cleared from both of their minds Mikhail steered his focus back to Claire.

"She's dying. I've got to get her out of here." Dead slayers littered the basement floor, a few dhampirs, too. Mikhail couldn't risk staying for another moment, not when Gregor's reinforcements might be on the way.

Jenner's expression was dead serious as he positioned his body between the staircase and Mikhail. "Just say the word and we're outta here."

Claire's lids were hooded, her eyes no longer tracking. A fear so intense gathered inside of Mikhail that it froze him in place. She'd said that he couldn't love her. That they hadn't known each other long enough for him to care about her so deeply. But what Claire hadn't realized was that he'd fallen hopelessly in love with her the first night they'd met, and not because of her blood or the power that her life's essence had given him.

He'd fallen in love with her fire. With the strength he'd seen in her eyes long before anything else. And he was relying on that strength and fire now. "Claire." She moaned at the sound of her name, barely audible to even his ears. "I'm going to move you, love. It's going to be painful, but I need you to stay with me no matter what. Don't retreat into your mind, don't close your eyes or shut me out, do you understand me? I need you to *feel,* Claire. To allow that pain to keep you going."

Her heart slowed to the point that Mikhail could barely discern its beat. Each breath dragged through her lungs was wet and ragged. A sickening gurgle that wracked her chest. She didn't respond; her body had gone deathly still on the table pooled with her blood. He couldn't waste another second and so Mikhail scooped her up in his arms, taking as much care as possible, but it jostled her enough to jolt her into awareness.

"Ahhh!" A tortured rasp tore from her throat and

Mikhail hugged her close. Crimson soaked into his shirt, dripped from her body. Gregor had nearly bled her dry.

"Go!" Mikhail's shout was answered by instant action as Jenner led the way up the stairs. Ronan fell into step behind Mikhail, offering protection from the rear. Despite his newly turned state, Ronan had fought with all of the speed and skill of a vampire of many years. His control was unflappable. The transformation for him had been smooth and flawless, like slipping into a warm pool. Thank the gods for small favors.

Claire cried out as Mikhail took the steps three at a time even though he leaped from one spot to the next with an agility that barely jostled his precious cargo. With her numerous injuries, Claire had sustained just about all her fragile human body and psyche could handle. It pained Mikhail that he would have to put her through more still, but there was no use for it. It was now or never, and instead of easing her pain he was about to add to it a thousandfold.

When they reached the ground-level floor Mikhail came to a skidding stop. Dawn's gray light filtered in from the high windows of the foyer, and his body heated as it sensed the coming of the sun. *Trapped!* Forced to remain in this gods-forsaken place with no chance of escape! This couldn't be. He couldn't allow for Claire to be turned here with their enemies still too close. The transformation would weaken them both, and if the Sortiari sent reinforcements—which Gregor would undoubtedly do—neither of them would survive the day.

"Wait here." Jenner threw open the door and disappeared into the murky morning.

"Claire, are you still with me?"

Blood matted the long strands of her hair, and for the first time Mikhail truly took stock of her injuries. Gregor had disfigured her. Cut into her without mercy. The only thing he'd left untouched was the area of her lower abdomen, and only because the death of Mikhail's child had been meant to be Gregor's crowning achievement. A lump the size of a baseball formed in Mikhail's throat and he tried without success to swallow it down. Emotion prickled behind his eyes, burned in his chest. Constricted everything inside of him until he thought he might implode from the pressure.

Alone. For centuries Mikhail had been hollow. Soulless. A male without family, allegiance, or honor. Isolated. Held apart from those who were his kind because of his own stubborn stupidity. Disconnected from emotion and living in a soulless, apathetic state for so damned long.

Now the floodgates were open. This beautiful, fiery female in his arms had done that. And he was about to fail her.

"Let's go!"

Jenner poked his head through the doorway and Mikhail didn't waste a single moment as he rushed outside. Sunlight be damned, he'd burn himself to a fucking crisp before he'd let Claire die. Parked outside the house was a windowless van with more than enough shelter from the sun and room to lay Claire down inside. *Thank the gods.*

Jenner pulled open the side door and Mikhail climbed in. Sunlight crept over the foothills, the bright yellow rays slicing across his forearm. Blisters boiled on his skin, and he locked his jaw down tight as he fought through the pain. It would heal in time. Right now his sole focus was Claire.

"Get them out of here," Ronan called out to Jenner from the cover of the doorway.

Mikhail looked up as he remembered his promise to his mate. "There's a human girl locked in one of the rooms, Ronan. Find her and protect her. I'll send Jenner back for you."

"Don't worry about me." Ronan's gaze landed on Claire. "Take care of your mate."

Mikhail gave a sharp nod of his head and Ronan turned, a flash of motion as he ran back into the house. Mikhail laid Claire down gently on the floor as Jenner slid the door shut, hopped in the driver's seat, and took off. Her heart had nearly ceased its beating and Mikhail could no longer hear the sound of air in her lungs, nor of blood pumping through her veins. Seconds hung in the balance.

Barely an inch of skin had gone untouched by Gregor's blade. As if the bastard had targeted every vein, giving Mikhail no place from which to drink. Did it matter? She'd left her life's blood on that damned table, the price paid for tethering his soul to hers. Mikhail closed his eyes, blocked out the sounds of the engine, the roadway passing beneath the tires, even the beating of Jenner's heart, as he focused solely on Claire. She had not a drop of blood left to spare.

Mikhail cradled Claire in his arms as he tore into his wrist with his fangs, opening the vein wide. He tipped her head back and her jaw hung slack, but he refused to acknowledge the possibility that it was already too late. The crimson rivulet poured over her teeth and coated her tongue. It pooled in her mouth. She wasn't swallowing and Mikhail was gripped with panic as he paused in feeding her to work her throat with his palm, urging the thick blood to flow down her throat.

Still, quiet seconds passed and Mikhail prayed to any god that might listen that Claire's life—and that of his child—be spared. "Don't leave me, Claire," he whispered close to her ear. "Please don't leave me here alone."

Her body seized. A violent spasm that bowed her back and contorted her limbs. Mikhail was reminded of the memory he'd found in the Collective. Of the human woman's violent reaction to the vampire blood before it killed her. *No. No, no, no!* The word ran a loop in Mikhail's mind, willing Claire to survive. To fight! She was the

Vessel. His *mate*. "You will not die." His declaration came from between his welded teeth, strained with unspent emotion. "I forbid it. Do you understand me?"

A glass-shattering scream tore from Claire's throat, followed by several gasping breaths. Her eyes rolled back in her head, nothing showing but stark white as she thrashed and clawed, the deep cuts that marred her skin further tearing with each violent spasm. He hadn't given her nearly enough of his blood. The wound on his wrist had already healed, but Mikhail opened it fresh. Even deeper this time, damn near exposing the bone. He pressed his bleeding wrist to Claire's mouth and a low moan of relief replaced her agonized scream.

"That's it, love. Drink."

Her arms still hung useless beside her, but Mikhail kept his wrist at her mouth. She swallowed greedily and mewling sounds vibrated along his flesh. Another spasm rocked her and Claire pulled away, tearing at Mikhail's skin with her blunt little teeth. He swayed on his knees, his vision darkening at the periphery. A rough shake of his head managed to clear some of the fog from his brain, but not much. Claire had nearly drained him, taken everything he had to offer. Whether she survived the transition or not was out of his hands.

Mikhail let loose an emotionless laugh when he realized that he had no choice but to leave her survival to Fate.

"Make it stop!"

Claire shot up from the bed, clawing at her throat. As though someone had force-fed her flaming charcoal, the unquenchable burn scalded her from the inside out. Vibrant colors burst in her vision, many of them foreign and nameless. New to her eyes and frightening. Her veins felt as if they were expanding, bulging against her skin until she felt too tight and uncomfortable in her own body. Someone smoothed her hair back from her face and she pulled away. Her sensitivity to even the slightest contact sent her into a state of sensory overload that pushed her composure to the breaking point.

"Don't touch me!"

She scrambled away, eyes squeezed shut, until her back met the headboard. Her mouth was too dry; her ears, too full of sound. And her throat . . . *Jesus fucking Christ!* If someone didn't put out the fire raging in her goddamned throat she was going to go ballistic!

"Claire, try to calm down." The voice was firm yet warm-chocolate smooth, and it caused a ripple of pleasure to vibrate through her that made her moan. "You need to feed."

Feed? Yessss. A primal urge built inside of her. Like the craving for a really good cheeseburger times a trillion. Claire had never known such all-consuming hunger, and she'd gone hungry more than her fair share of times.

A delicious aroma hit her nostrils and Claire's eyes flew open, only to slam back shut at the riotous assault of color. Whatever that smell was, she *wanted it*. Wanted it like her next breath. Wanted to bathe in it, roll around and coat herself in it. She'd go mad without it—

Strong arms encircled her, and Claire relaxed by small degrees. She didn't dare look to see who held her, but his scent captivated her. Male. Though she wasn't sure how she would recognize the fact. And this particular male belonged to *her*. She knew it like she knew her own soul. Felt him burning bright like a beacon inside of her. *Mikhail?* The name rang with familiarity. She knew this faceless man who held her. Cared for him. *But how?*

"Claire, I want you to listen to me. Can you do that?"

Anything. She'd do anything for him if he kept talking to her. His voice was like a caress and she felt it on every inch of her skin. She tried to answer, but her throat was too dry, too consumed by fire, so she gave a curt nod of her head instead.

"Good." *God, his voice.* She pressed her back tighter against his chest, gripped the strong arms that held her. "Dhampir blood won't sustain you and I don't know why. Likewise, my own blood hasn't been enough to sate your thirst. We're going to try something different, but you have to be gentle, Claire. Do you understand what I'm saying to you?"

No. Not even a little bit. The delicious scent distracted her and Claire bit down on her bottom lip, surprised at the sharp sting that penetrated her skin. *What the hell?* Did she chip a tooth in her sleep? A drop of blood welled and she licked it away. *Oh. My. God.* This was what she wanted. But somehow, not. Confusion built until the frustration was almost more painful than the inferno in her throat. She needed to see her surroundings. Look at the man holding her. At least try to make sense of the situation.

She cracked one lid and then the other. Her eyes felt dry in their sockets, scratchy. The overload of her heightened senses threatened to pull her under once again, but Claire locked herself down. A good hustler never lost control. And she'd be damned if she let any situation get away from her.

How could a run-of-the-mill bedroom be so breathtakingly *beautiful*? Claire gasped. Everything was clearer. Sharper. And the colors! As though she were seeing the world for the first time, she wanted to weep in appreciation of it. Long fingers stroked her bare skin and Claire shuddered, momentarily distracted from the sights around her. Need coiled within her, and she let her head fall back on a strong shoulder. Sex became so much more important than the burning in her throat or the hunger that gnawed at her. In fact, she couldn't get naked fast enough—

Low laughter rumbled at her ear and a pair of much larger hands came around hers, stopping her from stripping off her shirt. "Not yet, love. And certainly not with an audience."

Audience? Claire's brow puckered as she looked up into the face of a god. Dark hair that brushed his brows, clear turquoise blue eyes. Cheekbones you could cut a steak with, the sexiest dimple in his chin, and full lips that she couldn't wait to kiss. He smiled, revealing a row of straight white teeth and . . . fangs. Two sets, one longer than the other. The jaw of a predator. Claire reached up slowly, touched her fingertip to her lip and then the tooth she'd thought was broken. It curved into a perfect, razor-sharp point.

"Claire . . . try to stay calm."

She moved before her brain could give the command. The mahogany dresser cracked as she practically flew from the bed straight into it and she leaped away, propelling herself into the far wall. "Holy shit! What in the hell is going on?"

Was that her voice? Claire reached up and palmed her still-burning throat. Her voice was lower. Huskier. With an undertone that vibrated her eardrums on a level that she didn't think she should be able to hear. Not the way she remembered herself sounding. Adrenaline seeped into her bloodstream and she turned to face the man she knew as Mikhail Aristov. Claire's legs gave out as a sharp pain shot through her skull, accompanied by the sound of thousands of whispering voices. With her hands clasped tightly over her ears, her gaze met his. "Mikhail, what's happening to me?"

"The seers have seen it, Alexei, and the council is nervous. It could mean the evolution of a new species. They won't allow it to happen."

Through the vampire's eyes Claire regarded the man

sitting across from him, his fingers laced together on the worn oak table. Alexei scribbled something down on the blank pages of a large leather-bound book. The dark ink shone on the page and he scattered fine sand over the pages to encourage the ink to dry and set. "It's impossible," Alexei said, though he continued to put the other man's word to the record. "A human could never be turned. Without being part of the bloodline, no human could be a part of the Collective. Your seers are wrong."

"The Sortiari are never wrong," the man replied. "This human will be a Vessel, Alexei. A source of great power."

The vampire snorted. "The Sortiari have been keeping company with da Vinci for far too long, speaking of Vessels and untold power. Have you inducted him yet, Iago?"

The man—Iago—graced the vampire with an indulgent smile. "Leonardo's place within the guardians of Fate isn't your concern."

"And yet, here you are. Why tell me at all about this Vessel if the Sortiari won't suffer this so-called prophecy to come to fruition?"

"Out of respect for our friendship," Iago said. "War is coming, Alexei. It could be years or centuries from now. None will be spared."

The vampire leaned back in his chair as he contemplated his friend. "You would destroy us all based on conjecture?"

"I would not," Iago stressed. "But it is not my decision to make. And neither are our prophecies based on conjecture. We are Fate, my friend. There is no escaping what will come to pass."

"Oh no? You came here to warn me in the hopes that we'll hide ourselves away. If I'm not mistaken, aren't you trying to misalign Fate simply by coming here?"

Iago stood from his chair, his expression grave. "Don't

allow my goodwill to go to waste. Heed the warning I've given you."

Alexei didn't respond, simply watched his friend walk away. He dipped his quill in the ink and scribbled a single word on the vellum sheet: "Vessel."

Claire surfaced from the memory on a gasp of breath. Her heart threatened to burst from her chest as the panic of disorientation overtook her. The call of ethereal voices threatened to pull her under once again and she drank in lungsful of breath as she prepared to be submerged yet again, drowned in visions she was helpless to escape.

Mikhail pulled away from the woman in his embrace, his lips stained with her blood. She was lovely. Mocha brown hair that surrounded her naked body in a wild tangle, dark eyes, and creamy skin. She slung one slender arm over his shoulder, tilting her head to the side as his tongue passed over the four puncture marks on her throat. A slow, contented sigh slipped from between her lips.

"What worries you, Mikhail?"

"Our lack of a tether."

She answered with low, lazy laughter. "Do you wish to be tied to another in such a way? To be inextricably bound for the remainder of your existence?"

"I wish to have my soul returned to me," Mikhail replied. He traced an intricate pattern that wound a path from the curve of her hip to the swell of one breast. "I wish to feel whole again. Yes, I want to be bound to another. Do you not wish to be whole, Ilya?"

"Perhaps someday," she said on a wistful sigh. "But for now I am content."

"And if I should find my mate? Or you find yours? What then, Ilya, if one of us should become tethered to another?"

"My soul will be full." She leaned up and put her mouth to his. "But my heart will be broken."

The scent of blood pulled Claire back into the present. Mikhail came into focus looking just as vibrant and youthful as he had in her vision. Beside him, a young woman stood with her arm outstretched, blood trickling from four punctures at her wrist. Clarity returned, along with the burning thirst that scalded a path up Claire's throat. The woman smelled better than a box of hot Krispy Kremes and Claire was absolutely *starving*.

"Claire." Mikhail's warning tone gave her pause. A predatory growl echoed in the bedroom. Hers. "She's delicate. Easy to harm. If you feed from her, you must handle her as though she's a bird newly hatched from the nest."

Claire nodded, unable to speak through the fire in her throat. Voices of the past tugged at her consciousness, urging her to return, but the blood held her rapt.

"Good." Mikhail led the woman to where Claire sat against the far wall. With every step placed, her hunger mounted. *Delicate. Easy to harm.* Claire heeded the warning even though an instinct deep within her urged her to attack. To ravage.

He knelt beside Claire and guided the woman to do the same. Her eyes were glazed over, her pupils nothing more than pinpricks. A dreamy expression painted her sharp features, and as Mikhail guided her wrist to Claire's mouth the woman's arm seemed to float up as though resting on a cloud.

"Drink," he instructed.

Claire locked her gaze with Mikhail's as she took the woman's wrist into her palms. As if the woman were a baby bird, delicate and oh, so breakable, Claire cradled her as she lowered her mouth to the rivulets of blood that trickled from the wounds. Her own tiny fangs punctured the skin and the woman let out a low moan as Claire began to drink.

So *much better than Krispy Kremes.*

She bit down harder and Mikhail's brows drew down sharply. "Treat her with care, love. Or I'll punish you."

It should have scared her, but his dark warning sent a thrill through her center. Desire warred with the thirst that began to slowly abate with each deep pull on the woman's wrist. Her blood was thick and sweet. Extinguished the burn that radiated throughout Claire's body. She was flooded with a burst of energy and power unlike anything she'd ever felt. Strength, vitality, the very essence of life itself, coursed through her veins and Claire sucked harder, desperate for more of the high that dizzied her as the floor seemed to fall out from beneath her.

"That's enough."

Mikhail's command resonated in her mind and she released the woman in an instant.

"Close the wounds, Claire. Don't leave her to bleed out."

Instinct prompted Claire and through the vast memories of vampire-kind she found the instruction that she needed to proceed. She nicked her tongue with the tip of one sharp fang and sealed her mouth over the woman's wrist, closing the wounds with gentle passes of her tongue.

She looked at Mikhail to find him beaming, as though proud that she could properly feed herself. An infant in this new stage of existence, she might as well have used a fork for the first time.

"Very good, love."

Kudos to her! Another surge of power washed over her and Claire teetered into Mikhail's embrace. How she could be so full of energy and so exhausted at the same time was truly a wonder. But holy crap, did she need a nap.

CHAPTER
29

"I told you she'd survive."

Mikhail gave Ronan a sidelong glance. "She hasn't survived anything yet. She's insatiable, Ronan. We still don't know how much it will take to make her bloodlust abate."

"Oh, it'll abate." Ronan chuckled. Mikhail wanted to put a fist to the other male's face for his smug optimism. "It just might take a stadium's worth of humans to see it done."

So far, the attempts to satisfy Claire's bloodlust had ended with less-than-favorable results. Her body had rejected dhampir blood, and the seizures she experienced after her first feeding had been horrible to behold. She'd had no problem feeding from Mikhail, as he was not only her maker but also her mate. He was still too weak from turning her, though, and he'd fed her from his own vein until he had nothing left to give her and barely enough to sustain himself. As they searched for a solution, they came to the conclusion that human blood might nourish her. Claire was human after all. Or at least, she had been. It served to reason that she could feed from humans and get the sustenance she needed. And though this last attempt to feed her had been a success, they still didn't know how much it would take to sustain her. Would he have to employ a houseful of humans in order to keep her bloodlust at bay?

Ronan was sure that Claire would pull through. Mikhail was hopeful. That she'd survived the transition at all was a miracle. And he wasn't interested in testing fate with arrogant overconfidence. There were other differences, too. She didn't possess two sets of fangs like every other vampire he'd ever known but only one set with tiny, sharp points like a dhampir. Her eyes flashed with preternatural power, but rather than silver, Claire's eyes flashed a bright shining gold. And those were just the differences he could see. She seemed to be a species apart from all of them.

Mikhail's worry mounted with each new secret discovered, in every minute that passed. Her strength rivaled even his, and when possessed with thirst she was truly a sight to behold. Wild. Intimidating. With a sharp focus that sent a chill over his skin. The Collective pressed upon her mind, but she seemed to handle the burden well. The simple scent of blood had been enough to free her from its grip.

"You're going to need a good sub-contractor when all of this is said and done."

Mikhail looked around the wrecked bedroom. Broken furniture, five-foot holes in the walls. The floorboards cracked and sinking into the sub-floor. He scrubbed a hand over his face and let out a slow sigh as he set an unconscious Claire back onto the bed. At least there was one similarity between them. Adjusting to vampiric strength was hard enough for dhampirs. He could only imagine how difficult the transition must be for a human.

Too much. It's just too much.

Ronan sat in a crooked wing chair, the leg broken the

first time Claire had regained consciousness. He gave a sad shake of his head and scoffed. "You're so busy worrying about her, you haven't quieted your own mind long enough feel the change."

Mikhail arched a curious brow. "What are you talking about?" Besides the fact that Ronan looked ridiculous lounging in the ruined chair, that expression of superiority was about to snap the meager hold Mikhail had on his temper.

"It won't be long before the majority of dhampir society comes knocking at your door."

"For the love of the gods, Ronan!" Mikhail railed. "Stop being such an asinine tease and spit it out, already!"

Ronan snorted. "Isn't that the pot calling the kettle an ass."

Mikhail leveled his gaze.

"She's like the cold fusion of vampires!" Ronan finally exclaimed, throwing his arms up in frustration. "Jesus, Mikhail, are you seriously going to tell me that you haven't felt it?"

Mikhail went deathly still. He'd been so preoccupied with worry for Claire's well-being that he truly hadn't given any thought to her power once she'd been turned. In fact, he'd shut her out entirely, blocking the bond between them just in case he inadvertently took from her stores or she likewise funneled power to him.

Curiosity won out over anger at Ronan for drawing on Claire's energy so soon after her transition. Slowly, Mikhail lowered the barrier between them, opening himself fully to Claire. Their bond flared like a flash grenade on a darkened battlefield and he swayed on his feet from the impact.

"I told you," Ronan said with a smirk. "Cold. Fusion."

Mikhail had never felt so much concentrated power in all the centuries of his existence. It pulsed around him. Through him. Infusing him with strength and vitality the likes of which ignited his own spark, adding to her fire until they created a supernova. "My gods," he breathed. "It's—"

"Amazing?" Ronan ventured. "Indescribable? Better than an eight ball and a roomful of hookers?"

"It's miraculous." *Unreal. Wondrous.* Mikhail could go on and on.

"I found something in the codex," Ronan said. "A Vessel isn't just a unique human who can sustain the change and the Collective. I'd thought the reference alluded to the burden she'd be able to bear. But it doesn't."

"What does it mean, then?"

"She's a Vessel of *power.* A font that never runs dry. Those Sortiari fools thought that Fate wanted her dead. But I think that Fate sent her here to save us. To save you, Mikhail."

His wonder was quickly replaced by fear. "How can I possibly protect her, Ronan? Like you said, the dhampirs will come to her in droves. The fanatics will worship her like a goddess. Others—like Siobhan—will see her as a threat. And when the Sortiari piece it all together, they'll come after her with a ruthlessness that will make their last attack look like loving attention in comparison."

"Maybe she doesn't need you at all," Ronan suggested. Did the male live his life to deliver thinly veiled insults? "I'll be willing to bet that Claire can take care of herself."

"She's yet to remain conscious for more than fifteen minutes at a time," Mikhail countered. "And she has no recollection of what's happened to her as far as I can tell. I've no doubt that she's capable of taking care of herself. She was capable long before I met her. But how can she fight if she can't even keep her eyes open?"

"The transition has taken a lot out of her," Ronan replied. "And I know from experience that trying to adjust to the Collective is beyond challenging."

Mikhail snorted. *Challenging.* It was a gods-damned curse. "As soon as Claire is stronger, I'll turn Jenner." The male was formidable, honorable, and he'd been instrumental in saving Claire. If Ronan was Mikhail's right hand, then Jenner was certainly the weapon that arm wielded. Three vampire males did not an army make, however. In their history, no single male had ever had to rebuild the race. The bureaucracy of it all made Mikhail's head spin. First, he'd need candidates. Strong in both body and mind. Dhampirs who'd be thoroughly vetted. But he couldn't allow the process to be perceived as elitist. In his youth, each coven was responsible for deciding who would be turned and when. Petitions were made. Answers given by a council. There was so much more to consider. And of course there was: "Siobhan."

"What about her?" Ronan cast a suspicious glance Mikhail's way and pinned him with his stare. "We were talking about Jenner, remember? I think it's you who needs to feed, my friend."

"She wants you." Before he moved forward Mikhail needed to get to the bottom of Ronan's relationship with the female. She was a dangerous variable. One he didn't have time to address at the moment. "Why?"

Ronan's gaze narrowed. "You're a suspicious bastard, you know that?"

The question didn't warrant a response. He simply quirked a curious brow.

"She doesn't want me to fight for her or help to further her cause." Ronan squirmed in his seat and let out an aggrieved sigh. "Siobhan is shrewd. She knows how to get what she wants and isn't above extortion to get it."

"You bargained with her for the codex. What did you give her in return?"

"None of your fucking business, that's what." Ronan's tone darkened and storm clouds gathered in his expression.

"You can rest assured that my arrangement with Siobhan has nothing to do with you or yours. It doesn't compromise my oath of fealty to you."

"But she wants your oath to be hers," Mikhail said. "She told me as much."

"Yeah, well, what Siobhan wants from me and what she gets are two completely different things. She'll have to settle for what I've chosen to offer her. The rest is none of your concern."

Mikhail inclined his head. For what it was worth, he trusted Ronan. Reaching at least a temporary peace with the female was on Mikhail's quickly growing to-do list. But until he was assured that Claire was going to pull through the transition, many items were going to remain uncrossed off.

A vast, intricate web of bright color stretched out before Claire. She turned, only to see more of the interconnecting veins of light. Turned again. And again. She stood at its center, a bright field of gold beneath her feet. Solid. Like a well-tended plot of grass. Beside her, another field shone like a sheet of silver under the sun. The two melted together, stretching out through the veins, weaving and twining to form a perfect blend of the two colors that were so different and yet so alike. Silver and gold. Fire and ice. The sun and a heavy rain.

She traced the patterns with her gaze, marveling at them, form without end. Each vein connected to another, and another and another. And like all rivers flow to the sea, each tributary of the pattern ended at her feet.

For the first time in days, Claire's mind was clear. As her lids cracked, the image of the web vanished from her mind's eye. Though she couldn't see it, she felt it. In every fiber of her being, it pulsed around her. A living, breathing thing.

Mikhail's bedroom was dark, the heavy shutters pulled down over the windows. It was midday. The sun had reached its zenith and would soon begin its descent to make way for night. She didn't have to see the sun to know where it was. Her awareness of it was keen, prickling across her flesh. And yet she didn't fear its presence.

Her mind had never been so clear. So in tune with her body and soul. Details of memory began to unfurl in her mind starting from the moment Gregor had strapped her down to that damned table and ending now. Everything before that was still a blur, the memories just past her grasp. At the forefront of her thoughts was a truth that distracted her from what she couldn't yet remember. *Holy crap!* Mikhail had actually turned her.

She slid from beneath the covers, mindful of every motion. The room was in shambles, holes in the walls, furniture overturned and smashed. From the looks of it, she'd thrown one hell of a rager. No doubt she'd racked up the sort of repair bill that would make a rock star proud. Mikhail was probably pissed.

An unquenchable thirst burned at the back of her throat, but Claire no longer felt as though it mastered her. Instead, it was more like being really, really thirsty after running a marathon. You wanted to guzzle a gallon of water more than you wanted your next breath and all anyone would give you was one of those kiddie-sized paper Solo cups. Sure, it was frustrating. But it wasn't going to kill you.

In the corner of the room, in a broken wing chair, her vampire slept.

Her vision no longer hindered by the dark, Claire's gaze caressed the line of his jaw, the curve of his mouth, and lower, past the sexy dimple in his chin—the one she wanted to lick—to the column of his throat. She closed her eyes and listened to the slow, erratic beat of his heart, and behind her closed lids the web of gold and silver reappeared, and next to her the field of silver grew bright and dim in time with his heartbeat. Those lights that wove into the web were dimmer than the gold ones now. They sparked and sputtered, like a candle about to blow out.

That light was Mikhail. Beside the silver veins, the gold still burned brightly, pulsing with vitality. That light belonged to Claire. It surged through her veins in a delicious warm rush that relaxed her from head to toe. She had strength enough for all of them. Why hadn't Mikhail allowed her power to nourish him?

Awareness scratched at the back of her senses and Claire opened her eyes to find Mikhail's clear blue eyes fixed as he quietly studied her.

"You shouldn't be awake." Her husky, teasing tone was answered with a heady bloom of musky scent that stirred her body.

"Neither should you." His gaze burned, turquoise flames tipped with silver as he dragged his eyes down the length of her body. "Nor so lucid."

His voice shivered over her skin and a deep, throbbing ache settled between Claire's thighs. Her need for Mikhail's body far outweighed her need for blood. For anything, really. Just a look, the sound of his voice drove her far beyond reason. Like the first night they'd met, she found his pull irresistible. She would do anything for this man. *Anything.* All he had to do was ask.

"Your desire is the sweetest perfume." His voice was strained, the words choked out as his fingers curled tightly around the armrests. Claire watched with fascination as the cords of veins stood out on his forearms. God, to have him grip her so tightly . . . his hand wrapped possessively around her thighs. "Claire." She snapped to attention, her eyes going back to his like the recoil of a rubber band. "I'm holding on to my control by the barest of threads. And you should feed before I become too distracted to care."

She could sate her thirst later. It was her need for his body that required attention right now. A low purr vibrated in her chest and Mikhail's eyes widened a fraction of an inch. His fingers curled tighter into the armrests and Claire glanced down, a satisfied smirk pulling at her lips as she noticed the erection straining against the fly of his neatly pressed slacks.

A sly smile curved her lips and one sharp fang nicked her bottom lip. Mikhail's gaze wandered, locked where the blood began to well and Claire's tongue flicked out slowly to lick it from her skin. As she took the crimson droplet into her mouth Mikhail's scent grew stronger. A rich, intoxicating mixture of cinnamon and dark chocolate with the undertones of a cool spring rain. He craved her body as badly as he needed her blood. Her senses were so attuned to him now that she knew what he wanted without him having to say a single word and she was quickly becoming drunk on the sense of power and control that she felt.

Her shirt was torn and stained with her own blood. It was anyone's guess where her jeans had gotten off to. Clad in nothing but her underwear and shirt, she let her fingertips wander. Up her bare thighs, under the hem of her shirt, to the unmarred skin of her abdomen. Gregor had cut into her. Again and again. Opening veins and slicing through muscle as he used her pain to unravel Mikhail. Gregor had tried to take their son from them and Mikhail had broken loose of his bonds and protected them both. And thanks to her transformation, not even a single scar remained to betray her torture.

Bits of crusted blood still clung to her skin and Claire stripped off her shirt, unhooked her bra, and let them both fall to the floor before pushing her underwear down over her hips. Mikhail was rapt, his chest heaving with each breath as he took in the sight of her. Claire turned with a secretive smile and headed for the bathroom without uttering a single word.

Her stomach twisted into an anxious knot, the feeling of being pursued triggering something primal within her. Her footfalls were almost silent, whispering over the tile as she made her way to the enormous glass-enclosed shower.

Mikhail was right behind her. Closing in like a wolf on the hunt.

Excitement coursed through Claire's veins, the effects so powerful that she swayed on her feet. Her human emotions, feelings, sensations, seemed so gray and pale in comparison to this new existence. The intensity of it all stole her breath and sent her heart beating madly in her chest.

She opened the glass door and turned the knob on the shower while she waited for the water to warm. Showerheads covered the ceiling and two of the walls, creating a constant cascade of water that was sure to feel like heaven on her bare skin.

Strong arms encircled her and Mikhail cupped her breasts in his palms. He feathered his thumbs over her already erect nipples and Claire gasped, arching her back as he pinched lightly and then just hard enough to cause a rush of wetness to spread between her naked thighs. Steam billowed inside of the enclosed glass and Mikhail reached out to open the door.

The kiss of microscopic water droplets on her skin, like thousands of tiny caresses on her hypersensitive flesh, caused Claire to shudder. She let out a slow sigh that ended on a husky moan.

"Everything is more intense." She shivered at Mikhail's heated words in her ear. His bottom lip brushed her earlobe and a satisfied purr rumbled in Claire's throat. "I could make you come by doing nothing more than blowing lightly on your clit."

Holy hell. If he kept up with the dirty talk, it was going to take a hell of a lot less than a breath to make her come. The bond between them flared, opening a direct line between her emotions and his. "I can feel you," she gasped. Her fangs throbbed in her gums as the line between her needs for sex and blood blurred and became one and the same.

"Feeding and sex are closely tied," he said as though he knew her thoughts. "Which is why there is nothing better than having my fangs deep in your throat while I fuck you."

"Yes." Claire let out a breath on the word. She wanted to bite. To suck. To drink her fill, and even then she knew it wouldn't be enough.

"Bloodlust," Mikhail murmured against her temple. He urged her inside the shower and she took a step under the multiple jets, letting out an audible sigh as the myriad drops rained down on her skin. He stepped in behind her, the hard length of his erection sliding through the crease of her ass. "If you wait too long to feed, you'll succumb to the madness."

How could something so distressing sound so god-damned sexy? She wanted to lose it, to give herself over to base desires. To surrender completely, until there was nothing left of her but mindless need and want. Abandon herself to instinct. Only then would she truly connect to the animal side of her nature that Mikhail had brought to life.

"Careful, Claire." Mikhail threaded his fingers through her hair, wetting it under the spray. "I can feel you slipping away. You must always remain in control. No matter how badly you want to surrender."

His dark, seductive voice anchored her to the present. Kept her head as level as it was going to get. She tried to turn and face him, but Mikhail forced her shoulders back around and gave a shallow thrust of his hips, sliding his cock between her thighs and through her wet, swollen lips. "Gods, how I've missed you," he said against her throat. "Needed you. I worried . . ." He paused, his mouth hovering over her jugular. "That you wouldn't survive."

She rolled her hips, urging his cock to slip through her slick, sensitive flesh. "It's going to take a hell of a lot more than a few supernatural assassins to keep me from you, Mikhail."

CHAPTER
30

Mikhail wanted to roar his satisfaction. It appeared that all of his worry was for naught. Claire had handled the transition remarkably well, showing the kind of restraint most new vampires didn't master for weeks afterward. The Collective seemed to no longer press at the forefront of her mind, and though he could sense the bloodlust that crept upon her, she wasn't lost to it.

Her control amazed him.

Unfortunately, his was hanging on by the barest of threads. The need to take her vein overwhelmed him. Her scent, enhanced by the heat of the shower, intensified his need and he couldn't wait to taste the sweet nectar of her blood as it flowed over his tongue. The human's blood had sustained her. Had satisfied a thirst that Mikhail had thought unquenchable. What should have weakened her only made her stronger. A miracle if ever he'd seen one. Mikhail had fed from humans for centuries and it had nearly killed him. Claire suffered no such restriction. She was an anomaly. A species unique to herself.

Extraordinary.

He sealed his mouth over the vein on her throat, sucking gently to coax it to the surface of her skin. She let out a soft moan before turning abruptly. Her speed rivaled his own as she gripped his biceps and forced him against the cool marble wall. *Gods, such a female!* She heated what blood was left in his body to the boiling point.

"Not so fast, vampire." Her voice was a seductive purr that sparked every nerve ending of his body into awareness. Gold eyes sparked with mischief and his already-rigid cock hardened further. Claire drew her bottom lip between her teeth, giving him an unhindered view of her petite fangs. Gods, the sight of her . . . water sluicing off of her pert breasts, the slight roundness of her abdomen, and the flair of her hips that curved into thighs he wanted wrapped tightly around his waist. No female in all of his years of existence had stirred his lust to the degree that Claire did.

Mikhail didn't know what he needed more: to sink his fangs into her throat or his cock into the heat of her pussy.

She kept him pressed against the wall as she slid to her knees. The soft glide of her breasts and tight beads of her nipples moving down the length of his torso was a sweet torture that he couldn't get enough of. One hand reached up, splayed across his chest as she took the length of his cock in the other. Mikhail sucked in a sharp breath and his muscles tensed as she stroked him from the swollen head to throbbing base.

"Again."

The back of his skull knocked against the marble wall and she took the head of his cock in her hand, swirling her palm over the tip before squeezing him tightly in her fist. She stroked all the way down and his balls drew up tight. He thrust into her grip, eagerly pumping his hips in a desperate surge.

Claire's eyes met his, her seductive gaze alight with

gold fire. She leaned in and flicked out with her tongue, never looking away as she swirled it—*gods, so soft*—over the glossy head. A bead of moisture formed at the tip and she licked it away, a slow, sensual, deliberate motion that left him panting as her lids grew hooded just before she pulled away and licked her lips.

The pause was momentary. Water cascaded over them, the glass enclosure filled with steam, and Claire knelt before him, a goddess he was surely unworthy of, paying homage to his body with her mouth. The glide of her lips was heaven. The wet heat encasing his cock, perfection. She took him deep and he could do nothing about the low moan of approval that worked its way up his throat. As she pulled away, her little fangs dragged over his shaft and a pleasant shiver ran down Mikhail's spine. She plunged down again and fell into a steady rhythm that stole his breath. His hips thrust in time and Claire dug her nails into his ass as he fucked her mouth.

"You're so beautiful, Claire. So gods-damned perfect."

He wound his fists into the wet tangles of her hair and she pulled away. Water droplets clung to her dark lashes as she looked up at him, dotted her brow and cheeks, the gentle curve of her shoulders. She pushed him to his breaking point with teasing licks. She took him as deep as she could and then hollowed her cheeks as she sucked just the engorged head of his cock.

A half smile played on her lips as she bit down with only the blunt edges of her teeth. Mikhail's jaw locked down and his body went taut. Every corded muscle flexed as a shudder racked him from head to toe. "Yes, love," he said on a groan. "Gods, yes."

She bit down again, this time with the razor-sharp point of one fang. The skin broke and Mikhail was possessed by a delicious heat, flames of desire that licked at his skin until he thought he'd combust from the intense sensation.

He threw his head back as Claire lapped and sucked. A spasm traveled from his sac up his shaft and the backs of his thighs as he came. Claire didn't pull away; instead, she became greedier still, sucking deeply as she eagerly took everything he had to offer. The orgasm was intense, ripping through him and stealing every ounce of strength left in his legs.

No woman had pleasured him in such a way. None could compare to his mate. His Claire.

Becoming a vampire freaking rocked!

Claire had never experienced anything so intense in her entire life and she hadn't even been on the receiving end. Being with Mikhail had been unlike any other sexual encounter and that had been when she was human. But now . . . ? It was like sex times a trillion. Supersex. She couldn't get enough of him. His taste, the hard length of his cock that filled and stretched her mouth. A full-on religious experience. Unbelievable.

Mikhail pulled her to her feet and turned, slamming her against the marble wall with enough force to crack the tiles. He pressed his body against hers and kissed her with all of the ferocity of a starved animal consuming a meal. Each deep thrust of his tongue was surely a precursor to how unmercifully he planned to fuck her, and it sent a thrill through Claire to think of Mikhail, so desperate, so urgent, to take her that he would abandon all common sense.

She didn't want to be treated with care. Not this time.

Over the course of a week she'd been made into an animal. Plugged back into that primal aspect of her psyche that had been bred out of humanity over the course of millennia. She wanted to fuck and be fucked like an animal. With reckless abandon. Mikhail lifted her as though she weighed nothing, slinging her legs over his shoulders. He cradled her ass in his palms as Claire braced her back against the shower wall to steady them.

When the heat of his mouth met her sex, Claire cried out. Mikhail devoured her, lapped at her, with mindless desperation. The scent of his arousal mingled with the steam, creating a perfume that intoxicated Claire, and her head spun from the heady mixture of that delicious aroma, his taste that still lingered on her lips, and the sensation dancing across her flesh, radiating from her clit as he passed over it again and again with the flat of his tongue.

Stiff, wet, warm. Soft. Gentle and then forceful. He plunged his tongue into her channel before flicking out at her clit. Soon he fell into a rhythm, teasing her, bringing her close to the edge before pulling back, making only enough contact to give her pleasure. Not enough to bring the release she craved.

"Bite me, Mikhail. Now."

She couldn't wait another second. Refused to. He angled his head into her inner thigh and sank both pairs of fangs deep into her flesh while he worked her sensitive knot of nerves with the blunt pad of his thumb. Claire came in a violent spasm that sent her back arching away from the shower wall. Her ankles hooked between his shoulder blades, she sobbed her pleasure as one shock wave after the next broke her completely apart. Mikhail sucked greedily at her thigh and a surge of pure power infused every pore, every cell, every inch of her. The orgasm ebbed, the waves merely ripples now, but the power she felt through her bond with Mikhail left her breathless and shaking.

She now truly understood the depth and scope of their tether.

Her soul *knew* his. She'd scoffed at how quickly he could claim to love her, but now that she was turned she felt everything with so much more intensity. She recognized emotions in an entirely different way. Her human

brain wasn't weeding through logic anymore, trying to jus-
tify things that didn't need justification. Now she was
running on instinct. Could she love the man holding her?

Absolutely.

Water droplets clung to Mikhail's skin. Claire watched
with fascination, her new keen eyesight picking up on the
minute changes as the tiny drops grew fatter, heavier, before they released their hold on his skin and ran in tiny
rivulets over the dips and hills of sculpted muscle. She
looked down at him, combing her fingers through the wet
locks of his hair as his tongue passed over the two sets of
punctures his fangs had opened in her thigh. The skin
tightened as the wounds closed and he lingered, kissing,
licking, nipping at her sensitive flesh. Savoring her in the
way she'd savored him only moments before.

Claire never wanted this moment to end.

That delicious scent of his arousal billowed around her
in the steam and she swung her legs from around his shoulders as he lowered her to his waist. An almost impercep-
tible tremor shook Mikhail, vibrating into Claire. "What is
it?" she murmured close to his ear. His scent changed, an
almost citrus tang.

"You're changed. But not." Mikhail's large hand encircled her waist, holding her secure as he pulled back to
study her. Silver chased across his gaze and his brow furrowed. "Your scent, your taste . . . your blood. It's the
same. You were drained, Claire." His voice hitched. "Gregor bled you dry. I fed you from my vein, replenished
what you'd lost. You've fed from others and yet . . ." The
furrow in his brow cut deeper as the words died on his
tongue.

"Should I taste differently now?" She laughed. "Smell
like a vampire, maybe?"

"Yes," he said on an emphatic breath. "Claire, you
are—"

"A freak?" she ventured with a smile. "Such a screwup that I can't even turn into a vampire correctly?

"You are *extraordinary*."

The heat in his gaze sent a thrill of excitement through her. His mouth claimed hers, hungry and demanding. Desperate. Claire returned his ardor, her lips slanting over his as she thrust her tongue into his mouth in a wet, urgent tangle. He rolled his hips as he pushed down on hers, impaling her on his cock in a forceful thrust. Claire gasped, the intensity of sensation stealing her breath as the satiny glide of his rigid sex caressed her inner walls.

Sex had never felt so damned *good*.

This was beyond good. Surpassing emotion and sensation that Claire could form words for. Mikhail pulled out, thrust hard and deep, and a primal growl worked its way up his throat. But he was still too restrained for what she needed.

"Don't hold back." She fisted his hair, rolled her hips into his. "You never have to with me."

Her words sparked something in him and Mikhail's lips pulled back to reveal the vicious points of his fangs. He pressed her hard against the tiled wall, his fingers biting into her ass as he picked up his pace, fucking into her as though his very life depended on each desperate thrust. Claire's eyes drifted shut for a blissful moment before Mikhail's hand wound in the length of her hair. He jerked her head to the side, and she opened her eyes to find his gaze locked on the elongated column of her throat.

"What are you waiting for?" she panted. He pounded furiously into her, knocking her back against the shower wall. A snarl tore from his throat moments before he buried his fangs into her flesh. The sting of his bite coupled with the powerful suction sent a euphoric rush chasing through Claire's veins.

A scream erupted from her lips as she came. Deeper,

more intense, than the last orgasm, this one didn't simply shatter her; it ripped her apart. Something pulsed not just from her core outward but also from her soul outward. A ripple that disrupted the time and space of her tiny universe. "Harder! More! Don't stop!" The words seemed incomprehensible, tumbling from her lips in a desperate rush. She had no idea if her commands were in regards to his bite or the way he was fucking her, but it occurred to Claire that they were one and the same. An act of love, of their bond, and one would never occur without the other.

Her hips bucked as the orgasm continued to crest over her, wave after violent wave until Claire was shaking and her breath came in desperate, shuddering gasps. Mikhail disengaged from her throat with a roar and Claire's focus was drawn to his throat. *Oh, god.* If she didn't sink her fangs into that flesh, if she didn't taste him, now, she'd lose her mind.

She struck with the speed of a cobra, instinct guiding her as she latched on to the flesh that concealed the throbbing vein. The skin popped and a rush of sweet warmth cascaded over her tongue. Claire had never tasted anything so good as Mikhail's blood. His chest heaved with labored breath and Mikhail thrust harder, filling and stretching every inch of her pussy as he fucked her with wild abandon. Like an animal. Just how she wanted him.

She swallowed and the scratchy heat abated in her throat, a fire quenched in an instant. Even after the intensity of her orgasm, Claire felt a satiation that at once completed her and made her greedy for more. Another long pull brought with it another mouthful of the sweet nectar and Claire swallowed it down eagerly. No wonder Mikhail craved her blood like an alcoholic jonesing for his next drink. If there was anything she could ever become addicted to it was this. *Him.*

Mikhail's thrusts picked up in pace, his body jerking in

a disjointed rhythm. Claire kept her jaws locked firmly around his throat, one hand wound tightly in his hair and the other gripped so tightly to his shoulder that her nails penetrated the skin. A tremor shook his body and he called out as he came, jet after heated jet filling Claire, flooding her body with a radiant warmth that turned her muscles to mush.

His orgasm seemed to go on forever. Claire continued to drink from his vein, each deep suck matching the pulse of his cock inside of her. Claire's body grew heavy, her mind fuzzy. The hand at his shoulder fell limply to her side, and the one in his hair released its hold. The only things keeping her upright were Mikhail's palms cupping her ass.

He brought himself down from the moment slowly. Pulling almost completely out before sliding with languid ease as he sank back in. Claire was boneless. Thoughtless. A being without form or substance. A gossamer thing floating through a vast universe until she was slowly pulled back into orbit.

Tethered. To Mikhail Aristov. Her mate.

He pulled out completely and a sense of loss and emptiness opened up inside of her. She rolled her scored tongue over the punctures in his throat, the way he had done to her, and she felt them close with every gentle pass. Claire wobbled on her feet as he set her down and Mikhail steadied her. His expression was soft, full of unspoken emotion, as he leaned in toward her.

"Mine." The word rumbled in his chest and vibrated over her skin.

No truer words had ever been spoken. Emotion swelled in Claire's chest and rose as a lump in her throat. She reached up, cupped his cheek in her hand. "Mine," she repeated, feeling the truth of the word in the root of her soul.

Not another word was spoken between them. There was no need for any. Mikhail washed her, lathering her body with a bar of soap, his large palms working her body into a state of relaxation that made Claire wonder how she was still upright. He washed her hair, easing his fingers through its length as he maneuvered her under the spray, combing out the tangles as he rinsed it. She returned the favor, taking her time as she acquainted herself with every swell of muscle, every straight line and curve, as she used her sudsy hands to map his body, committing each detail to memory.

The water began to cool by the time they were both squeaky-clean. Claire had never had a more decadent shower, and the bathroom had officially become her favorite room in Mikhail's thousands of square feet of living space. He toweled her off and draped a fluffy terry-cloth robe over her shoulders. Claire quirked a brow as she slipped her arms into the soft fabric, cinching the belt tight around her waist.

"Did you just have this lying around?" she asked with a sly smile.

"I sent Alex out for a few things," he murmured, placing a light kiss on her lips. "We'll go out shopping together soon. When things have settled. Whatever you need. Want. It's yours."

She didn't care about clothes or anything else that could be bought in a store. She reached up on her tiptoes and returned his soft kiss with one of her own. "I have everything I need. Right here in front of me."

CHAPTER
31

After centuries of empty soullessness, Mikhail was finally whole. Nothing could have prepared him for what Claire had ignited in him. He no longer saw the future as an endless chasm, dark, cold, and as lonely as a tomb. And despite the danger that loomed, he no longer feared that, either. They had both survived their trials. Nothing in this world could separate them now.

That wasn't to say that there weren't many loose ends still to be tied up. One of them was currently sitting on the couch in the living room, tiny legs tucked beneath her as she channel surfed.

After her weeklong transition, Claire was still riding the high of her transformation. What had happened prior to that—the incident at her apartment building—hadn't even entered her mind. So far Mikhail hadn't sensed an ounce of distress in her, but when her memories of that time surfaced past the Collective it was sure to rekindle that distress.

"When can I see Claire?" The girl, Vanessa, had remained remarkably calm considering all she'd been put

through. She shared Claire's resilience, that spark of *otherness,* and that the Sortiari had spared the child only
served to pique Mikhail's curiosity.

"Soon." Alex had stocked the kitchen with kid-friendly
food, as he'd called it. Popcorn, soda, prepackaged pizzas,
and other such things that could be easily cooked in a
microwave. It all looked like junk to Mikhail, but he wasn't
about to argue. Not when the girl had already been through
so much. If she wanted to eat food that looked no better
than the cardboard it was packaged in, then so be it.

After their shower, Claire had collapsed back into their
bed, falling into a deep sleep almost before her head had
a chance to settle on the pillow. Their bed. The thought
filled Mikhail with a deep sense of satisfaction. There
would never be another sunset that he would awaken to
lonely. Incomplete. Perhaps even, with time, the night-
mares would fade and having Claire by his side would
banish those specters of his past spent in that damned tomb
beneath the ground.

Though until Gregor the Black died a bloody death not
much would serve to truly heal Mikhail from the ordeal.

Which led him to his second and third loose ends. "I
have a meeting now, Vanessa. Do you think you can entertain yourself for a while?" Alex had gone home. Ronan was
out on another errand, and Jenner was in the study, keeping
watch over Mikhail's reluctant guest. For the girl's safety,
Mikhail hoped there was enough on TV to keep her riveted
to the screen. At least until tonight's business was concluded.

"I'm fine," she said without looking away from the
teenage-fueled drama fest currently playing. Mikhail
pinched the bridge of his nose and let out a sigh. Was this
even appropriate for a girl her age to watch? He had no
fucking clue. "I've decided that since I'm staying here, I
should get to stay up all night and sleep all day, too. It's
totally cool with me."

Again, Mikhail felt entirely too unprepared to care for a human girl. Didn't she have school to attend? He'd have to check with Alex, since care of the girl had fallen to him in Claire's absence. He hoped that his mate would soon wake, because he had a feeling he was going to be in way over his head with this one. "We'll see what Claire thinks about it," he replied as he headed toward the study. "Stay put until my guest leaves. Yes?"

"Yes, sir," she said with a saucy salute and a wide smile. Something in Mikhail's chest tightened at her beaming expression and he wondered, would his own child have as instant an effect on him as this girl had?

Jenner stood outside the sliding doors that led to the study, his spine ramrod straight and his expression fierce. He was weighed down with an assortment of weapons: a saber strapped to his back, twin daggers at his thighs, and a pair of semiautos under each arm. The male meant business, and Mikhail couldn't be happier for Jenner's presence. In a few short days he'd undergo the transition, though Mikhail wouldn't let it happen as carelessly as he'd turned Ronan.

"She's playing nice." Jenner's voice grated like metal scraping over gravel as he let out a soft snort of derision. "But she doesn't really have a choice at this point, does she?"

Everyone had a choice. Including Siobhan. They would never be allies, but he hoped that they could reach a tentative peace at least for now. He left Jenner outside the door, confident the cagey female wouldn't try to kill him in his own home. She was here because she wanted to hear what he was about to say. And he was going to make the most of this reluctant meeting.

"Keeping the human girl as a snack for your mate?" Siobhan snickered at her own joke, tossing the thick mane of raven hair over her shoulder as she turned to face him.

Her emerald eyes sparked with an adversarial edge, though completely devoid of even a glint of silver. No matter how she felt, she was keeping her emotions in check. It was comforting to know she had at least a modicum of self-control. "You must be pleased with yourself, Mikhail. The city is abuzz with rumors. Some say she's vampire royalty hidden away and protected from Sortiari assassins for centuries. Others think she's some kind of mythical second coming." A dark brow arched elegantly over Siobhan's eye. "You've bagged the white stag of vampires, haven't you?"

There was no use downplaying Claire's power. Any dhampir living would be able to sense it, and even Siobhan in all of her disdain was benefiting from Claire's power as well. "And what is your opinion on the matter?" Not that he cared, but he was curious all the same.

She hiked a disinterested shoulder. "I don't care one way or another about your special snowflake of a mate or how she was turned. In fact, I couldn't care less if she was the first gods-damned vampire ever created and shat straight out of Egypt's ass. Your elitist hierarchy means nothing to me. I won't fall at your feet and beg for the opportunity to lose my soul until some worthless male stumbles along to tether me. Just like I'm not here to make any sort of peace with you tonight. The only reason I agreed to come is because Jenner said you had something to say that I would want to hear. And even though that bastard is dead to me for aligning himself with you, I trust him. So tell me, Mikhail. What is it that you have to tell me? Perhaps you've finally decided to reward me for saving you not once but twice in one week?"

She claimed not to care about how Claire had been turned, but he knew that wasn't entirely true. Siobhan might have been able to keep the silver from leaking into her emerald gaze, but her scent soured at the mention of his mate. She couldn't hide everything from him.

"What is your clan?" Mikhail asked as he took a seat at the desk that separated them.

Her gaze narrowed. "I have no clan. Only a coven."

She wanted him to believe that the only family she knew was the ragtag group of dhampirs she'd convinced to follow her. Mikhail didn't buy it. "I fought a Sortiari assassin a week ago." He leaned back in the chair and planted his arms on the rest, steepling his fingers before him as he spoke. "A berserker warlord that I suspect is Gregor the Black."

Her scent changed in an instant, the adrenaline that seeped into her bloodstream sending a sulfuric tang into the air. Without uttering a word she'd confirmed Mikhail's suspicion. "He told you that?"

Mikhail pursed his lips. "Not exactly." Though Gregor hadn't admitted to being the famed highland lord, his expression had spoken volumes.

"And here I thought you were finally going to show your gratitude." She let out a disgusted snort. "Do not speak to me of this again, Mikhail. I'll not entertain your fantasies. Likewise, leave me and mine be and I'll consider a tentative peace between us despite that you've cheated me of Ronan's fealty. The minute I suspect you're trying to influence any member of my coven, I'll come after you with a vengeance."

Like a shot she was out of her chair and stalking toward the door. "Agreed." Mikhail kept his voice low and even. "But don't forget what nourishes you and yours when you think to come after me," he added as she yanked the doors aside in a wide sweep of her arms and strode from the office, the stiletto heels of her boots clicking on the hardwood floor with her passing.

"That went well." Jenner strode through the open door and stopped short of the desk, folding his massive arms across his chest.

Mikhail snorted. "Better than I expected, actually."

"What do you think she'll do now?"

"Hunt the bastard down."

Jenner smirked. "And in the process lead you straight to him."

Mikhail flashed a wide smile, showing both sets of fangs. "Exactly."

"What is it that's between Siobhan and the berserker?" Jenner asked.

"A history too long and bloody for me to relay in a week of nights," Mikhail replied. "I should lay the blame of the berserker's rage at Siobhan's feet. Or at the very least her sire's." A low burst of anger rumbled in Mikhail's chest. "If you think her nasty streak runs hot, it's nothing more than a smolder in comparison to the berserker's rage."

Jenner let out a low whistle. "He's held on to his need for vengeance for a while, then?"

"Centuries," Mikhail said. "And anger like that only builds with time."

"It's good we're amassing an army, then. Because he won't stop until we're dead . . . or he is."

Mikhail sat in quiet contemplation. He'd set something in motion tonight. Something he couldn't undo. He just hoped that he hadn't inadvertently given his enemy the upper hand by steering Siobhan on the path to Gregor. "It is good," he replied. He'd need an army if he was going to protect any of them from not only the Sortiari's twisted view of Fate but that of a formidable berserker warlord, hell-bent on revenge.

Ronan closed the wounds on the female's throat before pulling away. A wistful smile complemented her dreamy expression. She licked her lips and sighed. "Mmmm."

She palmed his cock through his jeans and Ronan moved her hand aside. He was hard and needed to fuck like he'd needed her blood, but he'd given his troth to Siobhan and if he so much copped a feel of the female beside him it would be his ass.

"I can pleasure you," she said with a childlike pout that wasn't doing anything for him. Acting like a testy teenager was sure to guarantee that any thoughts of bedding the female would soon fizzle. "I know you want me, Ronan." She wiped a drop of blood from the corner of his mouth and sucked it from the tip of her finger. "You're hard."

No shit. But it wasn't because she was so gods-damned irresistible. It was simply because he'd fed. And the need for sex awakened with his body after he ingested blood. Came with the territory now.

Before Mikhail had turned Ronan, he would have felt bad for the female. He would have assuaged her ego as he gently turned her down. For decades, he'd wanted nothing more than to be turned. To know the strength and power of being a true vampire and not just a pathetic shadow of his true self. The prospect of losing his soul had seemed a small price to pay in comparison for what he'd gain. Besides, a vampire was only soulless until his mate tethered him. What were a few years—or a few hundred—when he had millennia ahead of him? He had plenty of distractions in the meantime: males and females alike lined up, ready and willing to let him feed from their veins, an army to amass, and a kingdom to help build. And even though he hated her, he had Siobhan to keep him occupied when his lust mounted. Surely those things would help to distract him from the emptiness that had opened up inside of him like an endless black chasm the day Mikhail turned him.

Ronan's phone vibrated in his pocket and he couldn't believe that he almost hoped it was Siobhan calling to summon him to her bed. He was wired, too keyed up from feeding, to call it a night. He was already pissed that she hadn't answered his earlier calls. The least she could do was be available, considering the oath she'd made him swear.

His skin tingled with foreboding as he noted the unidentified caller on the ID. "Hello?"

"I think I found it!"

It had been months since he'd heard his sister's voice, and it bubbled with barely contained excitement. The roar of traffic in the background nearly drowned out her words.

"Chelle?" *No, "Hey bro! How are ya?" Or, "Hey, long time no talk. What's new?"* "Where are you? What did you find? What in the hell is going on?"

Her excitement bordered on mania as uncontrolled laughter answered him. "I'm in Crescent City. Up by the California/Oregon border. I've been hiking, digging, talking to the locals all up and down the coast, and I finally have a lead on the chest! *Set's* chest, Ronan! Do you know what this means?"

Good gods. He was pretty sure that Chelle was actually the love child of Indiana Jones and Lara Croft. Her passion for the lost relics of vampire lore was rivaled only by her addiction to caramel macchiatos.

"Chelle, listen. A lot has changed since you left." He'd lost his soul for starters. . . . "Who are you working for? These relics, they have to be turned over to Mikhail. To me, at least. I need to tell you something about—"

Chelle's breath came in quick pants and her voice bounced as though she'd taken off at a sprint as she cut him off. "Ronan, there's no time for small talk! I'm in deep shit. Get your ass up here and—"

She let out a grunt and the sound of a scuffle rose above the din of traffic on the other end of the line. "Chelle?" Ronan clutched the phone tighter to his ear. "Chelle?" he shouted into the receiver. "Answer me, damn it."

Muffled voices grew silent. The sound of traffic disappeared. And the line went dead.

"Fuck!"

Ronan squeezed his phone so tightly that the plastic cracked in his palm. How could he possibly leave the city? He was newly turned, Mikhail and Claire had barely survived their ordeal with the slayers, and someone was going to have to help oversee Jenner's transition. Not to mention how Ronan was going to deal with Siobhan's ire if she discovered he'd ditched her. But how could he stay when Chelle could be someone's captive—or worse? What if the Sortiari had taken her to use as leverage against Mikhail? They could have been following her for weeks—months—for all he knew. And any relic, especially one rumored to be as powerful as Set's chest, would be dangerous in their enemies' hands.

How could he possibly leave? How could he not?

"Is everything okay, baby?"

Ronan looked down as though only now realizing he was still standing in the middle of a crowded nightclub with an eager dhampir waiting to get into his pants. "I'm out of here," he replied absently as he snatched the high-ball glass of scotch from the table and swallowed it down. He needed a little liquid courage if he was going to go to Mikhail and tell him that he was thanking him for the gift of transformation by abandoning him while the future of his kingdom was still so uncertain.

Shit.

He turned and stalked through the club. From behind him the female shouted in her infantile whine, "Call me!"

Yeah. Sure. Whatever.

Out front, he waited for the valet to bring his car around, his impatience mounting by the fucking nanosecond. The sun would be up in six hours and he had a hell of a lot of ground to cover between now and then. And once he got to Crescent City, what then? He had no leads, no information aside from his sister's name and the relic she'd been hunting, both of which, spoken to the wrong person, could get them both killed.

Mere weeks as a vampire, his soul lost to the void, and Ronan might just die before he could get it back. What happened to those who died untethered? Did he really want to know?

CHAPTER
32

Becoming a vampire sure took a lot out of a girl.

Claire stretched like a contented feline on the expanse of Mikhail's bed. Or was it *their* bed? The tether that bound his soul to hers gave a tug. Like an invisible length of rope that connected them no matter how far apart they might be. She smiled into the darkness as she remembered the intense moments of their lovemaking and the bliss of feeding from Mikhail's vein. As though her life had truly begun the moment she'd become a vampire, there was no empty, painful past, only the present and her future stretched out before her.

Her hands wandered over her bare collarbone, fingertips trailing between her breasts. A chill raced over her flesh as she ventured lower, revisiting all of the places Mikhail's hands had been before her palms settled on her belly.

The baby.

Her last human memory had been of lying on that damned table, eyes squeezed shut, as Gregor ripped scream after tortured scream from her with the razor-sharp edge of his blade. Mikhail had saved her. Saved their child before Gregor could hurt him. Her son floated safe and secure in her womb. And she had her mate to thank for that. But before the slayers had taken her to that shithole of a basement so much more had happened. Events that had been all but forgotten in the midst of her transition. *Jesus Christ*—"Vanessa!"

Claire flew from the bed and smashed into the opposite wall. A harsh breath of air left her lungs in a *woof!* as her ass made contact with the floor. Through the darkness, she caught sight of the wall. A large, Claire-shaped indentation marred the drywall. Holy shit, if she'd been going any faster she would have plowed right through it like some sort of deranged cartoon character.

After all of the damage she'd caused to Mikhail's posh digs, she had a feeling he'd want to reconsider keeping her around. At this rate, she was bound to cause thousands of dollars' worth of damage before she got a grip on her new supernatural speed and strength. Claire tried not to let the way the individual carpet fibers felt against her palms distract her as she pushed herself up from the floor. She shot straight up, her feet no longer making contact with the floor as she rocketed up toward the vaulted ceiling, missing the roughly hewn timber support beams by mere inches.

Her landing was considerably more graceful, and she lit back on the floor as easily as a cat jumping down from a tree. *Wow. Okay, Claire. Get a freaking grip and get your shit together.* There were too many distractions in this new state of existence. Her brain and thought patterns didn't even work in the same way. Her mind was cranking too quickly, probably what a kid with ADHD felt like when he was hopped up on sugar. Multitasking took on a whole new meaning as her thoughts wandered in multiple directions. Vampiric strength and speed weren't simply limited to her physical traits.

Right now she missed the calm and laser focus she'd had as a human. It was the one trait she'd been the most proud of. Well, that and her ability to pick the pockets of even the skinniest of jeans. Right now wasn't the time to lament those losses or ponder what she'd gained, however. There were so many unanswered questions. So many details she needed filled in from the days that she'd lost. And if any harm had come to Vanessa those Sortiari bastards were going to pay for it.

Claire gripped the knob of the door gingerly, turning it with just the tips of her fingers. The bolt released with ease and the wooden panel didn't even made a squeak as it whispered open. *Score!* Likewise, she kept her footfalls light, as though walking on thistledown, as she padded down the hallway to the staircase. Her feet whispered over the hardwood without a sound to betray her passage. Very cool. Step by step, she used her trek to the ground floor as a study in mastering her new gifts. Even her mind began to calm. No longer racing through thought after endless thought as she learned to ignore the Collective and filter through everything around her, taking it all in at once rather than trying to pick through and separate it all.

Really, it wasn't as tough as she thought it would be. Her fingers slipped through the strands of her hair, combing it out into some sort of order as she hit the last step. With any luck, she'd get this whole vampire thing down yet.

The upbeat sounds of the TV filtered from the living room into the foyer. Definitely not something Mikhail or Ronan would watch. Claire treaded softly, creeping into the other room as a predator approached potential prey. Her guard was up, but she didn't know why. Danger prickled along her skin like icy rain.

"Claire!"

Vanessa sat on the carpet, her legs crossed in front of her. She shot up with a wide smile on her face and sprinted the length of the living room, nearly taking Claire out in a huge tackle hug.

"Mikhail said you didn't feel good. Did those guys hurt you? Have you ever seen a house this big in your entire life? He has every channel on TV. Even the Disney Channel! Holy crap, Claire! Your eyes are all shiny and gold. You sort of look like Mikhail and Ronan and Jenner now. Oh, and this other lady who came over earlier, too. Do you have superpowers? Does it hurt? Mikhail says it hurts to become a vampire and that humans can't do it. But you did. Why do you think you can do it and no one else?"

If Vanessa didn't stop to take a breath soon she was going to pass out.

The gravity of the situation hit Claire like a five-ton mountain collapsing on top of her. Right now Vanessa was riding the high of the excitement; her little ten-year-old brain hadn't wrapped itself around everything that had happened yet. How could it? The human psyche could only take so much. Claire remembered feeling like she'd lost her own grip on reality from the moment she'd met Mikhail.

"Are you all right, kiddo?" Claire guided Vanessa back toward the TV and eased herself down on the floor. She patted the carpet beside her. "How are you holding up?"

Vanessa plopped down and fixed Claire with her wide brown eyes. "I'm okay. Sad. But I'm not scared, Claire. Not anymore."

Truth. Vanessa's scent was sweet, almost like too-ripe watermelon. There wasn't a trace of distress to sour it. A worry and a relief. "You're tough, kiddo." Claire pulled her in for a hug, so, *so* careful not to squeeze too hard.

"Mom's still in a coma." Vanessa sniffed and looked away. "Mikhail talked to the doctors about it, but they don't know when she'll wake up. She has a head injury."

Claire listened to Vanessa regurgitate words that she'd

no doubt been told several times over the past days. It could be months—or longer—before Carlene recovered, if at all. What would happen to Vanessa in the meantime? Where would she go? Claire pulled Vanessa in for a hug, careful to handle her as though she were made of cobwebs. "I'm so sorry, kiddo. She'll be okay. We just have to think positive thoughts."

"I like Mikhail." Vanessa's voice was muffled by Claire's shirt. "He reminds me a little of my principal at school, but he's nice."

Claire couldn't help but laugh. Mikhail would probably love to hear that he gave off an elementary school principal vibe. "How's he like your principal?"

"Sort of scary. Like, you know he's a nice guy, but if you get in trouble he's definitely not a nice guy."

Huh. Strangely accurate.

"Claire, are those guys who took us going to come get me?"

Claire pulled away, looked Vanessa in the eye. "Why would you ask that?"

"One of them said that no one should hurt me because I was special. Are they going to try to put me in jail?" Her voice broke, and for the first time Claire sensed her fear. "Or foster care?"

Claire thought back, slogging through the haze of her muddled human memory. Gregor had forbidden the other slayers from killing Vanessa. But why? What did they know about her that Claire didn't? How did this innocent child who wasn't even old enough for her first kiss fit into their grand notions of Fate?

"Don't worry about them," Claire said. A low growl vibrated in her throat and Vanessa's brow furrowed. *Whoops.* She was going to have to learn how to control her new animal impulses. Pushing thoughts of violence against the Sortiari to the back of her mind, she gave Vanessa a reassuring smile. "No one's going to make you do anything you don't want to do."

"Can I stay here?"

The hope in Vanessa's voice twisted Claire's heart in her chest. How could she answer that when she wasn't entirely sure if *she* was staying here? And for that matter, she couldn't just invite Vanessa to stay in a house that wasn't hers. "I'll talk to Mikhail about it," she said. "We'll figure it all out, don't worry."

Vanessa let out a sigh much too heavy for such a little girl. "Okay."

"Okay. You watch TV for a bit and I'm going to go find Mikhail. Holler if you need anything."

Vanessa flopped down on her tummy in front of the TV. "I will. But I pretty much already know where everything is."

The tether that bound Claire to Mikhail tugged at her chest and she let it lead her to her mate. *Mate*. The word was so foreign, even to her new vampire mind. But it rang with so much truth that it stole the air from her lungs. Like a mouse after a piece of cheese in a maze, she crossed the foyer, went past the staircase and down a long hallway, her feet taking her where she needed to go even though this was a section of the house she'd barely had time to explore when she'd been there last.

She turned toward a set of sliding doors and smiled. He was in that room. His presence burned in her soul like a flame.

Mikhail stopped midsentence and smiled. Her steps had been so light he hadn't heard her approach. But his mate stood on the other side of those doors just the same. He held up a hand to Jenner and said, "Come in, Claire."

She walked into the room, beaming. Mikhail's blood

stirred at the sight of her, and any thought of business took a backseat to his lust. Their moments in the shower had been far too fleeting to fully satisfy him, and he couldn't wait to take Claire back to their bedroom, where he could strip her bare and enjoy her body until the sun rose.

Jenner cleared his throat, breaking the spell, and Mikhail shifted in his seat, his hardening cock causing him discomfort in the restrictive cut of his pants. Damn it. "How are you feeling?"

"Good." She graced him with a knowing smile and a rush of pleasure flooded him.

"I'm glad."

"I just saw Vanessa." Claire gave Jenner a wide berth as she approached Mikhail's desk, as though she sensed that it would ignite tension to see her standing so close to another male. Mikhail marveled at her intuitiveness. Claire had indeed been born to become a vampire. "She's afraid that the Sortiari are going to take her away. Or that someone is going to make her go into foster care. I wasn't sure what to tell her—"

"The child can stay for as long as it pleases you, love." Mikhail leaned back in his chair and studied Claire. How could she think that he would turn away anyone she cared about? "This is her home as much as it is yours."

Claire smiled wide, the tiny tips of her fangs brushing her full bottom lip. Mikhail thought of those fangs scraping along his shaft and suppressed a pleasant shudder.

"Thank you." Her voice lowered an octave and the husky tone vibrated along his skin.

Jenner cleared his throat once again and shifted uncomfortably from one foot to the other. "Mikhail, if it's all right with you, I'd like to keep an eye on Siobhan. If you're right, she won't waste any time in going after Gregor."

"Yes." With Claire so close, it was hard for Mikhail to

remember that there were other people in the world, let alone the same room. "Go. We'll discuss the rest later."

Jenner gave a curt nod, turned toward Claire and nodded again, and took his leave.

"Come here," Mikhail commanded as soon as the doors were closed. It had only been a couple of hours since he'd taken her in the shower, but it felt like centuries. "Let me smell you, touch you, put my lips on your skin."

Claire giggled as she rounded the desk. He pulled her down into his lap and she leaned in to his chest. "You sort of make me sound like a gourmet meal when you talk about me that way."

"I could devour you like one," he murmured against her throat as he breathed her in.

Her previous pleasure evaporated under worry that soured the air and Mikhail tightened his grip, encircling Claire's waist. "I know this is going to take some adjustment, but you're through the worst of it."

"It's not that." Claire worried her bottom lip between her teeth and one sharp fang nicked the skin. She licked the blood away and Mikhail was disappointed he hadn't beat her to it. "It's Vanessa."

He stroked a loving hand over the silky length of Claire's hair. "I told you, love. She can stay with you."

"There's something wrong with her," Claire blurted. "No. Not wrong." She paused as though searching for the right word. *"Different."*

Mikhail had sensed it, too, but he hadn't said anything. Didn't want to pile anything more onto Claire's plate. "The Sortiari ordered Gregor to spare her. They think she's important. And that she plays a part in their plans is, at the very least, disconcerting."

Mikhail had managed to thwart Fate more than once in the course of his existence, however, despite the Sortiari's grand schemes. There was undoubtedly something otherworldly about the girl, though he couldn't put a finger on just what it was. Perhaps her father had been *other*. The world was thick with supernatural beings. If not her father, there was a possibility that someone in her bloodline had passed down whatever traits she now exhibited that not only piqued his enemies' interest but worried his mate as well.

"We'll keep her close, Claire. Care for her. I've arranged for her mother's care and we'll see this through. I promise you, this will all work out."

Claire graced him with a soft smile and leaned in for a kiss. "Have you always been such an optimist?"

An optimist? Mikhail thought back over the centuries, the many years of war and excess. The taking of physical pleasures in search of the one thing that would banish the emptiness that had swallowed him whole. He thought about that gods-forsaken tomb. The hole that Gregor had left him to rot in and the wound that still pulled at his chest after all of these years, a permanent reminder of the emptiness and despair that he thought would have no end.

"No, love. I have not been an optimistic male. Until now."

"Oh really?" Claire teased the strands of his hair, her nails scraping against the back of his neck. "And just who could have possibly instilled such a sunny outlook in such a broody vampire?"

Mikhail cupped the back of her neck and kissed her, coaxing her mouth to open for him with gentle flicks of his tongue. She responded, deepening the kiss as a purr vibrated in her chest. Ah, his mate. So full of fire and passion—

"Mikhail." Ronan burst into the room like a force of nature. A raging storm about to ravage the land.

Mikhail didn't pull away but kept his head bent close to Claire's. "As usual, Ronan, your timing is—"

"I'm leaving, Mikhail. Tonight. Now. I just came here to tell you in person so you wouldn't think I was committing treason."

"Treason? Ronan, what in the gods' names are you talking about?"

"It's Chelle."

Ronan's twin was a wandering spirit, a dhampir hellbent on uncovering all of the secrets of the vampire race. So many times he'd flown to her rescue when she got in over her head. Mikhail had hoped that she would settle down. Stay closer to her brother and out of trouble. "What's she done?"

"I don't know." Ronan raked his hands through his hair and his agitation burned Mikhail's nose like sulfur.

Claire placed a tentative hand on Mikhail's forearm, also in tune to the male's distress. She'd only been awake and alert for a few hours before she'd needed to rest and Mikhail had no idea how long she'd be able to sustain this time. He didn't want to waste a single moment on Chelle and whatever trouble she'd brought to her brother's door.

"What can I do to help?" Just because Mikhail didn't want to deal with Chelle didn't mean he wouldn't. Ronan might not have been Mikhail's brother by birth, but he was the closest thing Mikhail had ever had to one. He was part of the Collective now, an Ancient One in his own right. Ronan's problems were now Mikhail's and he was honor bound to give aid.

"Just give me your leave," Ronan replied. "Jenner is more than capable to protect you until I come back."

Mikhail scoffed. "Your ego's grown since your transition. I want you at my side, Ronan, but I don't need you to protect me."

A spark of amusement lit the male's eyes. "Not now that you have her," Ronan said with a nod toward Claire. "Because I have no doubt she'd gut even the fiercest creature that sought to do you harm."

She leaned into his touch as Mikhail brushed his thumb along her jaw. "He's right, you know," she said. "Anyone who wants you is going to have to go through me."

As if he'd ever allow her to put herself in the path of danger. "Go," he said to Ronan without making eye contact. "With my blessing. Good luck. And if you need help . . ."

"I know. Thanks. And Claire," Ronan added, "you're a serious badass now. Don't let all of that power go to your head."

The door closed to signal Ronan's exit, but Mikhail couldn't be persuaded to look away from his mate.

"He's right," Claire said. Her gaze flashed with liquid gold, the most beautiful thing Mikhail had ever seen. "I felt the truth in it. What does it mean, Mikhail?"

So much uncertainty. He wanted to reassure her. To make Claire believe that everything would be all right. "I don't know, love. But I do know that whatever happens from this day on, we'll face it together."

"I could be more trouble than I'm worth, you know." Claire kissed his temple and his cheek, took his earlobe between her lips, and sucked. "I mean, I am a reformed hustler and pickpocket. And not only that, I can't even seem to be a proper vampire."

Her hand wandered down to the fly of his pants and Mikhail swallowed a groan. "You were born to be a vampire." He cupped her cheek, seized her mouth in a tender kiss. "And with any luck, our son will take after his mother."

"Oh no." Claire leaned in, dragged her open mouth over his throat. Her fangs scraped against flesh. "He's going to take after his father. Brave." She flicked out with her tongue at his jugular. "Strong." Gentle suction tugged at his skin and he shuddered in anticipation of her bite. "A force to be reckoned with." She bit down and Mikhail's hips bucked as he ground his throbbing erection against her ass.

The bliss of feeding his mate was short-lived, however, as Claire sealed the punctures with her tongue. "That night in my apartment, you said that I would fall in love with you."

"I did."

"You were right, Mikhail."

"Our souls are tethered, love. Irrevocably braided into a single thread."

A surge of raw energy traveled through their bond from Claire into Mikhail. So much power. He reveled in it. Marveled at the strength of it. Of this female in his arms. For so long his soul had been lost and he had wandered the earth lonely, empty, untethered. But because of the wonderful, beautiful, perfect female he was whole. Complete.

"I love you, Mikhail." Gold light sparked in her eyes, shining with emotion.

"I will love you always, Claire. Forever."

And tonight was the first night of an eternity that he would spend proving it to her.

Read on for an excerpt from Kate Baxter's next book

THE WARRIOR VAMPIRE

Coming soon from St. Martin's Paperbacks

The doorknob turned and Ronan made his body go completely slack. He closed his eyes and focused his breathing so it would be deep and even. The hinges creaked as the door edged open, and the near-silent whisper of footfalls on carpet made his stomach coil into a tight knot. He let his senses do recon on the situation as his captor advanced. The footfalls were too light for anyone of substantial size and sounded more like tennis shoes or bare feet than the heavy thud of combat boots, which didn't rule out Sortiari involvement though he'd yet to see a slayer pad around in bare feet. If he could manage to free himself, he had no doubt he could at least physically overpower his captor. He'd take what he could get at this point. It might be the only factor to swing in his favor.

Ronan took a deep breath and held it for a brief moment. The scent that filled his lungs reminded him of the forest after a heavy rain. Clean. Naturally sweet. It stirred his body into awareness and remaining still became much more of a problem than it had previously been. Gods, that delicious scent. It was driving him out of his fucking mind. He wanted to bury his face in it. Roll around on it. He wanted to *drink* it. Thirst punched at his gut, scoured his throat, and Ronan swallowed against the sensation. How long had it been since he'd fed? His heart still beat, his lungs still functioned, so it couldn't have been too long ago. But the scent invading his nostrils now made his entire body ache with bloodlust.

The urge to steal a peek was overwhelming. An impulse built inside of him, one that once unleashed, could do some serious damage. And hell yeah, did he want to do some damage. But he'd spent years squashing that impulse, trained too well to act rashly. To fight blindly. He refused to lose control. It didn't matter if his situation was dire and his existence might very well be in danger. And so, he swallowed down that impulse that was as much a part of him as his own limbs—and waited.

Something cracked in front of his nose a split second before the noxious odor hit him. Too bad he was already conscious, because that smell made him wish he was passed the fuck out. He jerked his head away from the smell and let it loll to one side as if just barely coming to. The sound of a heavy sigh gave him another clue to his captor's identity: too light and airy to be male. Situation? Too soon to tell, but maybe not *altogether* hostile.

A dazed moan escaped Ronan's parted lips. His acting skills were killer. The soft staccato of a toe tapping on the carpet broke the silence followed by the sound of liquid being poured into a container—great, now he had to take a piss—as his kidnapper took a long swig of something. The suspense was killing him, and so he cracked one eye, just in time to see a sheet of water splash down on him. He gasped at the icy chill, choking as it splashed up his nose. Yeah, *so* not the wakeup call he wanted.

"Good. You're awake." As if she couldn't stand to waste any of the water, the woman standing over him shook the empty glass, sending a few stray drops onto his face. She seemed a little . . . pissed.

Ghosts of sensation whooshed through Ronan, filling his chest—his entire body—near to bursting. Emotion, strong and hot, choked the air from his lungs, and the emptiness that had consumed him vanished in the presence of this female who stood above him, her dark eyes flashing with indignant fire.

His back bowed off the bed and Ronan's teeth clamped down as his secondary fangs punched down from his gums. The thirst that burned in his throat raged. An inferno burning too hot to quench. Desire took him in its grasp, his cock hardening as his need for this female's body warred with his lust for her blood. Holy. Fucking. Shit.

This unknown female had *tethered* him.

Situation? *Proceed with extreme caution.*

How could this have happened? Though still hazy, Ronan knew that this female was the one from his memory of the previous night. She had returned his soul to him, made him whole in an instant. Whether or not she knew it, this female was *his*. Ronan cocked his head to the side, all thoughts of being bound and held against his will forgotten. Maybe the chains were left over from a wild night with a little light bondage? Doubtful, considering his aversion to being bound. Damn, he wished he could remember. It would take one hell of a woman to convince him to allow himself to be tied up. Then again, would he not do anything for his true mate? He let his gaze roam slowly from her knees up the curve of her slender thighs and well-rounded hips and paused at the swell of her breasts. Her V-neck tee provided the perfect amount of cleavage, and he let his eyes linger for a bit before he met her eyes. They reminded him of onyx, almost black and sparkling despite the meager light. Her skin was deep brown and flawless. Warm. Her mouth . . . Jesus Christ, her mouth was gorgeous. Full—her bottom lip only slightly fuller—and set in what he assumed was a perpetual pout. Had he kissed that mouth last night? Taken that delicious-looking bottom lip between his teeth? His want of her only intensified with the thought. Had he sunk his fangs into her throat while he fucked her?

Situation? *Maybe not as dire as I'd thought.*

"How do you know my name, vampire?"

Whoever she was, his mate was damned sexy when she tried to appear tough. Interesting question, though. She seemed unfazed by the fact that he was a vampire. This female was no dhampir, though. Nor was she human. Beneath her spring-rain scent, Ronan caught the tang of magic clinging to her skin. It sparked on his tongue like champagne. She was his. The knowledge of it was embedded in his very DNA. But as far as her name . . . he had no fucking clue. "I'm guessing we didn't have a wild, drunken one-nighter, then?" he drawled.

He couldn't help a triumphant smile as his words seemed to infuriate her even more. If he'd thought she was alluring when she was perturbed, she was fucking irresistible when enraged. "Look, why don't we start by unchaining me, yeah? I'm a lot more cooperative when I'm not tied to a bed and dripping wet." He quirked a brow at her dubious expression. "You might want to at least try the polite approach first. Flies, honey, and all that. I *am* chained to your bed after all. Before I jump to any"—his gaze drifted to her cleavage one more time—"conclusions about what happened last night, maybe you should fill me in first."

"Not a chance," she said flatly. "You answer *me*."

"Considering I'm the hostage here, and the events of last night have, ah, slipped my mind, I think maybe you ought to go first and tell me what I'm doing here."

She pulled a dagger from a sheath at her back and touched the point to his left pec, over his heart. The strange blade glowed like a damned canary diamond and practically screamed with energy. A warm tingle radiated from the tip of the blade as powerful magic flowed over his skin. The dagger was hungry for a kill. He didn't know how, but somehow, he could feel it.

She put pressure on the dagger, as if readying herself to drive the blade home. A thrill rushed through Ronan's veins that he'd be at her mercy and the scent of her blood blinded him with need. "How 'bout you tell me how you know my name and why you're in town—*now*—or I'll run this blade through your heart?"

Situation? *Definitely hostile.*

The song was unlike anything Naya had ever heard before. There was nothing corrupt about it, the notes pitch perfect, and the harmony so beautiful it threatened to bring tears to her eyes. A power resided in the notes, something so intense that it commanded her attention, and at the same time made her want to retreat in fear of that power. This was the song she'd heard calling to her last night, the melody that had robbed her of her senses and stolen her breath.

Naya's hand shook, the dagger becoming unsteady in her grasp. She'd known the first time she'd heard it last night that the music was too pure for the magic to be stolen goods. After she'd managed to get the bulk of his weight off of her, Naya had been prepared to extinguish the magic and call it a night. But his full lips had parted on a breath, revealing the porcelain points of his dual fangs. Vampires were supposed to be extinct. But there he was, his head resting on her legs, as real and tangible as she was. Curiosity had gotten the better of her. The magic's song was too pure for her to simply end his life. So she'd dragged him to her safe house and secured him with silver cuffs and chains. If the vampire hadn't stolen the magic, then how in the hell had he come by it? And why couldn't she shake the feeling that, somehow, she was meant to find this amazing specimen now at her mercy?

Naya shook herself from her stupor and willed her gaze from the hills and valleys of sculpted muscle beneath the dagger's point. "Did you not hear me? I said, answer me or I'll drive this dagger through your heart."

His calm demeanor scared her more than any shouts or threats might have. The vampire's brow creased in concentration as if he were trying to hold back a wall of water from a broken dam with nothing but the power of his mind. The way he looked at her was unnerving. Such deep intensity.

"I think a lot clearer when sharp objects aren't being jabbed into my skin."

Her eyes darted to his and she was momentarily taken aback by the beauty of them. As vibrant and green as the rain forest. His brows were tawny slashes, made slightly sinister by the look of concentration on his face, and he had the longest lashes she'd ever seen on any male. Plenty of women—including her—would gladly give up a limb to have eyelashes like those. She'd save a fortune in mascara. His cheekbones were sharp and his nose a fine, straight line. His jaw was equally strong, shadowed with stubble. Gods, but he was magnificent.

He cocked his head to the side and studied her with those gorgeous green eyes. "I'm going to assume that your silence means you're considering my request?"

She eased up on the dagger, pulling it away from his chest. The sound of the magic's song quieted and, after a moment, grew silent. Naya took a steadying breath as her own body calmed, no longer responding to the magic's call. All right, so the guy had been a little wound up. She guessed anyone would have been in his situation. "I'm not going to free you," she said as she took a couple of much-needed steps back. "But I still expect you to answer my questions."

"Magnanimous, aren't you?"

A lazy, tantalizing smile stretched across his mouth. So wicked. Naya's lower abdomen tightened and her fingernails bit into her palms. The vampire was built for sin, every inch of him tight and bulky with corded muscle. A killer, that much was apparent, and she couldn't help but wonder if his appetite for violence would rival his appetites for other . . . things. Naya swallowed, forced the lust rising up through her chest back to the soles of her feet. This male was dangerous. He could kill her before she even had a chance to defend herself. No matter how good he looked stretched out and bound to her bed, she couldn't forget that he was an unknown. And Naya couldn't afford unknowns.

The vampire sighed in resignation and tried to stretch his arms, wincing with discomfort. Raw, angry burns marred his skin where the silver made contact, but it couldn't be helped. The silver would weaken him and Naya needed an equalizer until she decided whether or not to alert the elders to the vampire's presence. "For starters, I don't know your name, so I'm not going to be able to help you on that one. I've never seen you before today."

Bullshit. After he'd sacked her like a quarterback, he'd said her name. And that he needed to protect her. A surge of emotion rose up in Naya's chest. Tenderness toward this male that she couldn't afford to feel. Protect her from what? Why? Who was he to her? And what did he know that she didn't? This was *her* town. Anything supernatural went down, and Naya knew about it. The only reason he was here now was because he'd passed out afterward. "You're lying. You said my name last night."

The vampire let out a measured breath and Naya had a feeling that if his hands were free, he would have raked his fingers through the tangle of his tawny hair. "I don't remember a goddamned thing about last night," he said. "I may be wrong, but I think we've been over this. I'm kind of drawing a blank here."

Amnesia? Sure, like she'd believe that pathetic excuse. "This isn't a soap opera, buddy. The my-memory-is-gone excuse is a little tired, don't you think?"

His mouth turned up in a half-smile and Naya's stomach did a little flip. Damn, he was sexy. The way she'd bound him showcased his muscled arms and chest in just the right way. His shirtless state was a bonus as far as she was concerned. Who cared where the garment had gotten to? His loss was her gain. She gave her head a shake and tore her gaze from his body. *Gods, Naya. Focus!*

"I never said my memory was completely gone. I just don't remember anything that's happened since I got to town." He let out a chuff of breath. "Hell, I don't even know why I'm in this town. Maybe you could help fill in those blanks, starting with why I'm chained to your bed?"

The question carried a decidedly sexual edge. Apparently he wasn't too nervous to nix the cocky attitude. "You're chained to my bed because I was feeling charitable last night and decided not to kill you on sight. I tracked you to an abandoned parking lot just past downtown. Unchecked magic was leeching from you. Before I could get the drop on you, you tackled me to the ground, said my name, and that you needed to protect me." She added, low, "And passed out. How's that for filling in the blanks?"

The mischievous glimmer in his emerald eyes dulled, and was replaced with a calculating light reminding Naya that, good looks or not, this male was an unknown variable she couldn't risk letting loose in the town. His arms pulled against the bindings, more of a knee-jerk reaction than anything, rattling the chains behind him. "Protect you from what?"

His tone vibrated through her, the rough edge coaxing a shiver to her skin. "I have no idea," she replied. "And since your memory has so conveniently failed you, I guess neither one of us will know anytime soon."

He studied her with that same inscrutable gaze, as though he were peering right into her soul. His expression softened and the tension in his shoulders relaxed a fraction or two. "Sounds like we didn't have a proper introduction. Aren't you even curious to know *my* name? Or are you more of a cut-to-the-chase sort of female?"

His patronizing tone did little for her mounting temper. Naya didn't care what his name was. If he was a threat, she'd have to put him down. Knowing his name wouldn't make that any easier. "I don't need or want your name. All I *want* to know is how you knew who I was, why you think I need protecting, and how you came by the magic so I can decide what to do with you."

"Aside from my good looks, I'm not sure what magic you're referring to." Gods, this male was insufferable! Arrogant, even at a disadvantage. Naya choked up on the hilt of her dagger and centered her energy, lest her own magic echo her emotions and become uncontrollable. "How do you know about vampires, female? And what are you that you could so readily identify me?" That half-smirk returned to his mouth, drawing her eyes away from his. His voice dropped to a smooth, mellow purr that made the tiny hairs on the back of Naya's neck stand on end. She felt that tug in her stomach again, a rush of excitement that had nothing to do with danger. Well, maybe it had a little bit to do with the danger. Sexy bastard.